SHAMANSLAYER

'This,' said Kat. 'This is unnatural. The beastmen don't travel like this.'

'Is it perhaps marauders instead?' asked Ilgner.

'Doesn't smell like marauders,' said Argrin.

Kat agreed. 'There are only hoof prints. No boots. It was a herd that did this, but I have never seen a herd cut down trees on the march. They are creatures of the forest. They move through trees like we move in the open. I don't understand it.'

'Perhaps they have a cannon,' said Felix.

Rodi laughed. 'Beastmen don't have cannon!' he said. 'They don't even have bows and arrows.'

'Listen to the beardling,' said Gotrek under his breath. 'He knows everything.'

'Those that lead the beasts sometimes have cannon,' said Felix, remembering the hellish weapon that the Chaos champion Justine had brought with the herd that had attacked Flensburg.

'It might be a cannon,' said Kat doubtfully. 'But where are the tracks of the wheels?'

'Unnatural or not,' said Ilgner, waving her on, 'we have found our quarry's spoor, and it does not appear to be hard to follow. Let the hunt begin.'

More Gotrek & Felix from the Black Library

GOTREK & FELIX: THE FIRST OMNIBUS
by William King
(Contains books 1-3: *Trollslayer, Skavenslayer & Daemonslayer*)

GOTREK & FELIX: THE SECOND OMNIBUS
by William King
(Contains books 4-6: *Dragonslayer, Beastslayer & Vampireslayer*)

GOTREK & FELIX: THE THIRD OMNIBUS
by William King and Nathan Long
(Contains books 7-9: *Giantslayer, Orcslayer & Manslayer*)

Book 10 – ELFSLAYER
by Nathan Long

More Nathan Long from the Black Library
BLACKHEARTS: THE OMNIBUS
(Contains the novels *Valnir's Bane, The Broken Lance & Tainted Blood*)

A WARHAMMER NOVEL

Gotrek and Felix

SHAMANSLAYER

Nathan Long

To Andy Law, my native guide.

A BLACK LIBRARY PUBLICATION

First published in Great Britain in 2009 by
BL Publishing,
Games Workshop Ltd.,
Willow Road, Nottingham,
NG7 2WS, UK

10 9 8 7 6 5 4 3 2 1

Cover illustration by Geoff Taylor
Map by Nuala Kinrade.

© Games Workshop Limited 2009. All rights reserved.

Black Library, the Black Library logo, Black Flame, BL Publishing, Games Workshop, the Games Workshop logo and all associated marks, names, characters, illustrations and images from the Warhammer universe are either ®, TM and/or © Games Workshop Ltd 2000-2009, variably registered in the UK and other countries around the world. All rights reserved.

A CIP record for this book is available from the British Library.

ISBN 13: 978 1 84416 773 9

Distributed in the US by Simon & Schuster
1230 Avenue of the Americas, New York, NY 10020.

No part of this publication may be reproduced, stored in a retrieval system, or transmitted in any form or by any means, electronic, mechanical, photocopying, recording or otherwise, without the prior permission of the publishers.

This is a work of fiction. All the characters and events portrayed in this book are fictional, and any resemblance to real people or incidents is purely coincidental.

See the Black Library on the Internet at
www.blacklibrary.com

Find out more about Games Workshop
and the world of Warhammer at
www.games-workshop.com

Printed and bound in the US.

This is a dark age, a bloody age, an age of daemons and of sorcery. It is an age of battle and death, and of the world's ending. Amidst all of the fire, flame and fury it is a time, too, of mighty heroes, of bold deeds and great courage.

At the heart of the Old World sprawls the Empire, the largest and most powerful of the human realms. Known for its engineers, sorcerers, traders and soldiers, it is a land of great mountains, mighty rivers, dark forests and vast cities. And from his throne in Altdorf reigns the Emperor Karl Franz, sacred descendant of the founder of these lands, Sigmar, and wielder of his magical warhammer.

But these are far from civilised times. Across the length and breadth of the Old World, from the knightly palaces of Bretonnia to ice-bound Kislev in the far north, come rumblings of war. In the towering Worlds Edge Mountains, the orc tribes are gathering for another assault. Bandits and renegades harry the wild southern lands of the Border Princes. There are rumours of rat-things, the skaven, emerging from the sewers and swamps across the land. And from the northern wildernesses there is the ever-present threat of Chaos, of daemons and beastmen corrupted by the foul powers of the Dark Gods.
As the time of battle draws ever nearer,
the Empire needs heroes
like never before.

'After our near-fatal encounter with the dark elves, I returned to Altdorf with the Slayer to discover that my greatest fears concerning my father were true. In my rage and guilt I made a vow then to destroy the shadowy nemesis that had killed him, no matter how long it took, or the cost incurred. But fate did not allow me to pursue this new quest. Instead, because of a long-forgotten pledge, the Slayer and I were swept up into a quest of another sort – one that led us into the darkest depths of the Drakwald to face the oldest and bitterest enemies of mankind, and a new threat of staggering proportions.

It was as we fought this horror that we were once again reunited with companions from our long ago past, and once again, those reunions were both sweet and bitter, joyous and heartrending, and both would change the nature of my travels with Gotrek for all time.'

– From *My Travels with Gotrek*, Vol VIII, by Herr Felix Jaeger (Altdorf Press, 2529)

ONE

FELIX JAEGER PAUSED as he looked up at his father's Altdorf mansion under the grey winter sky. Did it have an empty, shut-up look to it, or was he just imagining it? Surely the marble steps hadn't been so dirty the last time he had visited. Surely the curtains hadn't been drawn. He climbed the steps to the door, then stopped again.

Ever since he had found his father's ring on a cord around the neck of a skaven assassin on a beach by the Sea of Chaos, Felix had burned with fevered impatience to return to Altdorf to find out what the rat-faced villains had done to the old man. But now, on the doorstep of knowledge, he found it difficult to go on.

For more than a month his heart had been filled with dread and uncertainty. How did the skaven come to have the ring? Had they hurt his father for it? Had they killed him? Had they only stolen it and let him be? The questions had chased their tails inside Felix's head unceasingly as he and his companions had made their too-slow journey back to civilisation. But as much as the helplessness of not knowing had driven him mad, Felix suddenly feared knowing even more. If he knew, he would have to allow the emotions he had been stifling to come to the fore. If he knew, he would have to do something.

He cursed himself and squared his shoulders. He was like a man frightened of having a wound stitched shut – the anticipation was worse than the act. Better to take the pain and close it and heal.

He knocked on the door.

There was no answer. He knocked again, and waited again, trepidation rising in his heart. Then, just as he was wondering if he should find some way to break in, he heard locks turning and bolts drawing back. The door opened and the grave, grey face of his father's butler looked out at him.

'Is he…?' asked Felix hesitantly.

'Your father is dead, sir,' said the butler. 'I'm sorry, sir.'

A hot rush of anger and regret flooded through Felix. He had known it, of course – known it all along – but it was one thing to know it in one's heart and another to hear it spoken as fact.

'And…' he stammered. 'And how did it happen?'

The butler paused, a brief flash of fear disturbing his solemn features, then spoke again. 'Your brother is here, sir. Perhaps you should speak to him.'

Felix blanched. Otto was here? Speaking to him was the last thing he wanted to do! On the other hand, he would have to see him sometime. There were no doubt legalities to be attended to. He sighed. No point in avoiding the inevitable.

'Very well,' he said. 'Show me to him.'

THE BUTLER PUSHED open the door to Felix's father's study, a long dark room lined with ledger-filled bookcases and lit by a small fire in a large fireplace. Near the meagre blaze was a broad desk, almost buried in ledgers, stacks of papers, scrolls and leather folios, and surrounded by chests and strongboxes, all spilling even more papers and books. At the desk, almost entirely obscured by this mountain of paper, sat Otto, quill in one pudgy hand, bald head down, peering myopically at an open ledger by the light of a candle perched on top of the mess and muttering under his breath.

Felix stepped in and the butler closed the door behind him. Otto didn't look up. Felix paused, then cleared his throat and started forwards. Still Otto didn't look up, only kept murmuring and ticking things off with his quill.

Felix reached the foothills of the desk's clutter. He cleared his throat again. There was still no response.

'Ah, Otto...'

'Thirty-two thousand, nine hundred and... and... Damn you! You made me lose my count!' Otto looked up, his bearded jowls quivering with anger. 'Why couldn't you...?' He froze as he saw who he addressed. 'You.' Then again after a few seconds, 'You!'

'Hello, brother,' said Felix. 'I'm sorry to–'

'You dare to show your face here, you... you murderer!' said Otto, recovering.

'I didn't kill him!' exclaimed Felix, though he was suddenly bathed in a guilty sweat.

'Didn't you, by the gods? Didn't you?' cried Otto, rising up and stabbing towards him with his quill. 'You come to see him for the first time in over twenty years and that very night he is found butchered in his bed! Do you count that coincidence? No? You might not have done the cutting, but, by Sigmar, you brought the knives!'

Felix hung his head at that, for he could not deny it. Though he had not known it at the time, the skaven had been tailing him. They must have followed him to his father's house. 'What did they do to him?'

Otto glared at him. 'Schmidt found him in his bed, bound at the wrists and ankles. He... he had been tortured. There was no fatal wound. He seemed to have died of terror.'

Felix shuddered, remembering what the decrepit skaven seer had done to Aethenir and imagining it being done to his frail old father. Gustav Jaeger had not been a good man, but not even the worst of men deserved a death like that.

'I'm sorry, Otto. It was indeed my enemies that–'

'Sorry?' interrupted Otto. 'Do you think an apology will suffice? You caused the death of your father! Sigmar's blood, you're like a curse! I told you once before I never wanted to see you again. Everywhere you go, death and destruction follow. You can take your "sorry" and be damned with it. Now go, before you kill me too.'

Felix sighed. He couldn't blame Otto, really. He was right. He was a curse. He had exposed Otto and his family to danger, had nearly got him killed in an attack on the street in Nuln, and then had come to Altdorf and led his enemies to his father's house, where they had tortured him to death. And it wasn't just his own family

Felix's presence had destroyed. He and Gotrek had been in a fight that had burned down an entire neighbourhood in Nuln, the crew of the *Pride of Skintstaad* had been slaughtered, thousands of innocent slaves had drowned with the sinking of the black ark of the dark elves, and there were more – many more – an army of dead who marched behind him, pointing at his back and whispering, 'I would yet live if not for you...'

Felix bowed to Otto sadly, then stepped back from the desk and turned to go. He had learned what he had come to learn. There was no reason to stay. Except...

Felix turned back around. 'There is one last thing–'

Otto's eyes went wide with angry surprise. 'Sigmar, don't tell me you have the brass to ask for an inheritance! After what you've done? You should be paid with a hangman's noose, not the gold of the man you murdered!'

'I don't want his gold!' snapped Felix. 'Would you let me speak?'

Otto crossed his arms over his ponderous belly, glaring, but waiting.

Felix took an envelope from his doublet. 'Father asked me to do him a favour when I saw him. He wanted me to go to Marienburg and get back from Hans Euler an incriminating letter he had once written to Euler's father.'

'Euler,' spat Otto. 'That conniving little crook. I hope he rots.'

'Very likely,' said Felix, remembering his last duel with Euler where he had run him through. He held up the envelope. 'I recovered the letter. But–'

'But it's too late now, as Father is dead,' sneered Otto. 'Well done.'

Felix's hands clenched. He fought the urge to punch his brother in the nose. 'But,' he repeated as patiently as he could. 'When I read the letter, I was very disturbed.'

Otto beckoned impatiently and Felix handed him the envelope. He continued speaking as Otto opened it and unfolded the letter.

'Father said that it contained proof that he had smuggled goods into the Empire without paying the tariff, and that Euler meant to use it as blackmail to force him to sell him Jaeger and Sons.'

'The swine,' said Otto, beginning to read. 'He's ten times the smuggler Father ever was.'

'But that's not the worst of it,' said Felix. 'Look on the reverse. Father says that he has received from Euler's father six rare books from Tilea, but that some of them are in poor condition and he wants his money back.'

'So?' said Otto, holding the letter closer to the candle to read it. 'It wouldn't have been the first time that old pirate tried to pass shoddy goods.'

'The *Maelificarium* is a forbidden book,' said Felix. 'So is Urbanus's *The Seven Gates*. They are tomes of the blackest magic. Men have been burned at the stake just for knowing their names.'

Otto grew still, staring at the letter.

Felix stepped closer. 'This is more than mere smuggling, Otto. This is dangerous business. If Father made a habit of–'

Otto crumpled the letter and threw it into the fire.

Felix yelped. 'What are you doing?' He started towards the fireplace.

Otto stepped in his way, glaring into Felix's eyes. 'The letter was a forgery. A trick of Euler's to try to bring us down. Father never dealt in forbidden books. Never. Do you understand?'

'But how can you be sure?' asked Felix. 'Don't you think we ought to tell someone? The letter names the book dealer that–'

Otto shoved him, snarling. Felix stumbled back, nearly tripping over a satchel full of papers.

'By the gods!' Otto cried. 'Haven't you done enough? You killed the man once already. Do you want to dig him up and kill him all over again? Do you want to kill me? Do you want to ruin me?'

'Of course not,' said Felix. 'But…'

'Do you know what would happen if you were to "tell someone"?' sputtered Otto, limping forwards ponderously. Even in the ruddy light of the fire his skin looked pale. 'The witch hunters would be here before you could snap your fingers, and every book, every ledger, every letter owned by father, and by me, and by Jaeger and Sons, would be impounded and pored over for evidence of more witchery. They'd take me too, and Annabella, and my son, and you, if they could catch you, and what your "friends" did to Father would be nothing compared to what the witch hunters would do to us. Is that what you want? Do you want to see us racked and flayed?'

'Not at all,' said Felix. 'But–'

'But nothing!' said Otto. 'What Father did or didn't do doesn't matter. Jaeger and Sons is a legitimate company now. We deal in wholesome goods and honest services. Leave the past alone and go away, I beg you, Felix!' He caught at Felix's shirt front and stared pleadingly up at him. 'I beg you!'

Felix blinked, for the anger that had blazed within Otto's eyes was gone. All that was left was fear.

* * *

The streets of Altdorf were choked with refugees and soldiers returning from the war. Families with all their belongings on their backs wandered through the Konigsplatz staring up at the tall buildings in awe. Broken men with stumps for legs or hooks for hands begged in the shadow of the Temple of Sigmar. Mothers hugged weeping children to them to try and keep them warm in the winter wind that whistled through canyon-like alleys. Ragged columns of spearmen and crossbowmen shuffled after their sergeants with unshaven faces and thousand-yard stares.

Felix saw none of them as he wandered back from his father's house to the *Oxen's Yoke*, where he and Gotrek had taken a room upon returning to the city. He was still wondering if he had done the right thing by promising Otto not to tell anyone about the letter. As much as Otto seemed to think otherwise, he didn't truly wish his family any harm, but at the same time, books like those named in the letter were harmful to everyone. He wished now that he had shown it to Max. He wasn't the sort to bring the witch hunters into things. He would have taken care of things discreetly. Maybe he could still tell him. They had only said goodbye yesterday, though the magister had made it pretty clear that he hoped they wouldn't see each other again for a good long time.

Felix could understand why. Their sojourn on the Sea of Chaos had aged Max terribly. He had spent most of the trip back to Marienburg lying in a bunk in the captain's quarters of the dark elf galley they had taken, shaking and sweating with some sort of fever, while the flesh melted from his bones at an alarming rate.

Claudia Pallenberger, the seeress from the Celestial College whose premonitions had taken them there in the first place, had fared little better, raving and weeping in her sleep, and dull and unresponsive when awake. Felix had been more nursemaid than captain on that long, painful voyage, and he had feared many times during its course that his inexpert ministrations would kill the two mages, but they proved more resilient than he could have hoped, and by the time the ragged black ship had been accosted by the Marienburg Harbour Patrol they were able to come to the deck and make their way across the gangplank on their own power.

Neither, however, had fully recovered. Though Max's keen wit and his humour had returned to him, he remained terribly gaunt, even after a week of Marienburg chowders and black beer, and his hair, which had been brown streaked with grey before the dark elf sorceresses had shaved him bald, was growing in snow-white. Claudia's scars were more hidden. Except for her shorn hair, she quickly regained her beauty and health, but there was a gravity and sad understanding in her eyes that had not been there at the start of the trip. She had seen the cruelty and depravity of the world, and had been marked by it.

Felix was sorry to see it, for her innocence and youthful arrogance had been charming, but at the same time, it had got them all in a lot of trouble – and this experience, bitter as it might have been for her, had undoubtedly given her wisdom that would make her a better, more responsible seeress in the future.

Max and Claudia had spent the day they'd had to wait for a riverboat to take them to Altdorf recovering at an inn, while Gotrek and Felix went back to Euler's house to recover Felix's father's letter from Euler's safe. That had been an adventure in itself, complete with monsters and mayhem, but they had got it at last, and after a journey of twelve days toiling up the Reik, they had returned to Altdorf the previous evening.

Their leave-taking had been friendly, if a bit subdued. Max and Claudia thanked Felix and Gotrek for getting them through the adventure alive, Felix thanked Max and Claudia for the same thing, Gotrek grunted, and that was that. Max led Claudia away to face charges of misconduct and recklessness at her college, and Gotrek and Felix went to look for drinks and a room.

Felix was a little surprised – and a little disappointed – that Claudia hadn't tried to kiss him as they parted, but perhaps the streak of wild rebellion that had sent her into his arms had been burned out of her when the brand of hard-won wisdom had been burned in. As Max had said, given a second chance and the gift of forgiveness, we may all live long enough to learn from our mistakes, and make amends for them. He hoped it were so for Claudia.

Felix chuckled ruefully at the thought of all his recent goodbyes. It seemed he had only just got back to the Empire and everyone was telling him to leave again. But that wasn't a bad thing, for he had a debt with the skaven to settle that might just get him killed, and it wouldn't do to bring any innocents along for the ride.

FELIX PUSHED THROUGH the leather curtain of the *Oxen's Yoke* and strode to the table at the back where Gotrek sat alone, a stein in one fist and another brimming before him, waiting to be consumed. The Slayer too had been changed by their journey into the Sea of Chaos. Like Max and Claudia he had been scarred, the palms of his powerful hands melted to the smoothness of candlewax by the arcane power that had coursed through his rune axe when he had chopped the Harp of Ruin in half on the deck of the skaven submersible. But where the wizard and the seeress had been sobered by the danger of the experience, Gotrek had been revived. His single eye was once more bright and alert, his orange crest high and freshly dyed, his beard neatly plaited and his squat, powerful frame fairly vibrating with barely controlled violence.

Felix wasn't sure what had caused the change. The escape from the black ark had been one of the most gruelling challenges they had ever faced, and yet Gotrek seemed fitter and healthier than ever. Perhaps it had been the opportunity to fight the age-old nemesis of his race, the dark elves. Perhaps it had been the prophecy the daemon had spoken in the summoning chamber, that Gotrek was fated to die killing a daemon greater than itself. Whatever it was, Gotrek was in better spirits than he had been since they had left Karak Hirn.

The Slayer looked up as Felix motioned to the serving girl for an ale and sat down beside him.

'What did you learn, manling?' he asked.

Felix sighed. 'Everything I feared. My father is dead. The skaven tortured and killed him.' He clenched his fists and turned to look at the Slayer. 'I vow that I will have my revenge on that vile old rat or die in the attempt.'

Gotrek nodded approvingly. 'Well said.' He took a pull from his stein. 'Though he could already be dead. He fell into the sea.'

Felix shook his head. 'No. He lives. I know it. And I will kill him.'

The serving girl brought Felix's ale.

Gotrek raised his stein. 'To vengeance,' he said.

Felix did the same and they knocked them together. 'To vengeance!'

They both drank deep, then slammed the mugs down on the wooden table. Felix wiped his mouth with the back of his hand. He felt as if, after such a pronouncement, he should get up and stride off manfully towards his enemy, but he had no idea where the evil ratman might be.

'So, er, where do you suppose we find him?' he asked after an awkward minute.

Gotrek belched and started on his second beer. 'I wouldn't worry about it, manling. If he's alive, I'll wager he'll find us. All that is required is that we be ready.'

'Aye,' said Felix. 'Ever vigilant.'

'There he is!' said a high voice from the front of the tavern.

Gotrek and Felix jumped up, almost upsetting their steins as they drew sword and axe, but it was no skaven sorcerer who had cried out, but a youth in squire's livery, who was pointing directly at them.

Felix blinked in confusion. The boy had a bowl haircut, and was dressed in doublet and hose of deep blue, with a red heart haloed by fire emblazoned on the right breast. He stood with a tall, frail-looking old knight with a bald head and a magnificent white beard, whose pale blue eyes shone with the light of fanaticism. Under a heavy wool mantle, the knight wore clothes of the same blue. Felix had never seen either of them before in his life.

'Do you know them?' he asked Gotrek out of the side of his mouth.

'No,' said Gotrek. 'Do you?'

'Haven't a clue.'

The knight made his way across the taproom with stiff dignity, while the youth, who could have been no more than seventeen, followed in his wake.

Gotrek growled a warning as the two approached the table, but the old knight never took his angry eyes away from Felix's face.

'What do you want with me?' Felix asked.

The old knight reached into a pocket within his cloak and pulled out a book. He cast it on the table with a disdainful flick of the wrist. 'Are you he who wrote this dreck?'

Felix looked down at the book. It was the second volume of his travels with Gotrek. He blinked with surprise. It was the last thing he had been expecting.

'Well, I wouldn't call it dreck,' he said at last. 'But, yes. I wrote it.'

'And did you venture 'neath Karak Eight Peaks with the templar Aldred Keppler, of the Order of the Fiery Heart?'

This was getting stranger and stranger. Felix exchanged a glance with Gotrek. The Slayer shrugged.

'We did,' said Felix at last. 'What is this all about?'

'And did you take the sword Karaghul from his corpse, though it was not yours to take?'

'Uh, well...' said Felix.

'Answer not, craven,' cried the old knight. 'For I see it upon your person even now!' He thrust an accusatory finger at Felix, his eyes blazing with righteous fury. 'The sword belongs to the Order of the Fiery Heart! Your twenty-year thievery is at an end, Felix Jaeger. Return it to us at once!'

TWO

Felix stared at the ancient knight, utterly staggered. He had carried Karaghul for so long that he had almost forgotten that there was a time when it wasn't his. He couldn't imagine being parted with it. It was the best sword he had ever owned. Its runic power had once allowed him to slay a dragon, and do mortal harm to a sea serpent more recently. He might not have survived either encounter without it.

'I… I always meant to give it back,' he stuttered.

'A likely tale,' sneered the knight.

'I did,' said Felix. 'Only… only I haven't been to Altdorf in twenty years.' Which wasn't precisely true. He had been here for two months before leaving for Marienburg and the Wasteland, and he hadn't thought once of looking for the Order of the Fiery Heart and giving back the sword. That they had claim on it had slipped his mind long long ago.

That brought another question to Felix's mind. 'How did you know I was here?'

The old knight cast a baleful look at the boy at his side. 'The order's chapter house is nearby. My squire, Ortwin, may Sigmar have mercy on his soul for such a waste of hours, has read your braggart's tale, and recognised your companion in the street from the descriptions therein. Now, return the sword you stole.'

'He didn't steal the sword, knight,' said Gotrek, glaring up at him.

The knight glared back, apparently not one whit intimidated by Gotrek's fierce one-eyed gaze. 'Did he have Templar Keppler's permission to take it?'

Felix shivered, remembering how the troll had ripped Keppler's head clean off at exactly the moment that he had found the sword. 'Ah, he didn't get the chance,' he said. 'He was dead before he could say anything.'

'How can I know this to be true?' asked the knight. 'The whole tale might be false. You might have set upon the noble templar and robbed him of it.'

Gotrek gave him a level look. 'Dwarfs don't lie.'

This seemed to give the old knight pause. He inclined his head respectfully towards Gotrek. 'Your pardon, herr dwarf. The honesty and honour of your race is well known, and I would not question it under normal circumstances, but to hold something which belongs to another for more than twenty years...'

'I... I will give back the sword,' said Felix, though his heart sank when he said it. It was like saying he would cut off his leg. 'I never meant to keep it, but we were away for so long.' He began to unbuckle his sword belt from his waist. 'It became a part of me.'

'And in your absence, you have denied its power to a generation of Knights of the Fiery Heart. Who knows what prodigies they might have performed armed with such a noble sword. Far greater deeds than you ever assayed, I'll warrant.'

Felix paused as he wrapped the belt around the scabbard. There was no need for the old knight to be insulting. 'I slew a dragon,' he said.

'And scores of orcs and undead,' said Gotrek.

'And turned back the hordes of Chaos,' said Ortwin.

The knight shot the squire an angry look at this.

'It said so in the books,' the boy persisted.

Felix held out the sword, and something, perhaps the dignity of the old knight, or the solemnity of the occasion, compelled him to go down on one knee as he did so. 'Sir knight,' he said, 'I will return this sword to your order as I always meant to, but… you should know that I never dishonoured it, or the memory of Templar Keppler, and… and if there is any way that I might convince you to let me keep it, I promise I will not dishonour it in the future. I have grown so accustomed to it that I don't know what I would do without it.'

The knight raised an incredulous eyebrow. 'You want me to *give* you the sword? Which has been a relic of our order for nigh on five hundred years? No. You have held it long enough.'

'Well, er, perhaps I could, ah, buy it from you, or make some trade for it.'

Out of the corner of his eye Felix saw Gotrek wince at that, and the look on the old knight's face confirmed that he had said the wrong thing.

'Buy it!' cried the knight. 'Buy a holy relic? You might as well ask to purchase the honour of our order. Are you some base merchant? A sword such as this is not to be bought and sold. It is to be passed from templar to templar so that it may be used in the never-ending battle against the forces of darkness.'

Felix flushed, embarrassed, and scrambled for some better argument. 'I'm sorry, sir knight. I... I mis-spoke. What I meant to say was, ah, could I perform some service for you? Some, uh, deed of honour or quest, that would convince you I was worthy to carry the sword?'

The knight stared down at him for a moment, then snatched the sword from his upraised hands. 'No,' he said. 'I do not believe you mis-spoke. I believe you revealed your true nature in your first statement. The sword will return to the order, and to honour, at last.'

He turned away with a sweep of his heavy cloak and walked, stiff and proud, towards the door.

The squire hesitated, looking at Felix and Gotrek with an appraising eye, then snatched up his book and turned and hurried after the knight, calling to him in a loud whisper, 'Master Teobalt. Wait. Master.'

But the knight did not slow, and the curtain swished closed behind them as they pushed out into the street. Felix stared after them though they were already out of sight.

'Get off your knees, manling,' said Gotrek gruffly. 'They've gone.'

Felix had forgotten he was kneeling. He looked around. People were staring. He scrambled up, embarrassed, then sat back on the bench and patted his empty waist. Karaghul was gone. His sword. He felt naked without it. He didn't know what to do. He would have to get another sword, of course, but how could he replace it? Certainly he had hated Karaghul at times, when its dragon-loathing nature had invaded his mind and urged him into suicidal situations, but it had protected him as well, and defeated many a great and powerful enemy. He had had it so long, and it was so much a part of him, that he wasn't sure he would be himself without it.

'It... it seems I need a sword,' he said.

'Aye,' said Gotrek.

'And a drink,' he said.

'Aye,' said Gotrek. He pounded the table. 'Barkeep! Two more! No, four more!'

THE REST OF the night passed in a sodden blur of beer and bewilderment. Felix sat benumbed as Gotrek handed him mug after mug and ordered him to drink them down. He did so mechanically, staring into the middle distance as his mind spun in slow circles, like a wobbly cartwheel after the cart has tipped into a ditch.

He tried to focus on how he was going to reap his revenge on the skaven, but visions of bursting in on the grey seer in its lair and cutting its scabrous head off kept bringing him back to Karaghul, and he would mourn its loss all over again.

This grief took on different shades as he moved through the various stages of drunkenness. Sometimes he wanted to weep. Sometimes he laughed at the bitter humour of it. Other times he flushed with anger, and grew determined to stride to the templar's chapter house and demand the sword back. Still other times, he considered throwing himself at the templar's feet and begging.

In the end, he did none of those things, only took the next mug and methodically drank it dry, and the mug after that, on into the night.

* * *

THE NEXT MORNING he nearly did weep, for when he awoke at last, still dressed except for one boot, and with his head hammering like a cave full of dwarf smiths, he reached blindly for his sword belt, as he had done every day of his adult life, and found nothing.

He turned and stared at the bedpost, where he always hung his sword when he stayed in inns, and his heart dropped into his guts. It was gone! Someone had stolen Karaghul! He leapt up, about to call to Gotrek in the next room, and rouse him to go after the thief. But just as he filled his lungs to shout, he remembered, and his heart sank even further. The sword wasn't stolen. He had given it away. He would never see it again.

He sank back down on the bed and lowered his throbbing head into his hands. What had he done? What had honour made him do? How could he have been so foolish?

He sat there just breathing for quite a while, his mind drifting in a fugue of pain and regret, but then a sharp rap on the door jarred him awake again.

'Who is it?'

'Wake up, manling,' came Gotrek's voice. 'We must find you a sword today.'

Felix groaned and stood. 'Don't remind me.'

He straightened his clothes and crossed to the door, and even though he knew Karaghul was gone, even though he knew he was going out to look for a new sword, it still made his heart jump when his arms brushed his sides and he didn't feel the familiar shape of the old blade's pommel knocking against his wrist as it always did.

As it always *had*, he corrected himself. As it never would again. He took a deep breath and opened the door. It was going to be a long day.

* * *

Felix squinted against the light that streamed through the leaded windows as he and Gotrek shuffled down the stairs to the taproom. The smell of sausage and fritters and stale beer made his gorge rise, and he swallowed with difficulty. He needed fresh air and a walk, and perhaps a nice quiet puke in an alley somewhere.

A pair of fiery blue eyes caught him as he followed Gotrek towards the exit, and he stumbled as if he'd been hit. It was the old templar! The knight sat ramrod straight at the table nearest the door, glaring at Gotrek and Felix from under shaggy white brows. His squire stood behind him, gazing at them with a more anxious expression.

Felix's heart leapt as he saw that Karaghul was resting across the templar's knees. He had come to give it back! He had changed his mind! The sword would be Felix's again! But if that was the case, why was he looking at them so coldly?

'You rise late,' the old knight said as they stopped before him. 'I have waited here since dawn.'

'You just missed us, then,' said Gotrek. 'That's when we went to bed.'

The knight sniffed, disgusted, then turned to cast a baleful glance at his squire, as if it was somehow all his fault. The squire shrank before his displeasure.

Felix stepped forwards and inclined his head respectfully. 'You wanted to see us about something, sir knight?' he asked, trying to keep the pathetic hope out of his voice.

The knight did not look at him. Instead he turned and stared at Gotrek, who stood, arms crossed over his beard before him. 'Swear by the honour of your ancestors and your gods that you will answer me truthfully,' he said at last.

'I so swear,' said Gotrek, without hesitation.

The knight picked up the copy of *My Adventures with Gotrek – Vol II* which lay on the table beside him. 'Are the events in this book, and in the other volumes of your travels, true? Did you and your companion truly perform the deeds written of therein?'

Gotrek nodded. 'We did.'

'And there is no exaggeration, or embroidery in the telling?'

'None that I know of,' said Gotrek.

The knight continued to look hard at the Slayer for a long moment, then at last turned to Felix. The expression on his face said that he would rather be drinking urine. 'I will not give you the sword,' he said. 'But you may earn the right to carry it.'

Felix blinked, shocked but elated. 'H-how?'

'You spoke of doing some service for me,' said the knight. 'My squire assures me that you are a man of honour and valorous deeds, and your companion confirms it. Well, we shall see. If you wish to once again wield the sword, I would have you travel north with me into the Drakwald, to discover what has become of the rest of our order – brave templars who went north to fight Archaon's hordes and did not return. Be they alive, we must save them. Be they dead, we must recover the order's holy banner and regalia. If you prove yourself worthy on this quest, I will grant you the stewardship of Karaghul. If you are unworthy, I will take the sword from you, whether you would return it or not. Do you accept this venture?'

Felix paused, though every fibre of him wanted to scream, 'Yes!'

'What do you mean by "stewardship"?' he asked.

'The sword belongs to the order,' said the knight, raising his bearded chin. 'And always will. But if you show me that you are the hero this book claims, I will grant you the right to carry it until you die or dishonour it, or until the order requires it again, at which time it will be returned to us.'

Felix frowned. As much as he wanted the sword back, that sounded fishy. He had no objection to holding Karaghul as steward. He had no son to pass the sword to, and it was doubtful he ever would. But 'until the order requires it again,' could mean the day after he helped the templar find his fellow knights. It could be a trick.

And there was another consideration. Only last night he had made a vow to hunt down the evil old skaven who had slain his father, and kill it in its lair. Could he let a wild goose chase into the deep woods get in the way of that vow? It didn't seem right, even to win back Karaghul. On the other hand, as Gotrek had said, the skaven were likely to come to him. Perhaps it was better to stay in the wilderness until they did. Fewer innocent people would be endangered that way.

'Archaon's hordes still haunt the Drakwald?' asked Gotrek.

The knight nodded. 'So I have been told,' he said. 'As well as beastmen, orcs, goblins and horrors too strange to be described. It will be a perilous journey.'

Felix glanced at the Slayer, and saw his one eye shining with bloodthirsty anticipation. He sighed. Whatever he might have decided in the end, it didn't matter now. The decision had been made.

Felix turned back to the old knight and nodded. 'Very well,' he said. 'I will take this quest. And I will do my best to prove myself worthy of possessing, er, carrying Karaghul – for however long you are pleased to grant it to me.'

The old knight looked at him, almost disappointed, then after a reluctant pause, picked up the sword and thrust it out. 'Take it, then, and sit. I will tell you my tale.'

Felix bowed, then took the sword and began strapping it around his waist. He was embarrassed at how comforted he was to have it again.

When he was finished, he and Gotrek sat down across the table from the knight, while his squire remained standing at attendance behind him.

'My name,' said the knight, as Gotrek signalled the serving girl, 'is Sir Teobalt von Dreschler, templar and librarian of the Order of the Fiery Heart, and, I fear, its last living representative.'

Young Ortwin coughed at this and Teobalt sighed and corrected himself. 'With the exception, of course, of my squire, Ortwin Wielhaber, who is the last novitiate of the order.'

The serving girl brought steins for Gotrek and Felix. Felix's stomach churned at the smell and he pushed his across to Sir Teobalt.

The old knight nodded his thanks, took a sip, then continued. 'When Archaon's invasion began,' he said, 'it was decided that, because of my advanced age, I should stay behind and maintain the chapter house while the others went north with the Emperor to do battle. Ortwin remained to assist me. Since then we have waited for our brothers' return, but they have not come home, and I have begun to fear that they will not.'

'I'm sorry to hear it,' said Felix politely.

Sir Teobalt waved that away. 'If they died in battle, fighting bravely for their Emperor and their homeland, then they will have achieved all that a knight may wish. I do not grieve them. I envy them.'

Gotrek grunted approvingly at this.

'Still,' said Teobalt, 'it is my duty to learn what became of them and to recover, if possible, the regalia of the order. We have had word from others who returned that, while many of my brothers fell at the siege of Middenheim, the order as a whole survived to begin the march back to Altdorf in the train of Karl Franz. The last anyone heard of them came to us more than a month ago. They had answered the plea of some peasants from a town near the abandoned fort of Stangenschloss to help defend their village against a herd of beastmen.'

Teobalt took another sip and continued. 'I know not the name of the town, or whether my brothers succeeded in its defence, but we must find it and learn their fate. We shall make our way to Stangenschloss and enquire of them along the way.'

'What is the regalia of the order?' asked Felix.

Teobalt looked about to answer, then smiled slyly and looked at Ortwin. 'Squire, prove that you have been diligent in your studies. What is the regalia of the Order of the Fiery Heart?'

Ortwin snapped to attention and coughed nervously. 'The regalia of the Order of the Fiery Heart consists of two pieces,' he began in a high, clear voice, 'the Banner of Baldemar, made from the cloak of the mighty warrior who founded the order, and bearing the device of a heart surrounded by a halo of flames, and the Sword of Righteous Flame, wielded first by Baron Konrad von

Zechlin at the gates of Kislev during the Great War against Chaos. It is said that the blade of the sword bursts into flames in the presence of the unrighteous.'

Teobalt nodded. 'Very good, boy. Very good. You have learned well.' He turned to Gotrek and Felix. 'If my brothers yet live, then time is of the essence. I would therefore start on the morrow at dawn, if that is not *too early* for you,' he said, giving them a sharp look.

Gotrek grunted. 'We'll be ready.'

Felix would have liked another full night's sleep to recover from last night's excesses, but he knew it would never happen. No matter how much he drank, Gotrek would be up and ready to march before the cock crowed if there was any prospect of danger and doom in the offing.

'Aye,' he sighed. 'We'll be ready.'

THREE

It took three days' travel on the riverboat *Magnus the Pious* before Ortwin, the young squire, got up the courage to speak to Felix.

For some reason, Felix had pictured Sir Teobalt making the entire journey from Altdorf to Fort Stangenschloss dressed in full armour and astride his mighty warhorse. It suited his image of Teobalt as a mad old knight, clanking off on adventures far past his prime, but the reality was much more mundane. The old knight travelled by cart, with all his armour and lances and instruments of war piled on the back under canvas, and his warhorse hitched to the tailgate along with Ortwin's pony, and in the interests of speed, they didn't even take to the road until they were halfway to their destination. Using funds from the coffers of the Order of the Fiery Heart, Sir Teobalt paid for passage on the *Magnus the Pious* up the Talabec from Altdorf to the town of Ahlenhof. Fort Stangenschloss was apparently due north from there, deep within the woods near the head of the Zufuhr river, a tributary of the Talabec that passed by the town.

For the first three days of the voyage, Felix noticed young Ortwin peering at him whenever he thought he wasn't looking. He was always peeking out from behind the mast when Felix was walking the deck, or goggling at him from the door when he was sitting in the common area. It was unnerving. When Ortwin was with Sir Teobalt he kept his eyes to himself, but as soon as they were apart, Ortwin was stalking Felix again. The boy's stare was like an owl's, wide and intense, but whenever Felix turned towards him to ask him what he wanted, he flew off like a frightened sparrow.

Felix didn't understand what the boy wanted. Did he hate Felix for holding Karaghul for so long? Did he suspect he was going to betray his master and run off with it without completing his end of the bargain? Had Sir Teobalt told him to keep an eye on him? If so, he was being less than subtle about it.

Finally, on the third day, as Felix was updating his journal in the common room with a hot brandy to keep out the chill of the day, he noticed the squire hovering nearby, his skullcap in his hands. Felix sighed and looked up, ready for another scurrying retreat, but wonder of wonders, Ortwin didn't dart for the long grass this time, but only swallowed and stood on one foot.

'Yes, Ortwin?' Felix said. 'You want to speak to me?'

'If… if it's not too much trouble, m'lord,' Ortwin stammered.

'Not at all,' said Felix dryly. 'I was only writing. And it isn't m'lord. I'm a merchant's son.'

'Well, sir,' said Ortwin, swallowing again. 'I... I just wanted to say that... that you are my hero, Herr Jaeger! I have read every book you have published. Sir Teobalt frowns on books that aren't about Sigmar or the knightly virtues, but I think they're wonderful!'

Felix stared, surprised. It wasn't what he had expected to hear. 'Er, thank you,' he said at last. 'I'm glad you liked them.' He felt a bit uncomfortable with the praise, but it felt good too. His chest swelled. Someone liked his work! He hadn't had a favourable review since his poetry days.

'Uh, can you tell me, sir,' the boy continued, nervously. 'Can you tell me how you chose to become an adventurer?'

Felix frowned. 'You did read the books, yes?'

'Oh, yes!' said the squire. 'Many times!'

'Then you know that it wasn't precisely a choice. I swore to follow the Slayer, but... I didn't really know what I was letting myself in for.'

Ortwin laughed as if Felix had told a joke. 'You see,' he said, stuttering a little, 'I intend to become an adventurer too. When I have become a full knight of the order, I am going to go to the ends of the earth, seeking out ancient evils and destroying them, just like you.'

Felix's face fell. Was the boy a complete idiot? He sighed, then closed his journal and looked him right in the eye. 'Listen to me, Ortwin. I think you've got the wrong idea from the books. I have had a lot of exciting adventures, it's true.' Terrifying, near-death experiences, he thought to himself. 'But there's not a day that goes by that I don't regret making that vow. There's not a day that goes by that I don't wish that I had chosen the path of warm beds and regular meals, of a wife and children and a proper job. The books…' He waved a hand, wishing he had read more of them. He still had no idea what was in most of them. 'It's not that I don't enjoy it sometimes. I do. But quite a lot of the time, I don't. I… I don't put everything in the books. I leave out the bits about starving for days, sometimes weeks, at a time, and the bits about getting soaking wet and catching horrible colds.'

'No, that's in,' said Ortwin, smiling.

'Fine,' said Felix. 'What I am trying to say is that it is not a romantic thing to be an adventurer. You are going to have a dangerous enough life as it is, being a member of a knightly order, but you will at least have a home to go to, and a whole company of comrades to watch your back, and some sort of pension set aside for when you get old. An adventurer has none of that. It is a lonely life, uncomfortable, wounding to the body, the mind and the spirit, and more dangerous than you could ever imagine. It is not a thing that any sane man would wish for himself. The adventurers I have known, man, elf and dwarf, were driven, desperate people, either running from something terrible, or chasing something impossible. They were not adventuring for the fun of it, or for some noble purpose, but because life had left them no other option. And they were all, without exception, stark, raving mad. Do you understand what I'm saying?'

'Oh, yes, sir,' said the boy, with the same gleam in his eye he had had when he had first admitted his love for the books. 'Thank you. That is very good advice, sir. I will be sure to keep it in mind.' He looked over his shoulder, then smiled again. 'I have to go tend to Sir Teobalt's corns now. I won't keep you from your writing any further. Thank you, Herr Jaeger. It was an honour to meet you.'

He hurried off with a spring in his step. It was quite clear to Felix that not a single word of what he had said had penetrated the young squire's thick skull. He moaned. How many young idiots were reading his books and making plans to go a-roving? He could just picture Ortwin's snow-covered corpse curled up in his bedroll somewhere in the Worlds Edge Mountains with a goblin spear through his spine, his first adventure over before it had begun. If he died, and all the other idiots with him, was Felix responsible? Would he have set them on the road to a quick death?

The idea of recalling and burning all the copies of the books rose up in his head. He didn't want any more deaths on his conscience. But it would be impossible to get all the books back, and would it really be his fault if some fool ran off after reading his stories? After all, some people – perhaps most people – just laughed at the books. Who was to say that the Ortwins of the world would not have sought adventure anyway? Felix had certainly not read stirring tales of derring-do when he was young. He had read romantic poetry and great philosophical dissertations, and yet here he was, vowing eternal vengeance on vile ratmen, and following a mad old knight into the woods in dead of winter on a wild goose chase after a sword and an old cloak. So perhaps one thing had nothing to do with the other.

THEY DISEMBARKED IN the bustling trading town of Ahlenhof four days later and asked about for a boat to take them up the Zufuhr as far as it was possible to go, but there seemed to be no boats to be had, though Teobalt offered double the normal rate.

'I'm sorry, sir,' said the fifth boatman they approached, 'but we are all commandeered. Stangenschloss has been regarrisoned, and is getting in supplies for the winter. Their quartermasters have rented every northbound boat along the Zufuhr for themselves, and the refugees take every southbound one. I wait now for oat fodder bound for the fort and daren't let my boat to any other.'

'Stangenschloss regarrisoned?' said Teobalt, his ears perking up. 'Have you heard aught of the Knights of the Fiery Heart there? Or of who garrisons it?'

'No, m'lord,' said the boatman. 'I have not heard that name, or who commands there.'

And so, with similar answers everywhere they asked, and Sir Teobalt impatient to be started, they put their packs in the cart and began to make their way north by the rutted and muddy forest road that paralleled the little river instead.

With winter coming on, almost no one was going north, but many were coming south. Huddled refugees bundled in rags against the cold, trains of Shallyan hospital wagons, carrying the wounded and diseased down from the northern battlefields, soldiers from every province of the Empire, limping home after fighting all summer and autumn. Some were boisterous and prideful, for the Empire had won a great victory, and they sang jaunty marching songs and bragged amongst themselves about their kills and their conquests, but more were gaunt, sick, maimed or shattered in their minds, for the victory had come at a great cost, and against an enemy so strange and terrible that even to defeat them was to risk madness. It made Felix uneasy to see them.

The way was narrow and hemmed in by trees, and at every meeting, Sir Teobalt had to pull his cart to the side to let the southbound travellers pass. Sometimes they were met by jocularities – 'Off to fight at Middenheim, grandfather? You're a little late,' and, 'He may be old, but his lance is still hard! Just ask his squire!'

Just as often, however, they were met by warnings – 'Turn back, my lord. There is snow and ice north of Leer,' and, 'Beware the beasts! They ate half our party at Trenkenkraag,' and, 'Come back in the spring. Whatever you seek won't be found this winter. You will find only death.'

Sir Teobalt paid no attention to either jests or advice, just set his face in a look of dour disapproval and waited for whomever it might be to pass. Gotrek also made no comment, mostly because after one look at his crest and massive physique, no one was foolish enough to toss any jibes his way.

On the afternoon of the first day they came across a troop of Reikland archers surrounding a plump merchant and his four guards, who perched atop their ale wagon like cats treed by a pack of dogs. The archers were all clamouring to be given a drink, and some were trying to pull down kegs from the back as the guards shouted and banged at their fingers with cudgels.

'It's all spoken for, friends!' cried the merchant, wide-eyed with fear. 'I can't sell you any! I'm sorry!'

'Then give us some!' cried one of the archers. 'Do you want the boys who saved your sorry hide from the Kurgan to go thirsty?'

'Ungrateful lout,' said another. 'Fat while we're starving!'

'Only one barrel!' shouted several others.

Felix didn't like to see such bullying, but he might have passed by without interfering, as he could also see the archers' point of view, but Sir Teobalt, however, was incensed.

'Sergeant! Control your men!' he bellowed as he stood up on the buckboard of their cart.

The sergeant, who had been harrying the merchant just as strongly as his men, turned, sneering, but when he saw that he was addressing a nobleman he paused, then gave a hesitant salute.

'Sorry, m'lord,' he said. 'But the men are sore thirsty, and long on the road.'

'That is no excuse to rob an innocent merchant on the high road. By Sigmar, did you not go north to protect the people of our dear land? You might as well be Kurgan yourselves! Be off with you!'

Some of the archers growled under their breath at this, and none of them moved from the ale wagon.

The sergeant looked nervously from Teobalt to the archers and back. 'M'lord, I don't think they'll listen to me. They'll have my head if they don't have beer.'

Gotrek drew his axe and stood beside the templar. 'And I'll have their heads if they do!' he roared.

The sergeant's eyes bulged, and his men looked around and stared.

'Who wants a drink, then?' snarled Gotrek, slapping the haft of the axe against his palm.

The sergeant looked doleful, but finally sighed and turned to his men. 'All right then, lads. Let's away and leave this honest merchant to his journey. We was only teasing anyway.'

A chorus of 'aye' and 's'right' and 'only a bit of fun' followed this, and the archers formed up reluctantly behind the sergeant and began again to head south.

Teobalt regarded them disdainfully from under his shaggy white brows as they marched by. 'For shame,' he said. 'That soldiers of Karl Franz's Empire must be turned from evil by threat of violence. I despair for the modern age.'

The archers hung their heads as they passed under that penetrating gaze, but as they marched away, Felix thought he heard one of them say, 'Stick it in yer ear, m'lord.'

When they had gone, Teobalt turned to Gotrek and inclined his head. 'My thanks, herr dwarf. But for your timely interjection, things might have gone very differently.'

Gotrek shrugged. 'Forget it.'

Just then the merchant jumped down from his cart and hurried over to them, his eyes bright. 'My lord! My friends! Herr dwarf! Thank you! How can I ever repay you? I was in desperate danger of losing my stock and perhaps my life. Had you not come along, all would have been taken.'

'Do not trouble yourself, my good man,' said Teobalt. 'It is only what any man of the Empire would do, when faced with such injustice.'

'Not so, m'lord,' said the merchant. 'There are many who would have helped the soldiers against me and shared in the spoils.' He clasped Teobalt's boot upon the buckboard. 'I beg you, m'lord. If we travel the same road, might we not travel it together? This was not the first such trouble, and I fear it may not be the last, but with your presence, I may get my beer all the way to Bauholz in safety.'

'If Bauholz lies on the path to Fort Stangenschloss, then you are welcome to join our train,' said Sir Teobalt.

'It does, m'lord,' said the merchant eagerly. 'It is the town closest to it. The fort is just five days or so north of it, through the woods. And I thank you for your kindness.'

Sir Teobalt waved that aside and they got underway again, Teobalt's cart in the lead and the ale wagon following close behind.

As he walked beside the cart, Felix leaned in towards Gotrek, who sat beside the old knight. 'I've never seen you take such an interest in defending the common man when there wasn't a monster or daemon involved,' he said.

'It wasn't the common man I was defending,' said Gotrek, licking his lips. 'It was his beer.'

'Ah,' said Felix, and they travelled on.

NORTH OF THE little village of Leer, the road became no more than a track, with the trees drawn in closer on either side, making even high noon dark and full of shadows. Sir Teobalt ordered Ortwin to don his armour and helmet and to keep his sword at the ready. With the squire's help he did the same himself, strapping on his cuirass and vambraces and setting his helmet beside him on the buckboard. The merchant and his guards belted their leather jacks tighter underneath their woollen cloaks and heavy scarves. Felix followed their example, shrugging into his ringmail and loosening Karaghul in its scabbard, then tugging his old red cloak close around his shoulders. Gotrek had no armour to don, but he held his axe across his knees, not on his back.

At the same time it began to grow colder, with a few dry flakes of snow drifting down through the interwoven firs above them, and the thick mud of the track freezing into lumpy ridges and making it hard going for the carts. There were many times when they were obliged to get out and push, or lift their wheels out of some deep depression.

This was no problem with Teobalt's cart, which was almost empty, but the ale wagon was another matter, and the merchant, whose name was Dider Reidle, had many opportunities to thank Gotrek for his strength and Felix for his assistance; and that first night north of Leer, when they made camp, rewarded them all by broaching a cask of his precious cargo as they sat down to their dinner around the fire, and filling their cups and jacks.

Gotrek pronounced it 'not bad,' which was high praise coming from a dwarf.

Felix saluted the merchant. 'Thank you, Herr Reidle,' he said. 'It's very good.'

Reidle bowed his head. 'Thank *you*, sir. Without you I would have none to share.'

'I don't understand why you made the journey if it is so dangerous,' said Felix. 'Can the profit be so great that it's worth the risk?'

Reidle sighed. 'Well, had I been able to take the river, there would have been little risk, but all the boats are spoken for, and since I had already been partly paid for the shipment I felt I must try, dangerous though it may be.'

'Is Bauholz so large that it needs all this beer?' asked Sir Teobalt.

'Only recently, m'lord,' said Reidle. 'It was a tiny little village by all accounts, but since the war it has become a booming place. It is the last good port on the Zufuhr, and so has got a lot of traffic lately, with soldiers going one way, and refugees going the other. Before they had no inn, and only Taal's bower for a tavern. Now they have three inns, and beer and sausages for sale in every shack and tent that can hold two people.'

Sir Teobalt made a face. 'It sounds like a place of sin and depravity.'

'Oh aye,' said Reidle with a smile. 'But good for business.'

FOR FOUR MORE days they continued north into the woods towards Bauholz, and with every step Felix felt like he was pushing deeper into some web that he would not be able to walk out of again. He could not shake the feeling that the forest was watching them – that unseen presences were waiting for them to let down their guard so that they might pounce. He never saw anything, or heard anything more than birdcalls and the yelp of foxes or the bay of distant wolves, but always there was the same tingling between his shoulder blades that felt like hungry eyes upon him.

They spent their third night at a lumber camp on the banks of Zufuhr, little more than a few tents and stacks of trimmed tree trunks inside a temporary wooden palisade. The wood cutters knew Reidle from previous trips and welcomed him warmly, particularly after he rolled the broached barrel off the back of his cart and invited them all to share.

'Well worth it,' he whispered to Felix as they were sitting down to eat a hearty venison stew in the camp's mess tent, 'for the security of sleeping inside walls.'

Though he knew the safety of the camp was largely an illusion, Felix was inclined to agree. The feeling of being watched had diminished as soon as they had entered the palisade, and his shoulders had relaxed for the first time since they had left Leer.

'And with luck we'll be in Bauholz and journey's end before dark tomorrow,' Reidle continued. 'As long as the weather holds.'

It was too bad Bauholz was only the beginning of *his* journey, thought Felix. Sigmar only knew where Sir Teobalt's search for the missing templars would lead them. He had a sudden fantasy of finding them all waiting for them at the gates of Bauholz, healthy and happy and ready for Teobalt to lead them home. He chuckled at the foolishness of the vision. It was never that easy.

Never.

THE NEXT MORNING, as they shared a breakfast of river trout, porridge and beer with the camp foreman, Felix watched with interest as the wood cutters laid dozens of tree trunks side by side on the bank of the river, then lashed them together with sturdy ropes.

By the time they'd finished eating and hitched the horses again to the wagons, these log rafts had been pushed out onto the water, and as Felix and Gotrek and the rest rode out of the compound and turned north towards Bauholz, they had begun drifting south down the river towards Ahlenhof, each carrying two men armed with long hook-tipped poles who stood at the forward corners.

They're going the right way, thought Felix, as the flotilla vanished around a bend in the river, and the feeling of being watched settled between his shoulderblades once again, just as strongly as before.

BY LATE AFTERNOON it was clear that, though the weather had held, in all other ways, Reidle's luck had failed him. With the light of the sun turning from red to purple, they were still hours away from Bauholz and trying, for the fifth time that day, to rock the ale cart out of a deep frozen rut.

They were having little success.

Gotrek was under the wagon, muddy to the knees and lifting with his back pressed against the bottom of the bed, while Felix and Reidle hauled at the spokes of the back wheels and the rest pushed at the tail. Squire Ortwin held the leads of the carthorses while Sir Teobalt directed the whole operation from the side.

'Ortwin,' cried the old knight. 'On my mark, lead them forwards while the rest push. Ready? Heave!'

Felix heaved at the wagon along with Gotrek and the others, his feet slipping in the icy muck. It rolled forwards almost to the lip of the rut, then slid back again like it had the last seven times.

'Better,' called Teobalt encouragingly. 'Once more and we shall have it. Ready?'

Felix wiped mud from his eye and put his shoulder to the wagon again with the others, but just as Sir Teobalt was raising his hand to call 'heave,' one of the horses whickered and backed nervously in its traces while the other neighed and plunged ahead.

The wagon jolted forwards. Gotrek was knocked flat as the axle clipped his back and the others staggered and fell. Felix slipped too, banging his shoulder against the wheel and landing in the mud.

He jumped up cursing and rubbing his shoulder as Ortwin tried to calm the horses. 'Damn this cart!' he said. 'Damn these horses! We should take the damned barrels off and roll them to Bauholz!' He kicked the wagon wheel. 'I've had enough of this–'

'Quiet, manling,' said Gotrek, crawling out from under the wagon. He picked up his axe and looked around at the surrounding woods.

Felix stopped and listened as well, though it was hard to hear anything over the worried whickering of the wagon's horses. Their distress seemed to have spread to the other animals as well. Sir Teobalt's carthorses were throwing their heads and rolling their eyes, while Ortwin's pony was pulling at its lead. Only Sir Teobalt's charger remained calm, though its ears turned alertly.

Reidle's guards drew their swords, their heads on swivels.

'What is it?' whispered Reidle. 'Bandits?'

'Wolves?' asked one of his guards.

'Worse,' said Gotrek.

Sir Teobalt clapped on his helmet and took up his shield, then motioned them all to get between the two wagons. 'Face out from the centre. They may come from any side.'

They gathered behind Sir Teobalt's cart, which was in front of the ale wagon, and turned to either side, weapons at the ready. Teobalt began praying and Ortwin and Reidle's guards picked it up. 'Lord Sigmar grant us your strength in this our hour of need. Let us smite our enemies like your hammer. Let us push back the powers of darkness.'

Behind them, Reidle took his horses from Ortwin and did his best to calm them, whispering, 'There now, Bess.

Nothing to be afraid of,' and, 'Here, Pommertz, who's a brave boy then.'

For a moment, his murmurs and the shifting of the horses and the harsh breathing of the men was all that could be heard. The silence was unnerving. Felix and the others stared into the murk of shadows under the trees, their breath trailing away in steaming clouds, waiting for Sigmar only knew what. The tension made Felix grind his teeth.

'Which way are they coming from?' murmured Ortwin, adjusting a helmet that looked too big for him.

'Where are they?' asked one of the guards.

'Maybe the horses only spooked themselves,' said another.

'Silence,' said Sir Teobalt. 'Be ready.' A fine old long sword gleamed in his hand.

'Be ready for what?' asked one of the guards querulously.

He was cut off by a bloodcurdling roar from the woods to their left. Everyone jumped. The horses screamed and tore from Reidle's grasp.

'Steady!' cried Sir Teobalt.

With a thunder of hooves, the woods erupted with nightmares made flesh. Felix froze, terror gripping his heart. He had faced them before, but no amount of familiarity could breed contempt for such monsters. Five towering goat-legged, goat-headed monsters led the charge – two to the left of the carts, three on the right – followed by a swarm of smaller, more human horrors, mutated men with short, budding horns and mouths full of filed teeth. The behemoths rushed in, bellowing, their powerful limbs swinging huge spiked clubs and massive iron maces. Their smaller, scrawnier followers spread out behind them, knives and sickles and clubs clutched in their twisted claws.

Two of Reidle's guards died instantly, bodies pulped by a single swing of a beastman's mace. Gotrek leapt forwards before the monster had finished its swing and buried his axe in its stomach. He tore it out again with a spray of blood and was on the next before the first had begun to topple.

Teobalt ran out to meet another of the leaders, crying, 'To me, foul beast! Come face Sigmar's wrath!'

The beastman swung at him with a club that looked like a giant's femur, and Teobalt took it on his shield. The force of it slammed the old knight to the ground and the beast trampled over him and leapt at Reidle's horses, ripping old Bess's throat out with its teeth as the merchant fell back, screaming and throwing up his arms.

A beastman with a third horn sprouting from its forehead charged Felix. He flinched away from its gore-matted mace and crashed against Teobalt's cart to fall in the mud again. Three-Horn came on. Felix backhanded desperately with Karaghul and rolled under the cart as the beastman's sticky mace crashed down, splintering the planks of the cart. Felix hunched down, then lashed out from under the tailgate, hacking at the beastman's backward-bending legs. It jumped back.

All around, Felix could hear the screams of men and horses and the roaring cries of the beastmen and their followers. Quick glances showed him flashes of violence in every direction – the two remaining guards fighting for their lives in the midst of a handful of the lesser beasts, Teobalt's warhorse kicking the brains out of another, a lesser beast on the ale wagon, hacking at the straps that held the barrels tight, Gotrek exchanging clanging blows with a beastman three times his height, Reidle the merchant crawling on his belly, weeping like a baby, Ortwin slashing wildly at a pair of beast-followers as he tried to reach Sir Teobalt, who fought the beastman that had trampled him.

Then, with almost human screams, Teobalt's carthorses bolted as a pair of the scrawny beastlings leapt on their backs. With the horses went the cart, leaving Felix exposed again. The three-horned beastman loomed above him, swinging down with its mace. Felix rolled to the side and felt the ground shake as the massive iron weapon slammed down beside him. He jumped to his feet, slashing blindly around at the beastman's encroaching followers. The smell of them was overpowering. They reeked like a sewer full of dead dogs.

The three-horned beastman leapt at him again, swinging for his head. Felix ducked and lunged, stabbing forwards with all his might. Karaghul's point skidded across the beast's massive belly shield and punched through its ribs.

The monster howled and wrenched away violently. Felix held on, but could not pull his sword loose. Enraged and in pain, the beastman swung down at him. Felix let go of his sword and jumped back, slamming into a lesser beast who was trying to brain him from behind.

He grabbed the thing by its stubby horns and threw it in front of him. The three-horned beastman's mace crushed it, and it slumped to the ground like a bag of wet meat.

Three-Horn came on. Felix turned to run and found himself surrounded by its followers, all closing in on him. A sword! He needed a sword. One of the dead guards held on to one. Felix rolled to him, ducking a handful of attacks, ripped it from the guard's slack hand and lashed out all around. The lesser beasts dodged back then advanced again. There seemed no escape. Or was there?

Screaming he knew not what, Felix charged a man-beast that was between him and the ale wagon. The thing leapt aside and Felix sprang up onto the cart, kicking down the hideous thing that had been cutting at the leather straps. He climbed to the top of the barrels and turned to face his pursuers.

'Now try me!' he cried, triumphant.

The three-horned beastman slammed its mace into the cart so hard that it jumped. Felix staggered and almost lost his footing. His skinny followers started to climb the sides. Perhaps this hadn't been Felix's best idea.

A quick glance around told him that the rest of the wagon train was faring no better. Sir Teobalt and the beastman he had fought were both down, while Ortwin stood over the old knight's body, fighting a handful of lesser beasts. Only one of the guards remained standing, backed up by two more beastlings, and Reidle lay unmoving on the ground next to the ale cart. Only Gotrek was master of his situation, beating back his monstrous opponent with blow after blow.

Felix hacked at a climbing man-beast with his borrowed sword and bit deep into its shoulder. It screamed and fell off. But then Three-Horn swung again and Felix had to leap up to let the mace pass under his feet.

He knew before he landed that it would go wrong. His boot heels slipped on the curve of the barrel and he bounced down the side of the pyramid, knocking the wind from his lungs, and just barely catching himself at the wagon's rail.

The lesser beasts converged towards him, cackling. He kicked one in the chops and lashed out at another, but he was so precariously balanced that if he tried to move more than that he would fall between the barrels and the rail of the cart and be wedged tight.

The three-horned beastman pushed through its followers, Karaghul still sticking out of its ribs. Felix scrambled for purchase on the barrels and could find none. Behind Three-Horn he saw Gotrek running to help Ortwin. Couldn't the damn fool dwarf see that his old friend was in trouble?

'Gotrek! Help!' he called, but he was too winded, and it came out as a whisper. As Three-Horn loomed over him, raising its mace, Felix held up his short sword, knowing it would be like trying to stop an avalanche with a twig.

But then, as he waited cringing for the blow to fall, the beastman bellowed and arched its back in pain. Felix blinked. Karaghul was sticking from Three-Horn's ribs right in front of him. It was like the beastman was offering it to him.

Felix reached forwards with both hands and wrenched with all his might. The blade came free, causing the beastman to howl even louder. It also threw Felix's balance off, and he fell, just as he had feared, on his back between the barrels and the cart rail. He was trapped.

Three-Horn roared above him, blood flowing down its furred side like a river as it raised its mace once again. Felix did the only thing he could do, and thrust up fast and hard with Karaghul, aiming as best he could. The blade punched into the flesh below Three-Horn's lowest rib and sank deep.

With a whistling sigh, the beastman staggered sideways, its knees buckling. The bloody rent in its flesh ripped wider as its weight dragged at the sword, and its guts spilled out and slapped against its belt. It twisted as it fell, and Felix saw something thin and white sticking out of its back – an arrow!

Felix clawed at the rail, struggling up out of the confining space and looking around. The man-beasts that had been climbing the ale cart were on the ground, all writhing with arrows in their backs and necks.

As he turned towards Ortwin and Gotrek, he saw them cutting down the lesser beasts around them, half of which were also impaled with arrows, and as he watched, another arrow shot from the woods to the left and pierced the leg of one of the three beastlings fighting the last standing guard. The man killed it as it lost its balance, then turned on the others.

Felix vaulted the cart rail and ran to help him, but the lesser beastmen, seeing him coming, turned and fled for the woods – straight for where the arrows had come from. A third beastling picked itself up and joined them, squealing in fright.

Felix and the last guard started after them, but before they could take two steps, another arrow shot from the trees and took one of the man-beasts in the eye, dropping it. The other two kept running for the trees.

With a wail like a banshee, the hidden archer burst from the underbrush with a long, narrow-headed hatchet in each hand. He was small and quick and bundled in filthy furs, and ran straight at the escaping beastlings. They dodged right and left, too panicked to fight, but the archer side-armed one of the hatchets at the one on the left, then leapt at the one on the right. The thrown axe spun in a perfect arc and split the forehead of the left-hand man-beast. At the same time the archer kicked the right-hand monster full in the face with both feet, knocking it flat, then landed, turned and buried the second hatchet in its chest. The man-beast shrieked and tried to sit up, but the archer stomped on its throat and levered the axe free, then stepped back and let out a sigh of relief.

Felix looked around in the sudden silence. All the beastmen and their lesser followers were dead or fled, and he and at least some of the others still lived. Such an outcome hadn't seemed possible a moment ago. They had the archer to thank for that.

He and Gotrek started towards the figure as Ortwin knelt beside the fallen templar.

'Nice shooting,' said Gotrek.

'Thank you for the help,' added Felix.

The archer stood from prying the second axe from the other beastling and flipped back dirty, matted hair to peer at them. Felix stopped short, surprised.

Though she was bundled in thick leather armour and furs, with a scarf up to her narrow chin against the cold, and though her face was mottled with grime and scarred from hairline to the corner of her full lips on her left side, there was no mistaking the archer's sex at close range. Her fierce brown eyes flashed keenly under her unruly mass of hair, which was all black but for a lock over her left eye that was as white as snow. 'I... I have sworn an oath to...' Her words faded away as she looked closely at Gotrek for the first time.

'You,' she said, staring.

She turned and looked at Felix. 'And you!'

Felix exchanged a puzzled glance with Gotrek. Gotrek shrugged. He didn't know her either.

Suddenly the filthy girl fell to her knees before them. She grabbed Felix's hand and kissed it.

'My heroes!' she said.

FOUR

Felix stared down at the young woman as she covered his hand with kisses. He felt slightly dizzy. First Ortwin and now this strange forest creature. Had everyone read his books? Was he truly this famous?

'So... so you've read them too?' he asked.

She looked up at him curiously. 'Read? Read what?'

'My books,' he said. 'You've read my books.'

She shook her head. 'I don't know how to read.'

Felix felt even dizzier. 'Then how... uh, that is, why are we your heroes?'

She blinked, confused. 'You... But, I'm Kat. Katerina. You rescued me from the beastmen. You rescued me from... that woman.'

Felix looked at Gotrek again. The Slayer shrugged.

'We... we did?'

'Yes!' said the archer, a slight edge of desperation creeping into her voice. 'In Flensburg! It is because of you that I have become a slayer of beasts!' She looked worried now. 'You... you don't remember?'

Suddenly, with a flood of images and emotions, he *did* remember. The massacred village. The frightened little girl, hiding in the ruins of the inn. The desperate fight with the beastmen in the woods. The defence of Flensburg. The hideous strength of the woman with the white streak in her hair as she closed her hand around his throat. The little girl again, her eyes wide as she held the sword that had killed the woman, then once more as she begged and pleaded with Felix and Gotrek to take her with them, and then hugged them goodbye.

'You,' he said.

'You,' said Gotrek, and an uncharacteristic smile cracked his hard expression. 'You seem to have become a hero yourself, little one.'

Kat flushed at that, though it barely showed through the patina of dirt on her cheeks. 'I have vowed to rid all of the Drakwald of beastmen,' she said into her scarf.

'A noble ambition,' said Felix, his mind still reeling. 'I... I can't believe, after all this time...'

'Friends!' came Ortwin's voice from behind them. 'Help me. Sir Teobalt is sorely wounded.'

They turned. Ortwin was still kneeling by the old knight, who lay flat on the ground. Gotrek and Felix hurried towards them, Kat tailing behind.

On the way, Felix looked around at the aftermath of the battle and totalled the cost. Two guards dead and the other two wounded, one so badly he couldn't stand. Both of the ale cart horses mauled to death. Sir Teobalt's cart wedged between two trees, its wheels smashed and its horses missing. Ortwin's pony dead with its skull caved in, and Sir Teobalt's charger pacing nervously nearby with deep claw marks in its flanks. It occurred to Felix that if the beastmen hadn't been so hungry for horseflesh the battle might have gone much worse. At least the beer had been saved – and the beer merchant, it seemed, for Herr Reidle was groaning to his feet behind his wagon and peering around anxiously.

Sir Teobalt looked up as they gathered around him. He had a deep gash across one cheek where the edge of his helmet had cut him, and his armour was covered in dents. 'Right glad I am to see you alive, friends,' he said feebly. 'Valiantly fought.'

'How badly are you hurt, sir?' asked Felix, kneeling beside him.

'Mere inconveniences,' he said. 'My shoulder took a heavy blow, and I cannot at the moment move my left leg. Also, my vision is blurred. I fear I will need some rest.'

Felix turned to Kat. 'Do you know how far it is to Bauholz?'

'About an hour's walk,' she said. 'No more than two.'

Felix looked up at the few patches of purple sky that showed through the thick canopy of needles above them. 'Perhaps we should camp–' he began, but Kat cut him off.

'You must not stay here tonight. There are wolves and other beasts that will smell the blood. You will get no peace.'

Felix looked around, assessing their resources. One horse and a heavily laden wagon – that was all they had in the way of transport. He stood. It would have to do. 'Unload Herr Reidle's wagon and hitch Sir Teobalt's horse to it. We will lay Sir Teobalt and the other wounded men in it.'

Both Reidle and Teobalt erupted at this.

'Leave the beer?' cried the merchant. 'It'll be stolen!'

'Hitch Machtig to a cart!' complained Teobalt. 'Never! He is a warhorse. He has never stooped to such common duty, and never shall.'

'That common duty may save your life,' growled Gotrek.

'And do you expect us to carry your beer to Bauholz?' Felix asked Herr Reidle. 'Not even a warhorse has the strength to pull all that.'

'The horses from the other cart might come back,' insisted Reidle.

'They might,' said Felix. 'But I'm not waiting all night to find out.'

Both the merchant and the knight continued to complain, but there was little they could do. Gotrek, Felix, Ortwin and the less wounded guard set to unloading the beer from the cart and hitching the warhorse to it as Kat bound the wounds of Teobalt and the maimed guard as best she could with a field kit she wore at her belt. The proud charger complained almost as bitterly as its master when they laid the yoke across its neck, but with Ortwin whispering soothing words in his ears it finally acquiesced. Then they laid Sir Teobalt, the wounded guard and his dead companions on the back, and set off for Bauholz as the hidden sky above turned from violet to cobalt, and the shadows of the trees closed in around them.

FELIX HAD A thousand questions he wanted to ask Kat, for her transformation from a scared, sweet little girl to hardened beast-slayer was still a shock to him, but she had insisted on going ahead to scout the way and so he had no opportunity to talk to her. Instead he carried a lantern beside Ortwin as the youth led Machtig down the track. Gotrek took up the rear, keeping an eye out behind them in case more horrors came out of the woods.

After a half an hour or so during which Ortwin remained entirely silent, Felix looked over at him. The poor lad had had his first taste of adventure and it seemed to have stunned him a bit. Felix didn't blame him. Death and mutilation at close range were a far different thing than death and mutilation in a book. Felix had become somewhat inured to it over the years, but he could well remember the feelings of terror and nausea that used to overcome him before and after a fight. Maybe the boy was having second thoughts about a life of adventure. He hoped so.

'Not quite like it is in books, is it?' he said, smiling sadly.

'I'm sorry, sir?' said Ortwin, lifting his head from his thoughts.

'I was just wondering if our fight just now lived up to your expectations.'

Ortwin shook his head, eyes wide and far away. 'It was... it was glorious!'

Felix blinked at him, stunned. 'Uh... glorious?'

'Oh yes, sir!'

Felix frowned, anger stirring inside him. Was the boy bloodthirsty? Was he cold-hearted? 'You weren't frightened of the beasts? You weren't troubled by the slaughter of Reidle's guards, or the horses? Or by poor Sir Teobalt's grievous wounds?'

'Of course I was,' said Ortwin, not appearing to notice Felix's hard tone. 'I have never been so terrified in my life, Herr Jaeger. They were the foulest creatures I have ever set eyes upon, and they did vile, horrible things. My heart was near frozen with fear. But… but we vanquished them! We looked into the face of evil and though we were sorely tested, we did not flinch. We persevered! We have pushed back the forces of Chaos!'

A laugh burst from Felix though he tried to stop it. 'We haven't even given the forces of Chaos a paper-cut. And we didn't persevere over anything. We were about to die defending a wagonload of beer from a bunch of mindless beasts, when a girl with a good eye and a quick draw saved us. And I flinched plenty.'

Ortwin turned and stared at him, his eyes wide in the lantern light, his mouth open. Felix sighed. He shouldn't have been so harsh. He had broken the boy's poor sheltered heart with his hard-won bitterness.

He coughed. 'Listen, Ortwin, I…'

But then Ortwin laughed and grinned at him. 'Oh, but I see! This is the grim humour that I love so much in your books. The self-mocking jokes you use to disguise the true nobility of your acts.' He smiled sheepishly. 'Forgive me, sir. For a moment I almost thought you serious, but I see now that, like all good knights, you are truly humble, and do not wish to be praised for your deeds.'

It was Felix's turn to stare. The boy really thought he was joking. Felix opened his mouth to tell him that he wasn't kidding, and that he actually meant what he said, but then he closed it again. What was the point? Ortwin probably wouldn't believe him anyway, and besides, there was no need to shatter the boy's delusions about the world so quickly. He would find out for himself soon enough.

'Believe what you like, Ortwin,' said Felix, defeated. 'Just keep buying the books.'

Ortwin laughed. 'Very good, sir. Very good!'

Felix sighed and they walked on in silence.

AT LAST, AN hour into true night, the wagon came out of the forest into a narrow area of cleared land beside the Zufuhr river, and Felix saw, on its banks, the silhouette of a small, palisaded village in the distance, a faint glow of torchlight illuminating the tops of its squat wooden watch-towers. Felix noted that the fields were patchy with dead weeds and stray stalks of wheat, all gone to seed. It appeared that there had been no planting and no harvest this year. How had the village survived?

He turned away from Ortwin, looking around for Kat, and jumped when he discovered that she was already beside him. It was as if she had stepped out from behind a moonbeam. 'Oh!' he said, then lowered his voice. 'There you are.'

'I must warn you, Fel...' she paused suddenly and looked down. 'I... I'm sorry. I don't know what to call you now.'

Felix smiled as they started towards the town again. What a strange young woman she was, so vicious and yet so demure at the same time. 'You may still call me Felix, Kat,' he said. 'We've known each other for a long time, after all.'

'Thank you, Felix,' she said, smiling shyly.

His heart fluttered uncomfortably in his chest as her smile lanced through him. It seemed wrong to be stirred by someone you last knew as a seven-year-old, but filthy as she was, she was undeniably attractive.

'You're... most welcome,' he mumbled. 'Er, what was it you were saying?'

Her face grew grim and she nodded towards the village. 'Bauholz. I wanted to warn you that it is a bad town.'

'Oh?'

'It was good once,' she said. 'Before the war. It was my home from the woods. But the war killed it, and now the soldiers and bandits are feeding on the corpse.'

'Soldiers?' asked Felix.

'Aye. A man from the south and his men – Captain Ludeker.' She spat on the ground at the name. 'He was like all the others, coming back from the war on his way home, but then he decided to stay and rob all the rest. Now he runs the town.'

Felix frowned. He knew about those kinds of soldiers. They were in every war, and on every side. 'What has he done?'

'He steals from the supply boats going north and sells seats on all the boats going south. All the refugees must pay him to board, and he charges a fortune. He has turned the strong house and the temple of Sigmar into taverns, and he runs dice and card games in them, and keeps women upstairs. Every soldier that comes through town has his pocket picked.' She looked up into Felix's face, her eyes flashing. 'Beware of him, Felix, and tell Gotrek too. He will try to take everything you own.'

Felix chuckled, imagining anyone trying to take anything from Gotrek. 'I will be sure to warn him,' he said. 'But if the town is so bad, why are we going there?'

She pointed across the Zufuhr. 'We're not. We are going to the refugee camp on the other side of the river, but the only bridge is within the town. There is no other way across for miles.'

Felix frowned. 'You're taking us to a refugee camp?'

'Yes,' said Kat. 'To Herr Doktor Vinck. He is my friend. He will doctor your friends.'

Felix nodded, though he wondered how qualified a doctor that lived among refugees would be.

Kat turned to him, biting her lip, as the walls of the town loomed before them. 'Er, do you have any money?' she asked.

'Ah, a little. Why?'

'Ludeker has made a gate tax.'

'Who's that, then?' said a voice in the darkness.

Felix peered ahead to the big closed gate and saw two men in dirt-grimed uniforms that suggested they were from a company of Streissen handgunners strolling out from a small torchlit side door, naked swords dangling from casual hands.

'Travellers with wounded,' said Felix. 'Please let us in.'

'Wounded?' said the first man suspiciously. He was a thin-faced fellow with lank blond hair. 'What happened to ye?'

'We were attacked by beastmen in the woods,' said Reidle from where he sat on the buckboard. 'I beg you, sirs, be swift.'

The two men looked out into the night at the mention of beastmen, gripping their weapons tighter.

'There's beasts about and you want us to open the gate?' said the second man, a square-built tough with a three-day beard. He took a step back towards the little door.

'Please,' said Ortwin, stepping up beside Felix. 'They have hurt my master. He requires a doctor.'

'Open the gate, Wappler,' sighed Kat. 'The beastmen are dead. You've no need to fear.'

Wappler, the thinner man, peered towards her. 'Is it the she-beast, then? Brought us some more deadbeat refugees?'

The thick man laughed. 'Don't need any more of those. Town's full.'

'What are we waiting for?' asked Gotrek, coming from behind the wagon.

The two guards turned to him, then stared, their eyes drawn to the golden bracelets on his wrists, which gleamed warmly in the torchlight.

Wappler licked his lips. 'We'll open the gates, yer worships,' he said. 'But first there's the matter of the taxes.'

'Aye,' said the other, shouldering his sword. 'We have a foot tax here in Bauholz – for wear and tear on the public way. One pfennig per foot.'

Wappler walked among them, muttering under his breath. 'Two, four, six, eight, ten, twelve, and four for the horse makes sixteen. Now who do we have in the back?' He peered over the side of the beer wagon where Teobalt and the badly wounded guard dozed between the corpses of the others. 'Four more. That makes twenty-four. Two shillings.'

'Two of those men are dead,' said Felix.

'Still got feet, haven't they?'

'But they're not going to make much wear and tear on the public way,' Felix protested.

Wappler shrugged. 'I don't make the laws, mein herr, I just enforce 'em.' He smacked his lips. 'Now, there's also the danger tax – opening the gate when there's hostiles about. That's a shilling.'

'And the wounded tax,' said his companion. 'Four pennies each for each man who can't walk through the gate on his own. That's another eight pennies.'

'Right, that's three shillings and... aw, just round it up to four shillings, then,' said Wappler cheerily. 'That's easier.'

'A wounded tax?' rasped Gotrek menacingly.

'Aye, herr dwarf,' said Wappler. 'A man who's wounded can't work, and is therefore a burden on the community. Got to compensate for that, haven't we?'

Gotrek balled his fists, and his single eye sparked like a lit fuse in the torchlight. 'You can take your taxes and shove them up your skinny little human–'

'I'll pay, sirs!' said Ortwin, stepping forwards hastily. 'I would not argue while my master bleeds.'

He took a purse from his belt and shook out four silver shillings. Wappler took the money and signalled behind him, his eyes never leaving Gotrek. 'Be glad I didn't levy a resisting taxation tax on you, dwarf,' he said.

'You should be glad too,' growled Gotrek.

With a creaking of rope and timber, the big gates swung slowly open and the party started forwards into Bauholz.

Beyond the torches at the gate, the little village was dark, and it was hard to see many details, but Felix could see enough to realise that Bauholz was not a healthy town. The silhouettes of the little houses were lopsided and tumble-down, some with the ribs of their roof timbers naked to the sky. There was rubbish in the street and a stink of excrement, urine and rot all around. Things skittered away from them in the dark.

Towards the centre of the village there was more light – quite a bit of it in fact. Bright lanterns hung outside two large structures on opposite corners of the central intersection. To the right was a squat, stone strong house with a crenellated roof that must have been the town's last line of defence at one time. Now it seemed to be a bawdy house. There was a shield above the door that sported the coat of arms of Countess Emmanuelle von Liebewitz, and drunken songs and women's laughter came from within it. To the left was the old stone temple of Sigmar that Kat had said the soldiers had made into a tavern. The hammer had been taken down from above the door and replaced with a sign that showed a barrel of blackpowder with pyramids of cannon balls piled around it. Roaring laughter and heated argument spilled from its open door, and a man in the uniform of an Ostland spearman was being violently sick on the front steps.

'Ludeker's places,' whispered Kat.

'Lovely,' said Felix.

At the intersection, she led them to the right, down a dirty street that sloped towards the river. A sturdy warehouse – in better repair than any other building in the village – squatted to the left, and beyond it, the town's wall stretched out a little way into the water to guard the end of a wooden bridge. More guards stood before it, barring the way.

Felix raised an eyebrow. 'Don't tell me.'

Kat nodded, embarrassed. 'Aye. Another tax.'

If THE VILLAGE was a garbage dump, the refugee camp was a pigsty – a muddy field by the river with dozens of tents and makeshift shacks sticking up from it like broken kites trampled into a swamp.

'Are you sure this is best?' asked Reidle, looking around uncertainly from the bench of the wagon as he followed them.

'Your men will get no care in the village, mein herr,' said Kat. 'Not any worth the price, at least.' She looked around at the camp angrily. 'Doktor Vinck was once the mayor of Bauholz, the most respected man in town,' she said. 'Now he lives here. It isn't right.'

'What happened?' asked Ortwin.

Kat sighed. 'Marauders came during the invasion. The people hid in the woods. When they came back, they found it all ruined. Captain Ludeker came a while later with his men. He offered to rebuild the town and protect it. Doktor Vinck said no, they didn't need the help, but the rest of the people were scared. They asked Ludeker to stay, so he did.' She kicked a pebble. 'He tried to charge Doktor Vinck rent on his own house if he wanted to practise medicine there. Doktor Vinck refused. Now he is here and Ludeker lives in his house.'

'This Captain Ludeker sounds like a charming fellow,' said Felix.

Kat snorted and kicked another pebble.

The doctor lived near the centre of the ramshackle encampment, in a tent only slightly grander than those around it – its principal amenity being that it had a plank floor that mostly kept the mud out.

Kat rapped the edge of this floor with the toe of her boot as they drew the wagon up in the narrow street outside it. 'Herr Doktor, are you at home?' she called.

'Just a minute, just a minute,' came a reedy voice from within, and a few moments later the flap of the tent was pushed aside and a thin old man in a night shirt and a scarf looked out at them, wispy white hair floating in the night breeze. 'Ah,' he said. 'Young Kat. You have some business for me?'

Felix winced a little when he saw the man. There was thin and there was gaunt. Herr Doktor Vinck was gaunt. He looked of an age with Sir Teobalt, but he appeared to be starving to death. And maybe this was the case. If it cost so much just to get inside Bauholz, how much would it cost to get food? There was obviously none stored from the harvest. There had been no harvest. All the food in the town would have had to be imported from somewhere else, and Felix could not imagine that prices were cheap.

'These men fought beastmen in the forest,' said Kat. 'All are wounded. Two are dire.'

'Well, bring them in, bring them in,' said the doctor, holding aside the tent flap. 'And we shall see what we can do.'

Felix, Gotrek, Ortwin and the less wounded guard carried in Sir Teobalt and the other guard and laid them on the bare floorboards. There were two makeshift cots at the back of the tent, but they were already occupied, one with a young woman and a baby, the other with a man with a bandage around his head – all asleep. The rest of the tent was hardly better furnished – a small iron stove and a barrel of water on one side, a table and stool on the other, and a chair in the centre with a little tray full of barber and dentistry tools next to it. A curtain hung half-open before the entrance to another room. Felix saw another cot in it.

Doktor Vinck dragged a surgeon's bag out from behind the stove and then examined Teobalt and the unconscious guard, tsking and murmuring as he pulled back Kat's crude bandages and poked and prodded.

'Broken arm. Broken leg. Lacerations. Sigmar, that's a nasty cut.'

Teobalt woke with a hiss as the doctor turned to him and manipulated his shoulder.

'Good evening, sir knight,' said Doktor Vinck. 'Sorry to wake you.'

The templar lay back and composed himself. 'Not at all,' he said. 'Pray continue.'

The doctor smiled. 'Thank you. May I have a look at your eyes? Very good. And if you could move your fingers? Excellent. Well, I shall have a busy night tonight, and no mistake.'

He turned to Felix and the others. 'My friends, we will start with this fellow here,' he said, pointing to the unconscious guard, who had horrible gashes on his chest and arms, and a leg that was bent at an unnatural angle. 'If you would be so kind as to hold his arms and legs while I wash his wounds and sew them up?'

Ortwin sputtered at this. 'My master is a knight, sir. You will attend to him first!'

Doktor Vinck glared at him as he dipped a bucket in the barrel of water. 'Your master has only bruises, minor cuts, a concussion and a dislocated shoulder. He will not die if he waits a while. This man will.'

'But–' began Ortwin.

'Obey the doctor, novitiate,' said Teobalt. 'We are in his domain here.'

Doktor Vinck bowed to the knight, then collected a bottle of vinegar from the table. 'There is no hierarchy here but the hierarchy of need, young sir. Now, if you wish your master to be seen to quickly, then you would do well to assist me with the first.'

Ortwin frowned stubbornly at this and muttered under his breath, but after watching for a while, gave in and joined the others as they helped the doctor with his surgery.

MORE THAN TWO hours later, Felix lay down with the others on the bare floor beside the patched-up men and tried to sleep. The surgery had been long and unpleasant, and in the end the guard that Doktor Vinck had tried to patch first had died. He had lost too much blood. They had put him outside on the wagon with the other bodies and concentrated on saving Sir Teobalt, and then patching the rest of them. Teobalt had survived, at least for now. His arm had been set back in its socket and bound tightly. His lacerations had been bandaged and the hideous bruises on his legs where the beastman had trod on him and crushed his armour had been bled with leeches and salved. Doktor Vinck also gave him a draught of 'elixir of poppy' to help them sleep. Felix noticed that the good doctor had a gulp of it himself before he retired to his room.

Felix wouldn't have minded a sip himself, for the floor was hard and cold, and his aches and cuts and bruises from the fight were less than comfortable. It made it hard to sleep. He shifted, hissing, then rolled over – and found Kat staring at him from her space beside him on the floor.

His heart thudded at the intensity of her stare. 'Uh, hello?' he said uncertainly.

'Where have you been, Felix?' she asked in a whisper. 'And why have you come back again?'

Felix let out a sigh, then chuckled. What a question. 'It's too late in the evening to tell you everywhere I've been,

Kat. It's a long story. As to why I've come back to the Drakwald...' He paused, suddenly embarrassed. It sounded silly and old-fashioned to say it. 'I am on a quest,' he said at last, and waited for her to laugh, but she took it without even a smile. 'The sword I carry belongs to Sir Teobalt's knightly order. He has said that I can keep it if I help him find out what happened to his brother templars.'

'What was the name of the order?' Kat asked. 'I served as a scout during the fighting, and guided many knights north through the woods.'

'The Order of the Fiery Heart,' said Felix. 'Sir Teobalt told me he had word of them a month ago, defending a village near Fort Stangenschloss from beastmen.'

Kat nodded, her brow furrowing. 'I remember them, but from the beginning of the war. I did not see them or hear of them the last time I was at Stangenschloss.' She shrugged. 'They may have come and gone again while I was elsewhere. I am mostly in the woods.'

'When were you last there?' asked Felix.

'About two weeks ago,' she said. 'Since the end of the war I have made it my job to guide refugees from Stangenschloss to Bauholz, and supply trains from Bauholz to Stangenschloss.'

'How did you find us, then?' Felix asked, frowning. 'We weren't on your route.'

'There were rumours of beastmen near Bauholz, so I went hunting for them.' Her eyes glittered. 'That is my other job – my true job – finding the camps of the beastmen and leading the soldiers to them so that they can kill them all.'

Felix's eyes widened. He could think of no more dangerous profession. The girl was mad – valiant – but mad. 'That... that is very brave of you.'

'I only follow your example,' she said.

Felix groaned to himself. It was like Ortwin all over again! His was not a life to be emulated, particularly not by a petite young woman. He was about to say this when he saw she was yawning.

'Good night, Felix,' she said, closing her eyes.

'Good night, Kat,' he replied, but it took him a long time to go to sleep, and he looked over at her many times.

The next morning Felix woke so cold that he felt as if he were frozen to the floorboards. The others looked just as miserable – all except Gotrek, who might have been in Tilea in the summer for all the discomfort he showed.

Herr Reidle and the remaining guard went out as soon as they were up to try and find some horses and an escort to help them recover the barrels of beer they had left in the woods the night before, but Kat and Felix huddled around Doktor Vinck's little iron stove and stomped their feet to get their blood moving.

As the doctor made them all willow tea, which was all he had to give them, Sir Teobalt beckoned Felix and Gotrek to his cot, where Ortwin was sitting him up and bundling him with everyone else's blankets.

'Though it pains me, it seems I must stay here for some time until my shoulder heals,' Teobalt said in a tired voice. 'But I would not have the search for my brother templars wait with me. I bid you continue to look for them, and if you find them, return with them to me.'

'We will do our best, sir,' said Felix, though he had secretly hoped that, now that he was injured, the knight would declare the adventure over.

Teobalt inclined his head. 'My squire will accompany you to assist you.'

Felix paused at this. He didn't want to take Ortwin along. The boy was more likely to be a burden than an able assistant. His bright-eyed naïvety and his desperate longing for glory were a sure recipe for disaster, and Felix didn't want to have to keep an eye on him if things got rough. He had enough trouble looking after the Slayer.

'Sir,' he said at last. 'I thank you for your concern, but the search is likely to be hazardous, and I wouldn't like to endanger the life of your squire unnecessarily. The Slayer and I will be more effective on our own.'

The old knight's eyes flashed up at him, recovering something of their old fire. 'I am afraid I must insist, Herr Jaeger. Out of my sight, your enthusiasm for the vow you have made may wane. Ortwin shall be my eyes and ears, to see that you see the thing to its finish.'

Gotrek bristled at this. 'You doubt our honour? We have sworn.'

'You have done nothing yet to make me doubt it,' said Teobalt stiffly. 'But a man is entitled to ask for proof that a deed has been done. If you are truly honourable, you should have no objection to Ortwin's presence. Honesty fears no scrutiny, as the saying goes.'

Felix could see that Gotrek was going to make further objection. He couldn't let him. If they weren't careful the argument could get out of hand and Sir Teobalt could withdraw the quest – and Felix's chance to keep Karaghul.

'If you insist, Sir Teobalt,' Felix said. 'And if Ortwin is willing to take the risk, then we will take him.'

'I do insist,' said Teobalt. 'And I thank you for your acquiescence.'

Gotrek grunted unhappily, but then shrugged, resigned. Felix let out a relieved breath, but felt a pang of guilt as well. He had agreed to take the boy into danger just so he could get his sword back. That seemed a very callous thing to do. Of course, if Teobalt had forbidden them from searching for the templars, he would likely have sent Ortwin on the quest alone, so by bringing the squire along, Felix and Gotrek were actually protecting him. At least that's what Felix told himself.

They decided over their tea that the best course of action was to go back into Bauholz proper and ask the soldiers and southbound refugees there if any of them had heard news of the Order of the Fiery Heart. If they learned nothing, then tomorrow they would set off for Stangenschloss and enquire there.

At that, Kat said that if they could wait another day, she would guide them. 'I am to lead a supply train to the fort. They start the day after tomorrow, once one last supply boat from Ahlenhof arrives.'

Felix and Gotrek readily agreed. Neither of them was adept at navigating through deep woods.

WALKING THROUGH THE refugee camp on their way to the bridge to Bauholz, Felix could see that it was even worse than he had thought the night before. The inhabitants didn't just live in a garbage heap, they lived in garbage itself. Some of the shacks were made from broken carts, or stacks of broken barrels or crates. Some were no more than stained bedsheets draped over a line.

Even in the freezing cold, the smell was abominable, and ice-ringed latrine pits were everywhere. Felix saw men, women and children huddling around small fires, cooking rats and pigeons for their breakfasts. Others seemed to be eating leaves and brown grass. All of them had the near-death gauntness that Doktor Vinck had shown. He wondered how any of them were going to survive the winter.

Even as he thought it, he saw two men carrying a woman out of a tent. She was as stiff as a log, and frosted with ice. One of the men had tears frozen on his face.

Felix shivered, and not from the cold. The true horror of war was not the battlefield, no matter how bloody. It was the aftermath – the disease and famine and displacement that followed when a land was laid waste. The knights did not suffer. They either died or went home to their plenty. The enemy did the same. It was the poor damned souls in whose fields the battles were fought that suffered, and not for days or weeks, but for years. He hated the iniquity of it.

As they neared the bridge, Kat sucked in a breath and slowed her steps.

Felix looked ahead. 'What's the matter?' he asked.

'Noseless Milo,' she said, pointing with her chin. 'He runs the refugee camp like Ludeker runs the village. He may want to make trouble.'

'Good,' said Gotrek. 'I could use a warm-up.'

Felix looked to where Kat had pointed. A group of men in tattered leather jerkins lounged against the end posts of the bridge, swords and clubs dangling from their belts, watching everybody that passed. The passers-by all hunched their shoulders and ducked their heads as they edged by the men, as if they were afraid they were going to be hit. The men grinned and called out to some. Others they tripped and laughed at. One pinched a young girl on the behind as she went by and giggled as she scurried away across the bridge like a frightened rabbit.

'Scum,' said Gotrek.

'Varlets,' said Ortwin.

'Aye,' agreed Felix. After seeing the misery and deprivation around him, he too was angry enough to want a fight, particularly with anyone who was making life more miserable for these people.

'Please don't fight them,' begged Kat. 'You will only make trouble for Doktor Vinck and the knight if you do. And me,' she added.

Gotrek looked up at her. 'Do these villains have some hold on you, little one?'

She shook her head. 'No. But I cannot live completely in the woods. Sometimes I have to come back here. And I won't be able to if...'

'Aye,' said Gotrek. 'I see.'

The biggest of the men looked up as they approached, and a snag-toothed smile snaked across his face. It was one of the ugliest faces Felix had seen that wasn't on a mutant. The man was balding, with piggy little eyes in a moon face, but his most distinguishing feature was one he didn't have. Just as Kat's name for him suggested, he had no nose. It looked like it had been torn off a long while ago, and he was left now with nothing but two vertical slits in his face and a bit of white cartilage that poked out above them, all surrounded by a puckered sphincter of scar tissue.

"Lo, Kat,' he said, in a pleasant, mocking voice, as his eyes trailed over Gotrek, Felix and Ortwin. 'Looking lovely as always. Who's yer friends?'

His men sidled forwards, grinning and blocking the way.

FIVE

'Let us pass, Milo,' said Kat, sticking out her chin. 'We don't want any trouble.'

'Come in last night, didn't they?' said Milo, ignoring her. 'Stayed with Herr Doktor.' He smiled at her look of alarm. 'You think I wouldn't know? I may not have a nose, but I got eyes everywhere.'

His men laughed at that. Felix noticed that none of them appeared to be starving.

Milo looked from Gotrek's glowering face, to the gold on his wrists, and finally to Felix. 'You and yer mates staying in town long, sir?'

'They're just travellers going up to Stangenschloss, Milo,' said Kat before Felix could answer. 'They're no concern of yours.'

Milo raised his eyebrows. 'Going to Stangenschloss at this time of year? Y'must be hearty men, then. Regular champions, I'll wager.'

'Leave them alone, Milo,' sighed Kat. 'They won't work for you.'

Milo scowled. 'Why don't y'let the gentlemen speak for themselves, Kat?'

'We're not looking for work,' said Felix stiffly.

'Oh come now, sir,' said Milo, smiling. 'Stangenschloss is a hard berth in the winter. Likely to be the death of ye, what with all them northers and beastmen running about. Why slog all the way up there when there's good money to be made right here for a man who can use his fists? Or a dwarf,' he added with a wink to Gotrek.

He shot a sly glance over his shoulder at the walled village just over the bridge. 'And promise of even more money very soon, ain't that right, lads?' He swivelled his ugly head back to Felix as his men laughed evilly. 'So, what do y'say, sir? Spend the winter in comfort in lovely old Bauholz?'

'We already have employment,' said Felix. 'Sorry. Now, please, step aside.'

An angry twitch flickered across Milo's face for the briefest second at this, but it was covered instantly by a shrug and a rueful smile. 'All right, all right, no harm in asking, is there? If y'change yer minds, Kat knows where to find me.'

He stepped aside and shooed his men back so that the bridge was clear, then winked at Kat as she, Gotrek, Felix and Ortwin passed between them. 'Bye now, beloved. And if y'get tired of freezing yer tail off at Herr Doktor's, remember I've always got a warm bed waiting for ye if ye want it.' He chuckled, low and dirty. 'And all the sausage y'can eat.'

Gotrek growled at that, and Felix's fists clenched. Ortwin's eyes blazed. They made to turn around, but

Kat shook her head, and they kept walking. She let out a relieved breath as they reached the other side of the bridge and got out of earshot.

'He wouldn't be known as *nose*less Milo when I got through with him,' said Gotrek.

'Don't worry,' said Kat. 'I can take care of myself.'

'The villain,' said Ortwin, outraged. 'Hoarding sausage when all these poor souls are starving!'

Kat stifled a laugh. Felix blinked and almost said something, then let it go. Why dirty up a pristine mind?

Instead he turned to Kat. 'What did he want to hire us for?'

Kat looked back over her shoulder. 'Milo wants to run all of Bauholz. He is trying to get enough men and arms together to drive out Ludeker and take over. He makes the same offer to every able-bodied man who comes through town.' She turned to Gotrek. 'Be careful, Gotrek. They were looking at your bracelets.'

Gotrek snorted. 'They can look all they want, little one.'

She grinned at that, and Felix saw lines appear at the corners of her eyes and mouth. He looked her over again, as if seeing her for the first time. He had been thinking of her as a young girl, and with her shyness and her small frame she had appeared so under the shadows of the forest last night. But in the morning sun he could see that she was no longer in the first blush of youth. She would be twenty-six or twenty-seven now, he calculated, and though they looked good on her, they had not been easy years.

THEY PAID ANOTHER eight pfennig foot tax to get back through Bauholz's village gate, and then they were inside, where everything was a bustle of soldiers and boatmen and wagons being loaded into Ludeker's warehouse.

Kat told Gotrek, Felix and Ortwin that she knew some people in the village who she could ask about the Templars of the Fiery Heart, and it would be better if she went alone. She suggested they ask around in the *Powder and Shot*, the tavern that had once been the Sigmarite temple. It was always full of soldiers, either coming north or going south. 'But watch out,' she said as they parted at the intersection. 'Ludeker's men will try to get money out of you any way they can. And they don't take no for an answer.'

Gotrek snorted again, and Felix smiled.

'Don't worry, Kat,' he said with a chuckle. 'We can take care of ourselves too.'

'Aye,' said Ortwin, puffing up his chest. 'We can take care of ourselves.'

Felix and Gotrek exchanged a private look at that.

'How much?' asked Gotrek, with a dangerous rasp to his voice.

'A shilling a mug, herr dwarf,' said the barman.

Felix blinked as he fished in his belt pouch. 'Even the best dwarf beer in Altdorf only costs half that,' he said.

'Well, this ain't Altdorf, mein herr,' said the barman, pouring two pints. 'Costs an arm and a leg to get it up here – sometimes literally. One of our suppliers was just in here, said he lost three men last night trying to bring a shipment in. Now he's hired a cart and some bullies to fetch it out of the woods. You know he's going to add that to the price.'

Felix reluctantly put three shillings down on the bar, and he and Gotrek and Ortwin drank deep from the mugs the barman set in front of them. Felix made a face. It was flat and thin, as if they'd been mixing it with water.

Gotrek choked and set the mug down like he'd found rat droppings in it. 'How much is the good beer?' he asked.

'That's the only beer there is, herr dwarf,' said the barman.

Gotrek pushed the mug back towards the barman, stone-faced.

Felix did the same. 'We'll wait until Reidle brings the fresh barrels,' he said.

Ortwin kept drinking.

As they stepped away from the bar, two soldiers staggered past them and called for two beers. Felix shook his head as he heard the barman say, 'Here you are, gents. Already poured. I saw you coming. That'll be a shilling each.'

Gotrek and Felix surveyed the taproom. It still retained the shape of a temple of Sigmar, but trestle tables with little three-legged stools around them lined the nave, and the bar was where the altar had once been, with kegs lined up against the back wall, under the place where the golden hammer should have hung.

This early in the morning, the tavern wasn't terribly busy, only about a quarter full, with as many eating food as were drinking. Felix didn't like to think how much the food must cost if the beer was so expensive. He was glad they still had some of their road rations, or they would be broke before they left on the morrow.

On the left a crowd of young men in the colours of the town of Schmiedorf were talking animatedly amongst themselves as they drank and looked around with excited eyes. Beyond them were some river men, talking in low tones to a man in the same uniform as the men who had stopped Felix and the others at the gate the night before. He dismissed both groups. The soldiers were new recruits, just come north, and would have no information, and the river men would know of nothing north of Bauholz.

On the right side of the room was a more promising bunch. Spearmen of Wissenland practically asleep in their seats, with more scars and bandages among them than a Shallyan hospital. These men had been in the north. They might know.

Gotrek was already heading to them. Felix followed him, with Ortwin tailing behind. They sat down beside the weary men at one of the tables and Felix smiled at their sergeant, a red-headed man with only one ear.

'Heading home, sergeant?' he asked.

The sergeant nodded. 'Aye, sir, as soon as there's a space on a boat. Damned harbour master says it'll be a week.'

'Where were you fighting?' asked Ortwin eagerly. 'Did you kill many Kurgan?'

The soldiers turned dead eyes on him, staring in dull wonder.

'Aye,' said the sergeant. 'Plenty. From Middenheim to the Howling Hills. Chased 'em like hounds. Not that it made any difference. There was always more.'

His men murmured in agreement.

'Always more,' repeated one.

'Did you pass by Stangenschloss on your way here?' Felix asked.

The sergeant nodded. 'We was sent home from there. Service done. Pay coming. Go home and wait.'

'Did you by chance happen to see, or to hear of, a group of knights called the Order of the Fiery Heart on your travels?' Felix pressed. 'Their insignia is a heart with a halo of flame.'

The sergeant frowned and turned to his men. 'Any of you lot remember?'

They shrugged and muttered amongst themselves.

'Them jaggers at the Middenstag, was that them?'

'Nah, that were the Knights of the Silver Fist.'

'How about them fellows that got torn up by orcs in the hills?'

'I never heard their name, but they had a bird, didn't they?'

'Aye, a bird, not a heart.'

There was another minute of this, then the sergeant turned back to Felix. 'Sorry, mein herr. Don't think we saw them.'

Felix shrugged. 'Thank you anyway, sergeant.'

He and Gotrek were just turning to survey the room for someone else to ask when a big man in a barman's apron appeared beside them. They looked up. The man was Milo's height, but thicker in the chest and the arms. He smiled at them.

'Get you gentlemen a drink?' he asked politely.

'No thank you,' said Felix, and continued to look about the room.

The man didn't move. 'Have to have a drink if you want to sit at a table,' he said. 'What can I get you?' He was a little less polite this time.

Gotrek glared up at him.

Felix grunted. 'We paid for drinks less than five minutes ago,' he said. 'We left them at the bar.'

'Still need a drink to sit at a table,' said the man.

'You don't have any drinks worth the name,' said Gotrek. 'Get lost.'

The Wissenland spearmen were starting to take an interest.

'We don't want a drink,' said Felix quickly, before the man could say anything that would make Gotrek stand up. 'We just want to sit here.'

'Then there's a table tax,' said the man. 'Two shillings an hour, paid in advance.'

'A table tax?' said Gotrek dangerously. 'What kind of man-nonsense is that?'

'We're a tavern, sir,' said the man. 'Not a refugee camp. Tables are reserved for paying customers.'

Felix looked around the room again. It was still only a quarter full. There was plenty of room to sit. 'What if we leave when you need these seats?'

The barman crossed his brawny arms. 'I'm not going to argue with you, sir. If you won't drink and won't pay, you'll have to leave.'

Gotrek stood. The man stepped back warily.

'Listen, you clot,' said the Slayer, advancing on him. 'I will pay for a beer when you bring me a beer that doesn't taste like you pissed it into a mouldy rain-barrel!'

Ortwin stared. Felix groaned. The Wissenland spears laughed and applauded.

'That's exactly what it tastes like!' said the sergeant.

'Get out,' said the barman, stepping back again. 'We'll have no violence here.'

'If you want me out,' said Gotrek, still advancing, 'throw me out.'

The barman hesitated, his fists balled at his sides, but then turned and hurried back behind the bar as the soldiers jeered at him. He whispered to the other barman, then disappeared into the back room.

The Wissenland men began to pound the table with their mugs. 'Real beer! Real beer!'

'Come on, manling,' said Gotrek, turning away. 'There are more to talk to.'

He started across the tavern towards a trio of young pistoliers who had been watching the whole episode with amused eyes. Though they were dressed in the latest Altdorf fashions, Felix could see that their boots and clothes were worn, and had been patched extensively – as had they themselves. One had a parting in his hair that had been made with an axe, and another had a hook for a left hand.

He saluted Gotrek with it idly as the Slayer and Felix and Ortwin sat down at their table. 'Well done, herr dwarf!' he said in a noble accent. 'I've been wanting to express that particular opinion all week.'

'And I as well,' said his scalp-scarred companion. 'Damned busybodies won't give a man a moment's peace. 'Fill your cup, m'lord? Another beer, m'lord. Steal your wallet, m'lord?'

'Damned if I don't think they hold the boats on purpose so they can milk us for our last few crowns before we sail,' said Hook-Hand. He smiled at them, then indicated his friends and himself. 'Abelhoff, Kholer, and von Weist. Now, to what do we have the pleasure?'

'You've come from the fighting?' asked Felix.

Von Weist laughed and held up his stump. 'I didn't get this playing euchre, my lad.'

Felix flushed, embarrassed, and a bit irked that a boy twenty years his junior was calling him 'my lad', then let it go. 'We were wondering if, during your travels, you met an order of knights known as the Templars of the Fiery Heart?'

The three pistoliers looked at each other, frowning, then the third, Kholer, who hadn't spoken yet, nodded. He did not appear to have suffered the kind of wounds his companions had, but there was a gravity about him that suggested that he had seen his share of horrors.

'Aye,' he said. 'We met them. They were at Stangenschloss when we came through, about a month ago. Not many of them left as I recall. Lost half their number at Middenheim and Sokh, their bugler told me.'

'Were they still there when you left, m'lords?' asked Ortwin eagerly.

Abelhoff, the one with the scarred scalp, shook his head. 'They got wind of a village on the edge of the Howling Hills being threatened by some great herd of beastmen and went out to defend it.' He shook his head. 'Mad of course. All templars are. Took no support. No foot troops–'

Ortwin stood up hotly at this. 'I am a novitiate of the order, sir. We are not mad!'

'Easy, lad, easy,' said von Weist. 'No offence meant. We'd have been with 'em like a shot if we weren't all returned to store for want of parts.' He grinned like a cat. 'That kind of madness is our bread and butter.'

'And they didn't return?' asked Felix.

Kholer shook his head. 'Not before we continued south. Haven't heard what became of them. Sorry.'

Felix nodded. It looked like a trip to Stangenschloss was inevitable.

'I say,' said von Weist, turning to Gotrek. 'You're a trollslayer, aren't you?'

Gotrek looked at him with his single eye. 'And if I am?'

Von Weist smiled. 'Oh, nothing. Just an interesting coincidence, that's all. We saw three of your sort at Stangenschloss.' He laughed. 'They were mad too!'

'Aye,' said Abelhoff. 'Fiery fellows. Fight you as soon as look at you.'

'Except the one with the nails in his head,' said von Weist. 'He just drank, mostly.'

Felix and Gotrek both looked up at that.

'Nails in his head?' asked Felix.

Von Weist held up his stump. 'I swear to you it's true. He wore them like herr Slayer here wears his crest.'

Gotrek and Felix looked at each other, then Felix leaned forwards to question the pistoliers further, but just then there was a commotion in the street and a handful of men ran into the tavern.

Felix, Gotrek and Ortwin looked up with everyone else. Standing inside the door were a half-dozen men in the uniform of Ludeker's men, and with them stood the burly barman who Gotrek had menaced.

'There!' he said, pointing directly at Gotrek. 'Those are the ones! They threatened me and didn't pay the table tax.'

The leader of the guards nodded and swaggered forwards, his men spreading out behind him. He was a big man, with a bulging belly that spoke of three meals a day, with an occasional snack in between. In a starving town like Bauholz, Felix found that obscene.

'These tables are reserved for drinkers, lads,' he said. 'Buy a beer or go.' His men began to surround them.

'We bought a beer,' said Felix.

'And it wasn't a beer,' said Gotrek.

'You'll have to buy another,' said the guard. 'And while you're digging in your purses, there's a fine for disturbing the peace. Two shillings each.' He held out his hand.

Gotrek growled in his throat.

Felix and Ortwin shot him a nervous glance.

'Easy, Gotrek,' said Felix. 'We can't make trouble. We've got to stay here another day, and I want to talk to more people about the templars.'

'Then get him away from me,' said Gotrek.

Felix turned to the leader of the guards and opened his belt pouch. 'All right, we'll pay. Four shillings for the fine, and two for two more "beers".'

'It's six shillings for the fine, mein herr,' said the guard.

Felix frowned. 'You said two each.'

The guard pointed a stubby finger at Ortwin. 'Ain't he with you?'

'But he didn't do anything. It was only us.'

'Still a member of your party,' said the guard.

Gotrek stood and faced the guard. 'Take the four shillings and get out, before I throw you out.'

The guard stepped back. His men laid their hands on their truncheons.

'Threatening an officer of the law,' said the guard. 'That's an eight shilling fine.'

'And he's got a naked blade, sir,' said one of his men, pointing to the axe on Gotrek's back.

'Why, so he does,' said the leader. 'That's five shillings.'

Gotrek took a step forwards. 'I'll feed you your five shillings at the end of my–'

'Gotrek!' yelped Felix.

'Threatening again!' cried the guard, backing away. 'The fine's doubled for the second offence. Sixteen shillings! That's... that's...'

'One crown, fifteen shillings total,' said his man helpfully.

'Gotrek, don't,' said Felix as the Slayer raised his fist. 'I'll pay. We can't afford trouble. We...'

He paused as he heard the *shing* of drawn steel beside him. Everybody turned.

Ortwin stood with his sword drawn, glaring at the leader of the guards. 'You are dishonourable men!' he said in his high, clear voice. 'These are not the honest laws of the Empire, and you have no right to enforce–'

One of the guards clubbed him from behind and he fell forwards, his blade gouging the leader of the guards in the leg as he slumped to the ground.

'Committing violence upon an officer of the law!' roared the leader. 'Get them!'

His men charged in from all sides, clubs swinging. Gotrek blocked with his forearms as Felix ducked and snatched up a stool and the three pistoliers scattered away.

'Sorry, lads,' called von Weist. 'Not our fight.'

'Good luck to you!' cried Abelhoff.

Felix parried a club with his stool and kicked a guard in the knee. Gotrek buried his fist up to the wrist in the leader's soft belly, then swung at two more guards as the fat man crashed to the floor, puking. Felix cracked another guard on the helmet with his stool, then turned as a cudgel across the shoulders staggered him. One of the guards stood on the table, raising his arm for another strike.

Felix kicked the edge of the table and the man stumbled forwards. Felix swatted him with the stool as he fell. Gotrek shoved a guard into a stone pillar, then threw another over his shoulder, sending him crashing through another table.

In less than a minute Gotrek and Felix stood panting in the centre of a ring of bruised and fallen men, all groaning and holding various parts of their anatomies. The room burst out into spontaneous applause. The Wissenland spear company whistled and stomped their feet. The pistoliers clapped politely.

'Good show!' cried von Weist.

But before the cheering had died away, another crowd of guards had run through the door – a score at least – all breathing hard and with weapons drawn. At their head was a trim, compact man with a head that thrust forwards like a crow's. He wore a captain's uniform, and four pistols and an expensive rapier at his belt.

'What's all this?' he said, with a voice like a file scraping rusty iron.

SIX

THE BURLY BARMAN hurried out from behind the bar. 'Captain Ludeker! These men–'

'Never mind, Geert,' said Ludeker, his sharp eyes fixing on Gotrek and Felix. 'I see what they've done.' He stepped forwards, his hands behind his back, shaking his head as soldiers and curious citizens of Bauholz began to edge into the tavern to see what was going on.

'Disturbing the peace,' said Ludeker. 'Destroying private property. Drawing a sword within the boundaries of the town. Resisting arrest. Striking officers of the law. Damaging the uniforms and equipment of officers of the law.' He smiled darkly as he stopped in front of Gotrek and Felix. 'Such barbaric behaviour cannot go unpunished. Fifteen days in the strong house, and a fine of…' His eyes slanted to Gotrek's gold bracelets. 'Of twenty gold crowns, or the equivalent.'

Gotrek laughed, harsh and loud. He beckoned Ludeker forwards with a massive hand. 'Come and take it.'

Ludeker drew two of his pistols and aimed them both at the Slayer. 'You're making it worse for yourself, dwarf. Thirty crowns.'

Felix sneered. 'You're not an officer of the law,' he said. 'You're a thief in uniform.'

Ludeker turned one of the pistols towards Felix. 'Forty crowns. Do you want to go higher?'

Just then there was a commotion in the crowd and Kat pushed through to the front, her eyes wide.

'Felix! Gotrek! What happened?' she gasped.

Ludeker glanced at her. 'Take her too,' he said. 'She's the one who brought these troublemakers.'

Felix knew he shouldn't. He knew that the best thing to do was to try to talk their way out of the situation – to bargain with Ludeker, or find a way to buy some breathing room, but somehow he just couldn't help himself. He threw the stool at Ludeker's head.

Ludeker ducked and fired convulsively, his shots going wild.

Gotrek roared a laugh and charged. Felix was right behind him.

Ludeker scrambled back, tossing aside his spent guns and grabbing for the other two. 'Get them! Kill them!' he bellowed.

Gotrek knocked the captain's front teeth out and sent him skidding across the stone floor on his back.

There was a moment of shocked silence as the guards stared at the unmoving body of their leader, then they swarmed in, screaming, holding swords in their hands this time, not cudgels.

Gotrek pulled his axe from his back and swept it at the oncoming men. Felix ripped Karaghul from its scabbard and flashed it around him in a wide arc.

'Stay back!' he shouted. 'Do you want to die for this stupidity?'

They didn't listen. Felix parried and kicked and dodged as the guards mobbed him. Behind him he heard screams and shearing steel and snapping limbs as Gotrek went to work. Felix stabbed a man in the chest and elbowed another in the nose. A third man was coming up fast on his right. Then he fell, and Felix saw Kat standing behind him, holding a crimsoned hand-axe.

Surrounded by a distant wall of mesmerised onlookers, Felix, Gotrek and Kat fought in a whirlwind of Ludeker's men – kicking, swiping, ducking and lunging. Felix took a cut on the back and gave back a gash across the brow. Kat tripped a man and cut off the fingers of his sword hand. Gotrek took off the legs of another man with one swipe.

That was the end of it. The guards had expected a one-sided slaughter, but hadn't thought they would be on the receiving end. Those who could still run ran, shoving through the crowd to escape the terror of Gotrek's bloody axe. Those who couldn't run crawled away, weeping and begging for mercy.

'Blatth you, dwaaff!' lisped a hoarse voice.

Felix and Gotrek turned to see Ludeker, his four front teeth missing, aiming his second pair of pistols at them. Gotrek hurled his axe just as Ludeker fired.

Sparks flashed off the spinning axe and one of bullets ricocheted past Felix's ear, while another shattered a mug behind Gotrek. Ludeker was punched off his feet as the rune weapon caught him in the face and slammed him into the wall, his head split in two halves from crown to chin. He slid down the wall, his guns dropping from his slack hands, and slumped to the ground. Blood pumped from around the edges of the axe like a fountain and poured down Ludeker's neck, turning his uniform from grey to red.

The room was silent for a long moment. People were staring and backing away. Ortwin was sitting up and blinking around at the half-dozen corpses, bafflement and horror in his eyes. Felix felt like the squire looked. His stomach roiled with sudden nausea. No matter how corrupt, these had been Empire men. They had no doubt fought Archaon's hordes. It shouldn't have come to this.

Kat stumbled to him and clutched his arm. 'We'd better go,' she said, glancing towards the door. 'The others will be back before long, and with guns.' She shook her head as she watched Gotrek pull his axe from Ludeker's face. 'Can't wait two days any more. We'll have to leave for Stangenschloss right away.'

'Aye,' said Gotrek. 'I was sick of the place anyway.'

'How did this happen?' murmured Ortwin.

'Just go,' said Felix.

He steered the boy towards the door. Gotrek and Kat went with them. The crowd parted silently before them, frightened. Even the three pistoliers eyed them askance as they passed.

Felix was glad to have the air in his face as they stepped out onto the street, even if it was cold enough to freeze his snot.

AS THEY WERE running across the bridge to the refugee camp, they came upon Noseless Milo and his gang trotting the other way, all armed to the teeth. The big bandit gave them a grin and a jaunty salute. 'Hear I owe you lads a favour,' he said. 'Ta.'

His men laughed at that.

As they ran on, Milo turned and called after them. 'Herr Doktor's house will be mine now, Kat! A warm bed and a warm fire any time you want it!'

Kat curled her lip, not bothering to look back. 'He should give it back to the doctor,' she muttered.

'LUDEKER'S DEAD?' ASKED Doktor Vinck, shocked. He was giving a shave to a man in the uniform of the Talabheim city guard, and almost nicked his ear.

'Yes, doctor,' said Kat, angrily stuffing her belongings into her pack. 'But we didn't start it. He tried to kill Felix and Gotrek.'

'It was my fault,' said Ortwin, hanging his head where he knelt beside Sir Teobalt. 'Had I not drawn my sword, things might not have come to such a pass.'

Felix, off to one side tying up his bedroll, wished he could have told the boy it wasn't true, but really, it was. If the squire hadn't drawn steel, they might have got out of that tavern for a few shillings.

'My dear boy,' Vinck said, returning to the task at hand with renewed vigour. 'Don't apologise. I would rather Ludeker had faced the hangman's noose after a lawful trial, but he was a cancer upon the heart of this town that has sorely needed excising, and I am not sad to hear of his passing.'

'Milo is already trying to pick up the reins,' said Kat sadly, then looked up, eyes hard, as a thought occurred to her. 'And he might come looking for us afterwards. He might be worried we'll do the same to him.'

Sir Teobalt struggled up onto one elbow, wincing. 'You must leave the village with the others, young Ortwin, and quickly. Go north to Stangenschloss in my name and pursue these rumours you have heard. Perhaps, when you send word to me, I will be well enough to join you.'

'But we must take you with us!' said Ortwin. 'They may try to hurt you when they cannot find us.'

'He cannot be moved,' said Doktor Vinck. 'He must have rest.'

'I see no reason why they would try to hurt me,' said Teobalt. 'And even if they do, my life is not as important as the recovery of the order's regalia. I have said I would recover it or die in the attempt. The danger means nothing to me.'

Gotrek grunted approvingly.

Felix stood and shouldered his pack. 'We better go, then.'

Kat stood too. Her pack and bow were slung across her back. 'Aye,' she said.

'May Taal watch over you,' said Doktor Vinck.

'And Sigmar guide your path,' said Sir Teobalt.

Ortwin bowed low over Sir Teobalt's hand. 'I will not fail you, sir,' he said, then he turned and joined Felix and the others as they ducked through the tent flap and out into the cold white day.

It had begun to snow.

FELIX FOUND HIMSELF in a black mood as he and the others tramped north along the banks of the Zufuhr and deeper into the Drakwald. As the lazy snowflakes settled on his eyelashes and melted into his red Sudenland wool cloak, his mind turned sourly to the infinite corruptibility of man.

He had sensed no taint of Chaos in Bauholz, had seen nothing that reeked of cult activity, had found no vile altars or eldritch symbols daubed on the walls, and yet it was as foul a pit of villainy as any he had ever seen. Why was it that the corrupt were always strong and the good always weak? Why did the Ludekers and Noseless Milos of the world flourish while good men like Doktor Vinck were crushed and killed and shoved aside?

Felix sighed. He knew the answer, and it depressed him. It was because the good and strong went forth to battle the forces of darkness and died to defend mankind while the cowardly stayed at home and preyed on the weak who were left behind. In that way the corruption of Bauholz *was* the fault of Chaos, for though the vile forces of the Dark Gods had not reached the village, those that would have protected it against corruption from within had gone north and not come back, leaving it defenceless against the depredations of purely human predators who saw opportunity where others saw tragedy.

He wondered if perhaps greed was the unacknowledged fifth god of Chaos – some gold-skinned brother to lust, madness, disease and hate. Certainly greed seemed to do as much evil as the others, seducing men and women to steal from their brothers and sisters, to grind down those weaker than themselves, driving them into mad schemes and desperate gambles, birthing robbery, kidnapping, blackmail and murder.

But perhaps not. The fault might lie within the nature of man himself, for though the greed of the dwarfs was proverbial, Felix had never seen one so degraded by it that he would stoop to murdering one of his own to satisfy his lust for gold. The dwarfs might indulge in sharp dealing, or take advantage of outsiders, but dwarf thieves and murderers were rare, and kidnappers and blackmailers were, as far as he knew, unheard of. It was man – weak-willed, frightened and desperate – that made blood sacrifices to greed, and swore terrible oaths at its glittering altar.

His thoughts flew back again to his father, who, though he'd had a successful business in legitimate trade, and who had more money than he could have spent in two lifetimes, had still felt compelled to consort with smugglers and pirates, and to deal in forbidden books, because he must have more! And Felix's brother Otto looked set to follow his father's example. When Felix had shown him the letter that proved Gustav's crimes, Otto had been more concerned with losing the family business than restoring the family honour.

All his brooding left him with the glum belief that mankind would finally be dragged down into the pit, not by the gods of Chaos, but by its own frail, fallible nature, and that no amount of heroic victories over the marauders and the orcs and the skaven would save it from its self-inflicted demise.

Of course, that didn't mean one stopped fighting them – particularly not those scheming lurkers in the shadows, the skaven. His hand gripped his sword hilt hard as he thought again of what they had done to his father. Revenge would be sweet when he finally–

'Go carefully here, Felix,' said Kat.

Felix looked up, blinking. He had been following behind her blindly, lost in his thoughts, and hadn't been looking where he was going. They had come to a high-banked stream which fed into the Zufuhr. Someone had laid a log across the stream as a crude bridge, but the bark was glassy with ice and covered with a dusting of powdery snow. A false step and he might have plunged into the stream – not wise in weather like this. Being wet in freezing weather was a more certain death than a fight with beastmen.

'Thank you, Kat,' he said, as he picked his way across the log.

Gotrek followed onto the log behind him, stumping along without pause as if he were on solid ground. Ortwin came more hesitantly, but with a little tottering and arm-flapping he was across too, then Kat bounded effortlessly across like a, well, like a cat, and they were on their way again.

Felix looked at her as she took the lead again. She moved down the nearly non-existent path with perfect confidence and grace, her stride light and her head turning to one side and the other as she listened to the forest, her posture relaxed yet ready – a complete contrast to how she had been in Bauholz. There she had been nervous and ill at ease, afraid of Ludeker and Milo, uncertain how to deal with the people she spoke to. All the strength and calm she had shown in the battle with the beastmen had disappeared when they had approached the village gates – now it was back again.

Felix quickened his steps and caught up to her. 'Er, Kat,' he said.

She looked up. 'Yes, Felix?'

'How did you come to this?' he asked. 'Your profession, I mean. My last memory of you is seeing you and the old forester – I forget his name – waving goodbye to us as we left Flensburg for Nuln.'

'Papa,' she said, nodding. 'Herr Messner.' Then she smirked at him. 'I was mad at you when you went away. I wanted to go with you.'

Felix smiled. 'I remember.'

'It just seemed natural to me,' she said. 'Leaving with you, I mean. You saved my life. I saved yours. We'd killed that... that woman together.' She shivered. 'I didn't want to stay in another village. I'd felt safer travelling in the woods with you than when the beasts came to Kleindorf. There was somewhere to run in the woods. There was somewhere to hide.'

Felix paused, uncomfortable at the mention of the woman – the strange, beautiful champion of Chaos who had led the beasts during their pillaging of the two towns – who looked so much like the girl he walked beside now. 'That woman,' he said. 'I... Did anyone ever tell you about her? About who she was?'

Kat's eyes narrowed. 'You mean that she was my mother?'

Felix let out a relieved breath. He hadn't been sure he could have told her even now. He was glad she already knew. 'Messner told you?'

She shook her head. 'I figured it out.' She tugged out the long lock of white hair that grew among her dirty black tresses. 'My witch-lock.' She snorted and pulled off her stocking cap, then smoothed the lock back down and put it back on. 'I don't care about her. Herr Messner and his family were my real family – Magda and Hob and Gus. I'm Katerina Messner now.'

Felix chuckled. 'Ah. So you liked living with them after all.'

Kat nodded, her eyes faraway. 'I loved them. Herr Messner – well, at first he and Magda tried to get me to learn the things that other little girls learned, cooking, sewing, mending, but... I didn't like those things. I wanted to do what Hob and Gus did. I wanted to go out with Herr Messner and learn how to shoot rabbits, and follow trails, and kill beastmen.'

Felix looked at her. A hardness had come into her voice.

'They thought it was because of what I had seen in Kleindorf, and in the raid on Flensburg, and they hoped that I would forget it in time.' She gave a sad smile. 'It *was* because of that, because I never wanted to let anything like that ever happen again.' She shrugged. 'But I didn't forget it. It never left me. And when Herr Messner realised that I wouldn't change, he didn't try to turn me away from it any more. He took me out with Hob and Gus and taught me everything he knew.'

'He seems to have taught you well,' Felix said.

'Aye,' she said. 'He was a good man.'

Felix paused at the past tense. 'He's... he's dead, then?' asked Felix.

'Aye,' said Kat, her voice suddenly dull. 'They all are.'

Felix's eyes widened. 'All of them?'

Kat sighed. 'Flensburg was destroyed by beastmen, another great herd. There were just too many.'

'How terrible,' said Felix. 'Was this during the invasion?'

Kat shook her head. 'No. Long ago. I was seventeen. I was already part of the duke's rangers by then, and was out on a long patrol when it happened.' She hung her head. 'I should have been there.'

Felix opened his mouth, about to say something trite like, 'There was nothing you could have done,' then closed it again. No one was ever really comforted by that. 'I'm sorry,' he said instead.

She shrugged. 'After that I quit the rangers and went out on my own.'

'Why?' asked Felix.

'The rangers are good at what they do,' said Kat. 'But they have their duties. They must visit such-and-such a town once a month, and that town and then the next town. They must keep the roads clear and report bandits and catch outlaws. I only wanted to hunt beastmen.' She bared her teeth. 'So many times I would find a hoof print trail and want to follow it to the beasts' camp, but the patrol had to move on and I couldn't.'

She looked up at Felix. 'I wanted to be able to track them wherever they went, whether on the duke's land or not, and for however long it took. I was sure that was the only way to really get rid of them. You couldn't just kill a hunting party here and a warband there, you needed to find their secret places, where they lived, and bred, and destroy them utterly with fire and sword!'

Felix blinked, unnerved at her sudden fury. 'Er, yes,' he said.

'The first herd I tracked down was the one which had killed Papa and Mama and my brothers. I lived in the woods for months while I followed them. Never went near a town or a road until finally I found the camp and worked out a way that an army could surround it so that none of them could escape. Then I went to Magnusdorp, which was the nearest castle, and showed the lord my maps.' She glowered at a memory. 'He laughed at me. He didn't believe me. He didn't think a little girl could have found such a place.'

'Well,' said Felix carefully. 'You can't really blame him for that. You're a bit of an exception to the rule.'

Kat sniffed, dismissive. 'So I snuck back to the camp and cut off the head of a gor, then brought it back to him.'

'A gor?' Felix asked, confused.

'A beastman,' she said. 'The big ones, with the heads and legs of beasts, are called gors. The smaller, more human ones, are called ungors.'

Felix nodded. 'All these years fighting them and I didn't know. Sorry. Go on. You brought the head of one of the beasts back to the lord of Magnusdorp?'

'Aye.' She grinned, showing a lot of teeth. 'He listened to me then.' Her eyes grew dreamy and faraway, as if she were talking about attending a dance. 'His men wiped out the herd entirely. Their herdstone was crushed to dust.'

Felix swallowed. Kat was as driven as a slayer. It was a bit intimidating. 'So, uh, you've been tracking beastmen ever since?' he asked.

Kat nodded. 'Until Archaon's invasion. Then I thought it would be better if I helped the soldiers.' She straightened proudly. 'I was a scout for Count von Raukov from Wolfenburg all the way to Middenheim, spying on the hordes, scouring the woods during the retreat, bringing the army information on enemy positions.' She laughed. 'There were times when I was so close to the Kurgan that I could have patted them on the head, but they never found me.'

Felix shook his head. The girl didn't seem to know any fear at all – at least while she was in the woods.

She frowned again. 'I will go back to hunting beasts soon, but right now there are still too many people in the Drakwald who shouldn't be here – all these refugees and soldiers trying to get home. I will guide them until they are gone, then I will return to my true purpose.'

Felix swallowed, suddenly emotional, his depression at the sorry state of mankind lightening. Here was the counter to the greed and the corruption that had sickened him in Bauholz – the selflessness of a girl whose only thought was to help people return home and make the world a safer place. 'You are doing great work, Kat,' he said at last.

She blushed and tucked her nose down into her scarf. 'I am doing what I can.'

After they had walked a little while in silence, Felix spoke again. 'Is Bauholz your home now, then?' he asked. 'Do you live with Doktor Vinck?'

She shook her head. 'I haven't lived in a town since... since Flensburg was destroyed,' she said. 'I go to Bauholz and to other towns for supplies, but I live here.' She waved a hand around at the forest. 'This is my home.'

And welcome to it, thought Felix, staring around uneasily at the thick wall of trees on either side of the path.

'Doktor Vinck sewed me up a few years ago when a beastman gored me with its horns,' she continued. 'I would have died without his help, so I always try to look after him, and Bauholz.' She snorted bitterly, a great cloud of steam rising before her face. 'I wish I had dealt with Ludeker as I deal with the beasts.' She spat. 'I *should* have, but Herr Doktor said there are laws, and that the law should deal with him.' She looked back at the Slayer with a sly smile. 'I'm glad Gotrek thought otherwise.'

FOR FIVE DAYS Felix, Gotrek, Kat and Ortwin continued north and west through the deep forest, marching at a slow but steady pace. Their rate of travel was helped because the path they were on was the route by which supplies and reinforcements were brought to Fort

Stangenschloss, and was therefore relatively clear and well maintained. Had they been travelling in any other direction, they might have measured their day's travel in yards rather than miles, for the forest to either side of the path was an almost impenetrable undergrowth of brambles and intertwined tree roots.

Ease of travel, however, was countered by the fact that such a well-marked path was a target, watched by those who would prey upon those who used it. This had been why Kat had wanted to join the supply train that was to have left Bauholz two days after their arrival. A well-manned, well-guarded convoy would be a less attractive target than four travellers on foot. Twice in those five days she had asked them to wait, then disappeared into the woods in order to investigate further along the trail. The first time it had been bandits, waiting in the brush at a place where the path dipped down to go through a swift stream. The second time it had been mutants, hiding in overhanging trees for the unwary.

Both times, Gotrek had wanted to go fight the ambushers, and Ortwin had concurred, and both times it had fallen to Kat and Felix to discourage them. Felix reminded them that Sir Teobalt had charged them with finding the lost templars, not to fight random villains on the road. Kat had reminded them that Doktor Vinck was days behind them and the fort days ahead of them, and that even if they were victorious they would undoubtedly incur wounds that they might die from before they reached help.

Gotrek and Ortwin had reluctantly bowed to this combination of duty and cold logic, and had allowed Kat to lead them into the woods and around the ambushes, and they had escaped undetected.

At night, they made camp just off the path, hidden from it by a screen of brush. Kat always stopped before the sun went down, so that by the time it got dark their fire would have died down and the pulsing embers could warm them without bright flames giving away their position. As Felix, Gotrek and Ortwin made up their bedrolls and gathered firewood, Kat would vanish into the trees and return a half-hour later with rabbits or pheasants or a fox, each shot neatly through the skull with a steel-tipped arrow. These she would skin and gut with practiced precision and cook over the fire. They never went hungry.

On the night of the second day, the falling snow grew heavier, and they woke up the next morning with their bedrolls covered in two inches of dry powder, but with blue skies overhead. This distressed Kat, and not because it would slow them – the build-up was hardly enough to cover Felix's boots.

'We will leave tracks that will be easy to follow,' she said. 'It would be better if the snow continued, so it would cover them again.'

Later that day, they came to a place where the forest had been burned and saw signs that some great battle had occurred in the midst of the charred trees. Under the thin cover of snow, the ground was burned black, and ash-covered bones and dented, soot-blackened armour littered it like broken teeth.

Felix, Gotrek and Ortwin stared at the devastation.

'What happened here?' asked Ortwin, stunned.

Kat spat. 'This was the path of the army of Strykaar, one of Archaon's lieutenants. They say there were more than five thousand in his train.' She indicated the burned area with a sweep of her arm. 'Men from Stangenschloss met them here. They waited in ambush – archers and spearmen and men-at-arms. They wanted to strike and retreat into the woods, then continue to harry the marauders' line as they moved west.' She shook her head sadly. 'But Strykaar had things of Chaos with him, whispery things that could move through the woods like wind, dogs with skin like red scales, flying things. The men's first attack was their last. They could not retreat far enough or fast enough. They were hunted down and killed like vermin. Only a few made it back to Stangenschloss to tell the tale.'

Felix shivered as he pictured desperate men scrambling through the thick wood, running from silent, loping shadows.

'But their deaths were not in vain,' Kat continued as they started across the ugly burn. 'Their attack killed many of Strykaar's champions, and slowed his advance, giving Middenheim and the forts further east more time to prepare.'

Gotrek cursed and kicked the distorted skull of a dead Kurgan. 'Another worthy doom missed,' he muttered as it bounced across the snow. 'Damned weak-willed Kurgan. They couldn't have held on another two months.'

For the rest of the day the Slayer was in a foul mood, cursing under his breath and speaking to no one.

JUST AFTER NOON on the fourth day, they found the remains of a much more recent fight.

Kat, as usual, was scouting far out in front, and saw it first. Felix saw her go on guard, crouching and drawing her axes from her belt, then creep forwards steadily around a bend in the path.

'On guard, manling,' said Gotrek, and pulled his axe from his back.

Felix and Ortwin drew too, and they all moved quickly ahead, staring and listening all around them. As they came around the bend they saw what Kat had found.

She stood looking down at the ground beside a twisted line of smashed wagons, some of which had been tipped on their sides, all of them missing their horses and the supplies they had carried. As Felix got closer he saw that there were bodies lying by the carts, each covered in a thin white blanket of snow. Broken spears and bent swords littered the ground, and arrows stuck from the surrounding trees. But Kat was looking at none of it, only staring at a body at her feet – a middle-aged man in the colours of Averland.

'You know him?' asked Felix, approaching her.

'He was my friend,' she said, nodding listlessly. 'Sergeant Neff. He was a quartermaster for Stangenschloss. They left Bauholz a few days before you arrived.'

Sergeant Neff's left arm lay a few feet from the rest of him, and both he and it had been partially eaten by some forest predator. His face hadn't been touched, however, and looked up at Felix from under a cap of snow with an accusatory stare.

'I'm sorry,' said Felix.

Kat shrugged. 'It's what happens in the Drakwald,' she said. But as she turned away, Felix could see tears glittering on her cheeks.

'Did beastmen do this?' asked Ortwin, looking angrily around at the white-cloaked carnage.

'Kurgan,' said Gotrek. He held up a horned helmet that had a sword cut through it.

Felix swallowed and looked around at the woods at the mention of the northmen. Even in the middle of the day the shadows beneath the trees were impenetrable, and they might hide anything. He shivered as he imagined the mad red eyes of crazed barbarians staring at him from their depths. It took an effort of will to turn away from the trees and return his attention to the wagons.

As he walked around them, he counted seven bodies. It didn't seem enough. 'How many men guard these convoys?' he asked.

'Twenty, and two ostlers for each wagon,' said Kat.

'Then where are they?' asked Felix.

'Taken,' said Kat. 'For slaves.'

'Your friend was lucky, then,' said Gotrek.

Kat shuddered. 'Aye.'

'Do we go after them?' asked Ortwin.

Kat shook her head. 'This happened before it snowed, three days ago. They could be fifty miles from here, and the snow will have covered their trail.' She sighed and turned north again. 'I only hope someone got away to warn the fort.'

'Shouldn't we at least bury them?' asked Ortwin, as Kat started away from them. 'It goes against Morr's law to leave them here for the wolves.'

Kat turned on him, eyes dark. 'There is no time for things like that here. The ground is too frozen to dig, and we have too far to go.'

Ortwin looked for a moment like he was going to protest again, but then finally joined Gotrek and Felix as they followed the heavily bundled little figure north again.

* * *

The rest of the day passed without incident, and they made camp as usual just a few paces off the trail, collecting firewood and starting a fire as the light of the day began to turn from gold to red. A little while later, Kat brought them two squirrels, a rabbit and a pigeon, and set to cleaning and skinning them.

'Another day to Stangenschloss,' she said as she flensed the fur from the rabbit with quick, deft strokes of her hunting knife. She was always careful with these, because she sold the pelts of every one she ate. 'I wish I wasn't bringing bad news.'

'Another day still?' asked Ortwin. He looked around at the encroaching forest. 'I would have thought we'd have been in the Chaos Wastes by now.'

'That's because you've never left Altdorf,' said Felix with a smile.

'That's not true!' said Ortwin. 'I went to Carroburg once.'

Felix chuckled at that, but just then Gotrek rose from his seat and held up a hand.

'Quiet,' he said.

Everyone froze and looked around. Felix strained his ears. At first he heard nothing but the usual sounds of the forest – the crackling of the fire, the wind in the branches, the cries of wild animals in the distance. But then he heard it – a clash of steel, very faint, then another, and then an angry cry.

'Fighting,' said Ortwin.

'North and east,' said Kat. 'Deeper in the woods.'

'Shut up!' growled Gotrek.

They listened again. More clashes and clangs, then a howl of pain and a hoarse roar of triumph.

Gotrek pulled his axe off his back and turned in the direction of the sounds. 'That was a dwarf,' he said.

'Follow me,' said Kat, drawing her bow and diving into the woods.

Gotrek and Ortwin were right behind her. Felix snatched a burning branch from the fire for a torch, then hurried after them.

Running through the untamed forest was nothing like walking along the trail. The ground was a lumpy tangle of roots, creepers and dead branches that caught their feet and tripped them constantly. Thick undergrowth grew shoulder-high in places, but Kat led them unerringly around the worst of it, and they never had to stop or turn back. Still, thorns and nettles caught at them like claws and branches whipped their faces. The light of Felix's makeshift torch was almost more disorientating than it was helpful, for its bobbing, flickering light caused the shadows to dance, making it seem that the trees were looming out at them and jumping in their way.

Creatures of the night skittered away from them, screeching and yipping. An owl shot up in front of Felix, wings battering him as it tried to get away – and behind the crashing and thudding of their passage, still the ring and roar of distant battle.

Kat danced through it all without a mis-step, as if she had run this exact path a thousand times and knew every inch of it by heart. The others were not so nimble. Ortwin put a foot wrong and staggered to the side, slamming into a tree. He recovered and hurried on, weaving slightly. Felix jolted down into a hidden hollow, snapping his teeth shut and putting his foot into freezing mud. Gotrek hacked through the underbrush with his axe, clearing away great masses of black vines and leafless shrubs and shouldering on implacably.

Seconds later they could see an orange glow ahead, segmented by the vertical black bars of trees – a fire. They pounded on, and with each tree they passed, the light got brighter and the noise of battle louder, until, after dodging around the trunk of an ancient oak, Felix could see naked flames and surging shadows in a clearing up ahead, and make out individual voices in the torrent of sound.

'Stay together, curse you!' bawled an Empire voice. 'Hold your line!'

'Down here, you painted ape!' rasped a dwarf voice.

Kat paused at the edge of the clearing, laying an arrow to the string of her bow. Gotrek, Felix and Ortwin stopped around her, readying their weapons and catching their breath as they stared at the mad battle before them.

On the far side of a huge fire, a dozen or so Empire spearmen stood in a curving line before a clump of towering Kurgan marauders, who drove them back towards the trees with swipes from massive swords and axes. On the near side of the fire, two dwarf slayers fought back to back in the centre of four more Chaos warriors. To one side, horses bucked and screamed against their tethers and chained prisoners huddled together, the fire reflecting in their terrified eyes as they watched the fight. The ground was littered with the corpses of both men and marauders, all horribly mutilated.

'On, on,' said Ortwin, between gasps. 'Before another man falls.'

'Do not help the slayers,' said Gotrek, starting forwards. 'They will not thank you.'

There was a thrum at Felix's ear and one of the Kurgan who faced the spearmen barked in pain, an arrow sprouting from his back.

'Go,' whispered Kat. 'Go!'

Gotrek, Felix and Ortwin charged out of the trees, running low as more of Kat's shafts whistled past their heads. The Kurgan howled and turned as the shafts pincushioned them. Felix grimaced. They were hideous – impossibly muscular gargantuans in furs and rusty armour – but their bearded faces were painted up like fright masks. Felix hurled his flaming branch at one with striped cheeks and purple eyelids, then slashed at him with his sword. Ortwin dodged a blow from one with black lips and pink matted hair. Gotrek smashed through the shield of one who fought entirely naked, but with so many iron rings piercing his flesh that he looked like he wore chainmail.

The Empire spearmen cheered as they saw their enemies flanked, and the line pressed forwards with renewed energy.

'On them!' shouted a captain. 'Keep the advantage!'

The eyes of the painted Kurgan shone with berserk frenzy, and though the arrows had caught their attention, they didn't seem to have slowed them down. Felix blocked an axe blow from his opponent that nearly shivered Karaghul from his hands. Ortwin's blade bit deep into the pink-haired one's sword arm, but the giant only moaned as if in ecstasy and struck back savagely, knocking the boy to the ground with a blow that sent his helmet bouncing across the trampled earth. Felix cursed. He had forgotten how hard the Kurgan were to kill. They had hides like iron, and when their battle-madness was upon them, they seemed to feel no pain.

Gotrek killed the pierced one with a chop under the ribs that sunk to his spine, then backhanded the one who had flattened Ortwin, shearing through his pitch-smeared armour and biting into his back.

Felix stabbed his painted opponent through the leg, but he didn't even flinch, and Felix had to leap back ungracefully to avoid being gutted by his double-headed axe. As the huge weapon whipped by, Felix gashed the madman across the back of the wrist, cutting him to the bone. That the Kurgan felt. He howled and dropped his axe, but then drew two daggers the size of short swords and leapt again at Felix, still screaming wordlessly. Felix stabbed him in the sternum, trying to keep him at a distance, and felt Karaghul grate against thick bone. The marauder came on, pressing his breastbone against the tip of the sword and forcing Felix back with his weight as he swiped at him with his daggers, just out of range.

Suddenly Kat screamed up beside Felix and hacked the painted berserker in the shoulder with one of her hatchets. He swung a dagger at her face.

'No!' cried Felix, but the girl ducked it neatly and slashed at the marauder's knees.

The berserker jumped back and Kat and Felix advanced, pressing him back towards the Empire spearmen.

'Come on, then!' shouted Felix, trying to keep his attention fixed forwards.

It worked. The berserker didn't hear the spearmen behind him, and as he raised his axe to strike at Felix, a spearhead burst from his abdomen. He turned, roaring in pain and fury, and Felix jumped forwards and decapitated him with a whistling slash. The Kurgan's painted eyes stared with surprise as his head tumbled from his slumping body.

The head rolled to a rest against Ortwin just as the boy was sitting up and looking around. He yelped as it hit his leg and scrambled up, kicking at it.

Felix and Kat turned, searching for more opponents, but there were none. The spearmen had capitalised on the Kurgan's confusion and had slaughtered the rest while they were distracted. On the far side of the fire, however, the battle between the two slayers and their massive opponents still continued.

The spearmen turned towards it.

'Leave them be,' said Gotrek, holding out a warning hand.

'Not to worry, slayer,' said the captain, a long-jawed veteran with a battered helmet and a bloody face. 'We know the rules.' He grinned at Kat, throwing her a jaunty salute. "'Lo, Kat. Might have known. It is proof of Sigmar's grace that you found us in time.'

'It was Gotrek that heard the fight, Captain Haschke,' said Kat, humbly, then turned to watch the slayers fight.

Two of the marauders were down, one with his bald head cleft down to the neck, the other with his guts spilling out of his stomach and sizzling in the fire, but though the two slayers still stood and fought strongly, Felix could see they had paid for their victories.

The shorter, broader slayer, who wore his scarlet beard woven into two long thick plaits, and whose two side-by-side crests arced over his bald head to match, had a huge lump on the right side of his head and seemed to be having trouble remaining upright. He swung furiously but unsteadily at his enemy with a double-bladed axe, his head tilted at an odd angle. The taller, rounder slayer, who had a braided crest and a beard like an orange haystack, was bleeding freely from the stumps of two missing fingers on his right hand, and had a diagonal gash on his scalp that was flooding his eyes with blood. He could barely see to swing his long-hafted warhammer.

Still, both seemed to be in high spirits.

'Take a rest, Argrin,' said the double-crested slayer. 'I can take 'em both.'

'And give you my doom?' scoffed the braid-crested slayer. 'No fear, Rodi.'

Felix could see the spearmen inching forwards, wanting to help the dwarfs, but apparently their captain had schooled them, for they held back, though he could see it pained them to do it.

'Be ready if the slayers fall,' murmured Captain Haschke.

Then, abruptly, it was over. Rodi, the double-crested one, weaved drunkenly out of the way of an axe swing and found himself standing almost under the legs of his towering opponent. He hacked savagely at the marauder's inner knee with his axe, but overbalanced and cut off the Kurgan's foot instead.

The giant screamed and tried to take a step, but collapsed when he put his weight on his stump and crashed into the other Kurgan, sending him stumbling into the path of Argrin's warhammer. The massive weapon caught the second marauder in the ribs, knocking him flat. Argrin jumped up onto his chest and crushed his skull with a sickening pop, just as Rodi planted his axe deep in the chest of the first marauder, sending up a fountain of gore.

The spearmen cheered. The slayers didn't seem to notice. They were too busy complaining to each other.

'See now, Rodi Balkisson?' said Argrin, turning to Rodi, who was decapitating the footless Kurgan, just to be sure. 'You interfered in my fight. You've cost me another doom.'

Rodi sneered as he wiped his axe on his Kurgan's furs. 'You've a way to go before you reach the number of times you've cost me *my* doom, Argrin Crownforger. Nine times! I've kept count.' He turned to survey the rest of the clearing. 'Now where did...' He broke off as he saw Gotrek. 'Another slayer!' he said.

Argrin wrapped a cloth around the stumps of his two missing fingers and peered around. 'Where? Oh, so there is. By Grimnir, where did he come from?'

'No idea,' said Rodi. 'But where's old Father Rustskull? I lost track during the fight.'

'There he is,' said Argrin, pointing to a heap of dead Kurgan who lay piled on top of each other near the fire. Felix looked closer and saw that there was a pair of short, thick legs sticking out from under them.

The two slayers limped forwards and grabbed the dead marauders by the arms and legs.

Rodi beckoned to the others. 'Hoy. Help us shift these fat pig Kurgan.'

Gotrek, Felix and Ortwin and some of the spearmen came forwards to help. The Kurgan were unbelievably heavy, as if they were made of oak, not flesh, but finally, working together, they succeeded in rolling them off the dwarf who lay at the bottom of the pile, unmoving, his eyes closed.

Felix stared, stunned. The unconscious dwarf was a slayer with a huge white beard, an enormous warhammer held slack in one gnarled hand, an oft-broken nose, a cauliflower ear on one side of his head, no ear at all on the other, and a crest made of dozens and dozens of big iron nails, all rusted to a dirty brownish orange.

'Snorri Nosebiter,' said Gotrek softly. 'As I live and breathe.'

SEVEN

'I THINK HE'S dead,' said Argrin.

'The lucky bastard,' said Rodi. 'Found his doom at last.'

Gotrek grunted. 'He's not dead. He's out cold.' He slapped Snorri's cheek. It sounded like a pistol shot. 'Wake up, Nosebiter.'

Snorri didn't move.

'Maybe we should give him some air,' said Felix, stepping back.

'Aye,' said Rodi. 'He's been breathing Kurgan's armpit for the last ten minutes. That would kill anybody.'

'Chafe his wrists,' said the captain of the spearmen.

'Lift his legs,' said one of his men.

'Maybe we should give him a drink,' said Kat, reaching for her canteen.

'Snorri thinks that is a very good idea,' said Snorri.

'Ha!' said Argrin, as Snorri's eyes flickered open. 'He's alive!'

'The poor bastard,' said Rodi. 'Another doom missed.'

Gotrek helped Snorri sit up. The old slayer reached shakily for Kat's canteen and upended it over his mouth, guzzling greedily.

Then suddenly he was spitting it all out again, covering them all in spray and hacking and gasping so much that his eyes turned red. 'What... was that?' he sputtered.

'Only water,' said Kat, looking a little alarmed.

Snorri made a face. 'Snorri didn't like that at all.'

Argrin crossed to a pack with a small wooden keg strapped to the bottom of it. He brought it back and handed it to Snorri.

Snorri upended it like he had the canteen, but this time he drank smoothly and happily. After a very long pull, he lowered the keg, sighed happily and licked the foam off his white moustaches. 'That was much better.'

He handed the keg back to Argrin and looked around at everybody, ending on Gotrek. He blinked, a look of confusion on his face.

Gotrek grinned. 'Well met, Snorri Nosebiter.'

Snorri frowned. 'Snorri knows you,' he said slowly. 'Snorri knows he knows you.' He turned curious eyes to Felix. 'And you too.'

Gotrek's grin collapsed. 'Gotrek, son of Gurni,' he said quietly.

'And Felix Jaeger,' said Felix.

'It's only been twenty years,' said Gotrek. 'You don't remember?'

Snorri nodded. 'Snorri knows Gotrek Gurnisson and Felix Jaeger. They are his old friends.' he said. 'Are you them?'

Felix and Gotrek exchanged a glance. Felix wasn't sure if he had ever seen Gotrek look more unsettled.

'Please, sirs,' came a woman's voice from behind them. 'Please, can you free us from these chains?'

Everybody stood and turned. Felix flushed, ashamed. They had been so busy hovering over Snorri that they had forgotten the prisoners.

The slayers and the spearmen hurried to them and began breaking them loose. They were a pitiful lot – a flock of shivering half-naked men and women, all huddled around the tree they had been shackled to. The women wore the remnants of Shallyan robes, and some still had dove pendants hanging from their necks. They wept and thanked the spearmen for their release. The men wore the same uniform as the spearmen – those that wore anything at all – but they reacted almost not at all to being freed, only stared unseeing at their unshackled wrists or looked about them with dark, haunted eyes, murmuring under their breath.

Kat pressed her lips together as she looked at them. 'Neff's men,' she said. 'The guards of the supply caravan. What can have done that to them to make them like this?'

Felix shuddered. He didn't want to know.

Kat turned to the spear captain. 'Captain Haschke, how did you find them?'

Haschke grimaced. 'The Kurgan bastards attacked the Shallyan hospital wagons two days ago, while they were on the way south to Bauholz. One of their guards escaped and got back to the fort. He led us to the place where they were attacked, and we followed their trail here.' He nodded sadly at the supply train guards. 'I guess the Kurgan have been watching the trail.'

'Aye,' said Kat. 'We found the supply train earlier. Neff's dead. About seven others.'

Haschke sighed and shook his head. 'Ah, that's bad. I'll be sorry to tell Elfreda.'

'I... I'll tell her,' said Kat.

Haschke looked relieved.

ONCE THEY HAD freed all the prisoners and did what they could to get them up and moving – and put those who couldn't move on the backs of the stolen horses – Kat invited everyone back to the camp she had made by the road. The Kurgan camp was a charnel house, and not fit to stay the night in.

The undergrowth it had taken Kat, Gotrek, Felix and Ortwin two minutes to run through earlier took half an hour to lead the horses and the staggering victims through, but finally they made it back and got everyone around the fire and settled.

Gotrek watched Snorri as the old slayer nodded off, then crossed to Argrin and Rodi, who were cleaning and wrapping their wounds and combing out their beards and crests.

Gotrek nodded to them politely as Felix and Kat watched from nearby. 'Gotrek, son of Gurni, at your service,' he said.

The two dwarfs stood and bowed in return.

'Rodi, son of Balki, at yours,' said the short, double-crested slayer. He had arched black eyebrows and a sly look on his sharp-featured face.

'And I am Argrin Crownforger,' said the bigger slayer, whose braided crest was now unwound and hanging down over the left side of his square, lumpy face.

Gotrek acknowledged their names and they all sat again. Gotrek looked back at Snorri. 'How long has he been this way?' he asked. 'His memory.'

'Since we've known him,' said Argrin.

'Though that hasn't been long,' said Rodi. 'We met him at the siege of Middenheim, a few months back.'

Felix saw Gotrek's shoulders tense. 'You were at the siege?'

'Aye,' said Rodi, his powerful chest swelling with pride. 'Slew a daemon.'

Felix could hear Gotrek's knuckles crack over the popping of the fire. 'Did you?' he rumbled.

'It wasn't a daemon,' grunted Argrin, as if they had had this argument before. 'Not a real one.'

'It breathed fire and vanished into pink smoke when I hit it,' said Rodi, sticking his fork-bearded chin out.

'And it was the size of a cat,' said Argrin.

'Don't lie, curse you,' snarled Rodi. 'It was bigger than that! It was easily as big as–'

'A dog,' interjected Argrin.

'A wolf!' protested Rodi. 'It was as big as a wolf! A big wolf!'

Gotrek cleared his throat meaningfully. 'So, you don't know when Snorri Nosebiter started to lose his memory?'

The two slayers broke off their argument and shook their heads.

'He's always been that way,' said Rodi. 'As far as we know. We sometimes have to remind him who we are, and he sees us every day.'

'Too many bumps on the head,' said Argrin.

'Too many *nails* in the head,' said Rodi.

Argrin shrugged sadly. 'He remembers long ago like it was yesterday, and yesterday not at all.'

Gotrek cursed under his breath.

Argrin gave Gotrek an odd look. 'He certainly tells enough stories of you, Gotrek son of Gurni.'

'Aye,' laughed Rodi. 'And if they're all true, then you're the worst slayer of all time.'

'What was that?' growled Gotrek, balling his fists.

Kat sucked in a breath. Felix sat up, watching warily. This could be bad. His doom was a subject upon which the Slayer was notoriously touchy.

'Easy,' said Rodi, holding up his palms. 'A joke, that's all. I just mean that you must be too good. You should have been dead a dozen times over in the years you were with Snorri, and yet you defeated everything you met – daemons, dragons, vampires – and now it's twenty years later and you still live.'

'Do you question my dedication to seeking my doom?' said Gotrek, rising, his one eye flashing in the firelight.

Rodi stood too, chest to chest with Gotrek. 'Are you putting words in my mouth? I didn't say that.'

Felix put a hand on his sword. Kat looked from one slayer to the other. The spearmen from Stangenschloss were turning their heads.

'Then what *did* you say?' said Gotrek.

'Come now, lads,' said Argrin, rising and trying to step between them. 'Let's not fight over nothing.'

'My honour is not nothing, beardling,' said Gotrek, snarling at him.

Felix stepped forwards anxiously. 'I can confirm that the Slayer hasn't let a day go by in the last twenty years without actively seeking his doom.' Except for those months in Altdorf where he tried to drink himself to death, he thought, but he kept it to himself.

'Stay out of this, manling,' said Gotrek.

Argrin put a hand on Rodi's shoulder. 'Apologise, Rodi. Come now.'

'But, I didn't...' said Rodi.

'It doesn't matter,' said Argrin. 'A slayer's doom is between him and Grimnir, not anyone else. You shouldn't even have brought it up. Now apologise.'

Rodi made a sulky face, but finally bowed to Gotrek. 'Forgive me, Gotrek, son of Gurni, I should not have asked after that which is not my business. Please accept my apology.'

Gotrek hesitated, looking like he still wanted to punch the young slayer in the nose, but then nodded curtly. 'Accepted,' he said, and returned to Felix, still muttering under his breath.

SLOWED AS THEY were by the Shallyan sisters and the rescued men, all of whom were wounded and half-starved, it took two further days to reach Stangenschloss. Nothing happened on the journey, but it was still a difficult trip, at least for Gotrek and Felix. Felix spent the two days watching Gotrek watch Snorri, saddened to see the Slayer at such a loss.

Snorri was as cheerful as he had ever been, and seemed no less intelligent – and no more intelligent – than he had been before, but there was definitely something wrong with his mind. He greeted Gotrek and Felix as strangers each morning, and when they reminded him who they were, he would laugh and say of course they were and remember for the rest of the day, but at the same time, he would tell them stories of his old friends Gotrek and Felix, as if they were two completely different people from the man and the dwarf who walked beside him.

Gotrek nodded as Snorri told the stories – most of which were terribly mixed up and wrong – but his face was set in a grim scowl, as if he was trying to work out a puzzle. It hurt Felix to see it. This was not Gotrek's sort of problem. It was not a thing to be solved with an axe, or a daring rescue. There was nothing the Slayer could do to help his friend, and Felix could see it pained him. What should have been a joyous reunion with lots of drinking and property damage, had been instead an awkward and heart-breaking non-event.

Gotrek, being both a dwarf and a slayer, wasn't one to moan in the face of tragedy, however. Instead, Felix could see him getting angrier and angrier, and at the same time more frustrated that he had nothing to lash out at. Felix could hear him grinding his jaw as they walked, and he was constantly clenching and unclenching his fists. Given that they were going ever deeper into the Drakwald, it was inevitable that the Slayer would come across some evil that needed to be killed and he would finally find some release.

For Gotrek's sake, Felix hoped it would come soon.

STANGENSCHLOSS WASN'T QUITE as impressive as Felix had expected. He had been picturing some grim, monolithic bulwark against the forces of Chaos, its towering stone walls lined with massive engines of war and bristling with spearmen, swordsmen and handgunners. In reality, it was smaller than Bauholz, and though its walls were of stone, they weren't much taller than the village's wooden palisade, and had been knocked down in places. The garrison was less than five hundred men, most of them gaunt from hunger and weary from a hard year of war, and there were no catapults or trebuchets that Felix could see.

Captain Haschke caught him looking around as they crossed the yard and smiled grimly. 'It's better than it was.'

'You must have seen some fierce battles here,' said Felix.

'Not us,' said Haschke. 'At least not here. We were further north, with von Raukov. This place was garrisoned by a Lord von Lauterbach. They were overrun, killed to a man and the fort destroyed.'

'So how did you come to be here?' Felix asked.

Haschke grinned. 'Another of my lord Ilgner's brainstorms,' he said. 'We were returning south after the end, and came across this fort. It was abandoned, and all the nearby settlements ravaged by the loose ends of Archaon's army who had melted into the forest instead of going home. Well, Lord Ilgner can't stand to see a fly hurt, and so he says we must stay here until these horrors have been rooted out and the people can live in peace again.'

'A most noble sentiment,' said Ortwin, piping up.

'Aye,' said Haschke. 'Though many of the men didn't think so. They'd been fighting all year, and wanted to see their families in Averland again. There was a lot of grumbling at the first, I don't mind telling you.'

'Is he not well liked, then?' Felix asked.

'Oh no, they love him,' said Haschke. 'He gives 'em victories and keeps 'em fed – for the most part – and he has a way of making even the most mercenary soldier feel like he's part of a noble cause. We're proud of him, and proud to be holding the line. We're just a bit... tired, that's all.'

After he had found them a place to drop their packs, Captain Haschke brought Gotrek, Felix, Kat and Ortwin to Lord Ilgner, the commander of the fort, to give him the details of their encounter with the marauders. Abbess Mechtilde, the senior sister of the Shallyans, came too.

They found Ilgner sitting at a desk made from a heavy wooden door laid across two sawhorses. It was next to a little camp stove in a curtained-off portion of the keep's dining hall that served him as both office and sleeping quarters. The upper storeys of the keep had been shattered during the war and not yet rebuilt, so even the officers had to make do in the common areas.

Like his fort, Ilgner was not what Felix had expected. He had thought to find some ironclad giant of a man with a dour expression and the strength of ten. Instead Ilgner was short and bustling, and looked as if he would have tended towards the pudgy side if conditions at the fort hadn't been so dire. His hair was dark and thinning on top, his eyes were bright, and his teeth even brighter when he smiled, which was often.

'Sigmar preserve us,' he said when Haschke presented them. 'Another slayer. Y'don't drink like the other three, do you? As much as we have welcomed their prowess these last weeks, they have near to drunk us out of beer.'

'Slayers drink,' said Gotrek, shrugging.

'And not a little,' grinned Ilgner. 'They keep saying they're going off to find their doom, but they keep coming back, much to my cellarer's dismay.' He looked up at Haschke. 'They did come back again, didn't they?'

'Aye, my lord,' said Haschke. 'They're having a pint even now. Claim it helps their wounds heal faster.'

Ilgner sighed, then nodded respectfully to Gotrek and Felix and Ortwin. 'Well, you're all welcome here nonetheless. We can use all the proven veterans we can find.' He turned to Kat, his face growing suddenly sober. 'So, Neff's dead then?'

'Aye, my lord,' she said. 'A third of his men as well. And the supplies taken. I'm sorry.'

'And those that survived…' said Haschke, then bit his lip. 'Well, they were captured by the Kurgan, and… and they ain't themselves.'

'What's wrong with them?' asked Ilgner.

'They're… broken, sir,' said Haschke. 'Won't speak. Won't hardly eat. No life to them.'

'They were most cruelly abused, my lord,' said the abbess. She hesitated as all attention turned to her. Her face turned red. 'The marauders told us that they were taking me and my sisters to… to breed with, to make more of their kind, but the men, they used them as… as pets, or toys. That is–'

'No need to go on, sister,' said Ilgner, blushing. 'I understand your meaning. The villains were followers of the god of pleasure. They did as they do.'

Haschke put his hand on his sword hilt. 'My lord, I beg you to let me take a force of men and find the rest of these degenerates. We slaughtered those we found to the last man, but they were only a raiding party. I know the main body of their force must be somewhere near, with our supplies.'

Ilgner sat down at his desk wearily. 'Would that I could, captain. But I fear we have a more pressing problem that must be dealt with first.'

'What's that, my lord?'

Ilgner shoved aside the papers and mugs and dinner plates on his desk until he uncovered a map of the

Drakwald. He tapped it with a finger. 'We have reports of a great herd of beastmen, as big as anything we saw in the war, coming south out of the Howling Hills, destroying villages and settlements as they go.' His finger trailed down the map. 'We don't know where they're going, or what they want, but they're heading this way, and they must be stopped.'

Felix and Gotrek exchanged a look at this. Ortwin was holding his breath.

Felix stepped forwards. 'Forgive me, Lord Ilgner. We have come north seeking news of the templars of the Order of the Fiery Heart. Do you know if this is what they went to meet?'

Ilgner pursed his lips, nodding. 'Aye. The village they left to protect was the first hint of this trouble. The day they rode forth we received five more messenger pigeons begging for our aid – all from villages and timber camps on the edges of the hills.'

'Have you had word of the templars, sir?' blurted Ortwin.

Ilgner shook his head sympathetically. 'I'm sorry, lad. No one we have sent north has returned, and the refugees that stream south just babble with fear. I've heard nothing.' He returned his attention to the map, moving his finger again. 'Calls for help come from new villages every day, and each one further south than the last.' He looked around at them all. 'My estimate is that the herd is six days from here now. I am going north at dawn tomorrow to see for myself its size and nature.'

Haschke snapped to attention. He saluted. 'My lord, I would be at your side in this. Please allow me to accompany you.'

Ilgner chuckled. 'No, Haschke. You've only just returned from a desperate fight. You're wounded. You'll stay here. I'm only taking a few men anyway. It's a reconnaissance mission, not a war party.'

Haschke looked crushed.

Ilgner turned to Kat. 'Kat, if you're well, I'd have you as scout.'

'Of course, sir,' she said.

Ortwin stepped forwards, then went down on one knee. 'My lord Ilgner, my friends and I have vowed to discover the fate of the Templars of the Fiery Heart. We would be most grateful to be allowed to join you as you go north, and seek our answers there.'

Ilgner raised his eyebrows, seemingly amused at the boy's formality. He turned to Kat. 'And do you vouch for these noble seekers, scout?'

'Aye, my lord,' she said, her eyes bright. 'They are the finest warriors and bravest, most honourable friends I have ever known. And the boy can fight too.'

Ortwin glared at her as Ilgner grinned.

'Well then,' he said. 'It seems we'd better have them, hadn't we?'

AFTER THEY LEFT Lord Ilgner, the companions split up. Felix got a bucket of hot water from the cook and scrubbed himself clean behind the barracks, then went to the place that Haschke had found for them – a second-floor room in a half-demolished tower – and had a short nap, for it had been a gruelling trip from Bauholz.

He was plagued by dreams of skulking forms moving in shadows, and his father screaming curses as clawed hands ripped at his flesh. But his curses weren't directed at his torturers, but at Felix, who looked in at the window and shrank back as his father's bleeding eyes turned accusingly towards him, as he jerked at the bell rope by his bed, futilely ringing for help that would never come.

Felix woke to the jangling clang of a distant dinner bell and the smell of boiled cabbage. It was not the most appetising odour in the world, but it was a relief after the horrors of his nightmare. The dream lingered unpleasantly as he pulled his boots on, and he could still feel his father's eyes glaring at him as he started down to the dining hall, silently demanding to know why he had taken Sir Teobalt's quest and abandoned the vengeance that he was owed.

As he was crossing the muddy courtyard, Felix saw Kat standing by the kitchen door with a woman in an apron. The woman was looking down, her shoulders slumped, and Kat held one of her hands, patting it awkwardly. Felix slowed, struck by the seeming sadness of the scene. What had happened, he wondered? He realised he was staring and made to continue – he didn't want to intrude on someone else's misery – but then he saw Kat step back and say some final word to the woman, and he paused again. The woman nodded at Kat's words, but didn't look up, and after an awkward moment, Kat turned and walked away, her head down too.

Felix hesitated between withdrawing and going to her, and in that instant she looked up and saw him. She paused for a moment, then dropped her head again and continued towards him.

'Hello, Felix,' she said, not slowing as she reached him.

'Are you all right, Kat?' he asked. 'Who was that woman?'

Kat paused, then continued around him towards the dining hall, still not looking up. 'Neff's wife, Elfreda,' she said. 'She bakes our bread. I... I told her–' Her words cut off short and she broke into a sudden trot. 'Ex... excuse me.'

'Kat!' Felix hurried after her and caught her by the elbow.

She struggled for a moment, but when he turned her around she fell against his chest, knocking her forehead on his breastbone and sobbing silently. Felix wrapped his arms around her and held her tight. She clung to him, the front of his jerkin balled in her fists as her tears soaked the cloth.

'I'm sorry, Felix,' she mumpfed. 'It's only... only...' and then she was off again.

Felix patted her back and shushed her gently, marvelling again at her contrasts – so savage in battle, so sure of herself in the wild, so courageous in the face of death, and yet still so human beneath it all.

She head-butted his chest, angry. 'Why can I look at Neff's corpse without a tear, but when I go to tell 'Freda...' She sobbed again.

Felix stroked her filthy hair and decided not to remind her that she *had* cried then, if only silently. Instead he said, 'I suppose it's because the dead are past suffering. It is those who survive them who feel the pain of death.'

She nodded, still weeping. 'She wanted him to go south before winter locked them in, but he... but he was too loyal to Ilgner. He wouldn't go! Poor 'Freda.'

There were fresh sobs after that. Felix let her cry herself out, wrapping her in his red Sudenland cloak and looking sadly down at the top of her head. She weeps here because it is safe, he thought. In the Drakwald there is no room for tears. She has to be alert and on guard at all times. Emotion would kill her, so she saves it up until she is out from under the trees. He was oddly pleased that she felt safe enough in his arms to let herself go like this.

After a while her sobs subsided and she lay against him, sniffing. Finally she raised her head and looked up at him with a lopsided smile.

'I'm sorry, Felix,' she said. 'I think... I think I've ruined your jerkin.'

He chuckled. 'Tears are hardly the worst things that have stained this rag,' he said.

They stood that way for a moment, wrapped in each other's arms, smiling fondly at each other, but then, without anything changing, something changed, and Felix's heart lurched. One second, the embrace had been innocent, a brother hugging a sister, and then, without warning, it was innocent no longer.

It wasn't that Felix was suddenly overcome with lust. It was just that he had all at once remembered that he was a man and Kat was a woman and that it felt very nice to hold her like this. He paused, heart pounding, and felt Kat tense too. She had become aware of it as well.

Their eyes met, and for the briefest second an electric understanding passed between them, then they broke free of each other, practically leaping apart, suddenly unsure where to look.

'Er...' said Felix, apparently very interested in what was going on across the yard. 'Well, we'd best get to dinner then, eh?'

'Aye,' said Kat, intently rewrapping her scarf. 'Aye, dinner. Yes.'

They turned and hurried towards the dining hall, both looking straight ahead.

THINGS CONTINUED UNCOMFORTABLY at dinner. While Gotrek listened to Snorri's mixed-up stories of the siege of Middenheim, and Rodi and Argrin laughed and shared stories with their friends among the Stangenschloss garrison, Felix and Kat ate quietly, not speaking to one another, and shying away from eye contact. Every once in a while Felix would look up and find Kat staring at him, only to look away when he caught her. And at other times he would find himself staring at her, only to look away when she caught him.

Felix cursed himself each time. What was wrong with him? It wasn't right! The girl was almost half his age!

On the other hand, he told himself, she was older than Claudia, and he had allowed himself to be seduced by her. But he hadn't known Claudia when she was seven! Nor had he cared for Claudia the way he did for Kat. Claudia had been a manipulative fool who had wanted to use him as a way to rebel against the strictures of her cloistered life, and in a weak moment he had been ready to use her in return.

Kat was different. Felix felt responsible for her. He had shaped her past, and was concerned for her future. He didn't want to hurt her through some callous, casual lovemaking. She was no tavern girl or courtesan who gave her favours easily and often. She was... Kat, still in his mind the solemn little girl who had waved and cried when he and Gotrek had left her to go to Nuln all those years ago.

If he and Kat came together – and the brief electric look they had exchanged had made him unable to think of anything else – it would have to mean something. It would have to be as lovers, and not just as friendly sparring partners. And that, he feared, was impossible, for a number of reasons.

First were their oaths. Kat was bound to the Drakwald by her vow to rid it of beastmen. Felix was bound to Gotrek by his vow to follow him and record his doom. He could never tell one day to the next where he would be. Nothing he and Kat shared could last for long, for Gotrek never kept still.

Second was their ages, something that hadn't mattered so much with Claudia, who would have never been more than a momentary affair. It would be different if he remained with Kat. No matter what Max said about Felix's longevity, he would still be in his sixties when she was forty. It would be fair to neither of them.

Third, and now that he thought of it, most important, was the stark fact that he wasn't sure if he was in love with her. He loved her, certainly, but it was the tender, protective love one has for family, rather than the soul-piercing, heart-enflaming love that one had for... for...

Ulrika.

Felix cursed when he thought of her. Was he always going to be comparing other women to her? It would never be a fair test. They had been a perfect match of temperament and inclination. Restless wanderers who struck sparks off each other like flint and steel. Beside her, Claudia was a spoiled, snivelling brat, and Kat was a sweet-natured but unworldly yokel. It was hopeless. Neither woman could hold a candle to her, and yet love with them was possible, if he wanted it, where it never would be with Ulrika. Ulrika had been made a vampire. She no longer lived by the laws of the living. There could be nothing between her and Felix that would not lead to death or destruction for one or both of them. He had to forget her. It was imperative. Someday he would have to give up and settle for his second choice.

He looked at Kat again. He knew Ulrika would not begrudge him taking up with the girl. It had been she after all who had said that they must find solace among their own kind. But what solace could be had when he would be taking Kat's love without being able to return it in full? The guilt would kill him. She deserved more than what he could give.

She looked up, and again there was that arcing spark of attraction between them. He looked away quickly, pretending to look for more beer. He bit his cheek hard to drive away the flicker of lustful images that flared up before his eyes, then laughed at himself. So full of noble sentiments. He only hoped they would stand when put to the test.

Beside him Gotrek had turned away from Snorri and was staring at a soldier who sat across the table from Rodi and Argrin.

'Empty?' Gotrek was saying. 'Do you mean all dead?'

Felix turned to listen as the soldier shook his head. 'No, herr dwarf. The man said "empty". Him and his fellows is trappers, and they was out in the deep green when the big herd passed by. They never saw 'em, but when they got back to Weinig they could see that them beasties had been to call and no mistake. The whole place was mashed flat – gate, houses and temple – just as you'd expect. But the weird part...' The soldier leaned in and lowered his voice for effect. 'The eerie part, was that there was no people. Not a man, woman or child. They was all gone, and precious few corpses neither.'

Rodi shrugged. 'The beastmen took them,' he said. 'For food or for slaves.'

'No,' said Kat. 'You don't know them.'

Rodi's eyes widened to be challenged so bluntly by a woman, but Kat continued without looking at him.

'They might have taken some for food,' she said. 'But not many. They don't carry their larders with them. They eat as they go. And they don't take human slaves, because they can't keep up.'

'Then where did they go?' asked Argrin. 'The men, I mean.'

Kat shrugged. 'I don't know.'

'Neither did the trapper,' said the soldier, eager to get the attention back on himself. 'But he found the same thing in Bohrung and Grube further south. All vanished, like they was sucked up into the sky by a whirlwind.'

'Mayhap yer trapper was mad, Pfaltz,' said another soldier, laughing. 'A herd of beastmen that makes people disappear? Sounds like a tall tale to me.'

'Or a good doom,' muttered Gotrek, his one eye shining with the fire from the torches of the hall as the others laughed and insulted the storyteller.

Felix shivered. When Gotrek smelled a good doom, he knew trouble was sure to follow. He did not look forward to the morrow.

FOR THREE DAYS Lord Ilgner's party pushed ever deeper into the trackless heart of the Drakwald, a terrifying green vastness that seemed to Felix, his imagination fuelled by the stories of the tale-spinning soldier, to be one giant malevolent organism that watched them through half-slumbering eyes like some listless cat – too comfortable for the moment to bother going after the mouse that has entered its territory, but secure in the knowledge that its prey was trapped, and that it could reach out its paw and crush it any time it chose – or make it vanish.

There were no roads north of Stangenschloss, not even the meagre tracks that had served as such between Bauholz and the fort, and so the expedition travelled single file along faint game paths. Kat scouted the way far out in front, while Snorri, Rodi and Argrin – who had insisted on accompanying them despite their wounds – marched before Ilgner and ten picked knights leading their horses. Finally came Gotrek, Felix and Ortwin, bringing up the rear and keeping an eye out for anyone who might be following them.

Felix was relieved that Kat was taking point. She seemed to have regained her composure again swiftly, and had greeted him with a cheery and non-committal hello on the morning they had set out, but he found that he was still having difficulty keeping his eyes off her when she was around, and so welcomed anything that took her out of his sight.

Each day out of Stangenschloss the terrain grew hillier than the last, with much struggling up steep, brush-covered ridges, or pushing through thickly wooded ravines. Several times they came to places where they had to hack down the undergrowth to make a passage for the horses. Despite the bitter cold, the effort of the march made them sweat so much that they steamed.

On the third day they woke up to ominous clouds and whistling winds. Gusts of driving sleet lashed their faces as they broke camp and shouldered their packs. Felix wondered if Ilgner might give the order to return to Stangenschloss due to the threat of a storm, but the general didn't even discuss it, and they continued north as before.

'One advantage to travelling in the thick of the forest,' he said cheerily. 'Keeps the weather off!'

His knights laughed at that. Felix didn't find it particularly funny, or particularly true. Being under the trees did keep the wind and the sleet out of their faces, but the melting ice dripped from the needles and down the back of his neck, and turned the forest floor into a mouldy mulch of leaves and mud that made walking more like sliding and froze his feet through his boots.

Just before noon they at last found evidence of the mysterious herd's passage. It wasn't hard to miss. The party wormed their way down a densely wooded pine slope and discovered Kat at the base of it, squatting and staring at a river of crushed underbrush, hoof prints, beast-dung, gnawed animal bones and branch-shorn trees so wide that the far side of it was beyond the distance they could see into the wood. Her expression was dark and thoughtful.

'What troubles you, Kat?' asked Lord Ilgner. 'Is it a very big herd?'

She nodded, her mouth a flat line. 'I don't know if I've seen bigger, but that's not all of it.'

She beckoned them forwards, cutting across the beastmen's trampled path. As they went on, the murky leaf-shrouded light brightened, until, after twenty paces, they stepped out into a strange gap in the forest where the trees had been chopped down in a long straight line that followed the beastmen's line of march, and the sleet beat down at them from roiling grey sky above.

Felix shielded his eyes and looked up and down the line of felled trees. It went as far as he could see in both directions – like a furrow cut into the forest by some unimaginably large plough. It was not wide – no more than five or six paces from edge to edge – but there were fallen trees and ragged stumps all along it, the axe cuts that had felled them so fresh that thick sap welled up out of them like pus from a septic wound.

'This,' said Kat. 'This is unnatural. The beastmen don't travel like this.'

'Is it perhaps marauders instead?' asked Ilgner.

'Doesn't smell like marauders,' said Argrin.

Kat agreed. 'There are only hoof prints. No boots. It was a herd that did this, but I have never seen a herd cut down trees on the march. They are creatures of the forest. They move through trees like we move in the open. I don't understand it.'

'Perhaps they have a cannon,' said Felix.

Rodi laughed. 'Beastmen don't have cannon!' he said. 'They don't even have bows and arrows.'

'Listen to the beardling,' said Gotrek under his breath. 'He knows everything.'

'Those that lead the beasts sometimes have cannon,' said Felix, remembering the hellish weapon that the Chaos champion Justine had brought with the herd that had attacked Flensburg.

'It might be a cannon,' said Kat doubtfully. 'But where are the tracks of the wheels?'

'Unnatural or not,' said Ilgner, waving her on, 'we have found our quarry's spoor, and it does not appear to be hard to follow. Let the hunt begin.'

EIGHT

WHATEVER THE BEASTMEN'S reasons for clearing a path through the forest, Ilgner was right, it made them exceptionally easy to follow, and also allowed the party of knights and slayers to nearly double its speed. By midafternoon they had covered the same distance they had travelled the whole of the previous day, and Kat said that they were coming very near to catching up to the herd, for the dung and the half-eaten carcasses that littered the trail were still fresh. After that, they went with weapons drawn, and Ilgner and his knights stayed mounted, their helmets on and crossbows loaded and ready.

Felix was so focused on looking and listening to the front, worried that at any minute they were going to run into the back of the herd, that when trouble came from behind them, he failed to hear it. Only when Gotrek stopped and looked back did he hear the distant thudding of heavy hooves below the moaning of the wind and the rattle of the freezing rain. He followed Gotrek's gaze, wiping his eyes and peering through the slanting sleet, but the sound was coming from over the last ridge and there was nothing to see yet.

'Beastmen?' asked Ortwin, his voice wavering between anxious and eager.

'Aye,' rumbled Gotrek, his eyebrows dripping. 'Though not nearly enough.'

Even one beastman was more than Felix cared for, but he let it go. He ran up the line to Ilgner. 'Beastmen behind us,' he said. 'Gotrek thinks it's a small party.'

Ilgner looked back, cursing, then turned to his men. 'Into the trees to the left. We'll let them pass.' He looked down at Felix again. 'Herr Jaeger, if you would be so kind as to go ahead and tell the slayers and Kat.'

'Aye, general,' said Felix, and trotted forwards as the knights began leading their horses into the woods.

The slayers didn't like it.

'Hide from beastmen?' said Argrin. He looked genuinely shocked.

'We didn't join this squig chase to hide,' said Rodi, indignant. 'You want to rob us of a doom.'

'Ilgner came to scout the big herd,' said Felix, struggling for patience. 'Not die before he found it. If you want a doom, stay behind and fight the whole herd after we've returned to Stangenschloss.'

The two slayers grunted unhappily, but made for the trees. As Felix hurried forwards to find Kat, he heard Rodi mutter, 'Humans,' in a disgusted voice.

Kat looked grim when he told her.

'Foragers,' she said. 'A herd on the move has outriders that range for miles in all directions, hunting for food.'

They ran back and joined the others, who had disappeared into the trees on the left side of the ragged path. Lord Ilgner had ordered the knights not just out of the open cut, but beyond the edge of the wider swathe of flattened undergrowth that the herd had trampled on either side of it. They buried themselves in the heavy brush, the knights with their cloaks and hoods drawn over their armour and helmets so that they would not betray themselves with any stray reflections. They waited with shields on their arms and cocked crossbows in their sword hands.

Felix looked back at the path as he and Kat crouched down next to Gotrek and Ortwin in the bushes. It could be seen only in little slivers between the black silhouettes of the intervening trees. The sounds of the approaching beastmen were louder now – the clump, clump, clump of hooves on earth, the bawling and braying of their inhuman speech.

'Will they see our tracks?' whispered Felix.

'They might,' said Kat, laying an arrow on the string of her bow. 'But our prints will blend in with all of theirs, so they likely won't notice.'

'Let us pray they don't,' said Ilgner.

Rodi and Argrin snorted at that. Ortwin however seemed to be taking the general at his word, and was mumbling over his clasped hands, his head bowed.

As the sounds got louder, the horses began to shift nervously, but the knights held their bridles and murmured soothing words to them and they remained quiet.

Soon Felix saw flashes of movement between the trees, like glimpses through the cracks in a plank fence. A big beastman – a gor, Felix remembered – with a head like an antlered bear lumbered down the treeless path with a club over one shoulder, its hairy torso covered in rags and scraps of rusty armour. Four more big gors followed behind it in twos, each pair carrying a pole between them from which was hogtied the corpse of a giant boar. Behind these came a score of the smaller, more man-like beasts – those Kat had named ungors – all armed with spears, and some leading dogs – or things that might once have been dogs – on ropes.

Now it was the slayers' turn to get restless. Felix could hear them muttering.

'Dibs on the big one.'

'I called him first.'

'Abominations.'

'Snorri could use a good fight just now.'

'Quiet, sirs,' hissed Ilgner urgently. 'Their hearing is as good as their sense of smell.'

'We can only hope,' said Rodi, but the dwarfs' murmuring stopped.

Felix and the others watched in silence as the hunting party plodded along, snarling at each other and the weather and shaking the wet sleet from their fur. All Ilgner's party had to do was wait. Another minute and the beasts would be out of sight. A minute after that they would be out of earshot.

One of the dogs raised its tusked snout, sniffing, and Felix and the others held their breath. Had it scented them? It stopped and strained towards the trees. Its ungor master jerked its leash and cursed it. The dog barked and kept looking at the woods. The knights and the slayers white-knuckled their weapons. Kat raised her bow, though Felix doubted even she could hit a target through that thick screen of trees.

The dog barked again. The ungor snarled and kicked it, dragging it on. It growled at the abuse, then at last gave up and padded on.

Felix, Ortwin, Kat and the knights sighed with relief. The slayers cursed.

Gotrek sneered. 'Dogs on both ends of that leash–'

He was cut off by a crashing and a thudding at their backs. Everybody turned, peering into the depths of the forest with eyes blinded from staring towards the relative brightness of the path. Out of the shadows came two of the ungors, filthy, half-naked savages with tiny horns and pointed teeth. One had a brace of rabbits over its shoulder, the other carried a dead fox by the hind leg. They were running right for the hidden party.

'Kill them,' snapped Ilgner. 'Swiftly!'

The two ungors pulled up short as they saw the knights and the slayers standing before them in the darkness. Their eyes bulged and they opened their mouths to scream.

The one with the fox never got a chance. An arrow appeared in its throat and it toppled backwards without a sound. The other, however, lived a second longer, and spent it screaming and trying to run.

Two of Ilgner's men fired their crossbows. The two bolts vanished into the ungor's back and it went down thrashing and shrieking. Another shot from Kat silenced it, and everybody turned back to the path. Had the hunters heard over the wind?

There was a sound of bestial voices raised in the distance, and then the tread of heavy hooves coming nearer.

'They heard,' said Kat.

'Damn and blast,' said Ilgner.

'Grimnir be praised!' said Rodi and Argrin.

Ilgner started forwards, motioning for the rest to follow. 'Back to the open path. Hurry. They'll murder us in here. No, curse you! Leave the horses!'

The knights and the slayers shouldered through the maze of trees towards the cleared strip, but before they had made it halfway, a handful of the ungors came back down the path, dogs straining at their leashes as they peered into the woods and called out questions. Then one of them shouted and pointed directly at Felix – or so it seemed to him – and it and its comrades charged baying into the tree line, their massive dogs bounding before them.

'At them!' roared Ilgner. 'Push them out! Don't let them trap us in here!'

The knights shouted a battle cry and ran forwards, shields up and swords back. The slayers were just behind, axes and hammers high, roaring with joyous rage. Felix, Kat and Ortwin ran with them, screaming along with the rest.

The two sides crashed together just inside the tree line, swords and axes singing and blood flying. Felix grinned with grim pleasure as he saw that this would be no repeat of the fight around the ale wagon. The ungors were outnumbered and outfought. They weren't attacking hired bravos and old men this time, but well-trained, well-armoured men, and berserk, battle-hardened dwarfs, and they were getting the worst of it.

Felix cut down a dog with scales for skin, then gutted an ungor with bat ears and two rows of pointed teeth. Ortwin and Kat killed another dog. All around them axes fell and swords flashed and the ungors shrieked and died. Then they were stumbling out onto the cleared path with all the rest – and straight into the thundering charge of the five big beastmen and the rest of their ungor followers. Three of the knights went down instantly under the crushing blows of spiked clubs and crude axes.

'Dress ranks!' shouted Ilgner. 'Dress ranks!'

But it was too late. The gors were already in their midst, swinging in all directions as their smaller followers circled and struck from without. Another knight fell. Ilgner's visor was ripped away by a spiked club, and blood sprayed from his helmet like sweat as he fought the beastmen's bear-headed leader.

Then the slayers shoved to the fore, howling for blood. Gotrek's axe bit into a beastman's club and he wrenched the weapon out of its hands. Felix and Ortwin hacked the monster down then turned to fight the ungors that tried to flank them as Gotrek challenged another gor. Snorri elbowed Ilgner aside and crashed his hammer down on the bear-headed beastman's kneecap, shattering it. The big gor fell on its side and Ilgner and two of his knights stabbed it to death. Rodi and Argrin struck a beastman at exactly the same time and it crashed down onto its back.

'Mine!' cried Argrin, as he finished it off.

'No, mine!' roared Rodi, doing the same.

All around the melee, the ungors fell squealing as arrows whispered out of the woods and feathered their backs and sides. Good old Kat. Felix looked up as he stabbed a fallen ungor through the heart. The tide had turned. Now it was the beastmen who were surrounded and the slayers and the knights who were on the offensive. They were winning. It would be over in seconds.

But then, from the centre of the melee, Ilgner bellowed and pointed. 'Stop them! They'll warn the herd!'

Felix turned. Three of the ungors were running as fast as they could down the cleared path. Already they were hard to see through the sheets of slashing sleet. Two of the knights broke away and ran after them, but in their plate armour they were too slow. The dwarfs would be no better. Ortwin was still engaged. With a resigned grunt, Felix realised it would have to be him.

He charged down the path, slipping and slewing in the mud, but before he'd taken five steps, one of the ungors dropped with an arrow in its back. Felix looked around and saw Kat at the tree line, her feet braced wide as she nocked another arrow and drew back the string. He kept running just in case.

Another of the ungors fell, an arrow sticking from its arse like a tail, but the third one showed some intelligence and swerved for the woods. An arrow followed it and took it in the leg. It stumbled but ran on, vaulting over a felled tree and disappearing into the shadows.

Felix cursed. If they lost the thing they were doomed. The herd would know they were following them. The only sane option at that point would be to turn back – and Felix knew that was an option neither Ilgner nor the slayers would take. At least the man-beast was wounded. Felix had some chance of catching it.

He ran into the trees, glad that the herd's passage had made the area to either side of the cleared path marginally easier to navigate. All the undergrowth had been mashed flat and pounded into the earth, but the trees were still so closely spaced that it was impossible to see more than a dozen paces ahead. The ungor was out of sight, but Felix could still hear it, thudding and thrashing ahead of him.

Then there were footsteps behind him too. He looked back. Kat was darting through the trees towards him.

'Run!' she said as she passed him.

'I am... running,' he gasped. But not like Kat, he thought. She ran like a deer, as if she had no weight at all. He surged on, struggling to keep up with her.

A second later they dodged around an ancient tree and spied the ungor ahead of them, running with a hopping limp through the pines. It was a vile-looking thing, as lean as a starving wolf, with long greasy hair that flapped behind it as it ran. It had torn Kat's arrow out, and blood ran down its bare leg and soaked into its filthy buskins.

Kat drew an arrow and tried to fit it to her bow while she ran. The ungor looked back and shrieked, its black horse-eyes wide with fear, then dived into the thick brush at the edge of the trampled area, thrashing and kicking to get through.

Kat cursed and ran to the place it had entered, plunging in without slowing. Felix was right behind her. They shouldered together through brambles and bushes as the forest got darker around them. Felix could hear movement from in front of him, and could see the shaking of branches, but he had lost sight of their quarry.

After a moment they pushed out into a slightly more open area and Kat stopped, looking and listening. Felix could hear nothing over his own breathing and the rattle of the sleet on the overhanging needles, but apparently Kat had keener ears.

'This way,' she said, and started to the left.

They ran on, leaping gnarled roots and ducking overhanging branches as they raced up a slick, wooded hill. Felix had no sense of where the ungor was now.

They broke onto a narrow game trail and Kat followed it further up the hill, putting on more speed. At the crest of the hill, the ungor flashed through a shaft of grey light then disappeared beyond the ridge. It was lurching with every step.

'Ha,' said Kat. 'It's slowing.'

'Good,' said Felix. He felt like his throat was made of hot sand. 'So am I.'

They pounded after it, Felix slipping as they reached the top of the rise. Finally, as they came around a bend, it was before them, weaving wearily as it staggered down the path. Felix and Kat charged it. It screeched and dived into the thick brush again, like a rabbit into a hedgerow.

'After it,' shouted Kat.

They plunged in, fighting through the heavy growth as it struggled ahead of them. Then, with a surprised cry, it dropped out of sight, and they heard a heavy thud.

'Ha! It's fallen!' said Felix, and pressed forwards eagerly.

'Felix, wait!' barked Kat.

Felix burst through a screen of bushes and stumbled forwards into the clear, then back-pedalled desperately. There was a ravine directly in front of him, dropping down a rocky cliff to a tree-hemmed stream below. His foot slipped at the muddy edge. He fought for balance. Pebbles pattered away under his boot.

Then, just as he knew he was going to fall, Kat clutched his flailing hand and hauled him back. He toppled against her then fell to his knees.

Without a word, Kat stepped past him to the edge of the slope, readying an arrow.

'Thank you, Kat,' said Felix as he got to his feet and joined her. 'Is it dead?'

'I don't know,' she said, peering down into the ravine intently. 'I hope... No, Taal curse it, there it goes.'

Felix looked down where she pointed and saw the ungor just limping under the screen of trees, splashing down the centre of the ice-rimmed stream.

Felix eyed the sheer face of the sleet-slicked cliff uneasily. With some rope they might have descended, but with just hands and feet it would be treacherous. 'I don't know if we can–'

'But we must!' said Kat, angrily. 'If I fail in this we are dead!' She cursed with frustration and began trotting along the edge of the cliff in the direction the man-beast had gone, looking at the thick covering of trees that hid the bottom of the chasm.

'You set yourself a high mark,' said Felix, following her. 'You killed two of the three that ran, and wounded this one–'

'It won't be enough!' she said. Then suddenly she skidded to a stop, staring out into the ravine. 'Ha!'

Felix followed her gaze, trying to see what she saw through the gusts of sleet. At first he couldn't make out anything that would draw her attention, but then he saw that there was a break in the trees through which he could see the glint of the swift-flowing stream.

Felix shook his head. The gap was a good fifty yards from where they were, and at this distance he could have hidden it by holding out his arm and covering it with his palm. The ungor would walk past it in three strides. Could Kat even loose an arrow before it passed?

It seemed impossible, even without the wind and the sleet.

Nevertheless, she raised her bow and drew the arrow back to her ear, then stood as still as a statue while she waited.

Felix looked from her to the gap and back, not daring to speak for fear of ruining her concentration. How long could she hold the tension of the bow? How long could she keep her aim steady?

He scanned the trees before the gap, looking for some sign of the man-beast's passage, but the cover was too thick. He could see nothing until the break. He watched it like a cat watches a hole, trying not to blink.

Suddenly Kat loosed the arrow, and Felix gasped, thinking she had fired at nothing, but then, as he watched, astonished, the beast sloshed into the gap – and into the path of the arrow. The shaft caught it in the neck, betwixt shoulder and ear, and it splashed face first into the stream and lay there unmoving, its head and torso half under the water.

Kat let out a yelp of triumph and leapt into the air. 'Yes!' she said, then turned to the still-stunned Felix and hugged him, wrapping her arms around his neck.

Felix snapped out of his staring and burst out in astonished laughter as he hugged her back, lifting her off the ground. 'Well shot, Kat! Sigmar's hammer, what a shot! Never in my…'

His words trailed off as he realised that he was eye to eye with her, and that she was looking at him with the same strange intensity that she had when they had hugged before.

'Kat?' he said.

Suddenly she pushed her mouth to his and kissed him full on the lips, her tongue thrusting forwards to find his. For a moment he responded in kind, too shocked and too aroused to think what he was doing, and they grappled and crushed together like wrestlers.

But then his mind caught up with his body, and he pulled back from her, loosening his grip.

'Kat,' he said again. 'Listen. I... I don't think...'

She looked at him, blushing suddenly, and pushed out of his arms. 'I'm sorry,' she said, turning to hide her face. 'I... I didn't mean to do that. I just...'

She hurried to collect her bow, which she had dropped on the ground.

Felix stepped towards her. 'There's no need to apologise,' he said. 'You just... er, that is, I hadn't expected...'

'Forget it,' said Kat, not looking at him. 'Just forget it. I'm a fool.'

'You're not a fool,' said Felix, turning her around. 'I won't pretend I haven't felt the same... urges, but...' He paused, wondering if he should tell her all the things that had been roiling in his head since that first brief spark of awareness. Could he even articulate it? Better perhaps to keep it simple. 'I've known you since you were seven, Kat. It just feels... wrong.'

She looked up at him, then away again, nodding. 'I... I understand. Only...' She paused, looking as if she was going to continue speaking, but then just turned back the way they had come. 'We should get back to the others.'

She started into the bushes without a look back. Felix looked after her for a moment, wanting to say something to make her feel better, but still not knowing what that would be. He sighed and started after her.

After a while of walking together in silence he shook his head and laughed. 'I still don't understand how you made that shot. You loosed the arrow before the beast appeared.'

'It was walking in the stream,' she said, her voice dull. 'I shot when I saw the ripples of its steps. I knew it would follow behind them.'

By the time Felix and Kat made their way back to the others, the wind had become stronger and the sleet had turned to snow – great fat flakes that whirled before the gale to stick to their clothes and melt into the mud.

They found Ilgner and his knights and the slayers tending to their wounds in the midst of the bodies of the fallen beastmen.

'Excellent news,' said the general when Felix told him the runners were dead. 'Then we may proceed.' He had a bloody gash across his nose and cheeks that one of his knights was stitching up with needle and thread.

The sewing knight looked uneasily at the sky. 'This doesn't look like letting up, my lord,' he said. 'We could be in for a bad storm.'

Ilgner shrugged, seemingly entirely unaffected by the terrible cut on his face. 'We're stuck in it no matter if we go forwards or back, so... onwards.'

As the party hurried to finish binding their wounds, Felix noticed Ortwin off to one side, kneeling in the mud beside one of the beastmen, his head bowed mournfully.

Felix crossed to him. 'Everything all right, Ortwin?' he asked. 'Did you not find this battle as glorious as the others?'

Ortwin raised his head. There were tears in his eyes. 'It isn't that, Herr Jaeger,' he said. 'It is this.' He indicated the dead beastman he knelt beside.

Felix blinked in surprise as he realised that the rusty, dented breastplate that the monster wore strapped around its powerful furred torso was emblazoned with the insignia of the Order of the Fiery Heart.

NINE

'I FEAR WE have reached the end of our quest, Herr Jaeger,' said Ortwin with a break in his voice. 'I fear we have discovered the fate of Sir Teobalt's brother templars.'

Felix sighed, his shoulders slumping. It wasn't as if he hadn't expected this all along – it had almost been inevitable that they would find that the templars had been killed by the beastmen. Still it was one thing to expect a tragedy, and another to learn that it had actually occurred. The tiny spark of foolish hope he had carried with him from Altdorf guttered and went out. He might win Karaghul now, for he had done what Teobalt had asked of him, but there would be no joy in it.

'I'm sorry, Ortwin. Truly. At least we know they died fighting bravely,' he said, noting the battered state of the stolen breastplate. To his mind that was poor compensation, but it seemed to comfort Ortwin.

The young squire nodded and said, 'Aye. They would have wished for no better end than to die fighting the enemies of mankind. May Sigmar welcome them to his halls.'

Felix nodded and stood a moment in silence, then turned and left the boy to his prayers.

THREE OF ILGNER'S knights had to be left behind. One had been crushed to death by a beastman's mace, his armour so crumpled that he could not be removed from it. Another had a cracked skull and could not see straight, while the third had a shattered pelvis and could not walk or sit on a horse, let alone fight. Ilgner left the two wounded men with the corpse and some food and a fire, and said they would come back for them once they had seen what there was to see.

It seemed a polite abandonment to Felix, and he didn't doubt that the knights knew it. Even if Ilgner's party met no mishap while scouting the herd, it might be days before they returned, and both men were in need of immediate attention. Indeed, had Ilgner turned around and returned to Stangenschloss right then, it would still have been unlikely that the wounded knights would have survived the journey. Felix was impressed by how calmly the men accepted their fates, and it seemed the slayers were too.

Argrin left them his keg of ale – which was admittedly nearly empty, but still had enough for a few drinks each – and Rodi said he would pray to Grimnir for them.

He shook his head as the rest of the party got underway. 'I hope when it comes, my doom is clean,' he said. 'Starving to death is no way to die.'

'Maybe some more beastmen will come,' said Snorri.

'Aye,' said Argrin. 'That would be best.'

'Dying well no matter the circumstance – that is what is best.' said Gotrek. 'No one gets to choose their doom, only how they will face it.'

The other slayers nodded gravely at this. Even Rodi had no comment to make.

The party wasn't long on its march before the snow started sticking, turning the muddy track into dirty slush, and mantling the shoulders of the forest's green pines with epaulets of white. It fell so thickly and fiercely now that Felix found it impossible to see more than a few steps ahead, and he huddled inside his old red cloak and wished it had a hood. Fortunately, the path of the herd remained as easy to follow as ever – a raw gash of severed stumps that wound up and down wooded hillsides and between towering boulders through which the wind howled and the snow danced.

An hour on and the snow was covering even the muddy trail. An hour after that, in an open valley of scattered pines between high crags, Kat found hoof prints in the snow – a very different thing than finding snow in hoof prints. It meant that the herd had passed by so recently that the swiftly falling flakes had not yet had time to cover them.

'They are close, my lord,' she said to the general. 'Only minutes ahead.'

'Go find them and report back,' said Ilgner. 'We will follow slowly.'

Kat saluted and hurried off into the snow, disappearing almost instantly behind the slashing curtain of white. Felix shivered to see her going off into such danger, and glared at Ilgner for sending her on so blithely. Then he snorted angrily at himself. It was her job after all, and he had seen her do it before without worrying for her. Foolish how an unexpected spark and an unintended kiss had made him suddenly protective of her.

His mind continued to churn with thoughts of her. Damn the girl, why had she kissed him like that? The wildness of it! The sweet hunger of it! The urgent strength of her arms as she grappled herself to him! It made him dizzy just thinking about it.

He tried to calm himself. The reasons why being with her would be a bad idea were still as valid as they had been before, but now he found himself hunting for arguments that would poke holes in them. She wasn't *that* much younger than him, was she? And maybe it wasn't necessary that he love her. Perhaps she didn't love him. Perhaps all she wanted was a few nights together while they continued on the trail of the beasts.

He looked around at Ilgner and his knights, and Ortwin and the slayers. No. That wouldn't be such a good idea. He didn't want a repeat of the embarrassment he and Claudia had endured on board the *Pride of Skintstaad*. Whatever he decided, he would have to wait until they got back to civilisation. Perhaps by then his fever for the girl would have cooled somewhat and he would be able to think rationally again.

He breathed a sigh of relief and returned his attention to their surroundings, pleased to have defused his trouble, at least for now.

The knights and the slayers were following the beastmen's trail at a walk, not wanting to accidentally stumble into the tail of the herd. Here in this more open area, with only a few twisted pines dotting the valley floor, the true breadth of the herd's trail could be seen at last. The swathe of snow blackened by their passage was more than a hundred paces wide, and had been churned up by thousands of hooves. It was an intimidating sight.

Felix looked over to Ortwin to see how he was doing. He was worried about him. The boy had been praying constantly since Felix had left him to it back at the site of the fight with the foragers. Not only that, before they had resumed their hunt, Ortwin had stripped the breastplate with the insignia of the Order of the Fiery Heart from the dead beastman, and now wore it instead of his own.

'All right, Ortwin?' Felix asked.

'Yes, Herr Jaeger,' said Ortwin, breaking off his verses. 'Perfectly all right, thank you.'

'Not blaming yourself for the death of the templars or anything like that are you?'

'No, sir,' said Ortwin. 'It was the beastmen who slew them. And the order shall have its vengeance upon them, sir.'

'Of course they will,' said Felix. 'Of course they will.'

Less than an hour later, just as the grey day was darkening to a murky charcoal twilight, Kat's little bundled figure trotted out of the snow and waved them down. Felix and Gotrek and the others gathered around as she stood at Ilgner's stirrup to make her report. Her eyes were wide and fearful.

'I found them,' she said.

'And?' asked Ilgner, when she didn't go on.

'My lord, there are thousands of them. Thousands. I could not guess how many. I ran along the side of them for a quarter of an hour and still did not see the front of the herd. It wound away through the hills for... forever.'

'And did you see any champions among them? Any fiends of the Wastes?' Ilgner asked.

Kat shook her head. 'I didn't, my lord, but I did not reach the head, so did not see the leaders.'

Ilgner nodded, thinking, then sighed. 'There's no help for it. I must see them. I must know what we face.' He looked to Kat again. 'Can you bring us to the front of their line undetected?'

'I believe so, my lord,' said Kat after a moment. 'They are making their way over the hills by the broadest valleys. It takes them out of their way a bit. I think I may find a straighter line through smaller passes and get ahead of them, but it will be dangerous. They will have scouts and outriders moving before them and beside them. In this weather we won't know they are near us until they are on top of us.'

'Still we must risk it,' said Ilgner. 'It is that or risk doom for all the towns south of Stangenschloss.' He waved a gauntleted hand. 'Lead on, Kat. Lead on.'

AND SO THEY followed Kat's footprints up into the hills through narrow valleys and tree-choked canyons, all white and soft with snow that was now up to Felix's knees. It was hard slogging, and though the wind bit at his nose and cheeks, sweat was running down his back and ribs. The snow dragged at their legs and made it hard for them to judge their footing. More than once Felix slipped and fell and had to accept Gotrek's hand to stand again.

By the time they had reached the top of the hills, the snow had eased off somewhat, though the wind did not. It blasted straight over the crest, driving the flakes into their faces so hard that they felt more like sand than snow.

Rodi looked up as ragged clouds streamed across the sky, shredding like carded wool and revealing the sickly green light of Morrslieb behind them.

'Be easier to see them now,' he said.

'And easier for them to see us,' said Felix unhappily. Thousands of beastmen, Kat had said. A herd that went on forever. It seemed just the sort of doom Gotrek would be unable to resist – leagues from nowhere, in knee-deep snow, so that even if Felix wasn't killed by the beastmen who killed the Slayer, he would likely die from exposure before he made it back to civilisation. Wonderful.

They tucked their heads and started down the other side of the hill, and for another hour continued to go up and down smaller hills and in and out of wooded valleys until at last, just as it was becoming full dark, Gotrek lifted his head and inhaled.

'They're close,' he said. 'I can smell them.'

'No,' said Snorri, waving a hand behind him. 'That was Snorri. Sorry.'

'Unless you ate a wet fur coat,' said Rodi, 'it isn't just you. I smell them too.'

Just then Kat came back, appearing out of the trees to their left like a white ghost. 'They're coming,' she said, panting a bit. 'Down the length of the next valley.' She pointed back behind her. 'There is a stand of trees on the other side of this ridge. You may spy on them from there without being seen, my lord.'

'Excellent,' said Ilgner. 'Good work, Kat. Now we shall see what we shall see.'

THEY HEARD THEM before they saw them.

It was a quarter of an hour later. Felix was hunkered down at the edge of a pine wood that stretched down from the crest of the low hill behind them. He gazed with the others into a wide valley of jutting boulders and sparse, new-growth pine as the wind tore at his cloak and the steady snow slanted down ceaselessly from the charcoal sky and piled on his shoulders. It was full night now, but the white of the snow that blanketed the valley and the occasional light of Morrslieb piercing the torn and scudding clouds gave the scene the dim, colourless phosphorescence of a cave mushroom.

Despite his cloak, Felix was aching from the cold. His hands were stiff with it, and his face raw with it. Kat's hat was pulled down so low, and her scarf so high, that only her eyes were visible, flicking up and down the valley anxiously while Ilgner and the knights shuffled and stamped their feet to keep warm. Ortwin shivered, his teeth chattering as he continued his ceaseless praying. Only the slayers didn't seem to mind the cold. They squatted there shirtless, their eyebrows, beards and moustaches dusted with snow and crusted with ice, and didn't even shiver.

'Snorri forgets why we're here,' said Snorri after a while.

'Beastmen, Nosebiter,' said Gotrek. 'We hunt beastmen.'

'Ah,' said Snorri. 'Now Snorri remembers. Did Snorri ever tell you about the time he fought beastmen with his friends Gotrek and Felix?'

Gotrek grunted, but said nothing.

Then it came – a distant chanting brought on the wind, the sound of a thousand savage voices raised in unison.

Everyone looked up at once, then turned towards the north end of the valley. There was nothing to see yet, but the noise grew steadily louder, and was soon joined by a steady rumble that they could feel through the ground. The vibration was slow and rhythmic, like that of marching feet, but Felix knew the beasts didn't march – they shambled along in a disorganised mob – so what was it? The chanting kept time with the thudding rhythm – a single phrase, repeated over and over in the beasts' crude tongue, a vile gargle of harsh syllables and guttural grunts. And layered over it all were louder noises – whip cracks and roaring, wailing and smashing, and sounds of titanic tearing and snapping.

'What are they doing?' Felix wondered aloud.

No one had an answer for him.

Then, after minutes of staring, with the snow and the moonlight playing tricks on his eyes and making him see all sorts of things in the swirling flurries, Felix blinked and shook his head, for it seemed to him that the white distance was glowing yellow, like a candle set inside a porcelain bowl.

When he looked again the glow was brighter, and he knew it wasn't a trick of the eye.

'They're here,' whispered Kat.

Soon the silhouettes of young pines could be seen against the yellow light, and the snow flakes danced and glowed before it like fireflies, while the chanting and the thumping got louder, as did the syncopation of thuds and roars and cracks.

It seemed to take forever for the glow to get closer, and Felix wondered why. He knew from experience that beastmen could travel very quickly through the woods when they wanted to, but this herd seemed to be moving at a crawl. Even dwarfs marched faster.

Then, as Felix and the rest stared, one of the silhouetted trees shivered and thrashed like it was in a cyclone, then slowly toppled, accompanied by a horrendous splintering crash. Another tree fell the same way a moment later, and then, after a pause, another. It was as if some gigantic foot was crushing them to the earth.

Felix looked around at the others, his heart racing.

Ilgner's knights were wide-eyed and staring. Kat was shrinking back like a rabbit. The slayers were grinning with savage anticipation. Ortwin was still praying, his eyes closed.

'By all that's holy,' said Ilgner. 'What can flatten a tree like that?'

Felix looked back to the valley. The yellow light was brighter still, and had a shape now – long and sinuous, like some impossibly large glow-worm inching through the trees. The end of it faded into the snow-shrouded distance. It might have gone on forever.

More trees fell as the light crept ever closer. Felix began to see individual torches, and monstrous shadows moving around them, and now he could hear axes at work, which was almost a relief – for it was a much more mundane explanation for the toppling trees than the mad phantasms that had welled up unbidden in his mind.

"Ware the scouts,' said Kat.

Felix and the others looked where she pointed. Ahead of the crawling glow, dark shapes moved through the slender pines. Huge hunched shadows with giant axes and clubs in their hands, wading ponderously through the snowdrifts and looking all around them. Felix crouched lower instinctively as he saw them, but they continued on.

Then, finally, as more trees snapped and fell, through the swirling white veil of the snow came the column itself, and all Felix could do was stare.

First came the ungors, all carrying aloft burning brands to light the way. Just behind them lumbered a vanguard of huge, horn-headed gors, all in armour and carrying terrible weapons, which they raised over their heads and shook in time to the incessant chanting. There were hundreds of them, striding forwards in one ragged rank that stretched from just below Ilgner's position across to the far side of the valley for as far as Felix could see.

Behind them the trees fell. Felix squinted to make out the details in the bobbing lights of a moving mass of torches. The little shadows of hunched ungors scurried around the fallen trees, dragging them towards the sides of the valley, then running back for more as whip-wielding gors roared and lashed out at them.

Two more pines shivered and crashed to the ground with splintering screams, and four enormous horned shadows loomed through the gap they had made.

Kat gasped when she saw them, and Felix was afraid he had too. They were gigantic things, towering over the gors as the gors towered over the ungors, with shaggy, bull-shaped heads and heavy curling horns that stretched wider than a man might spread his arms. Each of them carried an axe taller than a beastman, with a double-bladed head that a dwarf could have hidden behind.

As the ungors hooked the branches of the fallen pines with chains and dragged them aside, the four great bulls strode to the next trees that stood in their way and hacked at their bases with slow, methodical strokes – one two, one two, one two. The trees were young and thin. It took no more than four bites of the massive axes for them to fall, then the bulls were onto the next group, with no more interest or emotion than a machine. It looked as if they had been doing this forever, and that they could go on doing it forever, never tiring, never slowing, never looking up from their work.

'Now they,' said Argrin, under his breath, 'would be a good doom.'

'For you?' said Rodi. 'Not if I reached 'em first.'

'Snorri thinks there is enough doom here for everybody,' said Snorri.

Felix wondered if the addled slayer had ever spoken a truer word.

Gotrek just grunted and watched.

'But I don't understand why they're doing it,' muttered Ilgner, seemingly to himself. 'Have they been cutting this path since the Howling Hills? What for?'

Two columns of ungor torchbearers filed from the gap that the monstrous minotaurs had cut in the trees. Between them capered a throng of wild-looking beastmen, all masked and bedecked with feathers and bones and strange fetishes – but otherwise entirely naked – and all shaking long staves capped with human and beast skulls and bits of crystal and brass that glittered and bounced in the torchlight. The dancing beastmen roared a guttural chant and thrust up their totems to the ponderous thudding rhythm, which continued to grow louder with each passing second. Some of them tore their flesh in ecstasy. Some of them burned themselves with torches, or butted heads with their fellows, their horns clashing with deafening cracks. Some fell, and scurrying ungors dragged them to the side, while new revellers jumped in to take their place.

And every few paces, following some rhythm Felix could not perceive, all of them would turn and bow behind them, wailing and shouting, then leap up again to dance on as before.

What comes now? Felix wondered anxiously. Are they bowing to some god? Has some champion of Chaos inspired this frenzy in them? If beasts as large as the minotaurs were toiling as lumberjacks, how terrible must the leader be?

Then Felix gasped again, as did all the other men, while the slayers swore in surprise.

For an instant, as it came out of the trees, Felix thought that his mad imagining had been true, and that it *was* a giant glow-worm that crawled among the herd, for the thing was long and round like a worm and had many legs, but then, as he focused through the blaze of torches that surrounded it, he saw that what he thought were the thing's legs were actually beastmen, all walking in file and in step, with heavy wooden yokes across their shoulders that carried what Felix had thought was the body of the worm, but which was in reality the largest henge stone Felix had ever seen.

'Sigmar's blood!' breathed Ilgner, as they watched it emerge from the trees. 'What is it?'

'It... it is a herdstone,' said Kat. 'The totem of the tribe. But... but it's too big. And they never move them.'

'They do now,' said Gotrek.

The stone was laid on its side, and was as long as the mast of a Bretonnian galleon. Its rune-daubed dark grey granite had been crudely shaped, starting narrow at the top, but thickening as it went along until it was perhaps eight feet in diameter near the centre. Jagged veins of quartz twisted through it, pulsing from within with a weird blue light in time with its bearers' chant.

Several of Ilgner's knights made the sign of the hammer as they stared down at the thing, and Felix understood why. It radiated fell power like an evil sun. He didn't just *see* the pulses of blue light, he felt them on his skin like a warm wind, and within his mind, like a whisper heard in a nightmare. It made him want to run away, but also to run to it, to throw down his weapon and join in the revellers' frenzied dance. It took an effort of will to remain where he was and only watch.

'Slayer Gurnisson,' said Ilgner. 'Your axe. Hide its glow.'

Felix turned to see Gotrek taking his axe off his back and burying the head in the snow at his feet. Its runes were blazing almost as brightly as a torch. Even through the snow Felix could see their glow.

Gotrek grunted, annoyed, then laid the axe flat and sat on it. The light disappeared.

Felix shared an amused smile with Kat, then turned back to the procession below.

Double columns of beastmen marched under the sturdy yokes on either side of the stone, all striding in unison to the rhythm, and shaking the ground with each ponderous step. There were at least two hundred of the monsters, a hundred per side, and more milled along beside them, chanting as well, their weapons out, the fur of their faces painted with blue stripes and symbols – an honour guard perhaps.

As the base of the stone appeared from between the trees, Felix and the others at last saw the leaders of the herd. The first was an enormous beastman, almost as large and muscular as the minotaurs, though leaner, who paced up and down on top of the stone, roaring at those who carried it. He had the blunt head and thick curling horns of a ram, but his teeth, when he snarled, were those of a predator, and his eyes glowed with the same blue light that pulsed from the stone.

The thick fur that covered his rippling muscles was coal-black, and criss-crossed with the white scars of a hundred battles. Over this natural armour he wore a suit of steel and bronze armour that fitted him perfectly, yet looked far beyond any beastman's ability to make. The axe he carried also bore the mark of the same sophisticated hand. It was a weapon as tall as Felix, crowned with a huge, single-bladed head with a deep notch in the cutting edge shaped so that it looked like the open beak of some screaming predatory bird. Fist-sized blue gems gleamed on each side of the axe like angry avian eyes.

'There now,' said Rodi, chuckling. 'I'll have a go at *him*.'

'I thought you wanted the bulls,' said Argrin.

'They'll be for afters,' said Rodi.

While the war-leader prowled up and down the stone, urging on his followers with hoarse bellows, the stone's other passenger stood stock still upon it, a gnarled staff raised high as he lifted his goatish head to exhort the heavens in a keening, high-pitched wail. He was half the size of the other, and appeared to be some sort of bestial holy man, grey of fur and gaunt with age, and dressed in long dirty robes, stitched over with crude symbols. On his cadaverous head he wore a leather mask with a sinuous blue symbol painted on the brow, and a crest of blue feathers that arced over his head and ran all the way down his back. One of his horns was bent at an odd angle, as if it had been damaged when he was young. The strangest part of his aspect, however, was the hundreds of severed bird claws that dangled from every part of his costume at the ends of strings and leather thongs. Eagle claws served him as earrings, crow feet as braid-locks in his straggly goat beard. Hawks' talons clutched every finger of his scrawny hands and shrivelled chicken feet fringed the arms of his robes. Even the head of his leather-wrapped, fetish-woven staff followed the motif, for it appeared to be the powerful fore-claw of a griffon, which clutched a pulsing blue orb.

'A shaman,' hissed Kat. She made a curious sign by hooking her thumbs and spreading her fingers so that her hands looked like antlers, then thrust them angrily in the robed beast's direction. 'Taal wither you, fiend. Rhya poison your fodder.'

'Is it a crusade of some kind, then?' asked Ilgner, again to himself. 'Do they do the bidding of their foul gods?'

The stone-bearers plodded slowly on, coming parallel with Ilgner's party's hiding place, with the main body of the herd appearing at last behind them. Felix stared as he watched them shamble out of the snow. For all the eldritch fear that the stone and its riders had inspired in Felix's heart, this was perhaps the most terrifying sight he had yet beheld.

The beastmen came down the valley like a slow brown tide, thousands upon thousands of them, an endless winding river vanishing into the opaque distance, and filling the valley from edge to edge so that the nearest beasts lapped halfway up the hill that Ilgner's party hid upon. Every single one of them croaked the shaman's chant, so that the air throbbed with it. Felix edged further back into the pines for fear of being seen. Not since his journey with Gotrek and Malakai over the Chaos Wastes had he seen so many of the monsters in one place.

Ilgner too seemed impressed. 'This beggars belief,' he whispered. 'Kat, have you ever seen the like?'

She shook her head. 'There are more here than all the herds I have spied upon combined.'

'But what is their purpose?' asked Ilgner again. 'Where do they go with the thing? What do they mean to do with it?'

'Whatever it is,' said Kat, 'they are heading south, into the lands of men. They must be stopped.'

'Aye,' said Ilgner. 'Aye.' And Felix could tell that he had left unspoken the simple question, 'How?'

For the slayers the question wasn't how, but when? They could barely contain their eagerness to be at the monsters. They shifted restlessly and toyed with their weapons.

Gotrek turned to Felix, Ilgner and the rest, a wild light in his single eye. 'You'd best get away,' he said. 'Return to the fort and prepare for what is to come. This is a true doom, a final doom at last. We four will die here.' He looked at Felix. 'Manling–'

But whatever he had been about to say was cut off as, behind him, Ortwin stood abruptly from his fevered praying and drew his sword, then stepped to the edge of the pines and held it aloft.

'The Order of the Fiery Heart shall have its vengeance!' he cried, and plunged down the hill, wading through the knee-deep snow straight towards the herdstone, as ten-score beastmen turned their heads his way.

For a stunned second, everyone just stared, and then they were all scrambling at once.

'Stop him!' hissed Ilgner.

'Kill him!' barked Rodi.

'Run!' whispered Kat.

Felix and some of the knights stood and started forwards, but hesitated at the edge of the woods. Kat half-drew an arrow, then stopped, uncertain. Only Gotrek acted. He scooped up some snow between his hands, packed it and hurled it. It caught the squire square on the back of the head and pitched him face first into the snow.

'Mad infant,' grunted Argrin.

'Forget him,' said Ilgner, staring at the beasts, more and more of which were turning and looking in their direction. 'We must go. Now!'

Felix was in hearty agreement, but he hesitated. Sir Teobalt had entrusted the boy to his care. He couldn't just leave him behind. With a curse, he ran down the hill, lifting his knees like a Kislevite dancer so that the snow wouldn't slow him.

'Felix! No!' called Kat.

Ortwin was just picking himself up when Felix reached him.

'Come on, you little idiot,' he snapped, and grabbed the squire's arm, pulling him back towards the top of the hill. The nearest gors and ungors were starting towards them, roaring and raising their weapons, and the ripple of turning heads had reached the herdstone.

Ortwin struggled to get away. 'No, I must avenge my masters!'

Felix cuffed his ear. 'What kind of vengeance is suicide? Come *on!*' He hauled on Ortwin's arm and the boy reluctantly allowed himself to be dragged up the hill.

Behind them, more of the beastmen were breaking from the column, their howls getting louder. At the crest, Kat was crouching and beckoning them on as Ilgner and his men backed away and the slayers readied their weapons.

'Hurry!' she cried.

Then a hair-raising shriek split the night and froze them all in their tracks. Felix turned as it echoed away down the valley, and saw that the beast-shaman was looking their way, his staff raised, and that the whole herd now stood staring at them, unmoving and utterly silent as the snow fell around them. The skin crawled on the back of Felix's neck as he looked at them. He could see the hate boiling in their glittering animal eyes, their hands tensing on the hafts of their weapons, but they remained where they were. Even the ones who had been chasing them stopped and fell silent.

'What are they doing?' asked Ortwin.

'I have no idea,' said Felix. 'Just keep moving.'

He turned up the hill as the shaman's voice rang out a second time, this time in a high chant, different from the one before, faster and more urgent. Then, like the murmur of thunder, the herd began to echo him, getting louder and more insistent with each repetition.

Felix could feel the air tingle around him, and the falling snow began to dance in wild eddies that bore no relation to the direction of the wind.

'Run!' he shouted, and shoved the boy ahead of him.

There was a crack like a pistol shot and Felix glanced back, fearful. The shaman was slamming the head of his orb-clutching griffon-claw staff against the herdstone in time to the new chant, and with each strike, the veins of quartz that ran through it flashed blue and bright.

'Faster!' Felix shouted.

At the top of the hill, Ilgner and his knights had recovered their surprise and were scrambling to mount their horses. Kat was backing away, open-mouthed, the flashes of blue reflecting in her white-rimmed eyes. The slayers were snarling and striding forwards, ready for battle.

Felix looked back again. The flashes from the stone were getting brighter and brighter as the old shaman struck harder and the chant got louder. The blue light lanced out in knife-sharp shafts, like bars of sunlight cutting through a dark room.

One shaft cut across the snow to Felix's right, turning it a blinding white. He pressed on, blinking and wincing as he herded Ortwin before him, then gaped when he saw that the snow where the light had touched it was melting, steam rising from it in wispy curls.

'Sigmar, he's aiming for us!' he said. He waved a wild hand at the knights on their horses. 'Down! Down! The light!'

Another crack came from behind them, and Felix threw himself to the snow, trying to knock Ortwin down with him, but the boy only stumbled and turned, reaching out a hand.

'Herr Jaeger, take my—'

'Ortwin! Curse you, get—'

A jagged bar of blue-white light flashed across Ortwin's eyes and he fell back with a cry, throwing his hands over his face. Felix looked away, expecting to hear the sizzle of cooking meat, or the crackle of charring skin, but it didn't come.

'My eyes!' wailed Ortwin. 'My eyes!'

Another shaft of light shot up the hill past them and Felix heard Ilgner and his knights cry out. He grabbed Ortwin's hand and dragged him on. Only a few more steps, a few more plodding, slogging steps.

Ortwin stumbled along blindly behind him, wailing, 'It burns! Oh, Sigmar protect me, it burns!' and dragging behind horribly. Did the boy want to die?

Felix turned, angry. 'Move, damn you! Pick up your–'

He stopped, staring, utterly stricken. 'By the gods,' he murmured. 'Your face.'

'What's wrong?' the boy asked. Then he shrieked in agony as he was wracked with convulsions.

Felix stumbled back from him, horrified. The boy was changing before his eyes. Hair grew on his cheeks and spread like fire to his hairline. His nose was lengthening and his chin receding. His ears were growing points. Lumps were beginning to form on either side of his brow.

Ortwin reached out trembling hands towards Felix as another spasm shook him. 'Please, Herr Jaeger. Help me! What's happening to me?'

Claws tore out through the fingers of the boy's gloves. Stubby horns burst from his forehead in sprays of blood, and his irises swelled to fill his whole eye.

The boy was becoming a beast.

TEN

THE SQUIRE'S YELLOW claws clutched at Felix's legs. 'Hllp me, Hrrr Jaegrr,' he pleaded. His voice was no longer human – more like the bleating of a goat. Felix could barely understand him.

'Ortwin,' said Felix in a whisper. 'I'm sorry.'

He kicked the boy in the chest, sending him tumbling down towards the herd, then turned and ran up the slope, his mind jagged with grief for the boy and fear for himself. What would he tell Sir Teobalt?

Fresh screams made him look up, and he moaned with despair. At the top of the hill, Ilgner's knights were writhing and falling from their rearing horses as Gotrek and the other slayers backed away from them. One of the knights was clawing at his face. Another was tearing at his breastplate, shrieking, 'Bees! Wasps! Get them off!' as fur grew from the joints of his armour. A third looked up from where he had fallen and Felix saw to his horror that he had a snout where his mouth had been, and the black, shining eyes of a goat. A warhorse danced in a circle, hooves flying as tusks grew from its mouth and bony spines rose from its mane.

'Slayers!' roared Gotrek. 'To work!'

Kat knelt over Lord Ilgner, who was curled and shaking in the snow. 'My lord,' she cried. 'My lord, are you all right?'

Lord Ilgner howled with pain and the back of his cuirass split down the middle. A sable-furred ridge like that of a boar ripped out from it. He turned, snarling from a bestial mouth, and swiped a gauntleted paw at her, knocking her onto her back.

Her eyes went wide with shock as the thing that had been Ilgner rose and advanced on her. 'Oh no, my lord,' she wept. 'Not you. Not you!'

Felix reached the crest of the hill and charged the general, sword high, but Gotrek was there first, his axe a blur. Ilgner's wolf-like head dropped from his shoulders in a shower of blood and thudded to the snowy ground between Kat's legs.

Felix groaned with misery. If the knights had only stayed low like Kat and the slayers, the fatal blue light would have flashed over their heads. 'The poor man,' he mumbled.

'No time for pity, manling,' said Gotrek, as a beast-knight charged him. 'Defend yourself.'

Felix turned just in time to take the sword of one of the changed knights on Karaghul's edge. Felix's arm stung as the force of the blow staggered him back. The thing's muscles had burst its armour and the sword looked like a plaything in its ham-hock hands. Behind it, he could see Snorri, Rodi and Argrin battling armoured monsters and slavering hell-horses in a mad scrum.

Felix slashed back at his opponent, cutting through the furred hide of its leg. It howled and attacked again.

Beside him, Kat chopped at it with her axes, weeping as she did. 'I know them,' she sobbed. 'I know them all.'

Felix ran the changed knight through and stole a glance down the hill as it fell.

Through the ever-swirling snow he could see that the beast-shaman and the war-leader had turned away from them as if they were of no more concern, and the giant herdstone was on the move again, as was the herd that followed behind it. Unfortunately, a dozen or so of the blue-painted honour guard had detached themselves from the rest, and were wading through the snow in their direction. Of Ortwin he could see no sign.

He turned back just as a horse with a mouth like a crocodile lunged and snapped at him. He stumbled aside and the thing shouldered him to the ground.

'Gotrek,' gasped Felix, trying to recover his breath. 'More coming.'

'I see them, manling,' said Gotrek.

'We have to get away!' said Kat. 'We have to warn the fort! We have to warn the villages!'

'Aye,' said Felix. He lurched up and faced the horse as it turned and charged again. He dodged away as it kicked at him with its forelegs, then darted in again and gored it in the belly. Kat cut the hamstrings of its back legs with her axes. It collapsed to the ground, screaming, still sounding much too much like a horse. Felix shivered with revulsion.

He and Kat looked around. The melee was over. The slayers stood shoulder-deep in a ring of dead horses and knights, but the blue-painted beastmen were halfway up the hill.

'Snorri has never killed a horse before,' said Snorri, sounding sad.

'Those weren't horses,' said Argrin.

'Now let's get the real beasts,' said Rodi, striding eagerly towards the edge of the hill.

'No,' said Gotrek grimly. 'This doom must be deferred.'

The two young slayers turned on him, staring.

'Are you mad, Gurnisson?' asked Rodi.

'This is a great doom,' said Argrin.

Felix looked down the hill. The blue-daubed beastmen were closing fast.

'It is a selfish doom,' said Gotrek. 'If we take it, the fort will not be warned. Thousands will die.'

Rodi snorted. 'A doom is a doom.'

'Aye,' said Gotrek. 'But a great doom makes a difference.'

'We're all doomed if we don't go now,' said Felix, exasperated. This was not the time to be arguing the finer points of slayer doctrine.

'We're doomed whether we go or stay,' said Rodi. 'The beasts are too fast. We might as well fight now as later.'

'We have to try,' said Kat. 'Please! Let's go!'

'There is one great doom here,' said Argrin solemnly. 'For the one who stays behind.'

'I'll stay!' said Rodi.

'No,' said Snorri. 'Snorri will stay.'

'There's no time for this!' said Felix.

'Let the slayer who suggested it stay,' said Gotrek. He nodded to Argrin approvingly. 'May Grimnir welcome you to his halls.'

Snorri shrugged. 'That seems fair to Snorri.'

Rodi looked about to burst, but then cursed and spat. 'Fine,' he said. 'But I will have the rear guard.' He bowed to Argrin. 'Die well, Argrin Crownforger.'

Argrin bowed back. 'We shall drink together at Grimnir's table.'

'Goodbye, Argrin,' said Snorri.

'Hurry!' said Kat.

Gotrek, Snorri and Rodi started into the pines without another look back as Argrin stepped to the edge of the hill and readied his steel-headed warhammer.

'Come on, you cow-faced dung piles!' he roared. 'I'll cut you into chops and cook you on Grungni's forge!'

Felix and Kat turned away and hurried after the slayers as they heard the beastmen bellow in response. Felix was afraid it was all for naught. Argrin wouldn't hold the beastmen for long, and even in the dark and through the whirling flakes, they would have little trouble following the party's footprints in the snow. They were only postponing the end.

'We're not going to be fast enough,' he said when he and Kat caught up to the slayers. 'They'll follow our footsteps and catch us.'

'Then another will stay behind to stop them,' said Gotrek. 'Until we have all met our doom.'

'If we can reach the deepest woods it might be possible to lose them,' said Kat. 'There are places where the snow never reaches the–'

She was cut off by the roaring of beasts and the clash of steel on steel, rising out of the wail of the wind in the trees.

Rodi paused and turned, but Gotrek shoved him on.

'Keep moving,' he growled.

They hurried up the hill through the darkness, silent and grim, following the footsteps they had made on the way here, and listening to the snatches of the fight that the wind brought them – screams and curses, clashes and thuds – and then, much too quickly, the triumphant howl of the beastmen.

The sound brought a lump to Felix's throat. He had barely known Argrin, but the young slayer had made a great sacrifice for them, and the fact that it had been very likely worthless just made it all the sadder.

'Lucky bastard,' snarled Rodi, with a rasp of emotion in his voice.

'Snorri is jealous,' said Snorri.

As they reached the top of the ridge and started down the other side, Felix strained his ears behind him. He could hear nothing. The wailing wind covered everything. Had the beastmen given up? Had they decided it was too much bother to give chase, and gone back to the herd? It was impossible to know.

The pines were thicker on this side of the hill, and the darkness beneath them was almost complete. Only the white of the snow gave some light, but not nearly enough. Felix followed Gotrek more by sound than sight. The crackle of branches and the slap of a twig against his cheek told him they were entering another tangle of brush before his eyes did. Felix would have loved to light a torch, but light would be their doom.

Six steps into the thicket, Kat hissed. 'Stop! Turn left!'

Gotrek obligingly turned left, and Felix followed, Kat, Rodi and Snorri crunching in behind him. The bracken grew even thicker here, and the faint light faded entirely. They might have been in a cave.

'Some trouble?' Gotrek asked.

'No,' Kat said. 'But deeper in the bracken, they might not see we've turned off our old path.'

'Ah,' said Gotrek. 'Smart.'

For a few minutes it seemed that the ruse had worked. As they broke out of the brush and continued along the steep shoulder of the hill they heard nothing behind them but the wind. It felt as if they might be entirely alone in the wood.

But then, as Felix followed Gotrek's steps through densely packed trees, feeling his way like a blind man, there was a distant crashing behind them, as of something big wading through bracken, just audible above the moan of the trees.

'Found us again,' called Rodi from the back.

Gotrek cursed and quickened his pace. Felix tried to do the same, flinching at the darkness that loomed up at him with every step. He could hear Kat picking up the pace behind him.

'Find an open space, Gurnisson,' Rodi called again. 'I'll need some room to swing my axe.'

They sped on, Felix stubbing his fingers and barking his knuckles on the trunks of trees he couldn't see, then pushing past. He shivered at the thought of fighting beastmen in the pitch dark. It would be short at least. And he wouldn't see it coming.

A guttural howl echoed from behind them, the baying of a beast that has caught the scent. Felix looked back – a stupid thing to do, since he could no more see behind him than in front. He turned back, and ran smack into a tree, cracking his head on some knot of wood. The world spun around him and he staggered, hissing in pain, then caught himself and felt his way around the tree one-handed as he massaged his temple with the other. There was blood, and a lump was rising. Touching it made his legs go wobbly and he had to steady himself again, fighting nausea.

He started on again, but after a few steps he realised he wasn't hearing Gotrek ahead of him any more. He paused. The noise of the others was off to his left, only a few feet. He edged in that direction, but ran into dense undergrowth. There was no way through. For an instant he thought about working his way back to where he had left the trail, but he didn't dare. The beastmen were in that direction. He'd have to keep going and angle back after the brush thinned.

'Felix?' came Kat's voice.

'Coming,' he called over the wind. 'Sorry.'

He pushed on faster, trying to go straight, but having to go out wider and wider to his right around the tangled brush. He fought for balance as the angle of the hill got steeper under his feet.

Then behind him he heard the thud of hooves and a garble of inhuman voices.

'Hurry, Felix,' Kat hissed. 'They're coming!'

'Move, girl!' shouted Rodi.

Felix shoved at the brush but it wouldn't give. He sidestepped desperately, trying to find a way through. His ankle banged into something hard and immovable on the ground. He fell sideways, flailing with his arms for purchase. His fingers caught at twigs but they snapped, and he was tumbling down the hill in a flopping sprawl of limbs, upside down, then right side up, then crashing into invisible tree trunks, rocks and bushes before slamming hard on his side at the bottom of the slope and cracking his head on another invisible obstacle.

The only thing he could see was stars.

* * *

HE WOKE AGAIN to the sound of distant fighting. For a long moment he had no idea where he was, or what the sound meant, or why he couldn't see, or what had caused the horrible throbbing in his head. He only knew that lying there in the dark was infinitely preferable to moving in any way. Moving hurt like a hangover, and he didn't care for it. Besides, the wind and the patter of snowflakes on his face were comforting somehow.

Then bubbles of memory began to float up through the mud of his brain and burst one by one on the surface. He had fallen. From where? A hill. Why had he been on a hill? There had been some desperate reason to get somewhere. At that memory his heart filled with dread, though he couldn't remember the cause. He had been trying to reach someone. Who? He knew he had to help them. Had to save them. A girl. She was running from...

Suddenly it all flooded back and he sat up with a gasp. At least he tried to. Really he flopped over on his side and vomited – while his brain smashed around inside his skull like an iron mace that might shatter it from the inside.

On a second try he made it to his hands and knees, which made it very convenient to vomit again – so he did. He was tempted to stay that way for a while, but the sounds of the fighting were still going on. Gotrek and Kat and the others still lived. He had to help them.

He forced himself to his feet with the aid of a tree. It was so black around him that he could see nothing at all – not the snow, not the sky, nothing. For all he knew the crack on the head might have blinded him. But he could hear the fight, above him and off to the left, some distance away.

He staggered forwards, wading through the snow and the blackness with his hands out in front of him. Every step hurt. He had bruises from head to toe, and he had smashed his left knee and twisted his right ankle. At least nothing seemed broken. He stumbled on at a snail's pace, feeling with both his hands and his feet. He wanted to run, but he wasn't sure he'd be able to get up if he fell again.

After a few more steps, the trees thinned out and the ground sloped down a little before him. This was encouraging. He might be able to make better speed in the clear. At the bottom of the little slope the ground under the snow became very flat and smooth. He took another step and his heel shot out to the side. He was on ice!

He scrambled to catch his balance, but his other foot went and he fell backwards. There was a loud crack and the ice gave beneath him. His heart stopped, as the image of plunging into some frozen lake or river and sinking to the bottom in his chainmail flashed through his mind.

Nothing so dramatic happened. He landed flat on his back in a foot of snow, and for a moment thought that he hadn't broken through the ice after all. Then he felt freezing cold water seeping though the seat of his breeches and the back of the leather jerkin he wore under his mail.

With a curse he fought to sit up. Soaking wet in the middle of a snowstorm was not good at all. He put his hand down on the ice to lever himself up. It broke through. His hand hit bottom almost instantly, his sleeve soaked to the elbow. He must be in some frozen pond or stream. He tried to be cautious, but no matter where he put his weight, the ice broke under it, and by the time he dragged himself to the edge he was soaked to the skin from the waist down. His cloak and both sleeves were wet through too.

'This is bad,' he murmured. And then he realised something worse.

He couldn't hear the fight any more. He paused and strained to listen over the howling and moaning of the wind, but there was nothing.

No. There it was. A clash.

He stood and started towards it. No. That way was the water. He'd have to go a little further down to the left. He stumbled on, his teeth chattering and his feet and leg joints aching with cold as his wet breeches slapped around them. His pack felt as if it weighed as much as Gotrek.

He listened again. 'Come on, curse you!' he muttered. 'Keep fighting! Let me hear you!'

He laughed as he realised that all of a sudden he was hurrying to the fight to be rescued, rather than to be the rescuer.

Another clang. He reorientated himself and started ahead again. At least he thought he was moving in the right direction. The wind made it hard to pinpoint the sound. After a few more steps he braved a move to the left and found the stream again. This time he shuffled across as cautiously as an old man – though to be honest, his wet clothes and his muscles were so stiff now he could hardly do anything else.

He reached the opposite bank without incident and listened again. He heard nothing. He moved a little further on. Still nothing. Had he got turned around? Shouldn't he have come to the hill by now? He pressed on, shivering as the wind pressed his ice-crusted clothes against his skin. Another ten steps. Still nothing. Was he even going in a straight line? He couldn't tell.

'Gotrek!' he called. 'Kat! Snorri!' But his voice came out in a plaintive whisper that was whipped away in the wind. He could hardly hear it over the ceaseless chattering of his teeth. And in this wind, he doubted his friends could have heard him even if he had shouted at the top of his lungs. Was that why he couldn't hear them? Or perhaps they were all dead, killed by the blue-painted monsters. Perhaps he was all alone in the Drakwald but for the beastmen – the only living man for a hundred miles.

It came to him then that he was going to die there – that his corpse would be buried in the snow, frozen to the marrow until the spring, when it would thaw and rot, to become food for the beetles and worms of the forest. Maybe some scout or forester would find his bones and wonder who they had belonged to. Just another victim of the war, they would say. And all because he had walked the wrong way around a tree and lost the others. It seemed an impossibly silly reason to die.

A sob lodged painfully in his throat as he thought of all the things he had left unfinished. He would never witness Gotrek's doom or complete his epic. He would never have vengeance upon the skaven sorcerer who had ordered his father's death. He would never see Ulrika again. He would never–

He shook himself. Sigmar, he was having brain fever! He had to stop ruminating and do something or he would die indeed. He had to make a fire and get warm. But, no, if he made a fire, the beastmen would find him.

He shrugged. He didn't care. He would rather die warm than frozen. Besides, if Gotrek and the others had won the fight, the light might lead them to him.

He stopped and struggled to take his pack off. He was shaking so violently now he could hardly get his arms out of the straps. Finally he got it off his shoulders and it thudded to the ground behind him. He turned and felt around until he found it. His heart sank. No wonder it had felt so heavy. The leather was wet and crackled with ice. The bedroll and blanket that he had strapped to the bottom of it were soaked through.

He groaned in despair. A wet blanket, no dry clothes to change into. He really was going to die.

He fumbled for the buckles of his pack with fingers so numb that he couldn't feel what he was touching. It seemed to take him an hour to get the straps loose and the flap open – an hour when the cold from his ice-hardened clothes seeped into his skin to the bone. He felt made of lead – cold lead. It was almost impossible to move his arms.

He dug painfully through the contents of the pack, all wet and ruined, until he found his flint and steel and tinderbox. The box was smashed, probably during his fall, and the little pine shavings wet and limp.

'It's not fair!' he said, sobbing, then was glad that no one had been there to hear him.

Pushing to his feet hurt more than a sword wound. It felt like he had Altdorf's temple of Sigmar on his back – like all his joints were wrapped tight with leather straps. He staggered around until he found a bush, then snapped twigs off it until he had a shaking fistful. He turned and went back to where his pack was. It wasn't there. He whimpered and started feeling around. He'd lost it in the dark. It was probably a foot from him and he'd lost it. He found it at last behind him, and knelt beside it, breathing a shuddering sigh of relief and sweeping away the snow in front of him so he could pile the little handful of twigs on the bare ground. Then he found the flint and steel again and struck them together. At least he tried to. His fingers were so stiff, and his shaking so violent, that he missed. He tried again. This time they clashed together, but they were too wet to strike a spark.

With a grunt of frustration he slipped them down between his jack and his shirt, the only place on him that was fully dry. The cold steel against his chest made him flinch, but it had to be done. After a second he fumbled them back out and tried again. A spark!

It flew away on the wind, never coming close to the twigs. He shifted around so that his back was to the gale and tried again. Still the spark flew. He sobbed. Every muscle in his body was cramping with cold. He felt made of wood now. His arms could barely hold their position. His fingers couldn't hold the steel. It slipped out of his hand and fell on the snowy ground. He struggled to pick it up again. It was like trying to grab something with one's elbow. He could only push it around.

At last he got the little bar trapped against his leg and fumbled it up into his grip. He struck it against the flint again, and again, and again. The sparks hopped onto the twigs and died – snuffed by the ice or blown out by the wind.

He paused. He was tired. He couldn't lift his arms any more. He needed to rest. Yes, that was it – a little rest and he would try again. He laid his arms on his knees and bowed his head. All he needed was a few minutes and he would get his strength back. Just a few minutes. He closed his eyes. That was better. He was feeling better already. Warmer even. A gentle heat seemed to be flowing through his veins. He felt cosy. Maybe he would just lie down for a bit. Yes, that was best. A little nap.

He eased over on his side, letting the flint and the steel fall from his fingers and curling into a ball. All was well. A cosy little nap and everything would be fine.

But then, just as he was drifting off into a drowsy dream of hearths and warm brandy, there was a noise in the darkness. His heart lurched. Something was coming for him. He tried to open his eyes, tried to move his arms and legs, to force himself to sit up, to draw his sword. He couldn't. He was pressed to the ground by weariness and petrified with stiffness. His body would not answer his call.

The thing in the darkness got closer. He could hear it behind him. He could hear it breathing.

ELEVEN

'Felix! Felix, wake up!'

Someone was shaking him. It hurt. His muscles screamed. He tried to shrug the person off, tried to complain, but he couldn't move, couldn't stop his jaws from trembling long enough to speak. The person stepped in front of him and held a slotted lantern to his face. Though the light was dim, after so long in the dark it blinded him. He cringed away.

'Rhya be praised.' said the person. 'You're alive!'

Felix knew the voice. A voice from the distant past. A girl he used to know. Kirsten? Ulrika? Was he dreaming? He couldn't tell.

A warm hand touched his face and felt at his neck.

'Gods, not by much. Wait here.'

He heard the person set down the lantern and move away. He squinted against the light, looking around only with his eyes, for he couldn't move his head. Through a screen of slashing snow he saw a little bundled-up form was bustling in and out of his field of vision, taking off her pack, looking though his.

Kat. It was Kat. He wasn't sure if he was disappointed or relieved.

'All wet,' she said to herself. 'Felix, what happened? How did you do this to yourself?'

There was a sharp scraping noise and a flash, and then after a moment, the space in front of him got brighter. Kat moved away and he saw she had started a little fire. It almost made him cry. How had she done it so easily? Why had it been so hard for him? He saw her digging away the snow around him as if she were a dog burying a bone, then she vanished again for a moment. Something was laid over him, and then Kat was kneeling beside him, raising it on sticks. She was making a tent around him.

Then she vanished again, and for long enough that he grew worried. Had she left him? Had something grabbed her?

Finally she stepped back in front of him, a big bundle of dead branches and twigs in her arms. She dropped them beside the little fire and then began to lay them carefully on top of it. The heat of it was reaching his face now. It stung like ice.

When she had built up the fire, she placed her canteen and his next to it, then crawled into the tent and spread out her bedroll beside him, then turned to him and pulled off his cloak, which was stiff and heavy with ice. She threw it out beside the fire, then started on the wool coat he wore over his chainmail.

'Wh... wh... what are you doing?' he managed.

'Your clothes are killing you,' she said. 'They are wet and frozen and taking your heat. You must get out of them or you will die.'

He tried to protest, but more for form's sake than anything else. He knew she was right, it was just that, though he had more than once pictured her taking his clothes off, it hadn't been like this. Not with him helpless as a baby. Not when it was a matter of life or death.

She had terrible trouble with his chainmail, but he could do little to help her. She had to raise his arms so that she could tug it off over his head, for he couldn't move them himself. At last, after much grunting and cursing, she dragged it off him and threw it aside. The rest came much easier, and soon he was lying naked under the tent with all his clothes drying around the fire.

Still he couldn't move except to shiver. Also, though he shook so much that he thought he would break his teeth with their chattering, he was burning up. He felt like he was back in the desert of Khemri, dying in the sun. With a grunt of effort, Kat rolled him onto her bedroll and pulled the blanket over him, then started taking off her hat and coat and scarf.

'Don't do that,' said Felix. 'You'll freeze too.'

'I am going to lie with you. The blankets are not enough. You need true warmth.'

Felix was alarmed. Again, he had dreamed of this, but not like this! 'But... but I'm too hot already.'

'You are not,' said Kat, unbuckling and shucking her leather armour. 'You're as cold as a fish. You only think you're hot. It is the madness that comes before the end.'

'M-madness?' stuttered Felix as Kat pulled her wool undertunic off over her head and revealed her naked torso.

She was as lean and wiry as a greyhound, but most definitely a woman. She shucked her boots and breeches, then reached out of the tent and grabbed her canteen from beside the fire. She hissed as it burned her fingers, then pulled it into the tent by the strap. When she had it, she quickly rolled under the blanket with him and wrapped an arm around him, while she gingerly unscrewed the cap of the canteen.

'Kat,' he said. 'I… this…'

'Shhhh,' she said, and lifted the canteen to his mouth. 'Drink this.'

He jerked back, yelping, as the water scalded his lips. 'It's too hot! I can't!'

'You must. You must warm your insides. Drink!'

Felix opened his mouth again and did his best to swallow as she poured it into him, though it felt as if the water were blistering his mouth and throat as it went down. Finally she relented and set the canteen aside, and he lay back, panting and gasping.

She rested her head on his chest and hugged him hard. It felt remarkably good, but Felix remained rigid. He wasn't sure if he should return the gesture, or if he wanted to, or even if he could.

'Listen, Kat…' he said, then couldn't think of what to say.

'Forget it, Felix,' she said. 'I remember what you said. Just rest.'

From the way that she said it he could tell it still stung her. He grunted, frustrated. He didn't want her thinking that he didn't love her. It wasn't that. It was… His mind was too jumbled with the cold and the warmth and the dizziness from drinking the hot water so fast. He gave up. He dragged his lumpish, unresponsive arms up and put them around her. She remained tense for a moment, but then relaxed and nestled her head under his chin, very like a cat indeed. It was such a sweet, cosy gesture he almost cried.

'Damn it, Kat,' he sighed, his words slurring a little with drowsiness. 'What is the matter with you?'

'What do you mean?' she murmured.

'Why do you like me? And don't say you're in love with the hero I was to you when you were young. You're smarter than that, and I was never that hero anyway.' He snorted. 'It was you who saved me that day, not the other way around. And...' His shivers overcame him again for a moment and he had to stop. 'And here you've done it again, so it can't be that.'

Kat was silent for a long time, and Felix wondered with mixed feelings if he had actually convinced her of her folly and that she would say, 'You're right, Felix. It was my memories of you I loved. I've been a foolish girl.'

But after a moment she squeezed him again and said, 'You *are* a hero to me, Felix. Not for killing that woman, but for trying to stop her even though you knew she would kill you. But...' She paused again. 'But it isn't that – not just that.' She stared out of the tent at the fire. 'There are many men I know who accept me as a scout, but not as a woman.' Her eyes narrowed. 'They call me she-beast, or tom-cat, or... other names.' She paused again, and Felix could feel angry tension in her arms, then she continued. 'And there are other men, like Milo, who would accept me as a woman, but not as a scout.' She turned her head and looked up at him, her brown eyes liquid in the glow of the fire. 'You accept me as both. That...' She swallowed, then buried her head against his chest again. 'That doesn't happen very often.'

A heart-sized lump welled up in his chest. 'Ah, Kat,' he said, and pulled her tighter against him. Why hadn't it occurred to him that all the time she spent alone in the forest might not have been entirely self-imposed? 'Ah, Kat.'

A snap of a twig from outside the tent brought her head up again, snapping his teeth shut as she cracked his chin with the top of her skull. Felix cursed, then tried to turn his head to look into the night.

Gotrek, Snorri and Rodi were stepping out of the darkness towards the fire. They were covered in minor cuts and bruises, but seemed otherwise whole.

Gotrek snorted when he saw Felix and Kat in the tent. 'Found him, then, did you?'

'I... I...' said Kat, pulling the blanket higher.

'It's... it's not what you think,' said Felix.

'It never is, manling,' said Gotrek. 'It never is.'

Rodi snickered.

Snorri shrugged. 'Snorri doesn't know what he thinks it is.'

'Don't let it trouble you, Father Rustskull,' said Rodi. 'But come spread your roll on this side of the fire. Give the poor skinny things some privacy.'

Felix groaned with embarrassment. 'It really isn't what–'

Kat stopped him with a shake of her head. 'Never mind, Felix,' she said. 'And it's time for you to drink again.'

He sighed. More torture. But now that he came to notice, he wasn't shivering nearly as much as before, and suddenly he felt very, very sleepy.

THE NEXT DAY, Felix woke alone. Kat was outside the tent, sitting with the slayers, cooking rabbit over the fire.

Felix's stomach growled at the smell of it and he tried to sit up. He hissed with pain. Everything hurt – his head, his joints, his muscles, but at least the terrible shaking and the frightening inability to think or move were gone.

After a few minutes of grunting and groaning, he got himself dressed and crawled out of the tent. The snow was piled high all around them, but the storm had stopped and it was a bright morning. He was greeted by a nod from Gotrek, a sly smirk from Rodi and a vacant grin from Snorri. Kat smiled at him, then looked away shyly.

'All right, manling?' asked Gotrek.

'I'll be fine,' said Felix, sitting down gingerly at the fire and warming his hands.

'Frozen stiff, were you?' asked Rodi.

'Nearly,' said Felix.

Felix jumped to his feet, though his muscles shrieked with complaint. 'Leave Kat out of this.'

Kat looked from one to the other of them, her eyes nervous.

Gotrek held up a hand. 'Easy, manling,' he said, then turned and gave Rodi a look with his one cold eye. 'He won't do it again.'

Rodi looked put out. 'Only making a joke.'

'A joke at the expense of my friends,' said Gotrek. 'There have been names penned in the book for less.'

Rodi glared at the Slayer sullenly for a moment, then had to look away. 'Aye, aye,' he said. 'Fair enough.'

'Snorri doesn't get the joke,' said Snorri.

Thankfully nobody tried to explain it to him.

As Felix and the slayers ate, Kat took down her tent and folded it into her pack.

'I'm leaving for Stangenschloss,' she said, when all was packed away. 'And then on to Bauholz. They must be warned before the herd arrives, and I can make better time on my own.'

'Aye,' said Gotrek. 'A good plan.'

Felix opened his mouth to object. She would be out in the wilderness on her own, without anyone to protect her! Then he paused, flushing. Who had saved who last night, exactly? And after what Kat had said as they lay together, about him being one of the few to accept her as both a scout and a woman, it wouldn't do to tell her he didn't want her to go. He closed his mouth.

'Can you find your way there without me?' Kat asked.

Rodi and Snorri shook their heads.

'Too many trees,' said Rodi. 'They all look alike.'

Felix wasn't sure he could get there either. After twenty years of wandering, he had learned quite a bit about travelling by the sun and the stars, but that was difficult under the forest canopy, and it helped to know where one was starting from. He had no idea where they were, or what direction they had travelled during the snowstorm the night before.

'We'll follow the herd,' said Gotrek.

Kat nodded sadly. 'Aye, I'm afraid the fort is exactly where they're heading.' She stood and shouldered her pack. 'Well, luck to you. See you there.'

The slayers grunted non-committally.

Kat turned to Felix. 'Goodbye, Felix,' she said.

Felix stood. 'Goodbye, Kat,' he replied. He wanted to go to her and embrace her, but he felt Rodi's eyes upon them, and didn't.

Kat waited for an awkward second, then turned away abruptly and headed into the trees.

Felix cursed himself inwardly as he sat down again. Was he really so concerned about what the dwarf thought, or was it that he still didn't know what he thought about her, and had been afraid that she would read too much into it if he had gone to her?

The girl was driving him mad.

THEY FOUND ARGRIN Crownforger's corpse on the way back to the wide valley that the herd had passed through the night before. It was buried by a deep layer of snow, a white hump surrounded by bigger humps, and they might not have found it at all had they not seen the haft of a beastman's spear sticking up out of the soft cover.

When they cleared it away they found that the spear was sticking up out of Argrin's chest, the point buried to the shaft between his ribs. All the snow around and below him was red crystals, and there were five dead beastmen surrounding him, as stiff and lifeless as he was.

Rodi tried to pry Argrin's warhammer from his hand, 'to return it to his kin,' but found that he couldn't. Argrin's death grip was too tight. He would have had to cut off Argrin's hand to do it.

'Leave it,' said Gotrek. 'And leave him. Let the beasts of this accursed forest see who killed their brothers. Let them see what a slayer can do.'

Rodi nodded, and he and Gotrek and Snorri bowed their heads over Argrin's body for a moment, then turned and started down the hill towards the herd's trail.

AS THEY STARTED along the beastmen's trail, Felix was afraid they would catch up to them again as they had before, and that the slayers might not this time be able to resist charging in to their doom. He needn't have worried. Though the storm had passed, it had left three feet of snow behind. Rodi was up to his fork-bearded chin in it, while Gotrek and Snorri were up to their chests and, strong as they were, it was still slow, weary work ploughing through it, with many stops to restore their strength. Felix doubted if they made ten miles that first day.

'This is rubbish,' snarled Rodi just after noon. 'Wading through leagues of snow to chase the doom we might have had last night.'

'A selfish doom,' rasped Gotrek. 'As I said before.'

Rodi snorted. 'I see now why you haven't found your doom in twenty years, Gurnisson.'

Gotrek turned a dangerous eye on him. 'What do you mean by that, beardling?'

'You are too choosy,' said Rodi. '"It must be an honourable doom, a great doom," says the great slayer. Bah! Those things mean nothing. A doom is a doom is a doom. It is the dying in battle that counts with Grimnir. Nothing else.'

Gotrek grunted and started forwards again. 'Grimnir asks only for death. Others ask for more.'

Rodi stared after him. 'What do you mean by that? A slayer answers only to Grimnir. He renounces all else.'

But Gotrek wouldn't answer him.

Felix followed wide-eyed. He had never heard the Slayer say anything like this before and he didn't know what it meant any more than Rodi did. Who were these others? What did they ask of Gotrek? Had the Slayer been the subject of some king all this time and never mentioned it to Felix? Did he worship some other god? Did it have something to do with the great shame that had made him a slayer in the first place? Felix grumbled with frustration. He might never know. Gotrek never spoke of these things and Felix knew better than to ask. Perhaps Rodi would goad it out of him as he had this. Felix would just have to keep his ears open.

A few minutes later, as if to change the subject, Gotrek turned to Felix. 'What happened to the squire, manling? I was fighting the knights and didn't see.'

'He changed,' said Felix. 'Along with the rest.'

'Did you slay him?'

Felix shook his head. 'I... I didn't have the heart.'

'It would have been kinder if you had.'

Felix sighed. He knew it was the truth. If the boy retained even a small portion of his mind, the life of a beastman would be torture to his Sigmarite soul. The thought brought Felix up short, for suddenly, with a sickening sinking of his stomach, he knew that the templars of the Order of the Fiery Heart had not died at the hands of the beastmen like Ortwin had thought. They had become beastmen themselves. The beastman that Ortwin had killed, who had worn the breastplate with the insignia of the order upon it, had not stolen it, it had been his all along.

'The templars didn't die, did they?' he said after a moment.

Gotrek shook his head. 'No, manling. But if we find them, I will give them peace.'

Felix nodded in agreement. It was the best that they could do for them. Next time he would not falter.

But as they continued on, a new thought gave Felix pause. How many of the massive herd had once been human? How many had been changed into monsters by the light flashing from the shaman's herdstone? The reports of empty villages that the soldier at Stangenschloss had spoken of – had the people all been slain? Had they all fled? Or had they changed as the blue light caught them, and followed obediently in the shaman's wake?

He shivered with fear. How could an army stand against such a thing? They might charge the herd as knights and spearmen and greatswords, but before they reached them, the blue light would sear their eyes and they would fall twisting and screaming, only to rise again as beastmen and turn on their fellows. It was something out of a nightmare, and if the nightmare were true, then Stangenschloss would be lost – and every village and town between it and the Talabec. Could even Talabheim or Altdorf repel such a threat? The wizards of the colleges would have to be mustered at once and the stone destroyed, before the herd numbered not thousands, but tens of thousands.

He slogged on, numb with the horror of it.

ON THE SECOND day, they came to the place where the herd had been when the snowstorm had stopped, and they found the snow on the path trampled to a blackened inch-thick crust that made travel easier. Felix again became afraid that they would catch up to the beastmen and that the slayers would do something rash, but on the morning of the second day they woke to their tents being ripped from the ground by another screaming gale, and the snow came down heavier than ever, once again blotting out the trail.

Felix began to wonder why he had ever longed to return to the land of his birth.

OUT OF THE blue on the morning of the fourth day, as they were making their slow way through an area of enormous oaks with the wind still blowing snow in their faces, Snorri chuckled and said, 'This reminds Snorri of fighting beastmen in the snow with his old friends Gotrek and Felix.'

Felix looked to Gotrek at this, and saw him wince.

'Snorri,' said Felix. 'We *are* your old friends Gotrek and Felix.'

Snorri looked at Felix with a puzzled frown, then smiled. 'Snorri knows that,' he said. 'But this was before. Snorri and Gotrek and Felix and their friend Max had just killed a vampire and then they were attacked by beastmen in the snow. Then Gotrek and Felix went through the door and never came back.'

'Snorri, listen to me,' said Felix, losing patience. Why couldn't the old slayer make the connection between then and now?

'There's no use telling him,' said Rodi. 'Poor Father Rustskull is a few bricks shy of a–'

'What happened after that, Nosebiter?' Gotrek interrupted. 'Where did you go?'

'Max and Snorri went back to Praag to fight the hordes of I-can't-remember-his-name,' said Snorri. 'But the cowards ran away as soon as they got there.' He paused. 'After that… After that…'

'After that you went beastman hunting with someone named Rag Neck Ruchendorf,' said Rodi impatiently. 'And killed a beast-lord in the forests of Ostermark.'

'Aye, that's right,' said Snorri. 'Now Snorri remembers.'

Felix looked at Rodi. 'You were there?'

'Nah,' said Rodi. 'But he's told it before. Sometimes he remembers. Sometimes he doesn't.'

'Rag Neck was a good man,' said Snorri, his eyes faraway. 'Drank almost as much as Snorri, which Snorri thinks is pretty good for a human.' The old slayer laughed. 'He made a contest with Snorri. Told him if he could take as many beastman heads as all of his men together he would give Snorri a keg of Karak Norn ale. Snorri killed ninety beastmen in three days – some big ones too – and won by fifteen kills!' He smiled.

'You still don't see it,' Rodi sighed. 'Your friend Rag Neck must have been collecting bounty for those heads. He robbed you of your share and fobbed you off with beer.'

'It was good beer,' protested Snorri.

Rodi shook his head, giving up.

'And after that?' asked Gotrek.

Snorri's heavy brows pulled together thoughtfully. 'Snorri was many places after that, slaying many things – orcs, beastmen, trolls, skaven. He even fought a dragon once, with his friends Gotrek and Felix.'

'No,' said Felix. 'That was before.'

'Oh yes,' said Snorri. 'That was before.'

He seemed troubled by that for a moment, then laughed uproariously. 'Did Snorri ever tell you about the time he was put in jail for killing beastmen?'

'Yes,' said Rodi grimly.

'No,' said Gotrek and Felix.

Snorri laughed again, then scratched among the nails of his crest and continued. 'Snorri was in some town of men – he can't remember the name. He and some others had been hired by the townsfolk to protect them from beastmen, and he had killed many. The night after he had driven the beastmen away, Snorri went to have a drink, then after ten or twenty beers he decided to go back to the army camp, which was in a field outside the village. On the way, Snorri saw a whole herd of beastmen standing in a meadow, looking towards the village. Snorri realised that the treacherous beastmen had come back, so he took out his axe and slew them all. Snorri took more than fifty heads that night.'

That sounded like an exaggeration to Felix. Still, it might have been twenty. 'But why did they arrest you for that?' he asked. 'Surely you had done them a great service.'

Snorri snorted. 'The mayor of the town told Snorri that they hadn't been beastmen, but cows, and put him in jail.' Snorri laughed. 'If they had been cows, then why would Snorri have slain them? There is no glory in slaying cows.'

'They *were* cows, you cloth-head,' said Rodi. 'They must have been. And you're lucky the mayor didn't hang you. You robbed the people of all their milk and meat. Half the town probably went hungry that winter because of you.'

Snorri shook his head. 'Snorri is pretty sure they were beastmen.'

Felix saw Gotrek shake his head at this, but he said nothing.

'So you've been fighting orcs and beastmen and trolls for twenty years and still haven't found your doom,' said Felix. It seemed amazing to him, but then, Gotrek had been fighting orcs and beastmen and trolls for twenty years, and he hadn't found his doom either.

Snorri nodded slowly. 'Snorri is sad about that. He has met many slayers, and they have all found their dooms, but Snorri has never found his.' He glared around at the woods with uncharacteristic anger. 'Snorri thinks it is the old lady's fault.'

Felix and Gotrek exchanged a look at this, then looked to Rodi. The young slayer shrugged and rolled his eyes.

'What old lady?' asked Gotrek.

'Snorri saved an old lady in the woods,' said Snorri. 'Spiders were attacking her. Big spiders, like the goblins ride. Snorri killed them all, but they bit him many times, and he got dizzy and couldn't walk. The lady took him to her house – Snorri thinks she lived in a tree – and she fed him and gave him terrible-tasting beer.' His brow furrowed in confusion. 'Snorri thinks he was there for a long time, but he can't remember, but when he left, the lady told him that he should have died from the spider bites. She said she gave him some medicines, but she was too late, and he should have died.'

'Well, she was obviously wrong, wasn't she?' said Felix.

Snorri nodded. 'Snorri wishes she would have been wronger. She said she looked at Snorri's stars and saw that he would not meet his doom for many years. She said Snorri had a great destiny.' He snorted, his anger returning. 'Snorri thinks the lady cursed him. Snorri thinks her stars have stopped him from finding his doom.'

Felix blinked at this. Snorri Nosebiter had a great destiny? Who would have thought it?

'Human nonsense,' said Rodi.

'Snorri wishes it was,' said Snorri. 'He has tried to prove her wrong many times, but he is still alive. Snorri is very angry with that lady.'

Gotrek frowned deeply at this.

Felix thought about trying to explain to Snorri that foretelling didn't work like that, and that he had it the wrong way around, but if the old slayer still believed that a herd of cows had been a herd of beastmen, the nuances of prophecy would undoubtedly be lost on him.

'Did the old lady say what this destiny was?' asked Gotrek.

'No,' said Snorri. 'But Snorri hopes it doesn't come soon.'

Gotrek turned, fixing Snorri with a hard stare. 'What? Why is that? Do you no longer seek your doom?'

A look of shame came upon Snorri's ugly face. He hung his head. 'Snorri shouldn't have said anything.'

Gotrek stopped walking and faced the old slayer, his one eye boring into him like an auger. 'Snorri Nosebiter, if you have renounced your vow to Grimnir, we will no longer walk together.'

'It isn't that, Gurnisson,' said Rodi. 'He–'

Gotrek held up a hand. 'I would hear it from his own mouth.'

Snorri continued to stare at the ground, a look of such lugubrious misery on his face that it was almost comic. 'Snorri has a great shame,' he said at last. 'A new great shame.'

'What shame is this?' growled Gotrek.

'Snorri…' The old slayer swallowed, then continued. 'Snorri has forgotten why he became a slayer.'

TWELVE

Gotrek blinked, a look of blank shock on his hard face. 'When did this happen?'

'Snorri doesn't know,' said Snorri. 'He tried to remember after the fighting at Middenheim but nothing came to his mind. There was nothing there.'

'Too many nails in the head,' muttered Rodi under his breath.

'It's shameful for a slayer to forget his shame?' asked Felix, confused.

'It is worse than shameful, manling,' said Gotrek, not taking his eye off Snorri. 'It is a crime against Grimnir.' He sighed. 'A dwarf becomes a slayer to atone for a great shame. If he forgets that shame, then he cannot atone for it. If he dies without remembering, he will not be admitted into Grimnir's halls. He will have no peace in death.'

It took a moment for the immensity of Snorri's plight to sink in, but then Felix saw that it was a terrible thing, the equivalent of a devout follower of Sigmar discovering that he was growing a tentacle or a third eye. Snorri was being denied salvation and forgiveness.

'Snorri is making a pilgrimage to Karak Kadrin,' said Snorri. 'To pray at the Shrine of Grimnir. He will ask Grimnir to give him his memory back so he can have his doom.'

Gotrek nodded. 'That is the right thing to do, Snorri Nosebiter. May Grimnir grant your boon.'

'But if you are afraid to meet your doom before you get your memory back,' said Felix as a thought came to him, 'why are you still fighting? Isn't it a terrible risk?'

Snorri shrugged. 'The old lady said that Snorri had a destiny, so he is safe until he finds it. And also,' he grinned, sheepish, 'when there are things to slay, Snorri gets excited and forgets that he has forgotten.'

'Forget his head if it wasn't attached to his shoulders,' said Rodi.

Gotrek shot the young slayer a hard look, then turned and started shouldering through the snow again. 'Come on,' he said. 'We have a long road ahead of us.'

A WHILE LATER, when Rodi and Snorri had fallen a little bit behind, Felix turned to Gotrek and lowered his voice.

'Gotrek, don't you know why Snorri became a slayer?' he asked. 'Couldn't you tell him and relieve him of his misery?'

Gotrek shook his head. 'A slayer does not tell of his shame,' he said. 'Not even to another slayer. He has not told me. And even if I did know, I would not tell him.'

'Sigmar, why not?'

'It is a slayer's responsibility to keep his shame firmly in mind,' Gotrek rumbled. 'If Snorri Nosebiter has forgotten his, then it is his burden to bear, and his problem to solve. To tell him would be as wrong as killing him to give him his doom. There is no easy path to Grimnir's hall.'

Felix thought this was cruel and unfair, but then, much of what passed for dwarf philosophy seemed harsh to him. He sighed and pushed on, suddenly depressed. Poor Snorri. He had never expected to feel sorry for the happy-go-lucky old slayer – he hadn't really thought Snorri had the capacity for sadness – but it seemed that the grimness of the Old World was great enough to touch even the most oblivious. It was too bad.

ON THE FIFTH day, the second storm cleared off, and by the middle of the sixth day they came again to flattened snow, which told them that the herd was no more than a day ahead. Felix began to worry about Stangenschloss. Even if Kat had made it in time to warn them, what could the fort do to prepare for the oncoming herd? Would the soldiers abandon it? Would they send south for a wizard? Would they hope that the herd would pass them by? Would they even believe Kat's story?

In the late afternoon of the seventh day, they saw the first signs of battle – a soldier's helmet tossed to one side, a trail of red in the snow, the scattered skeleton of a horse, scraps of meat still sticking to its bones. A little further on they found a headless corpse wearing the uniform of Ilgner's company. After that, the slayers readied their weapons and went more cautiously. Felix did the same. The herd might be just around the next bend, or the one after that.

An hour later, as the setting sun was turning the snow as red as the spilled blood, they came to the fort at last.

The beastmen's trail led right to it, entering the cleared fields that surrounded it from the rear.

Felix and the slayers paused before stepping out into the open area and surveyed the fort. The walls still stood, and there was no column of smoke rising from it, but there were also no signs of life – no glint of helmets from the walls, no kitchen smoke, no sound.

'Have they deserted it?' asked Felix.

'We'll see,' said Gotrek.

They started around the edge of the clearing, keeping within the tree line. The ground along the side of the fort was littered with a score of dead beastmen, all with arrows sticking from them, but no other signs of a battle. The walls were undamaged, and there were no dead soldiers.

Felix began to wonder if the herd had tramped past and not bothered to assault the fort, but when they could see around the corner tower, his heart sank, capsized with a flood of dread. The gates were wide open and no sentries stood before them.

'Look,' said Rodi.

Felix turned and followed his gaze with the others. On the far side of the cleared fields, a gap had been cut in the forest, just like the one they had entered from.

'The beastmen have moved on,' said the young slayer.

'But have they taken the garrison with them?' asked Gotrek.

Panic surged in Felix's chest. 'Kat,' he said, and he had to forcibly hold himself from racing towards the fort to look for her. If she were dead or changed it would have happened hours, maybe days ago. No mad charge now could change it.

He and the slayers crept warily towards the entrance, passing more arrow-studded beastmen as they went, and eyeing the battlements every step of the way. No arrows came from them, however, nor any spears or stones or shouted challenges.

Finally they reached the open gates and looked in. The courtyard was still and silent, but only because it was too cold for there to be flies. There were corpses everywhere – men and beastmen all hacked to gory pieces, some still locked in the struggle that had killed them, and bright blood mottling the snow between them like red islands in a frozen sea.

'Snorri missed a fight,' said Snorri.

'Not much of one,' said Rodi. 'There are barely a score of men dead here.'

'Two score,' said Gotrek.

Rodi snorted. 'Your eye is failing you, Gurnisson. I don't count more than–'

'Look at the beastmen,' said Gotrek. 'They wear the same uniform as the men they fought.'

Rodi turned and Felix followed his gaze. It was true, all the beastmen in the yard wore torn jerkins and dented breastplates, all marked with Ilgner's colours and device.

'The stone,' Felix groaned.

'Aye,' said Gotrek. 'It has done its evil work.'

Felix thought again of Kat and this time he could not restrain himself. 'Excuse me,' he said. 'I must…' and he ran off across the courtyard.

'Manling,' barked Gotrek. 'Wait.'

Felix hurried on, ignoring him, and looking fearfully at each beastman he passed to see if it wore a scarf and a hat and a heavy coat of wool.

As he turned the corner into the stable yard he saw a little figure in silhouette kneeling over a corpse and his heart gave a great leap, but then he saw that it was a boy, dressed in peasant rags, and that he was tugging at the rings on the hand of a dead knight.

'You, boy!' called Felix.

The boy looked up, eyes wide, then bolted for the kitchen yard, which was around another corner of the keep.

'Come back here!' called Felix and ran after him. He might have news of Kat!

He saw the boy disappear into a wooden storage barn built against the outer wall, and slowed to a trot. There was no exit from the shed. He was trapped.

'All right, then,' he said, stepping into the wide doorway. 'Come out. I only want to talk–'

He cut off abruptly when he saw that he was facing a bristling thicket of daggers and spears and clubs, with a gang of frightened-looking rustics behind them.

'This be our spoils,' said the one in front, a slope-shouldered fellow with a thatch of dirty yellow hair sticking out from under a stocking cap. 'Go find yer own.'

The boy was peeking out from behind him, glaring at Felix with angry eyes.

Felix looked past the men and saw that they had been loading bags of flour and jars of cooking oil onto a cart with a bony old plough horse hitched to it. He stepped back, lowering his sword and raising his free hand.

'Easy,' he said. 'I don't want your spoils. I... I only want to ask what happened here.'

The men looked at each other, then back at him, still suspicious. 'It weren't our doing,' said the leader. 'You can't blame us for what happened.'

'Of course not,' said Felix, as soothingly as he could. 'It was the beastmen. I just–'

'The blue light!' wailed a voice from a corner. 'The blue light!'

Felix's hair stood on end at the eerie sound. He turned with the others. Another peasant sat in the corner, hugging his knees. He was a big man, a smith's apron strapped around his barrel torso, but his face had the wide-eyed fear of a child woken from a nightmare. 'The blue light!' he said again.

'Quiet, Wattie,' snapped the leader. 'They're gone now, I told you.'

'And where's Hanna, Gus?' cried the big man. 'Where's Hanna gone?'

'She...' Gus looked over at a canvas tarpaulin that had been draped over something by the door. A cloven hoof, small for a beastman, stuck out from under it. 'She went on to Leer, Wattie. I told you. Now be quiet.'

Gus turned back to Felix. 'You best just go on yer way, mein herr. We don't want–' He broke off as footsteps crunched across the snow from outside.

The peasants' spears and daggers thrust back into guard.

'Who's that?' snarled Gus. 'Who's with you?'

Felix saw the shadows of the dwarfs stretch across the straw of the barn floor as they stepped into the door behind Felix.

'What's this, now?' asked Rodi.

Gus stared, then dropped his spear and stepped forwards. 'Master Rodi, you've come back!' Then, shooting a nervous look at the wagon full of plunder, 'Er, is m'lord with you?'

'No, master cook,' said Rodi. 'Lord Ilgner's dead. Argrin too. Killed by the beastmen.'

Gus's face fell. 'Aw, that's bad that is.'

The other peasants groaned.

'What happened here?' asked Rodi.

Gus sighed, and his shoulders slumped. 'Don't know, exactly. When the little forester girl brought word the beasts were coming, some of us was afraid and we went to hide in the old bandit caves.'

'So she made it here!' cried Felix.

'Aye,' said Gus. 'Though much good her warning did, as ye can see. Only Wattie stayed behind, but he won't say what happened. Something terrible though,' he said, glancing again at the form of the little beastman under the tarpaulin.

'The blue light,' moaned Wattie from his corner.

'When did this happen?' asked Gotrek.

'We hid in the caves last night,' said Gus. 'When we come back this morning, it was like this.'

'The girl who brought the news,' said Felix anxiously. 'Do you know what became of her?'

Gus and the others shook their heads.

'Saw her talking with Captain Haschke before we went to the caves,' said Gus. 'But not since.' He turned back to Rodi. 'Y'won't tell on us, will ye, Master Rodi? We're only fending for ourselves.'

Rodi shrugged. 'Who is there to tell?'

Felix's panic was returning. He backed out of the barn. 'I must see if she's here,' he said, and ran off again.

He searched the fort from battlements to dungeon, torn between fear of finding Kat, and the frustration of not knowing what had happened to her. Every new body he found quickened his heart and tightened his shoulders. Every fallen beastman he came to made him cringe in anxious anticipation. At last, as the purple sky blackened to full night, he gave up. She wasn't there, at least not that he could find, or in a condition he could recognise. Had she continued on to Bauholz? Had she gone out to fight the herd and died on the field or in the woods? He had to find out.

He ran back down to Gotrek, Snorri and Rodi, who were rolling a keg of beer up from the cellars as Gus and his followers prepared a meal.

'We have to leave for Bauholz,' said Felix. 'Now.'

'It's too late in the day, manling,' said Gotrek. 'We'll start in the morning.'

'We can't wait until morning,' cried Felix. 'We have to get to Bauholz before the herd does.'

'And we will,' said Gotrek, setting the barrel on its end. He nodded at Rodi. 'The beardling has bought the cook's horse and cart. We'll take it by the forest road while the beasts carve their way through the trees, foot by foot. We'll be ahead of them in a day.'

'But we should gain as much of a lead on them as possible!' Felix insisted. 'It will take some time to get everyone away.'

'Relax, Herr Jaeger,' said Rodi. 'A night under a roof will give us more stamina for the road. Besides, I'm hungry for a real meal.'

'And Snorri is thirsty for real drink,' said Snorri.

Felix growled with frustration, but he knew the dwarfs were right. A night wouldn't make much difference, but it just felt wrong not to be moving, not to be doing something to find Kat – and help Bauholz, of course.

* * *

It was a tortuous trip. Felix was cursing with impatience every minute of the five days it took. The bony old plough horse might have been quicker than the dwarfs on foot, but it was not fast enough. Every bump, every stop to ease the cart over a frozen rut, every time they had to tromp tracks in the heavy snow so that the wheels would not get stuck, drove Felix to nail-biting frustration. He wanted to run ahead and leave the slayers behind, and there were times when he almost gave into the urge and told them goodbye, but he knew it was folly. Without their protection he was prey to everything that lurked in the woods, and he would die not knowing if Kat lived. With them, as slow as they were, he was much more likely to get to Bauholz in one piece and be able to do something useful once he got there.

When at last, at noon on the fifth day, the snow-covered fields and timber walls of the little town hove into sight, Felix breathed a huge sigh of relief. The chimney smoke rising in little grey ribbons from its roof tops told him that the beasts had not touched it. He jumped down from the cart, unable to control his anxiety any longer, and jogged ahead to the gates.

'I'll just, uh, let them know we're coming,' he said over his shoulder as he ran.

'Aye, manling,' said Gotrek.

Rodi chuckled slyly.

The palisade walls were acrawl with villagers, retying the ropes that bound the logs together, setting new logs in the long-unrepaired gaps, building wooden mantlets at the tops to hide behind while firing bows. Felix nodded with surprised approval. It seemed that Noseless Milo had actually taken seriously his vow to protect the town when he took it over. Felix would not have thought it of him, though of course it would do no good in the end. Even without the foul stone, the shaman's massive herd could overrun the little village without breaking stride. The people should be leaving, not preparing to fight.

A pair of gaunt peasants were guarding the front gate, and only stared at him as he ran through. As he started down the main street, he saw that the village was as busy within as without. The townsfolk were doing what they could to strengthen their meagre houses – boarding up the windows, fitting the doors with crossbars and braces, making barricades to block the streets. Felix looked around for any sign of Milo or his men, and saw none. Were they all on the walls, helping with the defences? Or had the bandit failed to defeat Ludeker's soldiers after all? But Felix saw no Wissenland uniforms among the villagers either. Strange.

He ran to the *Powder and Shot*, the old Sigmarite temple turned beer hall, and stopped in wonder as he saw two men on ladders taking down the crudely painted tavern sign in preparation for replacing the gilded wooden hammer that had hung there before.

A gaunt old man stood on the steps of the temple, watching the proceedings, and Felix recognised him as Doktor Vinck.

'Herr Doktor!' he called as he ran towards him.

The old surgeon looked up, then smiled as he recognised Felix. 'Herr Jaeger, is it? Well met, sir. I confess I didn't expect you to return.'

'What are you doing here?' Felix asked. 'Are you working for Noseless Milo now? Is Kat here with you?'

Doktor Vinck's smile faded. 'I'm afraid the answers to all those questions are linked, my boy. I am here because Milo and his cronies left town as soon as Kat brought word that the beastman herd was coming this way. They have taken all the stolen supplies that Ludeker had gathered, put them on carts and headed south. We face our destiny with nothing but a few pitchforks and hunting bows.' He laughed and looked at the tavern sign, with its depiction of bullets and blackpowder barrel. 'The powder and shot is gone, and so we must put our trust in Sigmar.'

'But Kat,' said Felix impatiently. 'What of Kat?'

Doktor Vinck sighed. 'Milo took her with him.'

'What?' cried Felix. 'She went with that... filth?'

'Not willingly, I assure you.' The surgeon looked away, shame colouring his face. 'They took her while she was sleeping in my tent. Bound and gagged her and dragged her out. There... there was nothing I could do.'

THIRTEEN

Felix stared at the doctor, fear and rage rising in him like a boiling flood. 'When did they leave? How long ago?'

'Only a few hours ago,' said Doktor Vinck. 'No more than three.'

Felix turned and ran back towards the gate without another word. Halfway across the village's only intersection he heard a shout from his left and looked around. Sir Teobalt was limping up from the docks, leading a troop of peasants with makeshift spears over their shoulders. He seemed to have made an almost complete recovery.

'Herr Jaeger!' he called. 'You have returned.'

Felix stumbled, gulping with nervousness. Sir Teobalt was the last person he wanted to see at that moment.

'What news have you?' the old knight asked, coming on. 'Did you find my brothers? Did my squire acquit himself honourably?'

'I...' said Felix, edging sideways. 'I'll tell you later, sir. I must go.'

He sprinted away again, the templar's confused cries following him as he ran.

The slayers were just leading the cart through the village gate when he reached it.

'Gotrek, turn about,' said Felix, beckoning to the Slayer. 'We must go out again.'

'What's happened?' Gotrek asked.

'Milo has fled town and kidnapped Kat. They're three hours ahead of us.'

Gotrek looked around at the frantic efforts of the townsfolk to strengthen their walls. 'He's the only one with any sense. These people will all die if they stay here.'

'Then I will stay too,' said Rodi, his eyes lighting up. 'You get the girl and continue south to warn the armies of men. I will stay here and do my best to convince these fools to leave, and if they do not...' He smiled grimly. 'Then I will die defending them.'

'Snorri will stay too!' said Snorri, his eyes dancing with anticipation.

'No, Nosebiter,' said Gotrek, jumping down from the cart. 'You will not. You will come with us.'

'But Snorri wants to fight beastmen.'

Gotrek's jaws bulged under his beard. 'Have you forgotten your pilgrimage?'

Snorri frowned, then looked downcast. 'Yes, Snorri forgot. He will come with you.'

Gotrek turned and bowed to Rodi as Felix ground his teeth, impatient to go. 'May you find your doom, Rodi Balkisson.'

'And you as well, Gotrek Gurnisson,' said Rodi, bowing in return. He saluted Snorri too. 'May Grimnir favour you, Father Rustskull.'

'Goodbye, uh, what's-your-name,' said Snorri.

And with that eloquent farewell, Felix, Gotrek and Snorri turned and trotted south down the road.

KNOWING THAT MILO had a three-hour head start, Felix was afraid he and the slayers might never catch him, but to his surprise, only an hour later they heard curses and harsh voices coming to them across the silence of the snowbound forest.

Felix stopped and drew his sword, listening. Gotrek and Snorri stepped to either side of him and drew their weapons as well.

'Hold those horses still, curse you!' came a shout that Felix thought he recognised as Noseless Milo's. 'Anders, Uwe, lift together on my count. The rest of you lack-wits get behind and push.'

Felix and the two slayers started forwards again, moving slowly and quietly towards a bend in the track.

'It's hopeless, Milo,' whined another voice. 'We'll have to leave some of the loot behind. We'll never get it over this damned road.'

'You're a damned fool, Heiko!' barked Milo. 'This is our fortune! If we sell all this in Ahlenhof we never have to work again. I'm not leaving a stick behind.'

'Then it's you who's the fool, Milo,' said Heiko's voice. 'Because at this rate we'll have beastmen crawling up our fundaments before we get ten miles.'

There was a scrape of drawn steel, and Milo's voice raised to a shout. 'Are you challenging me, you mewling little turd?'

Gotrek chuckled darkly. 'They'll do our work for us.'

'Snorri hopes not,' said Snorri.

They were almost at the bend now. Felix craned his neck to the left, trying to see around the intervening trees.

'I'm only asking you to see sense, Milo,' came Heiko. 'I don't want to–'

He was cut off by a heavy thud and a shout of surprise. Someone cursed, and then came a babble of voices.

'She's loose, damn it!'

'I've got her!'

'Ow!'

'Damn the bitch!'

'She's breaking for the woods!'

Then Milo's angry roar. 'Get her! Get my wife!'

Felix could wait no more. He charged around the bend with the two slayers thundering at his heels. The scene that met his eyes was a frenzy of struggle and motion. Four wagons, heavily loaded with blackpowder kegs, crates, beer barrels and all manner of plunder – including Sir Teobalt's warhorse, Machtig, hitched to the last – sat in a crooked line along the trail, the first with its front right wheel down in a ditch and its back left raised like a dog cocking its leg to piss.

A dozen filthy men were breaking from the wagons and swarming after a little figure who plunged barefoot through the knee-high snow, dressed in nothing but a night shirt, her eyes burning with the savage desire for freedom. Felix's heart lurched. It was Kat, her wrists tied behind her back and a rope around her neck that dragged in her wake like a leash, and he knew at that moment that he loved her with all his heart and soul.

Just then the lead man leapt forwards and caught the end of the rope, jerking it tight. Kat's legs flew out in front of her and she went down flat on her back, yelping.

'No!' roared Felix, and bounded towards the man, the thudding footsteps of Gotrek and Snorri as they followed him barely registering through his rage.

The bandits turned at his yell.

'Ranald's luck,' spat Milo. 'It's the boyfriend. Stop him!'

Felix swung Karaghul around in a wide circle and it chimed off a half-dozen blades as he tried to break through the gangsters to Kat. He didn't get very far. Milo's men were well armed with swords, spears and rapiers that they must have taken from better men, and Felix could tell that some of them had been soldiers once, for they handled themselves well.

Felix parried two swords, but then had to jump back as a spearman stabbed at him from the second rank – proper military training.

None of that mattered once Gotrek and Snorri reached the fight. Swords shattered and men screamed as the slayers waded in, weapons blurring. Felix shoved past a man who was clutching the stump of his wrist, and aimed a slash at the man who was dragging Kat away from the melee by the rope around her neck.

A movement at the corner of his eye made him duck and something clipped him a glancing blow across the top of the head. Felix hit the ground and floundered in the snow, his head smarting and the world spinning around him. Noseless Milo was trudging towards him, a woodsman's axe in one hand, and a length of chain in the other.

'Come on, ye pretty little Altdorf milksop,' he snarled, raising the axe. 'Let's see how much she likes you when you've got a nose like mine!'

Felix threw up his sword just as the axe came down, and staggered to his feet as it shrieked down the length of his blade. Milo's chain cracked him on the side of the face, then whipped around the back of his head and snapped against his other ear.

Felix howled with pain and stumbled away, his sword up blindly behind him as Milo came on. He needed a second to shake it off. He didn't have it. Milo swung with the axe and chain again and Felix lurched aside once more. Out of the corner of his eye he saw Kat on her feet, kicking in the teeth of the man who held her rope.

The stinging ebbed enough for Felix to recover himself. He heard the axe and chain whistling behind him and spun and ducked at the same time, Karaghul lashing out high. The rune sword sheared through the haft of the axe and the heavy head bounced hard off Felix's shoulder. The chain wrapped around Karaghul and held it tight.

Milo laughed and yanked hard, hoping to pull Felix off balance. But Felix was ready and went with it, lunging forwards to slam into Milo's chest and knock him to the ground. The bandit swung his headless axe at Felix's legs, but Felix kicked it out of his hand and wrenched Karaghul from the coils of the chain. He raised the blade high for the death stroke, but suddenly a little figure blurred in from his right and shoved him aside.

'No!' cried Kat. 'He's mine!'

She kicked Milo in the face, then dropped down with both knees on his chest. Her hands were still tied, but somehow she had them in front of her now, and they held a bloody dagger.

'Kat...' said Felix.

There was no stopping her. She stabbed down with the little blade, plunging it into Milo's neck, and then his eye, and then his screaming mouth. 'No man ties me!' she hissed. 'No man holds me!'

Felix blinked, stunned by her fury. Milo was long past hearing her, but still she stabbed.

'Kat,' Felix said again, then, 'Kat! He's dead!'

The girl looked up at him with the wild eyes of an animal, her teeth bared in a feral snarl. Felix stepped back, unnerved, but after a moment her face softened and she came back to herself. She lowered the dagger, and hung her head.

'I'm sorry, Felix. He...' she paused, then shook her head. 'I'm sorry.'

'That's all right,' said Felix, still a little shaken. 'I'm sure he deserved all of it.'

He looked around. The battle was over. Gotrek and Snorri stood in the centre of a ring of dead bodies and red snow, while a handful of bandits legged it for the trees.

Felix knelt by Kat and took the dagger from her hands, then used it to saw at the ropes on her wrists. She was trembling so hard he was having difficulty not cutting her.

'He... he took my boots,' she said. 'So I wouldn't run. But I... I ran anyway.' A big sob erupted from her, then, and as he parted the last strand of rope she threw her arms around him and wept on his neck. Felix paused, bewildered by her sudden change from feral fury to frightened girl, but then he took off his cloak and wrapped it around her.

'It's all right,' he said, holding her and murmuring into her hair. 'It's all over now. We're going south to Ahlenhof to spread the word of the herd's coming. You'll come with us. Everything will be all right.'

She looked up at that, snuffling back her tears. 'But, but no. I can't go. I have to stay and protect Bauholz. I won't let another village fall.'

'But, Kat,' said Felix, as gently as he could. 'It's inevitable. The herd is ten thousand strong if it's a hundred. Stangenschloss fell before it. How can you expect Bauholz to stand? Rodi has stayed behind to convince everyone to leave.'

Kat shook her head. 'The herd will miss the village,' she said. 'The beastmen have gone due south from Stangenschloss. I've been watching them. If they stay on course, they will pass fifteen to twenty miles to the east of Bauholz. It is only the foragers we must worry about.' She stood and padded back to the wagons in her bare feet. 'And they may not come.'

Felix followed her. 'Even so,' he said, as she pulled her boots and clothes out from under the buckboard and started pulling them on. 'If the foragers come in force, you don't stand a chance. A bunch of starved peasants, one old knight, one slayer–'

'Three slayers,' said Gotrek, stepping up to him.

Felix turned on him, sighing. 'Come, Gotrek, you said that we must go south to warn the Empire.'

'That was before,' said the Slayer. 'When the town's doom was certain. 'This is a fight we can win.'

'You might survive it,' said Felix. 'But what about the villagers? Even a small force of beastmen will kill too many of them.'

'Perhaps not,' said Gotrek, stroking his beard and looking speculatively at the heavily loaded wagons with his single glittering eye.

* * *

It took almost two hours for them to turn the wagons around and ride them back to Bauholz, and by then the day was guttering down to a dull grey twilight.

'Sigmar be praised!' said one of the guards at the gate. 'You've brought the weapons back,' and waved them through the gates.

Rodi swaggered up to them as they led the wagons towards the centre of the village. 'So, you're not running away after all,' he grinned.

'We heard you crying and came back,' said Gotrek.

'Any more word of the herd?' asked Kat.

Rodi nodded, his face growing serious. 'A scout came an hour ago to say that they continue due south, but that a band of foragers was heading straight for us.'

'How many?' asked Gotrek. 'And how soon?'

'The scout reckoned about a hundred, and a few hours at most.'

'Snorri doesn't know if he can wait that long for a hundred beastmen,' said Snorri.

'Kat! You're safe!' came Doktor Vinck's voice.

The old surgeon was hobbling out of the temple of Sigmar, now properly fitted with its gilded hammer. Sir Teobalt walked beside him, tall and proud despite his limp. Felix avoided his eye.

'And you've brought back the wagons too,' said Vinck as he stepped up to them. 'My prayers to Sigmar have been answered.'

Kat hopped down from the first wagon and embraced the doctor as the others pulled to a halt.

Doktor Vinck returned the hug, but then pulled back and looked sadly at her. 'Though you should have kept going south and forgotten about us. It will end badly here, I think, despite your return.'

'Not necessarily,' said Gotrek. 'I have an idea.'

Doktor Vinck turned to him. 'If it is that we should leave the village, like your fellow slayer suggested, we will not do it. We have bowed before violence and savagery for too long. We will do so no longer.'

Gotrek shook his head. 'Not that. I have another way.' He turned and looked at the barrels stacked on the cart. 'We will put this looted blackpowder to its proper use at last.'

Sir Teobalt and Doktor Vinck frowned at him, confused.

'But we have no cannons,' said Sir Teobalt.

'And few guns,' said Doktor Vinck.

'We don't need them,' said Gotrek. 'All we need is all the drink in the village.'

FOURTEEN

As GOTREK BEGAN to outline his plan, Sir Teobalt finally caught Felix's eye and gestured for him to step into the temple of Sigmar with him. Felix's heart shrivelled in his chest as he did so. The moment had come to tell the old templar what had happened to Ortwin and the other brothers of the Order of the Fiery Heart, and he dreaded it.

Teobalt limped to the newly refurbished altar and turned, stiff. Felix noticed that, beneath his armour, his arm and shoulder were still wrapped with bandages. 'As you have returned,' he said, 'I wonder if you have time now to speak with me of the fate of my squire, Ortwin, who I see is not with you.'

'Yes, Sir Teobalt,' said Felix. 'I apologise for not telling you sooner, but…' He motioned back towards the door.

'It was a matter of great urgency, aye,' said Teobalt, his eyes never leaving Felix's. 'But now it is finished. So…'

He left it hanging. Felix nodded, but still hesitated. Should he lie? Should he tell the knight that Ortwin and the other templars had died nobly in battle fighting the beastmen? It was an attractive idea. It would be so simple, and so kind. It would ease the old man's heart and make him proud. But what if he should learn the truth? Ortwin and the templars couldn't tell, but Gotrek and Snorri had been there. They knew, and slayers never lied. Besides, Teobalt had asked for the truth. No matter how much of a kindness, to lie to him would not be honourable. It would not be a fitting way to win Karaghul. Felix would cringe at the taint of it for the rest of his life.

'Very well, Sir Teobalt,' he said at last. 'I will tell you. You... you heard from Kat how the herdstone that the beastmen carry changed Lord Ilgner and his men into beastmen?'

'I heard this from Doktor Vinck,' said Teobalt. 'Who heard it from her. A foulness. Did Ortwin die fighting these abominations, then?'

'No, sir,' said Felix lowering his head so he wouldn't have to meet Teobalt's eyes. 'He... he changed too. He became a beastman.'

There was silence from Sir Teobalt.

Felix swallowed and continued. 'And I fear that this is what happened to the Knights of the Fiery Heart as well. We killed a beastman wearing armour with the order's insignia upon it. At first we thought that the beast had stolen the armour, but having seen Ortwin change–'

Sir Teobalt's palm cracked Felix hard across the cheek, staggering him sideways. Felix caught himself and looked up, clutching his face.

Sir Teobalt advanced on him, his eyes blazing like blue suns. 'Lies!' he cried. 'Damned lies!'

'Sir Teobalt,' said Felix. 'I swear to you–'

'Will you perjure yourself in the house of Sigmar?' said the old templar. 'Cease, sir, lest his hammer strike you down!' He grabbed Felix by the front of his mail. 'The knights of the Order of the Fiery Heart were true followers of Sigmar. Devout, strong in their faith, and perfect in the observance of their duties. It is impossible that such as these could be corrupted by the foul touch of Chaos. I will not believe that they fell prey to such weakness of the flesh!'

'I'm sorry, Sir Teobalt,' said Felix, cringing away. 'But it's the truth.'

'It is not. You lie like a knave.'

'But why should I?'

'I know not. Perhaps to hide some fault of your own. Perhaps you failed to protect Squire Ortwin and now seek to blame him for your lapse. It matters not. You have betrayed my trust. And I will not have you by my side hereafter. Return the sword that you have taken unjustly and go from me.'

The knight held out an imperious hand. Felix hesitated, trembling with frustration. He wanted to try again to get the old templar to listen, but he knew that it would be fruitless. He doubted that even the testimony of Gotrek and Kat and Snorri would change his mind. What Felix had told him had broken the laws of Sir Teobalt's view of the world, and he would not believe it no matter what.

'Come, varlet,' barked Sir Teobalt, beckoning impatiently. 'Will you rob me as well as lie to me? Give me the sword or defend yourself with it.'

After another long moment, Felix sighed and began unbuckling the sword belt from around his waist. 'I have told the truth, Sir Teobalt,' he said. 'But since I cannot convince you, I will honour our agreement.' He pulled the belt free and wrapped it around the scabbard, then took a last look at the clawed crossguard and dragon-headed pommel of the ancient rune sword. He would miss it. With a catch in his throat, he held it out to the templar.

Sir Teobalt took it and pressed it against his breastplate. He nodded solemnly to Felix. 'You have honour at least in this, Herr Jaeger,' he said. 'Now go. I would pray.'

Felix bowed as the templar turned to the rebuilt altar, then he sighed and started for the door, his heart sick with regret.

He should have lied.

TWO HOURS LATER, under a sky of stars and scudding clouds, Felix leaned against the raw pine trunks of the battlements, above and to the right of the village gate, looking dully out at the black wall of the forest that waited in the darkness beyond the flickering bonfires the villagers had set in their fields. The beastmen were out in that darkness somewhere, and as much as he hoped that they would somehow pass them by and leave the village in peace, he also wished they would show up quickly and end the nervous tension that always came with waiting and vanished with action.

Kat sat cross-legged on the narrow walkway beside him, waxing her arrowheads with a candle stub and cutting the feathers at the ends of her shafts so that they were all even. Two nervous village boys knelt near her, watching intently and trying to copy what she did.

'Why do you wax the points?' asked one of the boys. 'Do they fly faster that way?'

Kat shook her head. 'They slip through skin and armour better. Important with beastmen, as they have tough hides.'

The boys' eyes widened at this, and they fell to waxing their own arrows with more vigour than skill.

Felix smiled down at her, and it was all he could do to not pull her up to her feet and kiss her then and there. He thought back to the moment when he had seen her fleeing Milo's wagons, her bare legs flashing as she pounded desperately through the snow. He wasn't sure why everything had changed then, but it had. All his worries, all his confusion about what he felt had evaporated, and he had known that despite it all, he loved her.

Unworldly yokel she might be, tied to the forest by her vows to save it, and too young for him by a decade. None of it mattered. What did matter was that she was neither a fool nor a manipulator like Claudia had been, nor did she constantly measure him and demand tests of his loyalty and worthiness like Ulrika had done. She neither overvalued or undervalued him, or loved some idea of him concocted from her memories and his unearned fame. Instead, to his confoundment, she seemed to accept him for who he was, and loved him for it.

She looked up at him, as if she could feel his eyes upon her, and gave him a lopsided smile that went through him as if it were the arrow she held in her hand.

He smiled back, then shook his head as she returned to showing the boys how to cut their fletches. It seemed complete madness to him, but when he looked in her eyes he found that he was ready to love her for as long as the world allowed them both to live, no matter what obstacles might get in their way.

Of course, he thought, looking out towards the vastness of the forest with a sigh, that might not be for very long at all. In fact, it was highly probable that they would both die tonight, no matter how well Gotrek's strategy worked.

When Felix had returned to the others after giving Karaghul to Teobalt, he had helped them put the plan into action. It had been fairly straightforward. They were making a beastman trap, and baiting it with alcohol. The idea was this. They would hide three of the wagons, leaving in the main intersection only the one that was loaded with barrels of blackpowder. These they would hide under barrels of beer, brandy and gin. When the beastmen came, they would lure them into the centre of the village, let them attack the wagon and try to steal the liquor, then – from a safe distance – fire the powder and blow as many of them as they could to smithereens.

If there were any survivors, Gotrek, Felix and the slayers, as well as Teobalt and whatever villagers they could muster, would finish them off before they recovered from the blast.

Felix was afraid that the blast would blow up the town as well, for Ludeker had amassed quite a little stockpile of powder during his tenure as 'protector' of Bauholz, and Milo had crammed every barrel of it onto the wagon. Gotrek assured him that all would be well.

The two structures closest to the intersection were the old strong house and the temple of Sigmar. Both made of stone and, in the Slayer's words, 'solid – at least by human standards.'

A shallow groove had been dug in the frozen earth of the intersection and match cord laid in it from the wagon to the strong house, where the slayers would be hiding. Then a line of planks was laid over the groove, to stop the beastmen from accidentally kicking or tripping over the cords and pulling them from the barrels.

When all had been prepared, Sir Teobalt and Doktor Vinck had directed the townsfolk in their duties. Those who could pull a bow would man the walls. Those that could fight would lie in wait in the temple of Sigmar, and those that could do neither would hide on the second floor of the strong house, with instructions to lock the bottom door and pray once the fighting started.

Gotrek gave Felix and Kat special duties, and sent them to the walls to wait with the archers. Felix could tell that Sir Teobalt wished that Felix would have left town entirely and not participated in such a noble enterprise, but the templar had said nothing, only pretended that Felix wasn't there.

Felix looked along the wall in the torchlight, sizing up the archers he could see. They didn't look like much. Their bows were new and well made, taken from the wagons along with their swords and helmets, but they themselves were mostly not of the same quality – a handful of village boys, a dozen refugees from the camp across the river, so starved that their bow staves seemed thicker than their wrists. But among them were a few old soldiers, trapped in town like the rest by recent events. From what Kat had said, the moment she had brought news of the herd, anyone with money or connections or a boat had taken to the river and sped south as quickly as possible, leaving only the poor and desperate behind.

The soldiers looked hardly more well fed than the refugees, but at least they knew their business. One of them, a hunched little man by the name of Weir, who sported a week's growth of beard and his own bow, had taken charge of the troops on this section of the wall, and was walking up and down the walkway with a profound limp, calling encouragement and cheerful abuse to his ungainly recruits.

'Keep yer bowstring away from the snow, ye daft bug,' he told a boy, 'If it gets wet ye won't be able to shoot five paces,' and, 'Can't bend yer bow, laddie? Are ye a maid? Here now, step through it and bend it across your hip. See it? Strength of Sigmar now, hey?' and, 'Don't stick 'em in the wood, ye lummox! Look ye, that won't cut yer beard now, will it? How's it to get through a beastman's scalp? Sharpen 'em again! Sharpen 'em again!' And on and on, keeping their minds away from the waiting and the fear of what was to come.

Felix sighed with uneasy impatience and put his hand on the pommel of his sword, then jerked it away again, surprised once more that he didn't feel the familiar serrated shape of the dragon head under his palm. He must have done this twenty times already, and still it alarmed and depressed him every time.

He had tried out a score of the swords that had been part of the plunder Milo had loaded on the four wagons, swinging them around and testing their balance, and had finally selected this one as the best of the lot, though really it felt just as wrong in his hand as all the others. He would have to get used to it though, or find a better sword if he ever made it back to civilisation. Karaghul wasn't his any more.

It was a very strange feeling. He had had the rune sword almost as long as he had known Gotrek, and in that time it had come to feel as much a part of him as his arm. He felt naked without it – almost amputated. It seemed unfair to have it taken from him like this. He had told the truth. He had done the right thing, and he had been punished for it. And yet there was nothing he could do. Sir Teobalt wasn't going to give the sword back to him – not unless he changed his mind, and that seemed unlikely. The old templar was hide-bound and stubborn. His faith, and his belief in the incorruptibility of his fellow knights, had blinded him more surely than the loss of his eyes might have done.

From the west wall of the village came a murmur of frightened voices. The archers all turned their heads and whispered questions at each other, then, after a moment, the news worked its way around the corner and the archers stood, snatching up their bows in nervous excitement.

'They're here!' said one. 'The boys on the west wall say they're circling in the woods.'

'But I'm not done waxing!' bleated another.

'Steady now, steady now,' said Weir. 'No need to rush. All the time in the world. String yer bows now, lads. Nice and easy. That's the way.'

Those that hadn't strung their bows, while the rest craned their necks to watch to the west, waiting to see movement beyond the edge of the corner platform.

Felix watched with them as Kat calmly strung her bow and slipped her arrows into a leather quiver at her hip.

The glare of the fires in the fields made it hard to see beyond them, but after a moment he thought he saw a suggestion of movement against the black of the woods – a glint of reflected flame, a ripple of shadow on shadow.

The archers saw it too, and their voices raised to a babble again. Weir, bless him, knew just what to say to calm them.

'There they are, lads. Have ye ever seen such big targets in yer lives? Sigmar, even bug-boy here ought to be able to hit something that size, eh?'

The boys chuckled and their babble subsided.

Felix, on the other hand, was growing uneasier by the second. The beastmen had come a little more into the light as they circled around to the south side of the village, and he could see their numbers now. There were scores of them! The scout had said a hundred. It looked to Felix like there were double that, but perhaps he was letting fear get the better of him.

The beasts were arcing in towards the gate now, and he could see that the first twenty or so carried something heavy between them. For a moment Felix's heart lurched at the idea that they were bringing some offspring of the giant herdstone to the village and were going to turn them all into beastmen after all, but then he saw that it was only a huge pine-tree, its branches trimmed to hand-hold stubs, and sharpened at its base.

He laughed a little wildly. What a state to come to when you were relieved that the beastmen coming to attack you were carrying *only* a battering ram.

The fires may have helped those on the wall see the beastmen, but they also made the fiends look more hellish then they already were, painting their fur blood-red and highlighting their cruel horns, their glittering eyes, and the curving teeth in their slavering black mouths.

The village boys whimpered at the sight, and a few of them put arrows on strings and raised their bows, but Weir barked angrily at them. 'Not yet, ye damned yokels! Have ye got so many arrows that ye can waste 'em? Wait! Ye see the fires? Well, do ye?'

The archers nodded sullenly, like schoolboys.

'Them fires are set at the edge of bow range,' he scolded. 'Ye fire now and ye'll hit naught but snow. Wait until they come past 'em, and then go on my word, aye?'

'Aye,' murmured his charges in return.

'Good,' said Weir. 'Now start to pick out yer targets. Pick a big one. The biggest one ye can see. These beasts, ye see, they follow the strongest. And if ye kill the leaders, the rest are lost and that much easier to beat. Have ye got a target?'

'Aye,' said the archers, more confident now.

'Good!' cried Weir. 'Then keep an eye on him, and listen for my call.'

The archers watched the beastmen in silence as they came. They were halfway between the tree line and the line of bonfires now, and coming fast, a jostling swarm of hulking monsters that strung out behind the ram-carriers in a long fanning tail.

'Wait for it!' cried Weir. 'Wait for it.'

Felix felt Kat's hand slip into his and give it a squeeze. He looked around at her and found her smiling up at him. He smiled back and returned her squeeze, then turned away. The thought that it might be the last smile he ever received from her nearly choked him, and he didn't want her to see the fear in his eyes.

Finally the beastmen carrying the felled pine trotted between two of the bonfires.

'Fire!' bellowed Weir. 'Cut them down!'

The archers raised their bows and loosed their arrows. It was a pathetic volley. Only Kat and Weir and a few of the other soldiers hit their marks. Most of the refugees and the village boys put their shafts in the snow. Some of their arrows failed to leave the bow, and they howled from stung fingers and wrists.

'Clumsy fools!' shouted Weir. 'Take it slow. Nock. Draw. Aim. Fire. And aim for their heads if you would hit their chests. Now fire!'

The boys tried again as Kat and the other trained archers fired at will, loosing five shafts to every one of theirs. Kat was concentrating on the gors carrying the battering ram, and had dropped the front three in six shots. More ran up to take their places and she rained shafts on them as well.

The biggest of the beastmen had fallen as well, pin-cushioned by a dozen arrows.

'All right, lads, all right,' said Weir, laughing. 'He's down. Now pick another.'

Kat grinned. 'The only good thing about beastmen,' she said to Felix out of the side of her mouth, 'is that they don't fire back. Imagine these boys trying to fire while ducking.'

Felix smiled, though he was secretly glad no one had asked him to take up a bow. She would be laughing at *him* then.

As they continued to fire, the village boys got more confident and their aim improved. Now at least their arrows were falling among the beastmen and not in front of them.

Unfortunately, the gors came so swiftly that the lads hadn't time for more than a few volleys before they were at the gates, and despite the help of Kat and the other trained archers, less than a score had fallen.

'Fall back!' called Weir, as the ram boomed against the great wooden doors. 'To your second positions!'

The boys and the refugees lowered their bows and scurried for the ladders as Kat and a few of the other archers took final shots, sinking arrows to the fletching in necks and the tops of bestial heads as they shot straight down.

'Come on, Kat,' said Felix nervously. 'We've got a job to do, remember.'

'Just one more,' said Kat, then 'Ha!' as she let fly a final time.

Then they were dropping down the ladders after the other archers and pounding up the street to the barricade that the villagers had built between the first two houses of the village.

As they took up their places behind it, Felix could hear the splintering of the flimsy bar Gotrek had ordered set across the doors of the gate. The bar was weak on purpose, because they wanted the beasts to succeed in coming through. The success of Gotrek's plan depended on all the beasts moving together, and it would fail if they were spread out around the walls, all trying to climb over at different spots.

'Arrows on strings, lads,' said Weir, as they watched the wooden doors shudder and flex in the torchlight. 'Two volleys and run again. No heroes here, aye?'

A splintering crack drowned out the archers' response. The bar had snapped and the beastmen were surging in, shouldering the doors aside and roaring in triumph.

Felix's stomach churned as they raced towards him, and he suddenly feared that the plan wasn't going to work. What could stop such a savage onslaught?

It seemed that the archers felt the same way, for only Kat and a few others fired. The rest just sat and stared, like rabbits before a wolf.

'Fire, curse you! Fire!' roared Weir, shooting into the stampede.

The villagers and refugees snapped out of their funk and fired, but poorly, and there was no time for a second volley. They had left it too long.

'Run!' shouted Weir.

The archers needed no further encouragement. They turned and fled down the street as fast as they could. Felix and Kat snatched up torches placed at the barricade just for the purpose and ran after them. Felix almost choked as he took a breath. The street reeked of spilled brandy – the breadcrumbs that would lead the gors to the trap if all else failed.

It seemed unnecessary at the moment. As Gotrek had predicted, the beastmen chased the fleeing villagers with murder in their savage eyes, leaping the barricade and closing the gap with frightening speed.

As they neared the village's main intersection, Weir looked back and waved his arms. 'Scatter! Scatter! To your third positions!'

Now was Felix and Kat's moment. As the archers broke left and right, dodging into the shadowed yards between the little houses, Felix and Kat continued forwards, waving their torches and shouting insults over their shoulders. It was imperative that the gors follow them and not split up to hunt down the fleeing archers.

Felix looked back, worried. A few were breaking off, but the majority were continuing after him and Kat. Good. He laughed hysterically. Again – what a state to come to when you were relieved that there was a herd of beastmen thundering after you.

Felix and Kat ran into the intersection, straight for the wagon that was parked in its centre. They jumped up onto its tailgate and clambered to the top of the barrels, then turned and waved their torches at the oncoming monsters. The brandy reek was even stronger here, for the casks had been opened so that the smell would be unavoidable. Felix was afraid his torch would light the fumes.

'Come on, you filthy scavengers!' Felix shouted.

'Catch me if you can!' shrilled Kat.

The beastmen did as they were ordered and surged forwards, straight for the wagon. From his high vantage point, Felix could see that the tail of the herd was only now coming through the gate. There were still so many of them! Too many! The powder couldn't possibly kill them all.

As the gors rushed to the wagon, Felix and Kat flung their torches at them, then leapt down and sprinted for the door of the strong house – praying now that the beastmen *didn't* follow them, and that they would be enticed by the trap they had set for them.

At first he thought they had failed, for he heard hooves clattering up the wooden steps behind him and heard the slayers curse as he and Kat dived through the door into the darkness of the stone house.

Three huge gors burst through the door behind them, but the slayers cut them down before they knew they were being attacked, and no more followed.

Felix and Kat caught their breath and joined the slayers at the door, where a savage joyful hooting was coming from outside. The first beastmen were surging around the cart, climbing on it and fighting each other to get to the brandy and beer, and more and more of them were pouring into the square and pushing forwards for their share. One gor had a brandy keg raised over its head and was pouring it down its throat.

'Well done, Gurnisson,' said Rodi. 'They've taken the bait.'

Gotrek only nodded, his eye never leaving the mob outside.

'Stupid beasts,' chuckled Snorri. 'Distracted by beer.'

Rodi laughed. 'That would never happen to you, Father Rustskull.'

'Snorri doesn't know what you mean,' said Snorri.

'Er, Gotrek,' said Felix. 'Shouldn't you light the fuse now?'

'Not yet,' said Gotrek.

'But what if they find the blackpowder?'

'They'll probably drink that too,' said Rodi.

Felix waited, tension gripping his shoulders as he watched the beastmen flood into the intersection and crowd around the wagon. The edges of the pack were starting to reach the sides of the street. It was a close game Gotrek was playing. If he waited too long, the gors on the periphery would lose interest and turn to other prey. They might also smell the blood of their fallen brothers in the strong house and come to investigate.

Finally, just as the urge to take the torch from Gotrek and light the fuses himself was becoming overwhelming, the Slayer lowered it to the ends of the bundled match cords on the floor. They flared to life and the flame crawled down their lengths towards the door, spitting as it went.

'Stand clear,' said Gotrek, and waved the others back.

Everybody stepped back, but not so far that they couldn't watch the flames' progress. It was too mesmerising.

Then, disaster.

Two gors were trying to carry a beer keg away from the rest, punching and kicking and butting as others tried to steal it from them. A clawed hand caught the top of the keg and pulled it down. The two gors lost their grip on it and it smashed down on its side. A wave of golden liquid poured from the smashed-in top.

The beastmen quickly righted the barrel, but not quickly enough. As they continued fighting over it, the spill of beer foamed towards the covered groove that the dwarfs had dug to protect the match cords. Unfortunately, the planks were no protection against liquid, and the beer bubbled down into the cut.

Felix and the others stared, stunned. Gotrek said something in Khazalid that Felix was glad he didn't understand.

'Right,' said Rodi, raising his axe. 'Give me the torch, Gurnisson. It's time for me to meet my doom.'

'No,' said Snorri. 'Snorri wants the torch.'

'It was my plan,' said Gotrek. 'It will be my–'

'Rhya's tits!' snapped Kat, and before any of them knew what she intended, she snatched the torch from Gotrek's hand and raced out the door with it.

'Kat!' screamed Felix, and charged out after her.

Kat dodged through the surging, brawling herd like a rabbit through a country dance, ducking elbows and skipping out of the way of heavy hooves. Felix wasn't quite so small or nimble and was knocked hither and thither by oblivious beastmen, still trying to reach the barrels of liquor.

As he stumbled on, he saw Kat run past the spill of beer and flip up one of the planks nearer the wagon with the toe of her boot. A gor saw her and let out a bellow. It was lost in the general uproar.

'Kat! Look out!' shouted Felix.

She was too intent. She didn't hear. More beastmen turned as she stabbed the torch down into the groove. Sparks shot up from it, racing towards the wagon between a gor's wide-spread hooves.

Another beastman grabbed Kat by the back of her coat and lifted her off the ground. Felix shoved between two big monsters and slashed at the gor's arm with his new sword. Karaghul would have had it off at the elbow, but the new blade lacked weight. He only bit to the bone.

Still, it was enough. The gor roared and dropped Kat to turn on Felix. Felix ducked a swipe of its tree-stump club and pulled Kat up.

'Run!' he roared.

She was already running, her axes in her hands. Felix turned and hurried after her, desperate to get her to safety. More of the gors were aware of them now, reaching and swinging for them, calling to their brothers. Kat danced away from every swipe, backhanding the beasts she passed with deft hacks. Felix chopped at them as they turned after her, then plunged through them as they howled and staggered aside.

Finally they broke out of the pack and ran up the stone steps of the strong house. A few of the gors chased them, and Felix felt the wind of a giant mace fan the back of his neck as he and Kat raced, side-by-side, over the threshold.

Then, just as Felix was letting out a sigh of relief, there was a deafening thunderclap and something hit him so hard in the back that he was thrown to the far end of the room and slammed against an interior wall. For a long black moment he thought that the gor had connected with its mace and sent him to some hellish afterlife, for he seemed to be in a world of darkness and flame and noise and could not tell up from down or cold from hot. His body seemed at once numb and on fire. His head spun as if he'd been in a drinking contest with Snorri Nosebiter.

Then his vision returned and he was even more confused. A ball of fire seemed to be coming from the ceiling and rising to the floor. The walls swayed as if they were made of mattresses. Heavy wet things thudded all around him like rotten fruit. A huge weight pressed on his shoulders. Finally equilibrium reasserted itself and he realised that he was propped head-down against the wall, his neck bent and all his weight on his shoulders with his arse sticking up in the air. The ball of fire was receding through the door, and there were bits and pieces of beastman lying around him like the leavings on a butcher's shop floor. A leg with a cloven hoof lay beside him, oozing blood, while a beastman's head hung from the wall above him, one horn impaling the plaster. Dust rained down from above.

There was a little moan from his right. He turned his head and his body slid down the wall and slumped to the floor in a painful heap. He grunted and sat up. Kat lay curled in a ball next to him. His heart turned to ice. Had the explosion killed her?

'Kat?' said Felix. 'Are you all right?'

Kat pried open one eye. 'Are we dead?'

Relief flooded through him like a river through a burst dam. 'No.'

'Then I'm fine–'

'Slayers!' roared Gotrek from the door. 'Attack!'

Felix looked up to see Gotrek, Snorri and Rodi charging through the door, weapons at the ready.

Kat slowly levered herself up, using the wall for balance. She was shaking like a leaf. 'Come on, Felix,' she said. 'There is slaying to be done.'

Felix stood as well. He felt as if he was made of matchsticks and rusty hinges. 'Aye,' he said. 'But you're to do yours from the roof, remember?'

'But I want to fight by your side,' she said.

And I want you to live, thought Felix, but he knew that wouldn't fly. Instead he said, 'No, Kat. The archers need you. You saw them on the wall. Go to them. Show them how it's done.'

She looked up at him with her lopsided smile. 'Is this how you make Gotrek do what you want?'

Felix opened his mouth, but before anything came out she laughed and started unsteadily up the steps to the upper floor.

Felix watched her go, then turned and hurried for the door, where the sounds of slaughter were rising.

The intersection was a charnel house. The pulped remains of scores of beastmen were piled up against the walls of the houses facing the street like drifts of crimson rubbish. Of the powder wagon there was no sign, only a smoking patch of earth where it had stood, surrounded by melting red snow, but bits of timber and barrel staves stuck out of the wattle-and-daub houses like straw blown by the wind.

And yet, astoundingly, some of the beastmen still lived. Felix saw Gotrek and Snorri and Rodi laying into them at the south end of the intersection – three squat whirlwinds wading into two score beastmen. And they weren't alone. Sir Teobalt, Karaghul in hand, fought at the head of a small group of soldiers, refugees and villagers, all armed with Ludeker's stolen weapons.

'Men of the Empire,' cried the templar in a high warble. 'Destroy the enemies of man! Defend your homes!'

As Felix ran – or rather staggered – towards the fight he saw beastman after beastman fall, and not all from the exertions of the dwarfs and men.

From every rooftop shot flashing shafts that buried themselves in beastman fur, and he could hear Weir shouting from somewhere above and behind him, 'That's the way, lads! Stick to the edges. Don't want to kill our own, do we?'

Felix ploughed into the fight, swinging high and low, and cutting down a beastman with almost every stroke. It was a dream of a battle – the kind of battle he had imagined being the hero of when he had read the old sagas as a little boy. Thus had Sigmar slain a thousand orcs at Black Fire Pass. Thus had Magnus smote the forces of Chaos before the gates of Kislev. The beasts practically fell over before he hit them, and Felix's allies were faring just as well, killing beastmen as if they had been lambs.

Of course it wasn't a fair fight and Felix knew it. The blast had dizzied the beastmen as it had him, only more so, as they had borne the brunt of it. They reeled as if drunk, and could barely hold on to their weapons. Some of them had smoking bits of timber sticking out of them. Still, it felt magnificent, a glorious vengeance for all the violence and misery the gors and the Drakwald had inflicted upon him and his companions since he had left Altdorf.

Only one thing marred the fight. Only one thing kept it from being the perfect battle – the paltry and unfamiliar sword with which he fought. It should have been Karaghul. Without it, nothing felt right. His blocks and parries were off, his attacks lacked force – in fact, it was a fortunate thing that the beasts were so disabled, for at full strength and with their wits unscrambled, he wasn't sure he could have prevailed against them with the new blade.

He glared at Sir Teobalt across the battle in between fighting. He supposed the templar had a right to take the blade from him, but it still stung. It still seemed unfair. He almost wished... but no, that was an unworthy thought. He pushed it away.

After only a few moments, the last few beastmen broke and ran for the gate. Felix and the slayers and Teobalt's ragtag company chased them all the way, cutting down all but the quickest. Only three remained when they reached the gate, and they quickly outdistanced their shorter-legged pursuers.

Gotrek heaved his axe at them as they ran across the field. It caught the slowest one in the left leg and it went down with a screech. The other two didn't look back, only sprinted for the black wall of the forest as quickly as they were able.

Felix and the others stopped just outside the gates of the village as Gotrek stumped forwards to retrieve his axe. Last came Sir Teobalt, limping and grimacing and wheezing like a bellows as he leaned against the gatepost and caught his breath.

'Well... well done, men,' he said to his troops. 'It was bravely fought. And well done to you as well, sons of Grimnir,' he added, turning to the slayers. 'Your plan worked in all particulars.'

Felix noticed that the old templar didn't mention him in his congratulations.

Teobalt turned to one of the soldiers. 'Anselem, close the doors, and place the heavy bar. They may come again–'

'Srr,' came a strange voice from the shadows beside the gate. 'Srr, pleese.'

Felix and the others turned at the sound. A horrible crouching figure shuffled out of the darkness. It was one of the ungors, with little sprouting horns and a furred face, but features still mostly human. It had been terribly abused, with great gashes and bruises on its face and shoulders, and its wiry arms were clutched around its belly, trying to keep in the intestines that threatened to slither out of a gash that slit it from privates to breastbone. It looked as if it could barely stand.

'A beast!' shouted Sir Teobalt. 'Kill it!'

His men stepped forwards, but Snorri and Rodi got there before them, raising their weapons.

The ungor staggered back, crying out, a look of fearful pleading on his half-human face, and suddenly Felix recognised him.

'Stop!' he shouted. 'It's Ortwin!'

FIFTEEN

Sir Teobalt stared.

The two slayers paused, but Gotrek, returning from retrieving his axe, did not. He pushed through them, preparing to strike. 'Not any more it isn't.'

The changed squire fell on his back, raising one hand in supplication. 'Pleese, no. I msst speek. I msst tell you.'

Gotrek stepped over him, axe high.

'Wait, Gotrek,' said Felix. 'Let him speak.'

'He is a beast,' said the Slayer. 'He must die.'

'Death is all I wssh,' mumbled Ortwin through his fangs. 'But I msst speek frrst.'

'It looks like he's going to die anyway,' said Felix.

Gotrek lowered his axe. 'Speak quickly then, beast,' he growled. 'My axe is impatient.'

Ortwin moaned with relief. 'Blsss you, Slayrr.'

Sir Teobalt stepped past the slayers and looked down at his former squire. Felix had never seen the old knight look so stricken or sad. 'Ortwin, is it truly you?'

The changed youth cringed away from the knight's gaze. 'Frrgive me, mastrr. Sigmar have mrrcy on me.'

Sir Teobalt's shoulders slumped, and he covered his eyes with a shaking hand. 'Sigmar have mercy on us all.'

The crunching of snowy footsteps came from the village. Felix turned to see Kat and Doktor Vinck leading forwards a crowd of nervous villagers.

'Are they all dead?' asked Doktor Vinck. 'Have you chased them all–'

He choked when he saw Ortwin. There was an angry murmur from the crowd.

'Keep them back, doctor,' said Felix. 'There is no need to fear.'

The doctor obligingly waved the villagers back, but Kat came forwards, staring wide-eyed at the dying squire.

'Is it…?' she asked in a trembling voice. 'Is it…?'

Felix nodded, then took her arm. Her hand circled his waist.

'Go on, Ortwin,' he said, turning back. 'Tell us.'

Ortwin nodded weakly and took a laboured breath. 'I know whrrr they… take the stone,' he wheezed. 'I know what they will… do with it. I came… to wrrn you but they caught me, and…' He looked down at the horrible wound in his belly. 'At leest it will be over soon.'

'Sooner than you expect if you don't speak quickly,' said Gotrek. 'Tell your tale, beast.'

Ortwin fought to focus. 'They go to hills in the south,' he said. 'Acrrss the Talabec. Thrrr is an old crrcle. They will raise the stone. On… on Witching Night – Hexensnacht.' He grimaced with pain.

'To what purpose?' asked Sir Teobalt.

'A crrimony,' breathed Ortwin. 'Urslak Cripplehorn was granted a vssion by the brrd-headed god. Thss crrimony, on thss niight... will trrn all men undrr the shadow of the forest to beestmen, like me.'

The men and dwarfs stared at him in disbelief.

'All men?' said Felix uncertainly. 'Everyone? He has the power to do this?'

'The stone givss him the powrr,' said Ortwin. 'His god givss him the powrr. His beesthrrd giives him the powrr.'

'Which forest?' asked Doktor Vinck. 'The Drakwald? The Great Forest? The Reikwald?'

'To the beestmen,' said Ortwin, 'all the frrests arr one.'

Felix and the others looked around at each other.

'This is dread news,' said Teobalt.

'It's bunk,' said Rodi. 'It's not possible. No beast has such power.'

'Can you say that with the evidence before you?' asked Doktor Vinck, indicating Ortwin.

'Changing a handful of men isn't the same as changing thousands, over hundreds of miles,' replied Rodi.

'Does it matter?' asked Gotrek. 'If this shaman can do a tenth of what he claims it will be too much. He must be stopped.'

'He must,' agreed Kat.

Rodi nodded. 'Aye. And there is a great doom to be had, win or fail.'

'Snorri wants it to be Witching Night now,' said Snorri.

The comment brought Felix up short. 'Wait,' he said. 'What day is it?'

Sir Teobalt looked up. 'It is the twenty-first of Vorhexen – fasting day of Walhemar the Valiant.'

Felix did a quick calculation in his head. 'Then there are fourteen days until Hexensnacht. I don't know where the beasts are going below the Talabec, but at the rate they're moving they'll never make it in time. It took us ten days from Ahlenhof, and we went by roads. They're cutting every step through the deep woods.'

Kat nodded. 'It's impossible.'

'Nno,' moaned Ortwin.

They turned back to him. The snow around where he lay was crimson with his blood.

'Evrry changed man Urslak adds to the hrrd adds knowing,' said the squire through bubbles of red phlegm. 'He sees our minds. He knew I would trry to come to you. He knows how to use the rrver.'

'How to use the river?' said Sir Teobalt. 'I don't understand.'

'The timbrr camp,' said Ortwin. 'On the rivrr.'

'Aye, I remember it,' said Teobalt, nodding. 'We passed the night there.'

'What has a timber camp got to do with it?' asked Rodi. 'The beast has stopped making sense.'

Felix gasped as understanding came to him. 'Logs!' he cried. 'Rafts! We saw them!'

'What are you saying, manling?' asked Gotrek.

Felix grunted with impatience. Dwarfs seemed to have a blind spot for the uses of trees. 'The shaman means to float the stone down the river,' he said. 'A few of those rafts we saw bound together, and he can move it at twice his speed. Maybe three times as fast. They'll tow it down the Zufuhr like a barge.'

'Yss,' said Ortwin from the ground. 'Yss.'

'But beastmen don't know how to make boats,' said Rodi. 'They can barely tie a rock to the end of a stick and call it a mace.'

'Beestmen do not,' whispered Ortwin. 'But beests who wrrr once men do. Urslak is...' He coughed, spilling blood down his furred chest. 'Urslak is... lrrrning.'

Felix stared dully as Ortwin fell silent. A beastman who learned was a nightmare – the doom of the human race. It had been the beasts' savagery and lack of discipline, more so than the superiority of the defences of man, that had stopped them from taking over the world. If the monsters began to learn to use wagons and boats and developed organisation and tactics, there would be no stopping them.

'Anything else, beast?' asked Gotrek, looking down at Ortwin.

The changed squire looked up through dimming eyes. 'Bewrre... bewrre the axe of Gargorath the God-Touched,' he said. 'It... it eats what it kills.'

'That is all?'

Ortwin nodded and sank back. 'I am rredy.'

Gotrek raised his axe, but Sir Teobalt stepped forwards.

'Wait, Slayer,' he said. 'It should be I that does this.'

Gotrek nodded and stepped back as the old templar stood over his former squire. 'I can offer you no salvation, squire,' said Teobalt. 'A beast is beyond Sigmar's mercy. But... but I give you my thanks. Though you have fallen, you sacrificed your life to return and warn us. It was a brave thing, bravely done.'

'Thank you, srr,' said Ortwin, and there seemed to be tears in his bestial eyes – though it might only have been blood. 'Sigmrr blsss you.'

Sir Teobalt lifted Karaghul with both hands. 'May you find in death the peace you lost in life.'

The changed boy closed his eyes. The sword came down. Kat turned away and pressed her face against Felix's chest as the shaggy horned head dropped softly into the snow. He pulled her close, stroking her hair as he grieved.

The squire had been a fool sometimes, and too concerned with honour and doing heroic deeds for his own good – or the good of his companions on more than one occasion – but at the same time that honour had proved stronger than the animal instincts that had come with his new shape, and he had died to maintain it. It was doubtful that anyone would write any ballads about a youth that turned into a beast, but he was a hero nonetheless. He might very well have saved the Empire. That is, he might have if the rest of them could warn Altdorf in time.

'I must go south at once,' said Sir Teobalt.

'Not alone, you won't,' said Gotrek.

'Aye,' said Rodi. 'We're coming too.'

'Snorri is ready,' said Snorri. 'Where are we going?'

'Is there a boat?' asked Felix. It seemed the only way to catch up to the beasts.

Doktor Vinck shook his head. 'There is not. They were all taken by the soldiers and the refugees when news of the herd reached us.' He frowned. 'There is one at the lumber camp, or there was. Perhaps the beasts have taken it.'

'Unless they haven't reached it yet,' said Kat, lifting her head from Felix's chest. 'If we take the river road, we may beat them.'

'We must try it!' said Sir Teobalt. 'We will leave immediately.'

* * *

Felix, Kat, Sir Teobalt and the three slayers left an hour later on a wagon to which they hitched four horses for greater speed – with Teobalt's Machtig tied behind. Though all were weary from the long day of preparing and defending the village, there was no alternative. They had to get ahead of the beastmen, and waiting until morning might make it impossible for them to catch up.

Doktor Vinck thanked them profusely for saving Bauholz, and gave them food and drink for the road. He begged Kat to be careful, and reminded Sir Teobalt to apply the ointment he had given him three times a day to his wounds, which were not yet fully healed, then waved goodbye to them until the wooden doors of the gate closed with a hollow boom.

Felix and Kat sat side by side in the back of the wagon as they rode out of town, alone – or at least nearly alone – for the first time since he had rescued her from Milo. Sir Teobalt, saying that he had done the least in the recent battle and would therefore take point, had unhitched Machtig and rode well ahead of the wagon, and the three slayers sat on the buckboard, Gotrek driving the horses while Rodi and Snorri kept watch.

Felix took a deep breath. This might be the best opportunity they would have for days.

He put a hand on her leg. 'Kat,' he said.

She turned and smiled up at him, and all the words went out of his head. He just stared.

Kat stared back, and, as the silence stretched and the seconds ticked by, she covered his hand with hers, then lifted it and pulled it over her shoulders so that she could lean against him underneath it. He pulled her tight and all at once they were kissing, long and deep, and the freezing night was suddenly as warm as a Tilean spring.

After a moment Felix pulled back, holding her away from him. 'Wait, Kat,' he said, panting. 'Wait.'

She scowled at him. 'Does it still feel wrong to you, then, Felix? I am no longer seven.'

'I know,' he said. 'I know. That's... that's not what I was going to say.'

'Then what?' she asked, her chin thrust out.

He hesitated again, not sure how to begin, but finally he spoke. 'I realised, when we were fighting Milo, that... that I cared more for you than I have for anyone for a long long time, and that all my... misgivings were gone.'

Kat dropped her eyes at that, smiling shyly.

'But...'

She looked up again, her brow lowering once more. 'But?' she said, warningly.

Felix sighed and sat back. 'Kat, I don't have a proper life. I have no employment, no home, no money. I follow the Slayer into certain death time and time again, and my vow to him means I'll keep doing it until he dies.' He looked sideways at her. 'I've got nothing to give you. Not even the certainty that I'll be here tomorrow.'

Kat smiled and let out a relieved breath. 'Is that all?' she said.

'Isn't that everything?' he asked.

'It's nothing, Felix. Nothing.' She leaned against him, resting her head on his chest. 'When Papa trained me to be a scout, he taught me the first rule of the Drakwald – the rule that every woodsman and beast-hunter lives by.'

'What rule is that?' asked Felix.

'Today is all there is,' she said. She circled her arms around him, looking out over the tailgate of the cart. 'We are all like you, Felix. No home, no money, and death always only an eye-blink away. None of us knows if we'll be here tomorrow, so we live by that rule.'

'Today is all there is,' Felix repeated.

'Yes,' she whispered, and raised her head and looked into his eyes, her lips parting. 'Today is all there is.'

Felix lowered his mouth to hers, closing his eyes. He could feel her breath on his lips. He could feel her straining upwards.

'Easy, Machtig!' said Sir Teobalt's voice.

Felix and Kat jerked apart guiltily and looked up. The old templar was pulling Machtig around the back of the wagon and trying to dismount while the horse skittered sideways. He smiled at them. 'Wilful beast. He has been too long without a bit in his mouth.'

Felix and Kat untangled themselves as Sir Teobalt let himself down and tied the warhorse to the tailgate, then climbed up into the wagon between them. 'I am too weary after the day's events to remind him of his training,' he said, unbuckling his breastplate. 'No matter. I will have plenty of opportunity in the days ahead.'

'No doubt,' said Felix, cursing the knight inwardly. Today might be all there was, but if Sir Teobalt was going to make himself a fixture, Felix and Kat would still have to wait until tomorrow.

The old templar looked from him to Kat and back with an odd expression on his gaunt face, then removed his breastplate and set it on the floor of the cart. 'Sigmar watch you whilst you rest, friends,' he said, then laid back on the breastplate like it was a pillow, folded his hands across his chest and closed his eyes.

Felix sighed and gave Kat an exasperated look. She smirked back at him across Sir Teobalt's body and stifled a laugh, then shrugged.

'Well, goodnight, Felix,' she said. 'Pleasant dreams.'

'I doubt it,' growled Felix, then flopped down and pulled his cloak tighter around his shoulders as the old knight began to snore.

FELIX DOZED ON and off, but unsurprisingly, he did not truly sleep. The bumping of the wagon and Teobalt's snoring, and Felix's frustrated thoughts of what might have been had the damned interfering old buzzard not been there didn't allow it. Towards morning, a particularly hard jolt woke him from a dream of Kat skinning out of her furs and stretching naked beside him, to find Sir Teobalt looking at him with thoughtful eyes.

Felix blinked at him sleepily. He was a jarring sight after his thoughts of Kat.

The templar kept staring.

'Are... are you well, Sir Teobalt?' Felix mumbled, as politely as he could manage.

'I have done you a disservice, Herr Jaeger,' he said after a long hesitation.

You certainly have, thought Felix, but all he said was, 'Have you?'

'I would have spoken of it earlier, but...' The templar looked over his shoulder at Kat. 'It is a private matter between us.'

'I'm not sure what you mean,' said Felix.

'You know of what I speak, Herr Jaeger.' Teobalt sighed and lowered his eyes. 'I could not allow myself to believe you when you told me of Ortwin's fate and the fate of my fellow templars. I... I see now that you told the truth.'

'It was a hard thing to believe,' said Felix.

'Aye.' The templar's brow furrowed. 'It pains me to think that such good men fell so far from the true faith that they could be twisted like this.'

Felix paused. Teobalt still didn't seem to understand. He was still looking to place blame. 'Forgive me, sir,' he said finally. 'But I'm not sure it is a matter of falling from faith. I think perhaps the shaman's power is just too strong. I wonder if even an arch lector could resist it.'

'You say this to hearten me,' said the templar. 'To allow me to think better of my brothers.'

'I say it because I believe it,' said Felix. 'I have seen the power of the stone. Lord Ilgner was a good man. He had fought the hordes and the herds with all his heart, and yet he changed with the rest.'

'Perhaps you are right,' said Teobalt, still not looking up.

He sank into a long silence, and Felix began to drift off again, thinking that the conversation was finished.

Then just as his head began dropping to his chest, the knight spoke again.

'You are an honourable man, Herr Jaeger,' he said.

Felix raised his eyes again and blinked. 'I am?'

'Aye,' said Sir Teobalt. 'You have done what I asked of you. You have discovered the fate of the templars of the Order of the Fiery Heart and, though you knew that I would not care to hear it, you told me the truth of that fate.'

Felix opened his mouth to speak, but the templar held up a hand.

'There still remains the task of recovering the regalia of the order, but I wonder if it is not lost forever. Or perhaps we will find it when we find the beastmen again. I know not.' He sat up, hissing and grimacing at his stiffness. 'Nevertheless, you have been true to your promise, and you do not deserve the punishment I meted out to you.'

He reached down and picked up Karaghul, which he had laid beside him as he slept, then held it out to Felix. 'Your sword, Herr Jaeger,' he said. 'And whether we find the regalia or not, you may carry it, as I had promised. You have already earned it.'

Felix's eyes moved from Teobalt's face to the sword and back. He almost didn't dare to reach for it, for fear it would be some kind of strange joke and the templar would pull it back. It was not a joke, and when Felix held out his hands, Teobalt laid the sword in them and inclined his head.

'Wear it with honour, Herr Jaeger,' he said. 'As I know you have until now.'

'Thank you, Sir Teobalt,' said Felix, shaking as he laid the sword at his side and ran a fond hand along its hilt. 'I will not disappoint you. I promise.'

WHEN FELIX NEXT awoke, it was to dwarfen cursing.

He sat up, groaning and stiff, and looked around as Kat and Sir Teobalt yawned and grumbled beside him. It was the dark grey of dawn, and a heavy mist swirled about the wagon. Nevertheless, he could see why Gotrek and Rodi were cursing.

They all climbed down stiffly from the wagon and looked around as they shook out their arms and legs. They were in the middle of the logging camp they had stopped at on their way north with Reidle the merchant, but the camp wasn't there any more. It had been levelled – the walls, the tents, the short docks that had once stuck out into the river like stubby thumbs, all crushed and shaken down by the hooves of ten thousand beastmen. The rafts and stacks of logs were gone – either taken by the beastmen or fallen into the river and washed away. For as far as the eye could see in every direction the muddy snow was covered by their heavy black prints. It looked like a parchment written over and over with letters by some mad author who couldn't stop his hand.

'They've been and gone,' said Kat, staring around bleakly.

'Aye, and only hours ago, by the smell of it,' said Rodi, spitting.

'Snorri thinks they could have waited,' said Snorri.

'There's our boat,' grunted Gotrek, nodding down the river.

Felix followed his gaze. Through the mist he could see a little riverboat sunk to its gunwales in the water just south of the timber camp. It had crashed into a big rock that rose from the side of the stream and shattered its prow. He wondered if the timber men had tried to escape in it, or if the beasts had made some ham-fisted attempt to pilot it. Whatever the case, it was beyond repair.

'Get back on the wagon,' said Gotrek. 'We won't be sailing.'

'Thank Grungni for that,' said Rodi with a shiver. 'Boats are for elves.'

SIXTEEN

THE TRAIL OF the herd was one of destruction and desolation. The road that paralleled the river was churned into a soup of mud and snow and the dung of ten thousand beastmen, and littered with abandoned wagons, mutilated corpses and half-eaten carcasses. The village of Leer was a shattered ghost town, its walls knocked flat and its buildings torn down, and entirely empty. There were a few corpses, but too few. Felix hoped they had fled into the woods, but he doubted it. More likely they had become the latest victims of the stone's mutating magic and had joined the herd, adding another few hundred to the shaman's endless train of followers.

He dreaded what would happen when the beastmen reached more civilised areas. He didn't see how anything could stop them, and as the wagon neared Ahlenhof after several days of hard, hurried travel, Felix feared the worst.

But when they came around the bend in the river and saw the town on the opposite bank, it appeared untouched. As they got closer, they saw why. The bridge that had spanned the Zufuhr had been demolished. Only the jagged stumps of the stone piers stuck up out of the water, all the rest had collapsed.

Hunching against the downpour of a cold, heavy rain, teams of labourers were hard at work fishing giant blocks of granite out of the freezing water and winching them up the banks to where foremen and engineers surveyed the damage on a promontory turned to a muddy hill by a million gouging hoof prints. A long line of carts and wagons and carriages that had come up the river road from Altdorf was stopped at the fallen span, and the drivers and passengers were milling about in the pouring rain, complaining to guardsmen from Ahlenhof and arguing amongst each other.

'What happened here?' Felix asked a young guard as they pulled up near the other wagons. 'Did the herd tear the bridge down?'

The guard shook his head. 'No,' he said wearily. 'The city did, for protection.' He pointed to the line of stopped traffic. 'If you want to cross to Ahlenhof, you'll have to go to the end of the queue. We've set up a ferry. Move along please.' It sounded like he'd been saying the same thing all day.

'We shall cross to Ahlenhof immediately, guardsman,' said Sir Teobalt, stepping down from the back of the wagon and limping forwards with his head high. 'I have news of greatest import for your mayor and for Emil von Kotzebue, your baron, concerning the herd.'

The guard blinked at the templar as if he'd sprouted from the ground, then bowed reflexively. 'Sorry, m'lord,' he said. 'Next ferry won't come for an hour.'

Teobalt pointed down to the bank of the river, where a long boat with eight oars was pulled up on the mud. 'Then I will take that,' he said.

The guard looked down at the boat, then hesitated. 'Er, I'll ask my captain.'

'At once, please,' said Teobalt.

Felix smiled as the guard scurried off. He didn't have much use for the noble classes as a rule, but they were handy to have around when one wanted to get things done in a hurry.

'Damned shame, isn't it?' said a halfling pushing a pie cart, nodding at the bridge. 'But it was the only way. Mined the pilings and blew it to pieces, they did. Fancy a hot pie?'

'Snorri doesn't want a pie,' said Snorri. 'Snorri wants a beer. He hasn't had a drink in a week.'

'Ah, you'll be wanting to speak to my darling wife then,' said the pie-seller. 'Hoy, Esme! These gentlemen would like a drink!'

A halfling woman further down the line waved to him and turned a wheelbarrow around, in the bed of which was an enormous barrel of ale. Gotrek, Rodi and Snorri licked their lips.

'And we was lucky,' said the halfling, leaning against his cart as he waited for his wife. 'For if the beasts had truly wanted the town, blowing up the bridge wouldn't have stopped them.'

'Why not?' asked Gotrek.

The halfling snorted. 'Well, they crossed the Talabec didn't they? Just jumped in and swam.'

Felix turned and looked at the wide, rushing river, more than a half-mile across here where the Zufuhr joined it. 'They swam the Talabec?' he said, unbelieving.

'Aye,' said the halfling. 'Or most of them did at any rate. Went across in a big clump, all clinging to each other, like. A lot of them still drowned. Hundreds, I hear. Swept away. Still, enough made it ashore to wipe Brasthof off the map. Trod it flat and kept on south like they was following a star.' He shivered. 'They say Brasthof's not there no more. Just... gone.'

Felix grimaced at the thought, but before he could ask the halfling any more questions, the guard returned with his captain, a round-faced, round-bodied fellow with a pointed beard and a nervous smile.

'Ah, m'lord,' he said, bowing to Sir Teobalt. 'Nesselbaum says you want to borrow our boat.'

'I wish to report to your mayor and your lord something of grave import concerning the beastman herd.'

'Thank you, m'lord,' said the captain. 'But a messenger was sent to Baron von Kotzebue yesterday, informing him of their passage.'

'It is not of their passage that I wish to inform him,' said Sir Teobalt, going a bit red in the face. 'He must hear of the threat the monsters pose, and of the danger involved in facing them. Is the baron on his way?'

'Er, no, m'lord,' said the captain. 'The mayor sent another messenger after the first telling him it wasn't necessary.'

'What?' The templar's eyes blazed. 'For what reason, in Sigmar's name?'

'Well, m'lord,' said the captain, shrinking back uneasily. 'They swam the river into Talabecland late last night. So they were no longer a threat to us.'

Felix stared, alarmed, as the veins bulged in Sir Teobalt's forehead and neck. He was afraid the old templar's heart was going to explode with fury.

'No longer a threat!' bellowed Sir Teobalt. 'Listen to me, you small-minded provincial buffoon. Has the late war taught you nothing? The Empire is strong only when it stands together! Had Middenland helped Ostland from the first, the invaders would have been stopped before they began!' He tugged off his riding gloves angrily, and Felix was afraid he was going to slap the fat captain with them, but after a moment he collected himself and took a deep breath.

'The leader of the beasts,' he said, speaking as one would speak to a small child, 'means to unleash a magic upon the Empire that will turn half of its citizens into beastmen and set them raging upon their neighbours. The spell will not stop at provincial borders. It will not respect the boundaries of any lord's land. It will touch anyone living under the shadow of the Empire's forests, be they in Talabecland, Reikland, Hochland, Middenland or anywhere else. Do you understand me?'

The captain's mouth opened and closed several times, but nothing came out.

'Now,' said the templar, 'you shall give this message to your mayor and tell him that he will send a third rider after the first two, and respectfully request Baron von Kotzebue come to the aid of his Talabecland neighbours before he and all his vassals start sprouting horns and hooves.'

'Ah... aye, m'lord,' said the captain, bowing convulsively. 'Right away, m'lord. But...' he hesitated, afraid to provoke the old knight's wrath any further.

'But?' said Teobalt, dangerously.

'But a military force must have permission from the ruling lord before entering his lands, m'lord. Baron von Kotzebue commands four thousand men. Talabecland would see it as an invasion. An invitation would have to be sent, and the baron surely wouldn't move his army before he had it.'

Sir Teobalt fought to control his temper. 'Then your messenger shall tell the baron that you have such an invitation already.'

'You ask us to lie to the baron?' said the captain, white as a sheet.

'It will not be a lie,' said the old knight. 'For you will this moment transport me and my companions across the river to Talabecland, so that I may speak to the lord there and procure the invitation you require.'

The captain hesitated, practically vibrating with fear at being the instrument that would carry a falsehood to his liege, but finally he bowed to Sir Teobalt. 'Very good, m'lord,' he said. 'I will find the oarsmen and have the boat prepared for you momentarily.' And with that he scurried off towards the riverbank, shouting for his subordinates.

Sir Teobalt let out a long sigh and sagged against the wagon, exhausted from his anger.

Rodi chuckled. 'That was telling him,' he said.

'Aye,' said Gotrek.

Felix put a hand on the knight's shoulder. 'Are you all right, sir?'

'I am fine, thank you, Herr Jaeger,' said Teobalt. 'I only hope I did some good. The message may yet fall foul of fools.'

Felix nodded and looked around. The halfling and his wife – who had come up during Teobalt's tirade – were staring open-mouthed at them all.

'Pardon, your worships,' said the pie-seller. 'Was all that true that you said just now? About everybody turning into beasts and killing each other?'

Felix hesitated and looked at the others. He could see the same thought in all their eyes. If this news were to spread there would be a terrible panic, and the halfling couple were just the ones to spread it, taking food, drink and gossip up and down the line of wagons, which would then travel to the ends of the Empire. It was a recipe for riot and rampage.

Gotrek fixed Felix with his single eye and gave him an almost imperceptible shake of the head.

'Nah. Not a word of it,' said Felix. 'Just something to get old Kotzebue moving a little faster.' He leaned in with what he hoped was a conspiratorial smile. 'Though don't tell the captain that. It'll spoil everything.'

The halfling and his wife grinned with relief.

'Not a word, squire,' said the little man. 'I know when to keep mum.'

'Thank you, sir.' said Felix, and then just to seal the deal, 'A pie and a pint all around while we wait for our boat.'

'It would be our pleasure, sir,' said the halfling.

THE MAYOR OF Esselfurt, the village almost directly across the Talabec from Ahlenhof, listened patiently as Sir Teobalt explained it all again. He was a big man, with a barrel chest, a booming voice and a chain of office around his neck that probably weighed more than Karaghul.

Felix almost dozed off in the middle of it. Esselfurt's council hall was warmed by a roaring fire, and he was basking in it. The crossing of the Talabec in a small boat had not been a pleasant experience. The battering wind had cuffed water off the waves and sprayed it in their faces. Felix, Kat and Sir Teobalt had hunched under their cloaks in the back of the boat, cold, wet and miserable, while Gotrek, Snorri and Rodi spent their time leaning over the side, giving their recently consumed pie and beer to the waves.

Now all was warmth and peace and the smell of wet wool drying by the fire – that is until Teobalt finished his tale and the mayor pounded the table he stood behind with a meaty fist, snapping Felix out of his nap.

'By Sigmar, Sir Teobalt,' he said. 'That's bad. A bad business. And Esselfurt stands behind you in your effort to defeat this terrible threat to our beloved Empire.'

'I thank you, Mayor Dindorf,' said the templar, relieved. 'Then you will send to your lord, and ask him to bring troops to face the herd before Hexensnacht?'

'Word was sent last night when the beasts crossed the Talabec, m'lord,' said Mayor Dindorf. 'And I will send messengers with this new information. But, er…'

'Is there a difficulty?' asked Sir Teobalt dangerously, as Dindorf faltered.

'Well, you see,' said the mayor, 'I'm not sure who will come. Or how soon.'

'I don't understand,' said the templar, his face clouding. 'Who would come but your lord?'

The mayor scratched the back of his head. 'Well, it's like this, m'lord. Count Feuerbach, the Elector of Talabecland is our liege here, but he hasn't returned from the fighting in the north. It is rumoured he might be dead. Most of the lords who would answer in his place are away in Talabheim, petitioning Countess Krieglitz-Untern to be his successor.'

'So you have sent to them there?' Sir Teobalt's shoulders sagged. 'Talabheim is days away. They will never return in time.'

'Word has also been sent to their castles, my lord,' said the mayor. 'But, well, there is no one at them but their sons and wives. I don't know who of them will answer.'

The templar sighed. 'Is there no one who can raise an army quickly?' he asked. 'We face the end of all things.'

'There is the Temple of Leopold in Priestlicheim,' said Mayor Dindorf, 'which trains warrior-priests. And the Monastery of the Tower of Vigilance further south. They're said to be a martial order, but they don't come out of the cloister much.'

Sir Teobalt nodded, though Felix could see that he was downhearted. 'Then I beg you, mayor, to send to them as well, and muster what militia you can from your people. Tell them to come to Brasthof. We will follow the herd's trail from there.'

'Aye, my lord,' said the mayor. 'I will do what I can.'

Felix wondered unhappily how much that might be.

SIR TEOBALT WAS torn between depression and fury as they made their way west along the south bank of the Talabec towards Brasthof in the driving rain, and it pained Felix to see it.

'Sigmar, I am sickened,' said the old knight, his eyes dull as he rode along on the horse that he had commandeered from Mayor Dindorf. He'd had to leave Machtig behind in Ahlenhof – the warhorse had been too big for the boat. 'These puffed-up popinjays fight over the holdings of Count Feuerbach like so many thieves, while the Empire is being lost behind their backs.' He sighed. 'Perhaps we deserve our fate. Though we have pushed back the hordes from the north there is still much wickedness abroad in the land. Perhaps it is right to wipe the slate clean and start again.'

Felix was more inclined to put it down to bad luck and human nature, but he didn't want to further upset the old templar with argument, so he said nothing.

As the pie-seller had said, there were huge shoals of dead beastmen floating in the river and washed up on the muddy banks all along the road to the village – Felix couldn't even have begun to count how many, but it was hundreds, not dozens – all bloated and grey from being long in the water, and stinking to the gushing clouds.

In Brasthof, however, there were no bodies. The town was Stangenschloss and Leer and the timber camp all over again – shattered and empty except for a few looters, with the same unnerving lack of corpses they had seen before – proof that there had been no slaughter, just the terrible magic of the stone, replacing those who had drowned with the changed.

It had been a small town – bigger than Bauholz, smaller than Leer – but like Leer it had been sorely damaged by the herd's passage. It looked as if the beastmen, frustrated because the stone's transformative power left them with no enemies to fight, had taken out their rage on the buildings instead. Little flattened cottages lay with their thatched roofs on top of them like scratchy blankets, stables and smithies torn apart, shops set on fire. Gaping holes had been smashed in the front of the one tavern. The few survivors sat among the ruins, weeping and calling out to loved ones who were no longer there, and likely no longer human.

The temple of Sigmar seemed to have seen special attention from the beasts. It had been daubed with faeces and all its symbols torn down and smashed. In front of it, Felix saw a corpse in the robes of a priest. Up close they could see that the man had died halfway through changing into a beastman. It looked as if he had stabbed himself in the neck to stop the transformation.

As they made their way around the piles of rubble, Gotrek stopped and held up a hand. Felix and the others paused, listening. From behind the temple came the clank and rattle of armour and heavy steps. Felix and Sir Teobalt drew their swords. Kat pulled her bow from her back. The slayers readied their weapons.

Then, around the corner crept four halberdiers in breastplates, morions and mustard-coloured uniforms slashed with burgundy. They stopped when they saw Teobalt's party and went on guard.

'Who are you?' asked the one in front. 'Scavengers?'

Sir Teobalt nudged his horse forwards a step. 'I am Sir Teobalt von Dreschler, templar of the Order of the Fiery Heart. I and my companions seek the doom of the beastmen.'

The men relaxed when they heard Teobalt speak, and the first one bowed. 'Soldiers of Lord Giselbert von Volgen, m'lord. You have knowledge of these beasts?'

'We have been following them for weeks,' said Teobalt.

'Then you had better come speak to our master.'

The soldiers led them out the other side of the village to a windmill around which about a hundred mustard-uniformed soldiers stood at ease while a hard-faced, beardless young lord in a suit of fluted plate armour sat upon a barded warhorse and spoke to a huddled collection of villagers who stood beside him. The lord had a handful of other knights with him, and they hemmed in the villagers on all sides. A tall, powerfully built captain of halberdiers held the reins of the lord's horse.

Felix was heartened to see so many uniformed men. It wasn't an army, but after the excuses and disappointments at Ahlenhof and Esselfurt, to find a band of fighting men of any size on the trail of the beastmen was a welcome surprise.

'Damn it, Thiessen,' the square-jawed young lord was saying as Felix and the others approached. 'Make them stop blubbing and talk sense. I don't understand a word they're saying.'

'Aye, lord,' said the big captain, then turned to the villagers. 'Come now,' he said kindly. 'We won't get it straight if you keep weeping. Take a breath and tell it again.'

'They changed, I tell you!' wailed a woman dressed only in a muddied shift. 'Before my eyes they changed. My husband, my son, my... my beautiful little Minna. Horns and hooves and teeth! They... they turned on me. My Minna bit me!' She burst out in fresh tears.

'It is true, my lord,' said an older man in torn clothes that had once been of fashionable cut. 'The whole town became beasts. Blue lightning flashed and they changed, then attacked all they had loved.'

The young lord stared down at the man, a flat look on his cold face. He turned to his knights, obviously annoyed. 'It must be nonsense,' he said. 'They are lying. It's not possible.'

'It is possible, my lord,' said Sir Teobalt, as the soldiers led them close. 'And they do not lie. I have seen the evidence of it with my own eyes.'

The young lord looked up at him with angry eyes as his knights turned their heads to stare. 'Who interrupts?'

Seeing him full-on at last, Felix guessed he might be twenty-two, and with the look of a young man with something to prove.

The soldier who had brought Teobalt and the rest saluted. 'My lord, this is Sir Teobalt von Dreschler, a templar, and his companions. They have been on the trail of the beasts for weeks.' He turned to Teobalt and bowed. 'My master, sir. Lord Giselbert von Volgen, heir to these lands.'

Von Volgen's face relaxed somewhat when he heard Sir Teobalt's title, and he inclined his head respectfully. 'Well met, templar,' he said. 'So this madness they speak of is true?'

'It is, my lord,' said Sir Teobalt. 'And there is worse.'

And so the old knight began to tell it all again, to fresh horror and shock, but before he had got very far, more of von Volgen's soldiers ran towards the windmill from the town.

'My lord,' called one. 'A column approaches! Fifty men!'

The soldiers by the mill straightened and looked to their weapons.

Von Volgen wheeled around. 'Who is it?' he barked. 'Friend or foe?'

'It is your cousin, my lord,' said the soldier. 'Lord Oktaf Plaschke-Miesner, come from Zeder.'

Von Volgen's face twisted into a cold sneer. 'Foe then,' he said.

As those by the windmill watched, a double file of knights rode out of the village with a column of spearmen at their back. Leading them was an exquisite vision in red, black and gold. He rode a midnight horse with gold trappings, and was dressed head to foot in red garments of the finest quality, over which he wore a gleaming golden breastplate that looked like it belonged on the wall of a prince's dining hall rather than upon the torso of a fighting soldier. His red doublet and puffed velvet breeches were slashed with cloth of gold, and he wore a yellow feather in a broad black hat.

When he saw von Volgen, he spurred his horse to the mill, his eyes flashing.

'What is this, cousin!' he cried, drawing up. 'Have you forgotten what side of Priestlicheim Brasthof lies on?' His voice was high and clear and matched his overly refined features and long blond hair perfectly. If he hadn't been horribly plagued with spots, he would have been as beautiful as a girl. Felix guessed him to be seventeen – possibly sixteen.

Von Volgen looked the youth up and down contemptuously. 'I do not ride for the house of Volgen, Oktaf,' he said, 'but for Count Feuerbach. I do my duty.'

'It is your duty to invade my lands?' said Plaschke-Miesner.

'It is my duty, as it is yours, to protect the lands of our liege,' said von Volgen. 'Had you been doing your duty, I would not be here.'

'Am I not here?' said Plaschke-Miesner, putting a beringed hand to his breastplate.

'Aye,' said von Volgen. 'An hour after me, when Zeder is half as far as Volgen. But then,' he added with a sneer, 'you weren't coming from Zeder, were you? How long is the ride from Suderberg, cousin?'

Plaschke-Miesner snarled and drew his sword at that, crying, 'Longer, it seems, than the one from Count Feuerbach's grave!'

'You dare, you dog?'

Von Volgen's blade sang from its scabbard as, all around them, knights and soldiers from both sides rushed forwards shouting, 'My lords! My lords!' and Felix's head spun with all the names.

He felt like he'd come in during the middle of a performance.

SEVENTEEN

Felix, Kat, Teobalt and the slayers stepped back as horses reared and soldiers and knights called out for calm. Von Volgen and Plaschke-Miesner were having none of it.

'Leave off, curse you,' called Plaschke-Miesner, waving his men back with a gold-hilted sword. 'He insults me on my own lands! I will have his blood.'

'Away,' roared von Volgen. 'I will not have my loyalty questioned!'

Suddenly Sir Teobalt pushed forwards, his face red with fury. 'My lords, there is no time for this! The threat of the beastmen–'

'Stay back, templar,' said von Volgen. 'This is a matter of honour.'

'It is indeed a matter of honour!' cried Teobalt. 'And you both dishonour your Empire and your names by–'

A sidestepping horse knocked him back. Felix and Kat jumped to catch him before he hit the cobblestones.

'Are you all right, Sir Teobalt?' asked Felix.

'Insolent little fighting cocks,' rasped the templar. He could hardly catch his breath.

Felix and Kat helped him away from the whirlwind that swept around the two nobles. Gotrek was growling under his breath as they passed him.

'Do you deny that you have come from Middenland, then?' called von Volgen, trying to control his plunging horse. 'Do you deny that you mean to marry a von Kotzebue and give your lands to the Middenlanders?'

'Love knows no borders, cousin,' shouted Plaschke-Miesner in return. 'Do you deny that your father is fitting himself for Feuerbach's mantle before it is certain that he is dead?'

'We only protect his lands in his absence,' said von Volgen. 'As we have for generations!'

'Liar,' shrilled Plaschke-Miesner, swiping wildly at von Volgen.

'Traitor!' bellowed von Volgen, slashing back.

'Enough!' roared Gotrek and, shoving forwards through the press of horses and men, he raised his axe then slammed it down between the two lords' horses with such force that it shook the ground and buried itself up to the heel in the hard-packed earth.

'If you want to tear each other to pieces,' said the Slayer into the sudden silence, 'wait until Witching Night, when you can do it with horns and hooves. Now stop this manling foolishness and listen to the templar or I'll give you a real fight!'

The knights and soldiers erupted in outrage at this.

'Kill the dwarf!' cried one. 'He threatens our lord!'

'Arrest them all!' said another.

'You shall hang for this, villain!' said a third.

'Come and try it,' growled the Slayer, pulling his axe from the earth in a spray of pebbles.

'And try me as well,' said Rodi, standing at Gotrek's shoulder.

'And Snorri too,' said Snorri.

Felix groaned. The slayers were going to end up killing the people they needed most. He stepped forwards, raising his arms and his voice.

'Friends! Don't do this! We must all save our strength to fight the beastmen.'

'Stand aside, vagabond,' said the burly captain. 'Our lords have been threatened.'

'Your *lands* are threatened!' cried Felix, feeling some of Sir Teobalt's righteous rage infecting him. 'The beastmen will take everything! Your homes, your families, your souls! Don't you understand? If you do not put aside your differences and unite now, you will have nothing left to fight over! We will all become beastmen! There will be no Middenland, no Talabecland, no lands for you to inherit – just one great forest where beasts who were once men fight each other over rocks and dirt and scraps of meat.'

The knights and soldiers started to shout him down, but both von Volgen and Plaschke-Miesner waved for silence.

'No Talabecland?' said von Volgen. 'There will always be a Talabecland.'

'And what do you mean, "we will all become beasts"?' said Plaschke-Miesner.

Sir Teobalt stepped forwards again. 'The beast-shaman who leads this mighty herd goes south to perform a vile ceremony that is meant to turn all men who dwell within the shadows of the Empire's forests into beastmen. If he succeeds, all of the north will be affected, from Middenland to Ostermark, and you can be sure that great herd of changed men will not stay in the forests. They will come south, into Wissenland, Averland and the Reik. No part of the Empire will be untouched.'

The two lords and their retinues stared, dumbstruck. Someone at the back giggled.

'But... but surely it's impossible,' said von Volgen.

'Aye!' said Plaschke-Miesner. 'A fairy tale. No beast of the forest ever had such power. This "shaman" of yours won't succeed.'

Sir Teobalt nodded gravely. 'Perhaps not. But will you allow him to try?' He swung his arm to encompass the ruins of Brasthof. 'Think wisely, my lords. For this is what awaits all of the Empire if he succeeds.'

The two lords hesitated upon their horses for a long moment, alternately looking around at the devastation and glaring at each other.

Finally von Volgen snorted and swung off his horse. 'Thiessen, find a hovel in this wreckage that still has some furniture and make it fit for company.' He turned to a knight. 'Albrecht, be so kind as to invite our cousin Oktaf to join me with his advisors for a discussion of the situation.'

Plaschke-Miesner rolled his eyes and turned to one of his knights. 'Creuzfeldt,' he said. 'Please inform our cousin's emissary that we accept his invitation and will be delighted to attend.' He shot a look at Teobalt. 'And ask the templar and his odd sorts if they will join us as well, since they seem to know so much of the matter.'

Felix and Teobalt and Kat let out long-held breaths. The slayers just grunted.

As they settled down on some nearby steps to wait for a meeting place to be prepared, Felix saw an old man in long dirty grey robes watching everything from the far side of the market square, but more particularly watching Gotrek.

Felix was about to say something to the Slayer, but just then the old man seemed to feel him watching and turned. For the briefest second, Felix felt their eyes meet, and he was jolted by the intensity of his stare. Then the man ducked back around the corner and the feeling faded.

HALF AN HOUR later everyone gathered around a long table in the tavern with the demolished front, von Volgen and four of his knights sitting on one side, Plaschke-Miesner and four of his knights sitting on the other, Gotrek, Felix and Sir Teobalt taking up the ends. Kat, Rodi and Snorri had declined to be there so that they could scavenge for food. Felix wished he had gone with them. Picking his way through unstable buildings searching for week-old meat would have been infinitely preferable to listening to the two young lords snipe at each other and protest every suggestion just for the sake of protesting.

The meeting was nearly over as soon as it began. Sir Teobalt started it by recounting their journey so far, and when he told of asking that Emil von Kotzebue and his army come aid in the fighting of the beastmen, Lord von Volgen jumped from his seat.

'By Sigmar, it is a plot after all!' he cried, hammering the table with his fist. 'These beastmen are a mere excuse to allow that damned Middenlander to cross the river while we are undermanned! I'll warrant he stirred up the beasts just for this.'

Sir Teobalt controlled his temper with an effort. 'Baron von Kotzebue would not be coming at all had I not invited him. Indeed, if we are unfortunate, he still may not come. But you are thinking only of yourself again, my lord. Can you not understand that we fight for the survival of the Empire itself?'

'Aye, with von Kotzebue as Elector Count of Talabecland, no doubt,' snarled von Volgen.

'You want the title for yourself perhaps?' sneered Plaschke-Miesner, throwing his blond hair back from his face.

Von Volgen was about to retort when Gotrek cleared his throat and both young men fell silent.

'It is a matter of numbers,' said Teobalt. 'Not politics.' He held up his fingers. 'The beastmen herd numbers between five and ten thousand. How many troops do you both command?'

'I can muster a thousand from Volgen within a day,' said von Volgen. 'Seasoned cavalry and spearmen just back from the war, as well as a few hundred militia.'

'I can bring seven hundred,' said Plaschke-Miesner. 'Swords, spears, handgunners, and my father's two Gunnery School cannons.'

'Then we are outnumbered by at least three to one,' said Sir Teobalt. 'It will not be enough. This is why we need von Kotzebue. He can bring four thousand men to the field.'

'It is too many,' growled von Volgen. 'We won't be able to fight him if he turns on us.' He glared at Plaschke-Miesner. 'Particularly not if he is joined by turncoats.'

'You have little choice,' said Sir Teobalt before young Oktaf could respond. 'Unless you know of some other lord who can muster the necessary troops by Hexensnacht.'

Von Volgen turned to his knights and they muttered amongst themselves, but none of them could think of anyone close enough who had enough men to make a difference, so at last, after more such convincing, the grim-faced young lord agreed that von Kotzebue's help was needed, and they were finally able to turn the discussion to where they would fight the beasts and how.

When Teobalt related what Ortwin had told him about the ceremony being performed in a stone circle atop a hill, one of Plaschke-Miesner's knights suggested that the herd must be heading for the Barren Hills, which was known to be littered with such remnants of the old religion.

Plaschke-Miesner was pleased to hear it. 'For it gets them out into the open where we can use our cavalry and artillery against them.'

'And my militia can rain a cloud of arrows down upon them,' said von Volgen.

The two lords agreed to set a combined force of scouts on the herd's trail while they gathered their forces and led them by road to the Monastery of the Tower of Vigilance, where the scouts would bring them word of the herd's final position. Then they would wait until von Kotzebue arrived with his army, at which point all would advance to do battle with the beastmen.

'And if the baron doesn't come?' asked von Volgen.

Plaschke-Miesner laughed musically. 'Oh, you want him to come now? There's a new tune.'

'If von Kotzebue fails to arrive,' said Sir Teobalt, 'then your fathers shall hail you as the heroes who saved the Empire with your brave sacrifice.'

Felix saw young Plaschke-Miesner pale at that, but von Volgen's chin raised, and there was a sudden fire in his eye.

'Of more concern than von Kotzebue's arrival, however,' said the old templar, 'is the stone that the beastmen carry. With it, they are nigh invincible, since all who charge against them are in danger of changing into beasts themselves, and turning on their fellows.'

Now von Volgen paled as well. 'How can we defend against such a thing? Should we summon priests? Shall I raise the brothers of the Temple of Leopold?'

'Can it be destroyed?' asked Plaschke-Miesner.

'We don't have to destroy it,' said Gotrek.

Everyone turned to him.

'What's this, herr Slayer?' asked Sir Teobalt, hopefully. 'You have some way to protect us? Some ancient dwarf rune of warding?'

Gotrek shook his head. 'The stone does nothing itself,' he said. 'Only when the shaman strikes it does the blue lightning flash. If the shaman dies, it is no longer a danger, and your armies may attack.'

The two lords looked at each other, frowning.

'But how can we kill the shaman without going to battle against the herd?' asked von Volgen.

Gotrek smiled a terrifying smile. 'Leave that to me,' he said.

And me, thought Felix with a resigned sigh. It was always the way.

'One moment,' said Plaschke-Miesner, licking his lips nervously. 'If this dwarf can render the stone harmless on his own, then what need is there to bring the herd to battle?'

He shrank back as everyone turned cold eyes on him.

'I will assume that it is out of concern for the lives of your men, rather than your own life that you ask this,' said Sir Teobalt stiffly. 'But there are several reasons.

First, stone or no, your land has been invaded by thousands of the vilest enemies of man, and left to their own devices, they will spread wrack and ruin amongst your people. Second, though the death of the shaman will take the stone out of the battle, it is still a thing of great and fell power and must be destroyed before another shaman rises, or its evil influence spreads. We cannot destroy the stone without first destroying the herd.'

The youth hung his head and thrust out his bottom lip. 'Very well,' he said. 'It was only a question.'

IN THE END it was decided that Gotrek, Rodi and Snorri would join von Volgen's and Plaschke-Miesner's scouts, and once the scouts found the beastmen's location, the three slayers would – no one was really certain how – infiltrate their camp and kill the shaman. Once this was done, the scouts would report back to the armies and the battle could commence.

Of course, where Gotrek went, Felix must follow, so he was going, and when Kat heard this, she said she wouldn't be left behind, so she was joining them as well.

Only Sir Teobalt was not coming. Instead he would be travelling with von Volgen and Plaschke-Miesner and their armies as military advisor. Felix was glad to hear the old man would be looking after them, for if the rivals' command of tactics was anything like their command of tact, the battle might go very poorly indeed.

Of course, if von Kotzebue's four thousand troops didn't show up, it would go even worse.

THE SCOUTS ASSEMBLED before dawn the next day – four from von Volgen's force, and four from

Plaschke-Miesner's – with Felix, Kat and the slayers yawning sleepily among them. Two of the lords' men held swift ponies, which they would use to bring messages to their masters once they had discovered the herd's position.

As they started south on their way out of town, a hunched silhouette stepped out of the swirling grey fog and approached them, bobbing its head submissively.

'Greetings, my masters, greetings,' it said in a high, wavery voice. 'I hear you go to the Barren Hills.'

The party stopped and looked around. Felix frowned. It was the old man in the dirty grey robes who he had seen watching them so intently the day before, though he couldn't imagine why he had earlier thought him sinister and suspicious. This morning he only looked harmless and slightly batty.

Gotrek, however, didn't seem to agree. 'Who are you?' he growled, reaching for his axe.

The old man shied back, cowering behind his hands. 'Please, your worships,' he wailed in a trembling voice. 'I mean you no harm! Please don't kill me!'

'Who are you?' repeated Gotrek, as cold as before.

'Only Hans the hermit, my masters,' said the old man. 'Who deals in rags, bones and trinkets.'

Felix stepped back and covered his nose as the man sidled closer. He certainly smelled like a scavenger. Kat waved her hand in front of her face and edged upwind.

'And what d'ye know about where we're going?' asked Plaschke-Miesner's sergeant of scouts, a lean, clean-shaven man named Huntzinger.

The hermit tittered. 'Soldiers talk, my master. Soldiers talk. I heard you go to fight the beasts that brought ruin to Brasthof.'

'What's that to you?' asked Felke, a ginger-moustached tough who was von Volgen's scout sergeant.

'Glad tidings is what it is!' cried the hermit, bobbing his head again. 'I hate them beasties. I want 'em dead. If you go to kill 'em, I want to help.'

The scouts guffawed at this, and Felke grinned.

'And what can you do, y'old bag of bones? Are ye hiding a sword under those rags?'

The hermit shrieked as if that was the best jest he'd ever heard. 'Oh no, your worship, old Hans can't fight,' he said, slapping his matchstick knees. 'But he does know the Barren Hills, and for a few coins, he would be pleased to serve your worships as a guide.'

Felke rolled his eyes. 'Ah, now we come to the real issue. A few coins.'

Huntzinger sneered. 'What need have we of a guide? We're all scouts here, old fool.'

'And the trail's as wide as a temple and straight as a pike,' added Felke. 'Be off with you, beggar.'

He turned and motioned his men forwards, and the party started off again. But the ancient was not to be denied. He stumbled after them, bleating piteously.

'But, my masters, please!' he cried. 'I know the hills. I know their dangers. I can keep you safe!'

Gotrek turned at this, though he did not slow. 'What dangers are these, old man?'

'Oh, herr dwarf,' chuckled the hermit, hobbling along beside him. 'The hills are a cursed place, withered by Morrslieb's glance, and filled with all manner of barrows and circles and stones of ancient and evil power. Why, a single mis-step, a wrong turn, and one might find oneself falling into an old tomb, trapped forever with nothing but dusty old skelingtons for company.

But with me to guide you, naught will befall you. Oh yes, old Hans will see you right, so he will.'

'And how do you know so much about it?' asked Rodi, sounding as if he didn't believe a word of it.

The hermit giggled. 'Why, the hills is where I find all my things. The trinkets and bits that I sell to the city men. I know them barrows like I know my own fingers and toes.'

'A grave robber,' spat Gotrek. 'Robbing from your own ancestors.'

Felix smiled at the Slayer's disgust. There had been more than one occasion that the two of them could have been accused of the same thing, but maybe Gotrek put robbing someone else's ancestors in a different category from robbing one's own.

'A recoverer of beauty,' said the old man proudly. 'Gold, gems, wondrous swords. What need have the dead for these things? I rescue them from their selfish grasp and return them to those who can appreciate them.'

'Aye, aye,' said Huntzinger dismissively. 'A turnip is still a turnip, no matter what y'call it. On yer way.'

'Just a minute,' said Felke, pausing and turning back. 'What's the harm in it? I don't want t'be falling down no holes. If he knows the lay of the land down there, why not bring him along?'

'Because the smell of him'll spoil our food,' said Rodi.

But Huntzinger was fondling his chin, thinking about it. He looked towards the hermit. 'How much d'ye want, grandfather?'

Old Hans smiled, showing the stumps of half a dozen teeth. 'Only a few pennies, my masters. Ye'll be doing me a service, so you will, if y'chase them beasties away from my hunting grounds. I'll not be able to go about my business 'til they're gone.'

Gotrek crossed his arms over his broad chest and shook his head. 'I don't want him,' he said.

'Snorri doesn't want him either,' said Snorri. 'He smells like cheese.'

'We don't need him,' said Rodi. 'Dwarfs know all about holes and barrows.'

'Aye,' said Huntzinger. 'But we ain't all dwarfs, are we?' He fished in his belt pouch and tossed the old hermit a few coins. 'Come along, grandfather,' he said. 'But stay at the back until we get to the hills, far to the back.'

Hans caught the coins and bowed and giggled with excitement. 'Oh, thank you, my masters. Thank you. Old Hans won't steer you wrong, no he won't.'

Gotrek growled as the scouts started forwards again, clearly unhappy. Felix felt the same. The old hermit unnerved him somehow. He didn't want him along either, but they weren't the leaders of the party, so there was nothing they could say.

He took a last slantwise look at the filthy old man, who was kissing each of the coins as he pocketed them, then turned and followed the rest as they started into the gaping gash that the beastmen had cut into the forest.

THE SCOUTS WERE as amazed and unsettled by the scar as Felix and Kat had been, and cursed aloud when Snorri told them how it had been made. They were wary of it too, for though they could make good speed on it, it left them exposed, and they posted men far ahead and far behind, and wide to the east and west as well, to keep an eye all around.

And it was well that they did, for halfway through the first day, one of von Volgen's scouts, a bearded, buckskinned woodsman with a Hochland long-rifle slung across his back, trotted up from the rear, a grim look on his face.

'They ain't all before us,' he said, jerking his thumb over his shoulder. 'I spotted fifty a'coming from the west, and Gillich saw twenty or so on a southbound tack t'other side of Bekker Ridge, just to the east. Seems the local herds are joining their friends from up north.'

After that Kat volunteered to scout as well, and they posted her and the two rear scouts even further behind them so they would have plenty of warning to find cover before the beastmen arrived.

The first day, however, passed without incident, and they made camp well off the cut, just in case any beastmen came down it during the night.

Despite the constant patrolling of the scouts, Felix had felt the whole day that something was watching them – a squirmy tingle between his shoulder blades that made him constantly look behind him. This was a different feeling than he'd experienced when they had travelled north into the Drakwald. Then it had seemed as if the forest itself was watching them, like some half-slumbering nature spirit irritated by their intrusion into its domain. The feeling he had now was of some sinister entity that was following them through the forest but was not *of* the forest – but no matter how hard he had stared into the shadows or listened for footsteps, he had seen nothing and heard nothing.

The sensation only increased as the twilight faded and the night closed in around their camp. With the fire banked low and the blackness of the forest as close as a smothering blanket, he felt as if the presence was hovering directly over him, near enough to breathe in his ear.

Kat rolled over as he raised his head to look around once again.

'Do you hear something, Felix?' she asked.

'No,' he said. 'Just... just a feeling, that's all.'

She nodded. 'I feel it too.'

He lay down again and forced a smile. 'Maybe it's just old Hans's stench. I wish he'd sleep a little further away.'

Kat giggled. 'He's already out beyond the pickets.'

Felix edged his bedroll closer to hers until they were shoulder to shoulder. They grinned like guilty children. He felt better already.

'Goodnight, Kat,' he said.

'Goodnight, Felix.'

But despite her warm, soothing presence, when he finally slept, his dreams were full of formless terrors and half-heard whispers, and he awoke morose and out of sorts the next morning.

MORE THAN ONCE on the second day they had to move off the path in order to let small groups of beastmen pass them by. The slayers hated this, but bowed to the necessity of staying alive until they had the opportunity to try to kill the shaman – at least Gotrek and Rodi did. Snorri had some difficulty comprehending why they should wait.

'But Snorri wants to kill *these* beastmen,' he muttered again as they listened to the grunting and tramping of a passing band.

'These aren't important, Father Rustskull,' said Rodi. 'And besides, there's only thirty of them.'

'Snorri will share,' said Snorri.

'When we get to the big herd there won't be any need to share,' said Rodi. 'There will be hundreds for each of us.'

'But why can't Snorri fight these, and then fight those?'

Rodi rolled his eyes and gave up.

THE NEXT NIGHT, as before, they made camp a good distance from the path, and banked their fire before it got dark. Felix was still plagued with the feeling of being observed, but he was weary enough from their long days of marching that when he bundled down next to Kat, sleep took him relatively quickly and returned him to his unquiet dreams.

He was awakened some time later by urgent whispers. He blinked open his eyes as Kat, the slayers and the scouts all sat up and looked around.

In the dim light of embers, Felix saw one of Plaschke-Miesner's scouts kneeling next to Huntzinger, panting heavily. 'More than two hundred,' he was saying. 'And spread very wide.'

'How far away?' asked Huntzinger.

The scout swallowed uneasily. 'No more than a half-mile.'

The sergeant frowned. 'How did they come so close?'

The scout hung his head. 'I... I must have dozed.'

Huntzinger cuffed his ear. 'You damned fool!'

Everyone stood and started talking at once.

'Cover the fire!'

'We'll have to run for it.'

'Damn you, Skall, you've killed us all!'

At the far edge of the camp, Hans the hermit listened with wide eyes.

Felke stepped past Huntzinger and grabbed the scout's jerkin. 'Can we get to one side of them?'

Huntzinger pushed Felke away. 'Lay off. He's my man, I'll question him.'

'Then, do it, curse you!' shouted Felke. 'We've got to move.'

Huntzinger turned to the scout. 'Well? Can we get around them?'

The scout shook his head. 'They're spread too wide. Foragers on either side.'

'Can we run?' asked one of von Volgen's scouts.

The scout sergeant looked down at the slayers' short legs. 'I don't think so.'

'We'll hide in the trees,' said another.

'Dwarfs don't climb trees,' growled Gotrek.

'They will scent us anyway,' said Kat. 'It is too late.'

'Sigmar's blood,' said another scout. 'We're doomed.'

'Good,' said Rodi.

Gotrek shot a grim look at Snorri at this pronouncement and grunted savagely. Then he shrugged and started throwing logs on the sleeping fire, so that it began to burn bright again.

'What are you doing?' cried Huntzinger and Felke simultaneously.

'There's nothing to do but fight,' said Gotrek, turning to them. 'Face the woods with the fire behind you and be ready.'

The scouts babbled at this, terrified, but finally they followed the Slayer's example and lined up facing the direction the beasts were coming from with the rekindling fire at their back so that it wouldn't blind them, and waited.

Felix found himself shocked by the suddenness and the stupidity of it – not that he could say he was surprised. He had known the Slayer's doom was going to come sooner or later. He had just expected it to be grander and have more meaning. He had imagined that Gotrek would die fighting some eldritch monster from the dawn of time, not just perishing because of simple human error, which was all this was. Because of the scout's lapse, they could not outrun the beastmen, or outflank them. Instead, they were going to face them, and not even Gotrek, Snorri and Rodi could defeat two hundred beastmen. They would die here in the middle of nowhere, for the most foolish of reasons, with nothing accomplished – the shaman undefeated, the stone undestroyed, the Empire unsaved. It felt wrong. It wasn't fitting. Felix wouldn't have written it that way in a million years.

Off in the distance they could hear the beastmen coming – the heavy tread of their hooves, the crashing and lowing as they pushed through the brush.

A scout whimpered. The slayers growled low in their throats and readied their weapons. Felix looked around and saw that the hermit had vanished – no doubt trying to run.

Kat took Felix's hand and squeezed it. 'At least we won't have to see our friends turned into beasts,' she said. 'At least we won't see the end.'

Felix swallowed. It was small compensation.

EIGHTEEN

THE SOUNDS OF the approaching beastmen got louder. Kat took her hand from Felix's and fitted an arrow to her bow. Snorri chuckled happily. Rodi slapped himself in the face a few times and snorted like a bull. Gotrek ran his thumb along the edge of his axe, drawing blood. The scouts shifted nervously, eyes darting hither and thither.

Felix readied Karaghul, then paused and looked at Kat. She stared into the wood, anxious but unafraid, her sharp chin firm. On a sudden impulse, he caught her shoulder and pulled her to him, then kissed her hard. She was stiff with surprise for a brief moment, but then relaxed into him and returned the kiss in full.

For a moment, there was nothing in the world but the pleasure of holding her and tasting her and feeling her push against him, but then after a moment he heard Rodi's dirty chuckle and they broke off. A few of the scouts were staring at them.

Felix smiled at Kat, embarrassed. 'I... I just didn't want to leave that undone,' he said.

She grinned and nodded, not quite able to look at him. 'Aye. Good thinking.'

They turned back to the woods. Moving yellow lights flickered in the depths – the torches of the beastmen. The scouts murmured and shifted, watching for the first of them to appear.

'Steady,' said Sergeant Huntzinger. 'Wait for your targets. We'll take as many of them with us as we can.'

Now Felix could see horned shadows rippling across the trunks of trees, grotesquely stretched. They were almost within sight. The time had come. Time to fight and die, after all these years. Strangely, there was no fear, only a sudden, almost overwhelming melancholy. He wanted to weep for all the things he would miss.

A banshee wail split the night right above their heads, rising like a steam whistle, and an icy, unnatural wind swept through the camp, snuffing out the fire and throwing them into instant darkness. The scouts jumped and cried out, and Felix was afraid he had too. The eerie shriek made his hair stand on end. Kat mumbled a prayer to Rhya.

'What is that?' cried Sergeant Felke from somewhere to Felix's left.

Felix could see nothing. The woods were pitch-black. The light from the beastmen's torches had vanished as well, leaving not even the glow of embers behind, but Felix could hear them thrashing and howling in the distance. They seemed as scared as the men.

Felix didn't blame them. The ear-splitting wail continued rising – a sound like a soul being ripped asunder by daemons – and a dread presence filled the wood. Felix felt flensed by it – as if the bones had been sucked from his body, leaving him as limp as a dead jellyfish. He couldn't move, couldn't think, could only hunch there next to Kat, quivering and twitching and staring about as the noise went on and on.

After a moment a dim red light gave Felix back his sight – the glow of the runes on Gotrek's axe. The Slayer glared, uncowed, up into the trees, with Snorri and Rodi at his side, as the men trembled all around them. There was nothing to see but shadows and mist drifting through the branches.

Out in the darkness the herd was running. Felix could hear their screams and their hooves thundering past to the right and left of them, and he saw a few shadows flicker past, but strangely none of the beastmen came through the camp. Whatever the evil thing was that had snuffed their torches, they were terrified of it and would not come near it. It felt to Felix like he stood on a stone in the middle of a river and watched the waters split to his left and right.

Then a single beastman did run into the camp, bellowing and stumbling wildly as it crashed through the bracken. It ran directly at the leftmost scouts, but didn't seem to see them, for when they dived out of the way it didn't turn on them, only staggered off into the trees again, clutching its head and screaming as if it were being chased by the contents of its nightmares.

For a few more minutes the sounds of the beasts passing them by continued, while the shrieking echoed from the branches above them and the enervating terror pinned Felix and the scouts to the ground. But then, as the last heavy hoof beats diminished into the distance, the hideous wail trailed off and the feeling of dread dissipated into a sense of trembling relief.

The runes of Gotrek's axe dimmed as the others recovered themselves and muttered prayers to Sigmar.

'Get that fire lit,' said the sergeant.

Felix let out a shaky breath as one of the scouts fumbled with his flint and steel to rekindle the flames. 'What *was* that?' he asked.

Gotrek glared up into the branches of the trees above them, his one eye searching. 'Something vile.'

'But it protected us,' said Kat. 'It chased the beastmen away.'

'Protected us?' snorted Rodi. 'It robbed us of our doom.' He spat on the ground.

'Aye,' said Gotrek. 'Why?'

'Maybe it wanted the beastmen for itself,' said Snorri. 'Snorri thinks that's greedy.'

Felix doubted that was the reason, but he couldn't think of a better one.

Just then, a rustling at the edge of the camp made everyone turn and go on guard again. Old Hans the Hermit poked his head out from behind a tree, his eyes as big as eggs. 'Is it over, my masters?' he quavered.

Everyone grunted with disgust and relief and settled back down to their bedrolls as the scouts who were on duty headed back out into the woods to continue their patrols. Felix doubted, however, that anyone except the slayers got any sleep. Felix certainly didn't. The memory of the shrieking and the cold, evil presence was too fresh. He knew if he closed his eyes they would return.

THE NEXT DAY, the ground began to rise and break up into rolling hills and winding valleys, all covered in oak and elm, and there was less undergrowth. The herd's axe-hewn trail twisted through the lumpy terrain like the path of a snake, avoiding the largest trees, which must have been too much bother to cut down, and sticking to riverbeds and areas of new growth.

After noon, the trees too began to grow more sparse, and those that remained had turned twisted and strange. The elms, which in the morning had been straight and tall, were now stunted and sickly, while the great spreading oaks had become black, tangle-rooted monsters with deformed branches and trunks that bulged with growths like bark-covered goitres. The beastmen's path grew straighter then, as they had fewer trees to fell, and veered to the south-east, cutting across the grain of the rise and fall of the hills.

A few hours later the trees gave out entirely, and they came at last to the northern edge of the Barren Hills. Felix thought they could not have been more aptly named. The land stretched out in an endless sea of low, mist-swathed ridges, mangy with dead winter grass and leafless thorn bushes, and bare of trees but for an occasional wind-bent pine hunched upon a rocky crest, like an old witch in a tattered cloak surveying her domain.

No birds sang here, and Felix saw no tracks of animals in the patches of snow that hid in the shadowed valleys. Even the light that came through the grey clouds seemed thin and sickly, as if not even the sun could bear to look directly upon such dismal desolation. It seemed a blighted land, nearly as lifeless as the deserts of Khemri. At least the herd's trail was still clear. The tread of ten thousand hooves had churned up a wide swathe of the hills' dry, powdery earth, and it wound away towards the horizon for as far as the eye could see.

'Long ago it was a lovely place,' said Hans, looking wistfully out over the stark landscape. 'The Green Hills, men called them, all meadows and lakes and the like. But then old Morrslieb spat a nasty green gob down in the middle of it, and everything for leagues around twisted and died – never to recover. Too bad, too bad. All dead.' He giggled suddenly. 'Though that's good for my business, isn't it?'

'Morrslieb spat?' Felix asked, sceptical.

'Aye,' said the hermit. 'A great flaming gobbet. Straight out of the sky.' He made a gesture like an arrow falling to earth.

'You sound as if you saw it,' said Kat.

Hans tittered. 'Oh, dearie me, child. Do I look as old as that?'

Huntzinger shrugged, making a face. 'Might have been beautiful once,' he said. 'But it's ugly now.'

'At least there aren't any trees,' said Rodi, cheerily.

'And no cover either,' said Kat with a shiver.

Felix turned and saw that she was eyeing the vast space before her like a mouse peeking out from its hole. It occurred to him that, living from girlhood in the Drakwald, she might never have seen so open a place in her whole life. He reached out and squeezed her arm reassuringly as they started forwards again.

'Not to worry,' he said. 'They don't have any cover either. We'll see them from miles away.'

She gave him a grateful smile in return, and they followed the others, walking side by side.

But though he had done his best to reassure Kat, Felix was far from being at ease himself. He had hoped that once they left the forest, the itchy feeling of being watched would cease, and he would be able to relax again, but it failed to go away. Even more so than before he felt that malevolent eyes were upon him, watching his every step, but when he looked around, he still saw nothing. It was impossible that anyone was following them or spying on them. As Kat had said, there was nothing to hide behind, and yet every time he turned his head he felt as if someone had just ducked out of sight a second before. Nor was the lack of trees a relief from the hemmed-in feeling of the forest. What with the grim grey sameness of the bleak hills below and the dull charcoal sky like a lowering ceiling above, Felix felt crushed between two vast millstones, and he found himself hunching his shoulders like he was carrying a heavy burden.

THEY SAW THE smoke of the beastmen's camp on the afternoon of the next day. It looked at first like the smoke from the chimneys of a small city – hundreds of narrow grey ribbons rising above the low hills – and Felix fancied they might find some mundane town there, Barrensburg, perhaps, with a wall and a gate and tavern named after the local landmark – but he knew he would not. There were no towns in this terrible place.

They went more cautiously then, looking for scouts and hunting parties and taking advantage of what meagre cover they could find. The land here was littered with the burial mounds and standing stones of long-forgotten races – lumpy grass-covered barrows like tumours rising from the turf, and lichen-blotched menhirs sticking up like rotting teeth bursting from an abscess – and the scouting party did their best to keep in their shadows, despite the miasma of ancient menace that seemed to emanate from them.

At last there was only one more ridge, and they crept up it through the dry snow and brittle grass on their bellies until they reached the crest and could look down the other side into a slayer's dream come true.

A diamond-shaped valley lay below them, perhaps a mile long and a half-mile wide, and narrowing at each end between the swelling flanks of the rolling hills, and it was filled from end to end and side to side with beastmen. Felix swallowed and shrank back at the sight. When he had seen the herd before, the forest had hidden its true size. Here, spread across the valley floor, its numbers were staggering. There had to be nearly ten thousand of the beasts – one vast camp made up of hundreds of smaller camps, each with a bonfire and a grisly standard stuck into the ground to let the others know who held sway there.

'Snorri thinks Rodi Balkisson was right,' said Snorri. 'There are enough beastmen for everybody.'

'So many,' murmured Kat, staring wide-eyed.

'Aye,' said Rodi, unusually subdued. 'This will do.'

'A certain doom,' said Gotrek, his eye gleaming.

Felix had to agree. It would doom all of them, and more than likely all the troops that von Volgen, Plaschke-Miesner and von Kotzebue could bring against them as well. He hadn't seen so many beastmen in one place since he and Gotrek and Snorri had flown over the Chaos Wastes in the *Spirit of Grungni*. There were beastmen fighting, beastmen feasting and drinking around the fires, but mostly there were beastmen facing towards the middle of the valley and shaking their weapons and raising their voices in a guttural chant that sounded like the song of the end of the world.

Felix turned to see what was holding their attention.

Out of the centre of the vast herd rose a single low hill, long and steeply sloped on its sides like a whale's back rising from the sea. Upon it, at the place where a whale would spout its steam, jutted an ancient stone circle, its rough black menhirs weathered with age and capped with snow. It was to this that the beastmen had carried their sacred stone from the depths of the Drakwald. Indeed, they were bringing it to the circle even as Felix and the others watched.

The hill was aswarm with beastmen, all thronging around the huge herdstone as it crawled up its flanks, borne upon the backs of its chosen carriers. The scene looked to Felix like ants carrying a dead grasshopper up their mound to the opening of their hole, but the stone did not vanish when it reached the top of the hill. Instead, the beastmen carried it into the centre of the stone circle, and then, with nothing but brute force and sheer numbers, pushed it upright.

Felix prayed to Sigmar that the evil thing would slip from their grasp and shatter upon the menhirs of the ring, but that prayer went unanswered. In the space of ten minutes the beastmen had righted and secured the stone, and the whole valley erupted in a howl of triumph that Felix thought must have been heard in Altdorf. He shivered as the implications of his thoughtless exaggeration sank home. If the slayers and the three armies failed here, the beastmen's triumph would certainly be *felt* in Altdorf.

And it seemed inevitable that the men and dwarfs would fail. Even the slayers seemed to have no illusions about that.

'It will be a grand doom,' said Rodi. 'But...'

Gotrek cocked his one eye at him. 'But? What happened to "A doom is a doom is a doom", Balkisson?'

Rodi grunted morosely. 'You've infected me with your pride, Gurnisson. Because of you, I want my doom to mean something. And this…' He shrugged. 'We may kill many, but we will never reach the shaman. Not by fighting, at least, and I was never any good at sneaking.'

'Not even the best scout in the world could sneak through that,' said Kat. 'They are too close together. Even if they didn't see us, they would smell us.'

'Can we wait until they're asleep?' asked Felix.

'They will likely carouse all night,' said Kat.

'And the ones on the hill will never sleep,' said Gotrek. 'You can be certain of that.'

Felix looked again to the central hill. There was a camp within the camp there – Urslak Cripplehorn's true herd – more numerous and tightly packed than the rest of the herds at the gathering. Felix could see patrols of massive beastmen circling the camp and the base of the hill, and more standing guard on its slopes. At the top of the hill, still more danced around and within the stone circle, waving torches and weapons.

'We may win the first charge,' said Gotrek. 'But once the alarm is raised, they will all come.'

'Snorri thinks that's a good idea,' said Snorri.

'Aye, Nosebiter,' said Gotrek, nodding. 'We'll have our doom then, but the stone will stand.'

'What is the date?' asked Felix.

'The thirtieth of Vorhexen,' said Sergeant Felke.

Felix sighed and rested his chin on his crossed arms. 'We have three nights then, to find a way.'

The hermit giggled behind them. 'Oh, my masters, have y'forgotten about me so soon? Don't worry yourselves so. Old Hans knows a way. Of course he does.'

NINETEEN

THE PARTY TURNED to face the hermit, staring.

'What's this?' asked Gotrek.

'A way to the hill!' Hans cackled. 'Without a beastman the wiser!'

'How?' asked Rodi, looking curious in spite of himself.

The old man cackled again and looked sly. 'Ye sons of earth may call me grave robber if you like, but if I weren't, you'd be in a pickle, eh? I know the barrows around these parts like the back of my hand, and the tunnels that link 'em too.'

'Tunnels,' said Gotrek, interested at last.

'Aye,' said the hermit, lowering his voice to a whisper. 'The old kings, they built not just for the dead, but for the living.' He turned and pointed down the hill, where old mounds snaked through the dead valleys like veins under the skin. 'Each barrow was an escape, and a place to hide in times of trouble. All led through secret doors to the old keep, built around yon sacred circle.' He turned back and nodded in the direction of the hill with the stone circle. 'Tarnhalt's Crown they called it then. Named for the last king that lived there.' He giggled again. 'His walls are fallen now, as do all works of men, the stones taken by folk for other things – all but the ring stones, which none dared touch – but the tunnels and cellars of the keep still sit under the hill. And there is a way out to the surface. A hidden way, not ten paces from the circle.'

The slayers had gathered around the old man now, drawn by his words, their eyes eager.

'Show us the way, hermit,' said Rodi.

'Bring Snorri to the beastmen,' said Snorri.

'Aye, grave robber,' said Gotrek. 'Lead us to these tunnels.'

The old man's eyes narrowed with sudden suspicion. 'You will remove the beasts, yes? You'll smash their stone. You won't rob old Hans of his treasures, will you?'

Rodi sneered. 'Do you think we've come all this way to steal from *you*?'

'What do dwarfs care for human treasures?' said Gotrek. 'Your pathetic hoard is safe from us.'

Hans hesitated a moment, stroking his stringy white beard, but at last nodded. 'Very well, I will risk it. The beasts must go.' He turned and started down the hill at a sprightly pace that belied his age, lifting the skirts of his robe as he went. 'Follow me! Follow me!'

Felix and Kat looked to Gotrek as the scouts muttered amongst themselves.

The Slayer shrugged. 'It's worth a try.'

Huntzinger and Felke looked less than happy, but finally shrugged, and the party turned and followed the old hermit as he led them down the slope and along the base of the hills until he came to an overgrown old barrow mound that stuck out from one like a blunt finger. Dry old bracken covered the front of the tomb, but it wasn't growing from the earth. It had been placed there. The old hermit pulled it all aside and revealed a small black hole behind it, low to the ground, and so narrow Felix wasn't sure the slayers would be able to get their wide shoulders through it.

'There, your worships,' he said gleefully. 'There is the hole that will lead you to the hill. Now, if you can give poor Hans a pen and paper, he will draw you a map of the way.'

Gotrek snorted. 'Dwarfs need no maps for tunnels, grave robber. We will find the way.'

'No no no!' said Hans, his eyes suddenly wide with alarm. 'A map is best, my masters. You don't want to go where you shouldn't.'

Everyone paused at that, and Gotrek gave him a dead-eyed stare.

'What's this?' he asked.

'What are you hiding there?' asked Sergeant Felke.

'Are there ghosts?' asked Huntzinger, biting his lip.

'Traps?' asked Felix.

The old man shrank back, eyes darting from one to the other. 'No no! No traps, my masters. Not if you go where I say. I... I only fear that you... that you will try to take my things. I have protected them, and they–'

'They're trapped,' said Felix.

'Lead us, then,' said Gotrek.

'Aye,' said Rodi. 'That's the best plan. That way we'll stay out of mischief, and so will you.'

'No!' said the old man, suddenly frantic. 'I cannot! I have tarried with you long enough. I must continue my work! I must go!'

'I thought the beasts were keeping you from your work,' said Felix, getting more suspicious by the second.

'There are other barrows,' said Hans. 'I work all over these hills.'

'It'll wait,' said Gotrek. 'You're staying.'

The others encircled the old man. He shrunk away from them, trembling and shielding his head, and for the briefest second, Felix thought he saw a look of pure hatred flash in his eyes, but it was gone before he could be sure, and then Hans was smiling meekly again.

'Very well, your worships,' he bleated. 'I will stay. I will stay.'

WITH OLD HANS in tow, the party scouted the valleys around the beastmen's gathering place until they found a suitable site to stage the armies of the three nobles when, and if, they arrived. Then von Volgen's and Plaschke-Miesner's messengers readied their horses for their run back to their masters at the Monastery of the Tower of Vigilance so that they could tell them that the slayers had found a way to reach the shaman and kill him, and that it would be safe to engage the herd.

'We will wait as long as possible,' Gotrek said. 'But if the armies are not here by sunset on Hexensnacht's eve, we start without them.'

Felke held up the hunter's horn he had slung around his neck. 'I will blow a blast when the shaman is killed,' he said. 'That will be their signal.'

Felix stepped forwards. 'And be sure to tell them not to attack before they hear it, or…' He shivered, remembering Ortwin's face changing before him. 'Or it may not go well.'

The messengers nodded, then mounted their horses and galloped away across the bare hills. At least, thought Felix, they will make good speed on such open ground, and with luck, the armies will make good speed back. The question was, would it be only von Volgen and Plaschke-Miesner, or would von Kotzebue and his four thousand men arrive with them?

'Right,' said Huntzinger, turning away. 'Now to find a place to lay low until the time comes.'

'The hermit's barrow,' said Gotrek without hesitation.

Huntzinger stared at him. So did Felke. Their men murmured uneasily.

'You can't be serious,' they said in unison.

Gotrek scowled. 'I am. It's warm. It's out of the wind. It's close to the beasts' camp, and they'll never find us there. It's perfect.'

'But... but it's a tomb,' said Huntzinger. 'We can't stay in a tomb.'

'Why not?'

'The old kings,' Huntzinger continued. 'They don't like being disturbed. They'll wake up and kill us in our sleep.'

'Aye,' said Felke. 'I'll go in at the end, to get to the beasts, but I'll not make camp there. I'll not sleep there.'

Their men murmured in agreement.

Gotrek rolled his eyes. 'Are you more afraid of a pile of dusty old bones than of ten thousand beastmen?'

Huntzinger and Felke exchanged a glance, then looked back towards Gotrek.

'Aye,' said Huntzinger. 'We won't do it, and that's that.'

'There are some things a man won't do,' said Felke.

Gotrek snorted with disgust, then shrugged his massive shoulders and turned away. 'There are some things a coward won't do,' he said under his breath.

Rodi and Snorri nodded in agreement.

Felix glanced at Huntzinger and Felke, afraid they'd heard the Slayer. From the scowls on their faces, it appeared they had, but it also appeared that they didn't look prepared to do anything about it.

AFTER AN HOUR of searching, the scout captains found a deep gorge about a half-mile from the valley that held Tarnhalt's Crown, and announced that this was where they would make camp. The dwarfs' silence on the matter was eloquent, as was the fact that they laid out their bedrolls as far from the scouts' tents as possible. They didn't go so far, however, as to not take part in the protection of the camp, and stood their watches without complaint.

Felix kept his mouth shut too. As much as he understood the dwarfs' view that going underground would be the best way to keep out of the way of the beasts, he wouldn't have relished spending a long period of time in the burial chambers of some ancient king either. He had done that once before. It hadn't gone well.

The scouts didn't dare start a fire until after dark for fear that smoke rising above the hills would give away their position. This meant a long day of shivering and stamping their feet, trying to keep out of the steady, ceaseless wind, and glaring at the slayers, who paced around the camp bare-chested, seemingly as comfortable as if they were in a warm tavern.

For their part, Gotrek and Rodi were restless and irritable. They knew their doom was only a few valleys away, and it appeared to be testing their patience to wait for it. Only Snorri seemed at ease, following the other two slayers around and telling them stories about his days with Gotrek as if Gotrek wasn't the one the events had happened to. Felix saw the Slayer's shoulders hunch at each new tale, but he never snapped at Snorri, only nodded and grunted non-committally, his brow furrowed and his mouth set in a grim line.

Felix did his best to ignore all the tension, and sat in the shelter of a big boulder, updating his journal with shivering hands, and wondering if he would be able to decipher the shaky lines he had written when he reread them later. He wished he could have waited out the day bundled in a tent with Kat – a much warmer and more pleasant way to pass the time – but she was doing her duty with the rest of the scouts, patrolling on a wide perimeter and keeping a constant eye on the herd, so he hardly saw her.

After a meagre dinner cooked over the low fire, Felix did his turn at watching on the lip of the gorge, looking and listening for approaching beasts, and watching as Morrslieb chased Mannslieb up the sky and then passed it by, so close that the edges of the two moons seemed to almost touch, before racing on and leaving its bigger, more distant brother in the dust of stars.

At midnight, with Mannslieb directly above and Morrslieb already setting over the eastern hills, his time was done, and he picked his way back down into the gorge to the camp and shook Gotrek by the shoulder.

'Your turn, Gotrek,' he said.

The Slayer sat up, awake instantly, and looked around. Then he stood and grabbed his axe.

'Where is the hermit?' he asked.

Felix looked to where they had leashed the old man to a stunted tree to make sure he didn't slip away. The rope that had gone around his wrists lay on the ground, but of Hans himself there was no sign.

Felix cursed. How had the hermit escaped? He looked around. Sergeant Huntzinger was on watch, the same man who had cuffed his scout for letting the beasts creep up on them. He crossed to him as Gotrek stepped to the empty leash.

'You let the old hermit go,' said Felix. 'Were you asleep?'

'What's this?' said the sergeant, standing and turning. He cursed as well. 'How can it be? I looked at him just before you came down the slope. He was lying there, asleep.'

Their voices were waking the rest of the camp, and sleepy questions followed them as they crossed to Gotrek, who was looking down at the leash. The sergeant made the sign of the hammer, for the knots that had tied the rope around Hans's wrists were intact.

'Sorcery,' said Huntzinger.

A scrap of parchment was rolled up in the loops. Gotrek picked it up and unrolled it. It was a crudely drawn map, showing rooms and corridors, and done apparently in blood.

'Or the ropes weren't tight enough,' said Sergeant Felke, sneering as he joined them. 'Looks like you're just as lax as your men, Huntzinger.'

'I tied those ropes myself,' protested Sergeant Huntzinger. 'He could not have escaped them.'

'But he did,' said Gotrek.

Felix looked over the Slayer's shoulder at the map. 'It looks like he still wants us to go after the beasts.'

'Or walk into a trap,' said Rodi, joining them and looking too.

Felix swallowed. Was that it after all? Was Hans's whole reason for joining him as their guide just a ruse to trick them into entering some underground trap? Perhaps he wasn't a grave robber after all. Perhaps he preyed on grave robbers. Perhaps the gold and trinkets he sold were stolen from the bodies of his victims rather than the tombs of the old kings.

Gotrek handed the map to Felix and turned away. 'Spread out and look for him,' he said. 'But watch for beasts.'

Huntzinger and Felke looked affronted at this casual assumption of command, but only turned to their men and chose who would go and who would stay.

Felix, Kat, Gotrek, Rodi and the four chosen scouts spread out on different headings, leaving Snorri – who couldn't be trusted to remember what he was searching for – and the rest to guard the camp. It was a fruitless search. Felix staggered back after two hours, half-asleep and two-thirds frozen, with nothing to report. The others came in soon after him with the same report. Hans had vanished. He was not to be found.

'Probably gone to ground in another barrow,' said Kat.

'Will he try anything?' asked Huntzinger.

Rodi shrugged. 'What could an old man do?'

'He could lead the beasts down on us,' the sergeant replied.

Felix frowned. 'I don't know about that. He seemed genuinely angry with them. And he left the map. I think he truly wants us to drive them away, though I can't guess what else he might want.'

'Do we still use the map, then?' asked Felke.

'What choice do we have?' said Rodi. 'There is no other way to get to the shaman.'

'We use it,' said Gotrek. 'But not blindly.' He nodded to Rodi and Snorri. 'We will scout the tunnels tomorrow so that we find no surprises on the night.'

THE NEXT MORNING, Felix, Kat and the three slayers made their way back through the hills to the barrow that old Hans had shown them. As they approached it, Felix had the sudden irrational fear that they would find the hole into the crypt gone as if it never was, like some mysterious door in a hill in a fairy tale, but when they pulled away the bracken it was still there, an irregular black shadow in the face of the mound. Felix wasn't sure if he was relieved or not.

'I'll go first,' said Rodi.

'No, Snorri will,' said Snorri.

'I will,' said Gotrek, and stepped in front of them before they could stop him.

Felix didn't know how the Slayer was going to fit – his shoulders looked wider than the hole by a foot – but Gotrek didn't even hesitate. He knelt down, stuck his head and his axe arm in, then twisted and propelled himself through with his feet. A rattle and hiss of pebbles and dirt rained down after his passage and for a second Felix thought the opening was going to collapse, but then the rain eased up and Gotrek's voice echoed hollowly from within.

'It's safe.'

Snorri went next, widening the hole even more as he shoved through it, then Kat, who didn't even touch the sides.

'After you, Herr Jaeger,' said Rodi.

Felix took a breath, then knelt and crawled forwards. There was an awkward moment when his hands couldn't feel any floor and his legs were hemmed in by the sides of the hole, but then strong hands were pulling him out and setting him on his feet in utter darkness.

Felix stood and cracked his head on something above him. He hissed and hunched down, rubbing his crown.

There was a sharp scraping from nearby and then a torch kindled and glowed in Kat's hands, just in time to show Rodi crawling out of the hole like an ugly, crested mole.

'Ah,' said the young slayer as he picked himself up and dusted himself off. 'Nice to be underground again.'

'Aye,' said Gotrek.

Felix looked around. They were in a long, low chamber – so low in fact that he could not stand straight in it. It seemed to have been built by people of Kat's stature. The stone walls were carved with crude wolf's heads and skulls, as well as angular intertwining runes and symbols. Against the long walls were four stone biers, old bones in rotting, dusty clothes scattered upon them, but not a single piece of armour or weaponry or jewellery. If old Hans wasn't a grave robber, someone else certainly had been.

Felix turned to the back of the barrow, where Hans had said the entrance to the tunnels would be. His heart sank. There was nothing but a stone wall with a crumbling relief of a running wolf. He was about to curse Hans for misleading them when Rodi laughed.

'The old man calls that a secret door?' he said. 'A blind elf could find that.'

'Snorri thinks a dead elf could find it,' said Snorri.

Felix closed his mouth again, chagrined, and followed the others to the back wall, thanking Sigmar he hadn't spoken.

Gotrek reached out and pulled a stone from the wall that looked no different to Felix than any other stone, and reached into the hole that resulted. He pulled at something inside the hole, and there was a grating of iron on stone. Then he pushed at the wall with the running wolf on it with his other hand and a narrow door swung open, revealing blackness behind.

'Come on then,' said Rodi, shoving in first.

Gotrek and Snorri gave him dirty looks, then followed after, and the three of them set off into the darkness without hesitation. Felix and Kat hurried after them, looking around warily in the light of Kat's torch. The tunnel beyond the door was as low as the barrow, and nothing more than a raw hole in the rock and dirt, kept from collapse by heavy wooden beams and posts. It smelled of mould and damp earth and decay. Spider webs hung like shrouds from the ceiling and fluttered in a constant moaning breeze. Felix hunched his head and kept one hand out to tear them down before he walked into them.

After no more than ten paces, Gotrek's steps slowed and he looked down at the floor. He stamped the floor with his boot heel, then did it again.

'There are many levels below us,' he said.

'Aye,' said Rodi, nodding in agreement. 'At least six.' He sniffed the air. 'And they touch bedrock.'

'What were they used for?' asked Felix.

'Burying the dead, by the smell of it,' said Rodi.

Felix shivered, the idea of countless ancient corpses flaking to dust in the silent tombs below him giving him a sudden chill.

As they continued on, they passed other tunnels that intersected with theirs, black maws yawning in the rock walls that seemed to swallow the light of the torch, and from which Felix imagined he heard soft scuttlings and whisperings. He tensed at each one, fearing that some trap or ambush would spring out at them, and that they would hear old Hans's mad titter echoing from the distance.

The dwarfs took lefts and rights without pausing, never once consulting Hans's map or conferring amongst themselves. They seemed to know the way by heart, despite never having been here before.

At one intersection, wider than the rest, Gotrek looked at some symbols carved in the wooden support posts. He spat, disgusted. 'These tunnels weren't only used for escape. Vile things were done here.'

He took his axe off his back and shaved away some of the symbols with the razor-sharp blade. 'Foolish manlings,' he growled.

They walked on, Felix even more uneasy than before. Perhaps the dead in the halls below weren't in tombs after all. Visions of crowds of weeping captives driven to mass sacrifice in some deep chamber came unbidden to his mind, and he found it hard to banish them.

A little later, Gotrek held up a hand and they stopped. The dwarfs cocked their ears to the ceiling. Felix listened too. There was a faint tremor in the air, and a distant muffled thumping that never ceased.

'We are under the herd now,' said Gotrek.

A short while later, they came to a place where the walls and floor became mortared stone. These halls were painted with browns and blues and yellows – crude faded murals of men in horned helmets and long beards fighting orcs and beastmen in great battles, and other murals of the same men on their knees, offering meat and drink to a white wolf with a moon over its left shoulder and the sun over its right.

'The catacombs of Tarnhalt's castle,' said Rodi. 'Not the best painters, were they?'

After a few more turnings, they came to an ancient stairwell. Air poured down from above, bringing with it the reek of animal fur and wood smoke. The constant vibration of the walls and ceiling was echoed by far-off roars and wails. It sounded like there was no door between them and the herd.

Gotrek stopped. 'The circle is above us.'

'Looks like the old man led us true after all,' said Rodi.

'Praise Taal for that,' said Kat.

Snorri raised his head and inhaled at the bottom of the stairs. 'Snorri smells beastmen,' he said. 'Time to go fight them, aye?'

'No, Nosebiter,' said Gotrek. 'Time to turn around and go back.'

The sudden sadness on Snorri's face was so comical that Felix had to turn away to keep from laughing.

THE REST OF the day was as cold and boring as the previous one had been – more endless grey hours without news or incident. Felix had known they would hear nothing from von Volgen and Plaschke-Miesner. It was impossible that the messengers could ride to the monastery and the armies advance to the herd's position in a single day, and yet the waiting still set his teeth on edge and tightened his shoulders into knots. When would the armies come? How many would come? Would they come at all? Having had a sample of their bickering, he knew it was entirely possible that the two young lords had fought again and that one or the other or both had decided not to come as a result.

There was also the nagging worry that – despite the encouraging evidence of the map – old Hans was lurking in the background somewhere, planning some revenge on them for holding him against his will. Felix could not imagine that the frail old man's vengeance would be anything but petty spite, but even something seemingly insignificant might inadvertently alert the beasts to their presence and bring them crashing down upon them.

Felix made more notes in his journal, and watched again as Snorri followed Gotrek and Rodi around, babbling cheerfully. But this time he noticed that Gotrek was shooting hard, surreptitious glances at the old slayer when he wasn't looking, and once, when Snorri had gone off to relieve himself away from the camp, Felix saw Gotrek talking earnestly with Rodi as the young slayer nodded gravely, fingering his plaited beard. When Snorri returned, the two stepped apart, for all the world like guilty schoolboys, and greeted him with painfully affected false cheer.

From this, Felix was certain that they had been talking about the old slayer behind his back, but as to the nature of their conversation, he hadn't a clue.

VON VOLGEN'S MESSENGER returned at last at dawn on Hexensnacht eve with news that the two lords' armies would be in position by noon.

'How many men?' asked Gotrek.

'Lord von Volgen says that he has found fifteen hundred men, herr Slayer,' said the messenger. 'Mostly spearmen and archers, but with three hundred mounted men-at-arms, and Lord Plaschke-Miesner brings almost a thousand, two hundred of them knights, as well as two cannon.'

Felix winced. It was more than the lords had promised, but it was still far from enough. The beasts would slaughter them all. 'Any news of von Kotzebue?' he asked.

'Aye sir,' said the messenger. 'And good news at that. The baron has sent a messenger forwards to say that he crossed the Talabec with more than four thousand men two days behind my lord's march, and he is pressing south as quickly as he may.'

Felix exchanged looks with Gotrek, Rodi and Kat. Kotzebue's four thousand men would be welcome – even though they would still not put them at even odds with the beasts – but if they were two days behind at the outset, would they be here in time? It didn't seem likely.

'My lord and Lord Plaschke-Miesner beg you to wait as long as you dare to begin your mission,' the messenger continued, 'in order to give Lord von Kotzebue time to get into position.'

Felix didn't wonder at the request. Without von Kotzebue's troops backing them up, any attack the two young lords made would be nothing more than suicide.

'We will wait,' said Gotrek. 'But if he doesn't show by full dark, we will wait no more.' He turned to Sergeant Huntzinger and Sergeant Felke and their scouts. 'Go back with the messenger. The time for scouting is done. Better to die with your comrades than with us.'

The scouts paled at this malediction, but lost no time gathering up their gear.

As they watched them pack, Felix bit his lip and turned to Kat. 'You should go with them,' he said.

She looked like he had hit her. 'I'll not leave your side, Felix.'

'But, Kat–'

'I will not take the woman's part in this,' she continued, cutting him off. Felix could hear her fighting to control her voice. 'I... I thought you understood.'

The hurt in her eyes was like a dagger in his heart. 'I do,' he said. 'I don't ask it because you are a woman. I ask it because...' He looked around at the staring scouts and lowered his voice. 'Because I love you, and I don't want you to die.'

'I am not afraid,' she said, lifting her chin.

'It's not a question of that.' He sighed, then took her arm and led her away from the others. 'Kat, I know you are brave, but this...' He shook his head. 'It is impossible that any of us will survive. I have made a vow that I will follow the Slayer and witness his death, and I know I will die doing it. But you... you don't need to die here. You have so much life ahead of you.'

She glared at him. 'You forget I have a vow too.'

'I know you do,' he said. 'But there will be other herds, and other fights, fights where your help will make a difference.'

He knew as he said it that it was the wrong thing to say.

Kat's eyes got colder still and she drew herself up. 'You doubt my skills?' she asked, stiffly.

Felix ground his teeth. 'That's not what I meant, and you know it. The time for scouts is done, just as

Gotrek said.' He nodded towards Felke and Huntzinger's men, who were lining up in preparation to march. 'I only want you to do what they are doing.' I only want to save your life, he cried inwardly, but did not speak it.

Kat hung her head and nodded. 'You are right, Felix. This is no place for scouts. I should go.'

Felix let out a sigh of relief. At last she was seeing sense.

'But,' she said, and all of Felix's tension returned as if it had never left. 'But still I cannot leave you.'

'Sigmar's blood, why not?' Felix cried.

She looked up at him with liquid brown eyes. 'Because I do not want you to die either.'

'But Kat,' he said, exasperated. 'I *will* die! There is no question.'

She shook her head. 'I have heard your stories. You have faced certain death before, and always there has been one little thing that saved you.' She swallowed and put her hand on his chest. 'What if, this time, I am that one little thing?'

Felix choked down a wave of emotion. The girl didn't want to die by his side. She wanted to protect him. It broke his heart. 'It's impossible,' he said. 'There's no chance. None.'

She stepped closer to him. 'How many times have I saved your life?'

He coughed. 'Er, twice? Three times? More than that?'

She looked directly into his eyes. 'There is always a chance, Felix. Always.'

Felix sighed, despairing that he had failed to convince her, but at the same time overwhelmed by how much she cared for him.

Their men assembled, Felke and Huntzinger stepped forwards and saluted Felix, Kat and the slayers.

'Luck to you,' said Felke. He took off his hunting horn and passed it to Kat.

'And to you,' said Kat, taking it.

'Give our regards to Sir Teobalt,' said Felix.

The slayers just nodded.

A FEW HOURS later, Felix stood watch again at the lip of the ravine, his mind still so full of worry for Kat and self-loathing for himself that it was doubtful that he would have spotted a beastman unless it had trodden on his foot.

It was just after noon and the day had so far been torture. While the slayers had paced and griped and waited for news of the armies, Felix's mind had churned ceaselessly, trying to think of new arguments that would send Kat to safety, but failing again and again. He knew she would not leave, no matter what he said, and he watched her come and go from her patrols in a bitter, brooding melancholy. She was such a strange, unique creature – so fierce and bloodthirsty and confident, and yet so shy and good and uncertain at the same time – that it seemed a tragedy beyond all measure that she should be snuffed from the world like this, and he had spent the morning despising himself for not being able to think of a way to avert that tragedy.

Pebbles rattled behind him, waking him from his unhappy reverie. He turned to see Gotrek climbing up the steep slope to join him.

'Something wrong?' he asked as the Slayer pulled himself up the last few feet and stopped beside him, dusting his palms.

'Aye,' said Gotrek.

Felix expected him to continue, but the Slayer just stood there, looking out across the endless hills. Felix frowned, wondering if he was supposed to guess the trouble. Had Hans the Hermit returned? Had beastmen found a way into the ravine? Had something happened to Kat?

Finally the Slayer spoke. 'Snorri Nosebiter will not find his doom here,' he said.

Felix raised his eyebrows. This sounded like prophecy. 'How can you be certain of that?' he asked.

'I'm going to *make* certain,' said Gotrek. 'He will not die without remembering why he took the slayer's oath.'

'Ah,' said Felix. 'I see.' He was quietly shocked at this pronouncement. Gotrek rarely thought of anything other than his own doom. To see him actively concerned about someone else's troubles, even another slayer's, was rare. Felix recalled that Gotrek had helped Heinz when the *Blind Pig* had burned down, but he suspected the Slayer had felt partially responsible for the fire. This was different. Gotrek hadn't caused Snorri to lose his memory. This was an actual, unasked for, act of kindness.

The Slayer kicked distractedly at the ground, his head low. 'I am releasing you from your vow, manling. You do not have to witness my doom, nor write of it. Instead, you will stay with Snorri Nosebiter, out of the battle, and when it is done, you will see him to Karak Kadrin and the Shrine of Grimnir. Then you are free.'

Felix choked, stunned. He couldn't believe what the Slayer was saying. 'Are… are you sure?'

Gotrek raised his head and glared at him with his single angry eye. 'Would I say it if I wasn't?'

And with that he turned and stumped back down into the gorge.

Felix stared after him, blinking with shock. His mind whirled with a hundred questions and emotions, all fighting for his attention at once. Gotrek had released him from his vow – or rather he had given Felix a task that would give it a definite ending. He was so surprised that he wasn't sure how he felt about it. Was he elated? That he knew he wouldn't die beside the Slayer was a relief, he supposed, and finally putting an end to the uncertainty of when his long, mad journey would be over was a weight off his shoulders, but he couldn't say either thing made him happy.

Did he feel angry? Not precisely. Cheated perhaps? To have dutifully followed the Slayer for more than twenty years, waiting for him to die, only to be told at the end, 'never mind, you don't have to record it after all,' rankled a bit.

But thinking about that made him realise the true enormity of the Slayer's decision. Since Felix had known him, Gotrek had wanted only two things out of life – a good doom, and an epic poem to immortalise his legend and bring it to the world. That desire for fame was why he had asked Felix to join him on his quest for death all those years ago. It was, in a way, the Slayer's greatest weakness – a flaw of the ego that at once drove him headlong into impossible danger, and held him back from less worthy dooms. That he was now willing to give up that dream of glory, to go to his doom without any record of it being made, to die anonymously and alone, was proof to Felix of how deeply he cared for Snorri Nosebiter. He was sacrificing the fame he had spent more than twenty years accumulating in order to try to safeguard Snorri's afterlife, and without any certain knowledge that it would work. Felix was sure that Gotrek knew as well as anyone that Snorri's prayers might be unanswered at Grimnir's shrine, and yet he was willing to forego his remembrance for that faint, forlorn hope.

Understanding this, all of Felix's initial misgivings vanished. He was not angry that Gotrek had dismissed him. He did not feel cheated. Instead his chest swelled with pride, for that dismissal meant that Gotrek trusted him enough to put Snorri's salvation – a thing apparently more precious to him than his own fame – in Felix's hands. It was the greatest honour Felix had ever been given.

He swore then and there that he would see it through without fail. He would hide Snorri during the upcoming battle, he would see him safely through the Worlds Edge Mountains to Karak Kadrin, he would accompany him to the shrine, and then...

Felix paused, frowning.

And then... what?

And then he would be free of his vow to Gotrek for the first time in his adult life. He would have... a future.

A new thought exploded in his head as that sank in. Gotrek had asked him to sit out the battle and stay with Snorri for the duration. If he would not be in the battle, then Kat would not be in the battle! She would live! They both would live!

Suddenly his mind was ablaze. A future! He and Kat could be together! They could *live* together, have normal lives together – well, no, not that. He still had his vow to take vengeance upon the skaven sorcerer who had brought about his father's death, and she still had her vow to vanquish the beastmen of the Drakwald, but why couldn't they travel the Empire and the forests together for the rest of their lives, hunting skaven and beastmen and sleeping in Taal's bower, living the simple life of the wanderer and the woodsman? It wasn't as if he would have to change his life much. He would still be a vagabond, as he had been for the last two decades. Only now he wouldn't be sharing the road with a surly, monosyllabic dwarf, but instead with a sweet, beautiful girl with whom he could also share his bed.

That brought him up sharp. He was actually looking forward to Gotrek's death! And the honour of bringing Snorri to Grimnir's shrine had become a mere stepping stone to his selfish dreams of happiness. He cringed with shame. What kind of friend was he? He should be mourning the Slayer's imminent passing and praying for Snorri's recovery, not gleefully planning the life he and Kat would have once he was free of both of them. How could he betray such lifelong friendships so callously? It wasn't right.

On the other hand, Snorri wasn't the sort to deny another person happiness because he couldn't find his own, and Gotrek was a slayer. He wanted to die. He wouldn't want his death mourned. He would want it celebrated. Of course, dancing on his grave before he was even dead probably wasn't exactly what the Slayer had in mind.

Felix sighed, conflicted. There was no question that he would mourn the Slayer's passing – *and* celebrate it. Gotrek had often been hard to understand, and harder to like, but their friendship, though rarely expressed, had been real, and Felix would miss it when it was gone. But he could not pretend that he wasn't pleased and relieved that his life after Gotrek's death, which he had often feared would be an empty and meaningless shuffle to the grave, would instead be full of love and life and joy.

He was suddenly impatient for his watch to be over. He couldn't wait to tell Kat the news.

'This isn't a trick, is it, Felix?' Kat asked warily. 'You're not still trying to send me away?'

'It's no trick. I promise you.' Felix looked over his shoulder to where the three slayers were sitting around the cold fire pit, cleaning their weapons for what must have been the fifth time that day. They were all out of earshot. He turned back to Kat. 'Gotrek doesn't want Snorri to find his doom until he has recovered his memory, so he has excused me from the battle so that I can bring him to Karak Kadrin to pray at the Shrine of Grimnir. I will not be fighting. You'll have no need to protect me.'

'And when you have brought Snorri to the shrine?' asked Kat.

'I'll be free to do as I please,' said Felix, smiling. 'And what I please, is to be with you.'

Kat shivered and shook her head. 'I'm sorry, Felix. I want it to be true, but I can't let myself believe it yet. It seems impossible.'

Felix chuckled and pulled her close. 'Not to worry,' he said. 'I understand. There is nothing worse than hope. Forget it. We won't speak of it until it has happened.' He kissed her on the forehead, then pulled back and gazed into her worried eyes. 'Just remember something that someone said to me not long ago.'

'What's that?' she asked.

Felix grinned. 'There is always a chance.'

A slow smile broke through Kat's cloudy demeanour and she hugged him hard. 'Aye,' she said. 'Always.'

JUST AS THE last crimson sliver of the sun sank behind blood-coloured hills, a messenger finally arrived from the armies. Felix knew the news was not good when the man saluted from his horse, but did not dismount.

'Lord von Volgen and Lord Plaschke-Miesner's compliments,' said the messenger as they gathered around him. 'And they regret to inform you that no sign of Baron von Kotzebue's army has yet been sighted.'

'Then they will have to go without him,' said Gotrek.

'No, herr dwarf,' said the messenger. 'My lords have determined that the risk is too great. If von Kotzebue does not arrive before your signal, they will retire.'

Gotrek snorted and turned away. 'So much for the courage of men.'

'This is madness,' said Kat. 'They must attack. They must!'

Felix stepped up to the messenger. 'I thought they understood that it was vital to attack the herd while it was all in one spot. If they let them disperse, the beasts will pillage the countryside for hundreds of miles in every direction, and they will be almost impossible to root out. If von Volgen and Plaschke-Miesner retreat, they are dooming Talabecland to years of raids and slaughter.'

The messenger nodded, very stiff. 'My lords are aware of this, and will go therefore to look to their own lands and strengthen the defences of their keeps.'

Rodi spat on the ground. 'Tell them from me that they are cowards, and deserve the fate that this tail-turning will bring them.'

The messenger bowed in the saddle. 'I will do so.'

And with that he wheeled his horse around and galloped off into the crimson twilight.

MORRSLIEB AND MANNSLIEB were again rising together over the hills as Felix, Kat and the three slayers crawled towards the top of the ridge again. The guttural chanting of ten thousand savage throats floated over the summit and raised the hairs on the back of Felix's neck. That such a huge herd of beastmen, a race famous for their fractiousness and infighting, should be in such accord that they could all chant in unison, was a terrifying thing. If this Urslak could continue to keep them unified and fixed on a single objective they would be unstoppable.

The five companions reached the top of the ridge and went forwards on knees and elbows until they could look down into the valley of Tarnhalt's Crown. The camps of the outlying herds were deserted, their bonfires dark. All the beastmen were pressing close around the base of the central hill from all sides, a shifting, undulating carpet of horned heads and hairy shoulders, with here and there torches sticking up to cast a ruddy glow on spear-tips and broad, armoured backs.

The hill itself was ablaze with yellow light. Roaring bonfires had been set all around the towering herdstone, causing the monoliths of the stone circle to cast thick black bars of shadow down the hill and across the swarm of beastmen that thronged it. A ring of blue-daubed guards protected the circle, lashing out at the teeming, chanting mob with blazing firebrands, keeping them back.

'Sigmar preserve us,' said Felix. It was like a scene out of the Chaos Wastes, transported to the centre of the Empire.

'He better not,' said Rodi.

'Snorri thinks it's nice of them to stay so close together,' said Snorri. 'Saves running after them.'

Felix, Gotrek and Rodi exchanged a look, but said nothing. Felix felt strangely guilty in the wake of that look, like he was in some conspiracy to murder Snorri, rather than save him.

Kat's keen eyes saw through all the flickering chaos to the centre. 'The shaman has already begun his ceremony,' she said.

Felix peered towards the circle again. He couldn't see the hunched old beastman, but he could see, through the haze of smoke and roaring flames, the occasional pulse of blue light from the jagged veins of the herdstone.

'It's time, then,' said Gotrek, then turned and started back down the hill.

Felix followed him with the others, fighting down waves of conflicting emotions. The time of Gotrek's doom was fast approaching. After all these years, he found it hard to imagine that it would really happen this time, but it was harder to see how it wouldn't.

FELIX ONCE AGAIN felt a chill of dread as they squirmed, one at a time, through the hole in the hill that led to the ancient burial chamber and the tunnels beyond. But though the fears of some strange vengeance by old Hans made him turn anxiously at every rustle and rattle that echoed in the dark as they hurried through the subterranean labyrinth, nothing happened. They came without incident to the catacombs of Tarnhalt's castle, and then to the ancient stairwell that led to the surface and the stone circle where the beasts performed their dread ceremony.

Kat passed her torch to Felix and drew her bow off her back as the dwarfs started up the square stone spiral. Felix followed her up, holding the torch to one side. The stairs crackled with dead leaves and dry twigs, blown down by the winds of ages, but as they got closer to the surface, the noises from above began to drown out all else – the stamping of thousands of hooves in unison, the hoarse chanting, now quickening to a frenzied pitch, the high wail of the old shaman rising above it all.

Felix found himself clutching his sword in a death grip, and his teeth were locked together like a vice. He had to keep reminding himself that he wasn't going out to fight the herd. He was going to stay hidden with Snorri and Kat while Gotrek and Rodi went to kill the shaman and meet their doom. It still felt unlikely. Would things really be different this time?

They turned up a final flight and saw a square of night sky above them. Torchlight flickered off the stairwell's crumbling walls. Gotrek slowed his pace and crept to the top, raising his head cautiously, then beckoning the rest up after him. They came out in the midst of a dense thicket of brambles that grew over and around broken knee-high walls – all that remained of the tower that had once surrounded the stairs.

Over their heads, Mannslieb and Morrslieb stared down, casting double shadows, and were even closer together tonight than they had been the night before, and from all around came bestial voices and the light of many fires. Felix and the others crouched down and peered through the criss-cross screen of thorny twigs to the scene beyond. Felix's heart pounded in his chest as he saw how close they were to the circle and the beasts.

The ring of stones rose only twenty paces away, and the circle of torch-wielding, blue-painted gors that guarded it was only ten paces away. The mob that the guards were holding back was even closer. In fact the stairwell was within their front ranks. The mob stretched out to both sides of it and behind it all the way down the hill to the valley floor. Only the mass of bushes and the tower's broken walls had stopped the beastmen from standing directly on top of it.

Felix heard Kat whispering frightened prayers to Taal and Rhya, and he did the same to Sigmar, all the while trying to keep his knees from shaking. It wouldn't take more than a cough or a loud sneeze to alert the beasts to their presence, and then they would be dead in seconds.

Gotrek pushed a little way forwards through the bushes, peering more closely at the circle. The others crept cautiously after him. Through the gaps between the standing stones Felix could see the blue quartz veins of the massive herdstone pulsing like a heart in time with the rhythm of the herd's chant, and before it, the twist-horned shaman, Urslak, standing in supplication, arms outstretched, his bird-claw robe flapping in an eldritch wind as he wailed a profane prayer. For a moment Felix thought he saw enormous blue-feathered wings sprouting from the shaman's shoulders, but then they vanished, and he decided it had only been a trick of the flames that surrounded him.

There were two ranks of beastmen between the slayers and the shaman. The closest rank were the blue-daubed guardians. They were widely spaced, and faced out towards the herd, brandishing torches to keep them back. The massive war-leader – who Ortwin had named Gargorath the God-Touched – stood with them on the east side of the circle, his powerful arms folded as he looked down on the sea of upturned goat-like faces that stretched away from him to the base of the hill and beyond into the camp. The second rank of beastmen stood just within the monoliths, blue-robed initiates that faced in towards the shaman, chanting and shaking strange fetishes over their heads – bones, feathers, gnarled staffs and skulls of different animals and races. Felix remembered them. They had been the dancers that had preceded the stone when it was on the march.

'It is possible,' muttered Gotrek.

'Aye,' said Rodi, nodding. 'Only a handful to kill before we reach the old goat – if we're quick. After that...' He shrugged and smiled savagely.

'Snorri is ready,' said Snorri eagerly. 'Snorri thinks this is going to be a good fight.'

Gotrek and Rodi exchanged another glance, then backed towards the stairs, beckoning to Snorri to follow.

'Come here, Snorri Nosebiter,' said Gotrek, looking uncomfortable. 'I want to speak of your part in this.'

A look of impatience passed over Snorri's ugly face, but he followed Gotrek, stepping past Rodi, who hung back behind him.

'Why waste time talking?' said Snorri. 'Snorri knows what to–'

With a sound like a cannon ball hitting a wooden floor, Rodi struck Snorri with the heavy iron pommel of his axe, just below the lowest nail on the back of his skull. The old slayer's eyes rolled up into his head and he sank to his knees, then pitched forwards, flat on his face. Rodi looked down at him, shame and sadness mixing in his eyes.

'Sorry, Father Rustskull,' he said. 'It had to be done.'

'Have…?' said Kat. 'Have you killed him?'

'Do you think a little tap like that could kill Snorri Nosebiter?' asked Gotrek.

But nevertheless, the Slayer felt Snorri's pulse, then he and Rodi lifted his limp body and rolled him down the stairs.

The two slayers stood for a long moment, looking down into the darkness at their friend, then Gotrek turned to Kat.

'You have the horn?'

She unslung it from where it hung at her waist and held it up.

'Good,' said Gotrek, then looked to Felix and fixed him with a hard bright eye.

'And you know what to do?'

'Aye, Gotrek,' said Felix. 'I do.'

Gotrek nodded, then turned with Rodi towards Tarnhalt's Crown, running his thumb down the blade of his axe so that it bled, but then, after a step, he paused and turned back. He crossed to Felix and held out his hand. Felix took it, a lump suddenly constricting his throat.

'Goodbye, manling,' said Gotrek. 'You have been a true dwarf-friend.'

'Thank… thank you, Gotrek,' said Felix, hardly able to speak. 'I–'

But Gotrek had already turned away and joined Rodi as he pushed towards the edge of the thicket.

Felix looked at his hand. There was a streak of blood across the back of it where Gotrek's sliced thumb had pressed it. He blinked his eyes and turned away, emotion threatening to overwhelm him, only to find himself facing Kat, looking up at him with sad eyes. He turned from her too, afraid she was going to say something comforting, but she seemed to know better. She only put her hand on his back and kept silent.

'Now!' came Gotrek's harsh whisper.

Felix looked up in time to see Gotrek and Rodi streaking out of the bushes fast and low, straight for the two outer circle guards who stood between them and the stone circle.

The noise of the chanting and the darkness near the bushes covered the slayers' approach, and the gors were dead before they even knew they were being attacked. Gotrek cut the legs out from under his, then chopped off its head as it hit the ground. Rodi gutted his with the leading blade of his double-headed axe, then severed its spine with the back blade as he shouldered past it.

The slayers ran on. Felix looked around. It seemed none of the other beastmen had noticed them yet. He clenched his sword in anxiety. They just might make it. If they could get through the robed beastmen that stood within the stones–

A roar from the right brought his head around. One of the outer guardians had seen the slayers and was running after them, calling to its comrades.

Kat sent an arrow at it. The gor stumbled but kept going. More were following him. She drew another arrow.

Gotrek and Rodi reached the circle and slammed into the backs of the chanting initiates who danced in the gaps between the stones. Three went down instantly, taken completely by surprise, but three more turned and gave battle, striking out with staves and sickle-shaped daggers. Bellows of anger came from those in nearby gaps as they saw what was happening to their fellows, and a few surged towards the slayers, but the old shaman in the centre was too focused on his ritual to notice, and most of the chanters were the same, so transported by the frenzy of their invocation that they continued on, oblivious.

The two slayers were making short work of the robed beastmen, but not short enough. The blue-painted guardians were coming swiftly behind them and would reach them before they were clear. Kat poured more arrows into the guards and a few fell, but she was only one archer. Most did not.

'They're not going to make it,' she said.

Felix knew it, and he fought the urge to rush out and help them. It was wrong for him not to be at the Slayer's side. He felt guilty and ashamed, but Gotrek had told him to stay with Snorri, and he had sworn he would do so.

'Where are the dirty beastmen that hit Snorri on the head?' said a blurry voice behind them.

Felix and Kat turned to see the old slayer standing at the top of the stairs, rubbing the back of his head with a meaty hand and weaving slightly as he blinked around.

'Ah! There they are!' he said, squinting ahead. 'And Snorri's friends are taking them all!'

The old slayer started forwards, wading through the brush towards the fight, a lump the size of an apple on the back of his skull.

TWENTY

'Snorri, wait!' hissed Felix, dogging the slayer's steps as he pushed through the brambles. 'You can't go, remember? You must recover your memory first.'

'Aye, slayer,' said Kat, following on his other side. 'You won't be allowed into Grimnir's hall.'

'Snorri knows,' said Snorri. 'He'll take care of that just as soon as he sorts out these beastmen.'

'But the beastmen will sort you out!' said Felix, exasperated. 'You'll meet your doom here, Snorri!'

'And it will be too soon,' said Kat.

'But there are beastmen,' said Snorri, breaking through the last of the bushes.

Felix looked around to see if any beastmen had noticed them. They were all looking towards Gotrek and Rodi. He grabbed Snorri's arm as Kat caught the wrist of his hammer hand.

'Snorri, please!' said Felix.

Snorri shrugged off Felix as if he were a fly, then gently pried Kat's hand away, all without breaking stride. 'You don't have to hold Snorri back,' said Snorri. 'There are plenty of beastmen for all of us.'

Felix and Kat made another grab for him, but just then Snorri swept his hammer up over his head and charged forwards, bellowing a Khazalid war cry.

Felix groaned, all his dreams of escaping Gotrek's doom and starting a new life vanishing in an instant. The cheese-brained old idiot had ruined everything. He turned to Kat. 'I... I'm sorry. I have to protect him. I promised.'

Kat shrugged and gave him a sad half-smile as she settled her bow over her shoulders and drew her axes. 'And I promised to fight at your side.'

He wanted to tell her no, and send her back to the stairs, but there was no time for argument. If this suicide was going to mean anything, he had to help the slayers reach the shaman. As one, he and Kat sprinted after Snorri into the fight, roaring and screaming and slashing at the backs of the blue-painted beastmen that surrounded Rodi and Gotrek. Felix was so full of rage that he cut down two beastmen in one savage stroke. He just imagined they were Snorri.

As the beasts fell, Felix saw Gotrek look up from slaying a beast-initiate to see Snorri fighting beside him. Gotrek snarled and looked around. He found Felix and glared at him with his one angry eye.

Felix shrunk from his displeasure. 'He woke up,' he called, ducking a huge club. 'I couldn't–'

Gotrek cursed and gutted another beastman with an unnecessarily vicious twist of his axe. Beside him, Snorri dashed out the brains of another, while Rodi head-butted a third between the legs. All at once they were through the initiates and stumbling into the middle of the stone circle. Gotrek, Rodi and Snorri turned to face the blue-painted guardians who had been fighting so hard to stop them from entering it, but the beastmen skidded to a stop at the line of standing stones, staring at the huge glowing herdstone in abject fear, and would come no further.

'Ha!' barked Gotrek. 'To the shaman!'

The runes on the Slayer's axe flared white-hot as he turned, and Felix didn't wonder why. Entering the circle of menhirs was like stepping into an arcane furnace. Chaos energy radiated from the blazing blue veins of the herdstone in great pulsing waves, making his skin itch as if he was being eaten by ants and filling his mind with chittering, bird-like voices.

Gotrek, Rodi and Snorri ran directly for Urslak, and Felix and Kat followed. There was no one to stop them. The crooked-horned shaman continued his invocation, entirely unaware of their presence. The rest of the chanting initiates remained transfixed as well, and the guardians remained at the edge of the circle, fearing to come in. Felix's heart pounded with unexpected hope. They were going to make it!

But then, into the circle charged Gargorath the God-Touched, the hulking black-furred, blue-eyed war-leader, with five blue-painted, heavily armoured gors at his back.

Gargorath roared a challenge at the slayers, his hate-filled eyes glowing with the same fire that emanated from the herdstone as he raised his vulture-headed axe above his head. Felix heard the weapon scream – the high, harsh shriek of a bird of prey. He shivered as he recalled poor Ortwin's last words – the axe ate what it killed. He wasn't sure what that meant, and he hoped he would never find out.

The slayers answered the challenge with roars of their own, and with a deafening crunch of steel and bone the two sides slammed together. Felix and Kat swung at a brass-armoured elk-man as Snorri, Gotrek and Rodi piled into the others. The elk-man smashed aside Felix's puny attacks with a crusty black iron mace that likely weighed more than Kat. Felix staggered back, his hands stinging from the impact. Kat leapt aside, one of her axes snapped in half, and before they could recover the elk-man was on them again, sending them diving away. Felix's palms turned slick with fear. The elk-man was stronger and more skilled than any other beastman he had ever faced – an actual warrior, rather than just a brawling animal.

The slayers were having the same difficulty. Gotrek blocked Gargorath's strike but was driven back several feet by the strength of the blow, the vulture-headed axe screaming in his face. Snorri was bleeding from a deep cut on his arm and was backing away from two bellowing beasts. Rodi's face was a mask of blood as he fought two more. Red sprayed from his braided beard with every swing of his axe.

'Felix! Look out!'

Kat shoved Felix and he staggered aside just as the elk-man's club whistled past his cheekbone, so close it made him blink. He returned his attention to the fight, aiming a cut at the beastman's eyes as Kat swiped at its ankles. The gor jumped back before this coordinated attack, and they pressed forwards.

On the other side of the fight, Gotrek's and Gargorath's axes met blade to blade and Gotrek's axe was caught in the vulture-headed weapon's beak notch. Gargorath tried to twist Gotrek's axe out of his hands, but the Slayer reversed the twist, his muscles bulging, and Gargorath's axe spun past Snorri's head to land on the ground.

The Slayer aimed a cut at the defenceless Gargorath, but when the big beastman leapt aside, Gotrek charged past him, straight for the shaman.

Felix stole glances from his own fight as Gargorath chased after the Slayer. Gotrek swiped behind him with his axe, ringing it off the war-leader's leg armour, but the beast caught him by the neck and shoulder and lifted him over his head.

'Gotrek!' cried Felix. Then to Kat, 'We have to help him!'

He and Kat jumped back from the elk-man and ran to Gotrek's aid, but before they could take three steps, they saw the Slayer chop down wildly at Gargorath's head. His rune axe sheered off one of the war-leader's curling horns and part of his ram-like snout. The beast howled in agony and flung the Slayer from him as hard as he could – right at the herdstone.

'No!'

Felix and Kat chopped at Gargorath as Gotrek sailed over the chanting shaman's head to crash down hard at the base of the looming herdstone. Kat's axe glanced off the war-leader's steel and brass breastplate, not even scratching it. Karaghul bit into the armour but did not touch flesh. The massive gor flattened them both with a careless backhand, then ran to snatch up his fallen axe.

Felix struggled up, trying to block Gargorath's way, but the elk-man was on him again and he had to fall back, the mace shivering his blade and turning his arms to jelly. Behind him, Kat sat up, shaking her head woozily.

Gargorath roared by her, axe in hand, charging towards Gotrek and the stone as Felix parried another brutal blow from the elk-man.

Gotrek stood to meet the war-leader, beckoning with his off hand and swinging his arm back in preparation for a powerful slash. As he did, his rune axe grazed the herdstone – the merest touch – but there was a sudden sparking crack and a flash of pure white light, and the ground slipped sideways beneath Felix's feet.

Felix caught himself before he fell and blinked his eyes to clear the after-images that danced before them. He looked around, his head throbbing. Gotrek was doubled up, his right arm cradled against his chest, while his axe lay smoking at his feet. Everybody else – man, dwarf and beastman – stood frozen, looking up at the herdstone. It was steaming and hissing, and little crumbling shards were flaking from it and raining down on the ground while the blue quartz veins that ran through it flickered and flashed like a torch in a windstorm.

The first to recover his composure was the beast-shaman, Urslak, who backed away and pointed a clawed finger at Gotrek, shrieking for his blood. The ring of robed initiates heeded his call, casting down their fetishes and drawing crude weapons as they surged forwards, braying their rage. Gargorath and his lieutenants added their voices to the howl and charged for the Slayer, but Rodi and Snorri had recovered as well, and leapt to stop them.

'Unfaithful beasts!' roared Rodi. 'You are *my* doom!'

'And Snorri's!' called Snorri.

Felix and Kat joined the slayers, slashing at Gargorath and the elk-man and trying to keep them from Gotrek until he recovered, but the war-leader was too strong. He knocked Felix aside and he and the elk-man bounded over Kat towards the stunned Slayer while Snorri and Rodi engaged the others.

"Ware the leader, Gotrek,' called Felix from the ground.

But Gotrek paid Gargorath and his followers no attention. Instead, as he shook off his shock, he looked from his axe to the herdstone and back again, a cunning glint kindling in his single eye.

Felix knew that look of old, and it never boded well for anybody in the vicinity.

'Gotrek, that is a very bad idea,' he shouted, picking himself up.

Gotrek snatched up his axe and dodged Gargorath's charge, laughing darkly. 'No, manling,' he laughed. 'It is a very *good* idea.'

Gargorath and the elk-man slashed down at the Slayer with their weapons. Gotrek knocked both attacks aside with a whistling backhand, then swung upwards, decapitating the elk-man's mace and tearing through its armour and flesh like a plough through soft earth. As the beast toppled to the ground in an explosion of blood, Gotrek aimed another cut at Gargorath. The beastman desperately threw himself back to avoid the strike and it clashed off his breastplate, raising sparks and knocking him flat on his back.

Gotrek did not follow up. Instead, he turned to the herdstone again and swung his axe at it with all his might.

For a brief second Felix thought the world had ended. The thundercrack flash of the strike blinded and deafened him, and he lost all sense of up or down. He opened his eyes to find himself sprawled on the ground, along with all his friends and foes. The beasts lay everywhere, writhing and clutching their horned heads. The shaman was shrieking as if he'd been stabbed in the eyes. Kat was curled in a ball. Gotrek was flat on his back, spread-eagled, his eyebrows and the ends of his beard and crest smoking, ten feet from the stone. His axe lay beside him, the head glowing as if it had just left the forge.

The herdstone was shaking itself to pieces. Large chunks were breaking off and crumbling to dust as they fell, and the quartz veins were starred with fissures, like thick glass under pressure. Felix felt an unnatural wind blowing – not from the stone, but towards it – and he saw that the dust and pebbles that were falling from the stone were being sucked into the cracks in the quartz.

Gotrek groaned and sat up, as stiff and slow as an old man. He took up his axe and used it to lever himself to his feet. 'One more ought to do it,' he grunted.

'Wait, Gotrek!' shouted Felix over the wind and the rising hum of the stone. 'You'll kill us!'

'Then you'd better run, manling,' said Gotrek, and he limped towards the stone as if his legs were made of lead.

Felix cursed as he forced himself to his feet – nor was he the only one less than happy with Gotrek's course of action. Gargorath and his remaining lieutenants were rising and staggering towards him, and Urslak, the shaman, was raising his arms and snarling out a vile incantation as the claw-clutched blue orb at the top of his staff began to glow and pulse. Felix noted with horror that all the bird-claw fetishes that dangled from his robes were clutching and unclutching their talons in time to his chant.

'Hurry,' said Felix, lifting Kat to her feet and urging her forwards. 'Run.'

'Is he really going to...?' she asked, looking back.

'Without a doubt,' said Felix.

He and Kat turned and ran as Rodi and Snorri lurched up to intercept Gargorath and his warriors, and Urslak stalked towards Gotrek, who was still limping doggedly towards the stone.

The initiate beastmen had recovered now, and were charging forwards again too. Felix and Kat lashed out at them as they came, but the gors hardly paid them notice. All their attention was focused on Gotrek and the stone.

A crazy hope flared in Felix's heart as the way cleared before them. The stair to the tunnels was only a few paces beyond the stone circle. If they were lucky, and the rest of the beasts ignored them as well, they might just survive this mad folly after all.

Felix looked back. Beyond Rodi and Snorri's battle with the beastmen, Urslak swung his staff at Gotrek, the blue orb glowing like an azure sun. Gotrek hacked the staff in two, then gutted the shaman and kicked him back before the claw-held orb had stopped bouncing across the rocky ground.

The Slayer spat on the dying shaman, then turned back to the herdstone, raising his axe.

'Faster!' said Felix, and sprinted with Kat for the ring of monoliths.

They weren't fast enough.

With another deafening crack, he and Kat were knocked flat again by a jolt stronger than all the others. It felt as if a giant had hit him in the back with an enormous shovel, knocking the wind out of him and pushing him to the brink of unconsciousness. He thought of trying to move, but it seemed too much effort. Easier to just lie there. Then Kat whimpered beside him. The thought of her galvanised him. He had to get her to safety.

As Felix fought to regain his senses, gasping and groaning and blinking the glare from his eyes, he became aware of a thunderous roaring behind him, and of a hard wind battering his face. He raised himself on shaking arms and looked back – then froze at what he saw.

The towering herdstone was rising from the ground and expanding – the jagged lines that had been the seams of quartz now widened into gaps between huge floating shards of granite that moved outwards from the core of the stone. And through these gaps shone a terrible blue light that bathed the inside of the stone circle in a harsh sapphire glow.

The impossible wind blew towards the widening cracks from all directions, as if they were chimney flues sucking smoke from a fireplace. Felix's hair streamed towards it. Leaves and branches whirled towards it. The wind tore at the floating granite shards of the herdstone too, crumbling their edges and sucking in the pebbles so that they shrank even as the gaps between them grew ever wider.

Felix squinted into the light that streamed from the expanding cracks, and a sickening dread swallowed all his other fears as he saw its source. Hanging within the core of the fragmenting herdstone was a hole in the world, a gash in reality that looked into some other place. Blue swirls of every shade wove a hypnotising dance inside the rift, blue swirls that looked at him with fierce intelligence, and begged him to join them in their search for ultimate knowledge.

Kat whimpered again beside him. 'It's... it's beautiful.'

Felix turned and clapped a hand over her eyes. 'Don't look!' he cried. 'It will take your mind.'

He fought to his feet, the unnatural wind pulling at him, then dragged her up too. 'Come on. Turn away from it. Run!'

And yet, even as he followed her, pushing hard against the rising wind, Felix found it impossible not to look back himself.

The beastmen were running from the stone, the initiates screaming with fear as the sucking wind dragged them back, Gargorath and his surviving lieutenants trampling them and hurling them aside in their eagerness to get away.

Chasing them came Gotrek, Rodi and Snorri, all roaring insults over the shrieking gale.

'Come back, you cowards!' called Gotrek.

'Are you afraid of a little wind?' bellowed Rodi.

'Snorri has seen squirrels with more courage!' shouted Snorri.

Felix could feel the wind trying to lift him off the ground as he leaned against it, and it was getting worse. It was going to suck him into the rift! Only two more yards to the menhirs, but it might have been two miles. He put Kat in front of him to shield her and they pressed on, fighting for every inch. More debris whipped past them, flying towards the vortex. One of the beasts they had killed as they fought their way into the circle rolled by, flopping loosely, over and over.

Finally they reached the ring of monoliths and Felix pushed Kat into the shadow of one, where the wind was less, then struggled to pull himself behind it as well. Kat caught his arms and hauled with all her strength. With a final grunt of effort he stumbled behind the stone and collapsed against it, breathing heavily.

The shadow of their stone shelter was as sharp as a knife in the harsh light of the vortex, and stretched away with the shadows of the other stones down the sloping sides of the hill to the valley below. Nothing could be seen within the shadows, but the light that blazed from between the stones illuminated a roiling sea of beastmen backing away from Tarnhalt's Crown with naked terror showing in their glittering black eyes. Felix couldn't blame them. If he could have run, he would have been over the hills and gone long ago.

'Are we safe even here?' asked Kat.

Felix shrugged weakly. 'I don't know. But I can go no further.'

A movement in the corner of his eye made him turn his head. Gargorath and his lieutenants had escaped the circle and were straining to reach the slope down into the valley as the gale tore at their armour and their fur.

Felix put his head around the corner of the standing stone, looking into the circle for Gotrek, Snorri and Rodi. The three slayers were ploughing on, slowly but steadily, against the wind, cursing lustily all the while.

Behind them, the initiate beastmen weren't doing as well. Felix saw one fall backwards and roll head over heels towards the howling stone. Another was lifted bodily and spun away through the air to be sucked into the fissures between the shards – breaking up into its component parts as it went. The wind was too loud to hear its screams.

Then Felix saw a lone figure rise before the stone. It was Urslak. It seemed impossible for him to be alive, after the evisceration Gotrek had given him. It seemed even more impossible that he was able to stand steady so close to the stone and the vacuum of the vortex. And yet he did. Though buffeted cruelly by the wind, he straightened his hunched form and spread his arms wide, calling out some incantation that was lost in the roaring rush of air. His claw-festooned robe flapped and fluttered around him like a living thing, and his intestines, which had spilled through the cut made by Gotrek's axe, streamed out in front of him, drawn towards the glowing void and waving like some grisly banner.

Felix wasn't sure if the old shaman was trying to repair the damage that Gotrek had done, or was simply praying to his god. Whatever the case, neither the wind nor the light diminished. In fact both grew stronger, rising to an unbearable intensity as the granite shards began to crumble away to mere slivers.

The slayers were on their hands and knees now, crawling with their heads down away from the herdstone. Gotrek was in the lead, only two strides away from Felix, but Felix was afraid they wouldn't make it.

'Come on, Gotrek!' shouted Felix. But he doubted the Slayer could hear him. He couldn't hear himself.

More of the initiate beastmen fell back and flew away, vanishing into the vortex in flashes of blue-white. Felix felt the massive monolith he leaned against shift under his shoulder as the wind pulled at it. Sigmar! The rift was going to suck in the whole world! It would swallow everything.

Finally, after a handful of lip-chewing seconds, as the wind shrieked louder and the light grew still brighter, Gotrek and Rodi dragged themselves behind the monolith just to the left of the one Felix and Kat hid behind. Only Snorri remained in the light. He looked back over his shoulder and shook his hammer at the vortex, shouting something Felix couldn't hear. But then big hands reached out of the shadow and jerked him back, and he vanished into the blackness behind the stone.

Felix was sure it wouldn't matter. They would all be pulled into the glittering void – all their hopes and dreams for the future ended here in a blinding flash of blue. He looked back towards the stone, shielding his eyes from the glare, and saw Urslak still standing there, a black silhouette against the bright blue, his arms wide, chanting ceaselessly as the wind tore at him.

The shaman grew thinner as Felix watched. The light was eating him. He was disintegrating, his flapping intestines and his flesh tearing away in chunks and vanishing into the swirling core, leaving at last nothing but his skeleton, and then that went too, flaking away like ash until there was nothing left.

Felix pulled back behind the monolith, unable to look any more as the light blazed from blue to white and the wind rose to an apocalyptic shriek. He wrapped Kat in his arms and hugged her tight, certain that these were their last moments together, and content – or nearly content – that his life should end that way.

Faces flashed before him like wreckage in the wind. Gotrek, Snorri. They were here. At least he was with them at their end. But there was no Max. No Malakai.

No... no Ulrika. He cursed himself for thinking of her. Kat was here. Kat who loved him, and who he loved. He should be content. He should be ready.

A clap like thunder shook the ground and made him slap his hands to his ears. It felt as if his head was going to implode. Kat did the same, screaming inaudibly.

And then, utter silence. Utter blackness. Utter stillness. He lay in it a moment, stunned into motionlessness. Had the thunderclap broken his eardrums? Had it killed him? Was this some empty afterlife? He tried to feel his arms and legs, but he wasn't sure he even had any any more. 'Is this death, then?' he whispered, looking around at the impenetrable darkness. 'Is this the endless sleep of eternity?'

'What did you say?' said a voice from nearby. 'Snorri can't hear a thing.'

Felix frowned. He was pretty certain that the endless sleep of eternity wouldn't have Snorri Nosebiter in it. Then Kat shifted against him and he realised that he was alive.

After another moment of quiet contemplation, he finally found the wherewithal to sit up. The blackness, which had seemed absolute after so much light, was now penetrable, showing stars above and far-off torches and fires down in the valley, and the faint glow of the moons that showed Felix the line of Kat's cheekbone and the white streak in her hair.

'What happened?' she asked.

'I don't know,' said Felix.

To their left, Gotrek, Rodi and Snorri were grunting to their feet. Felix and Kat did the same, groaning and weaving dizzily. Felix felt like he was on a ship in heavy seas. The ground wouldn't stay still under his feet.

After a moment with his head down, he straightened and followed the dwarfs as they stepped out from behind the monoliths and looked into the circle.

The vortex was gone, and so was the herdstone. No trace of it remained. It had been sucked into the rift.

'What happened to it?' Felix asked. 'I thought it was going to swallow us all.'

'Things of Chaos are unstable, manling,' said Gotrek. 'It swallowed itself.'

'Then the Empire is safe,' said Felix with a relieved sigh. 'The shaman is dead. The herdstone is gone. The people of the Drakwald will not become beasts–'

'Taal and Rhya, look at the menhirs,' breathed Kat, interrupting him.

Felix and the others turned to look at the ring of monoliths. They were all leaning in towards the centre of the circle, like fingers closing, or like old crones whispering to each other. He shivered. The vortex had nearly succeeded in pulling the massive slabs of stone from the ground – and if they had gone, Felix and the others would have been quick to follow.

'Never mind the stones,' said Rodi. 'Look at the bodies.'

Felix looked where the young slayer pointed. On the ground close to the centre of the circle, the bodies of a few beastmen remained, fallen where they had dropped when the vortex closed. There was nothing left of them but skeletons, but the skeletons were odd. They did not gleam white in the light of the two moons. They gleamed yellow – golden yellow.

'Gold, by Grungni!' cried Rodi, stepping forwards, his eyes gleaming with dwarfish lust. 'And of the purest too, by the look of it.'

'Snorri sees sapphires too,' said Snorri, stepping closer and pointing to a golden skull.

Felix stared at the thing, amazed. The horns and claws and hooves of the skeleton were indeed deep, star-crossed sapphire, polished as if by a master jeweller.

Gotrek put his arms out and held Snorri and Rodi back. 'You want nothing to do with that gold, nor that sapphire,' he said.

'But why not?' said Rodi, his eyes glazed with desire. 'It will solve everything. I can go back. I can pay the debt. I can…'

Gotrek slapped him hard across the cheek. Rodi snarled and doubled his fists.

Gotrek just glared at him, his single eye as cold as ice. 'It has already made you forget your oath,' he said. 'And you haven't yet touched it. Can you not see it for what it is?'

Rodi remained with his fists up for a long moment, then at last he sighed and lowered his hands. 'You are right, Gurnisson. Gold born of such an abomination could only ever bring misery. Forgive me.'

'Snorri still thinks it's pretty,' said Snorri.

Gotrek grunted and turned to Kat. 'It is time to blow your horn, little one,' he said, then looked to Felix and Snorri, his brow lowering. 'And it is time for you–'

He was interrupted by a bright tantara of rally horns blaring from the north. Everyone turned. The thunder of guns and cannons echoed off the stones around them, and the roar of angry beasts filled the valley.

'The armies!' said Kat. 'They're attacking!'

TWENTY-ONE

FELIX, GOTREK AND the others ran out of the circle to the north end of the hill. By the torches and fires of the beastmen, and by the light of the two moons rising side by side in the black sky, they could see the surging movements of the forces in the valley below them.

The whole of the herd was pressing forwards towards the narrow north end of the valley where regimented ranks of cavalry and infantry were stabbing into their milling mass. Felix's heart leapt at the sight.

'Hurrah!' cried Kat, throwing up a fist. 'They have come! The beasts are smashed!'

Gotrek grunted. 'Not with that force, they're not.'

'Aye,' said Rodi. 'Nor those tactics.'

Felix looked again, and his elation at the arrival of the armies faded. The slayers were right. Everything was wrong.

It was difficult to tell in the uncertain light how many troops were cutting into the herd's side, but there were certainly not seven thousand. For some reason, despite their earlier statements, it seemed Plaschke-Miesner and von Volgen had attacked without waiting for von Kotzebue to arrive. Worse, Felix saw that Gargorath the God-Touched and his lieutenants had escaped the herdstone's implosion, and were at the forefront of their followers, urging them on and wreaking terrible damage in the human army's front ranks.

'What are they doing?' Felix asked. 'The lords said they wouldn't engage without Kotzebue's reinforcements.'

'And they were to wait for the horn,' said Kat.

'It seems they found their courage after all,' said Gotrek. 'Though not their wits.'

It was true. The two lords' armies were driving forwards so strongly that they were losing all advantage of terrain. If they had stayed in the narrow end of the valley and let the beasts come to them, they could have kept them all on their front, with their cannons, handguns and crossbows positioned on the steep hills to either side to keep the beasts from flanking them. Instead, the armies had stabbed so deeply into the mass of the herd that already the beastmen were curling around the ends of their lines to encircle them, and the cannons and guns were forced to fire at the edges of the herd so as not to hit their own troops. The lords had lost tactical superiority – the only advantage they had – within the first minute of the attack.

'It's madness!' said Felix. 'They've killed themselves, and taken all their men with them.'

'Aye,' said Rodi. 'They're acting like slayers. A thing only slayers should do.'

Snorri chuckled and smacked the haft of his hammer into his left hand. 'Snorri thinks this will be a proper fight,' he said, then plunged down the hill, bellowing a savage war cry.

'Nosebiter, stop!' shouted Gotrek.

It was too late. Snorri was already halfway down and didn't hear him. Gotrek growled.

'We better go keep him alive,' said Rodi, grinning.

'Aye,' said Gotrek.

And with that they charged after Snorri, roaring war cries of their own.

Felix wanted to call out after them, but knew it would not change their minds to remind them that they had already done their part – that they had killed the shaman and destroyed the stone and could retire from the field with honour for those accomplishments. That was not the slayer way. By the slayers' logic, having saved the day, they were now free to die gloriously.

With sudden shock, Felix realised that he was miraculously free *not* to die gloriously. By some mad mischance, he had ended up in a position where he wasn't in danger of being swallowed by Gotrek's doom. He was up above the fray while the Slayer ran towards it. He could observe from here and then slip away with Kat to the barrow tunnels and to freedom where he could record Gotrek's doom later at his leisure. He would have fulfilled his vow and lived to tell of it, and he could take Kat with him. He could have a life beyond his travels with Gotrek.

He turned to Kat, opening his mouth to tell her to come away with him, but then paused.

It felt wrong. He knew that he had vowed to Gotrek only to record his death, not die himself, but it still felt disloyal not to be fighting at the Slayer's side at the end. Their relationship, whatever it was, had become more than just that of slayer and rememberer. It wasn't that they were friends in any way most men would recognise. They did not share their thoughts and inner turmoil with each other. They did not profess bonds of undying loyalty to each other. To the outside observer, and sometimes even to Felix himself, they seemed little more than master and servant. If Felix wanted to go somewhere and Gotrek didn't, they didn't go. It was not an equal partnership.

And yet, it *was* a partnership. They relied on each other, and trusted each other more than most so-called friends ever did. They knew each other better than they knew themselves, and certainly better than either of them knew anybody else. Like it or not, he and the Slayer were bound to each other by a bond not easily broken.

'You want to go with them,' said Kat, looking at him.

'I don't *want* to,' said Felix. 'But...'

Kat nodded. 'But you have to.'

Felix grunted, angry with himself. 'It's ridiculous. I don't understand it. I should be running away with you.'

'You have known the Slayer for a long time,' said Kat, smiling sadly. 'You can't leave him now.'

'But...' But, nothing. She was right. As stupid as it was, she spoke the truth. Felix sighed. 'Go back to the stairs,' he said. 'Get away from here. This is a fool's death.'

Kat shook her head. 'My life began with you, Felix,' she said, looking at him steadily. 'It will end with you.'

'Kat,' said Felix. 'Don't be an ass. Live your life–'

But she was already screaming down the hill after the slayers.

'Kat!'

She did not slow. With a groan he charged down after her, but he cried no war cry.

In the minute since they had first looked down upon the battle it had become even worse. Plaschke-Miesner's and von Volgen's combined forces were completely surrounded by the herd, and the firing of the cannons and handguns was even more sporadic, as the gunners tried to aim around the central melee. But despite the insanity of the position the two young lords had put them in, Felix had to admit that their troops were maintaining good discipline. The wings of their formations had folded back and around as the beasts had swarmed them, and the army was now a neat square, bristling with spears on all four sides, with the sea of beastmen breaking against it and falling back as if it were a stone pier. Unfortunately, this formation had completely hemmed in the knights and mounted men-at-arms, making them almost useless. Felix saw a wedge of them struggling to reach Gargorath and his lieutenants on foot, their warhorses left with their squires in the centre of the square. At this rate, the army could not hope to last – and of course, the slayers were driving right towards it.

With their longer legs, Felix and Kat caught up to Gotrek, Rodi and Snorri just as they reached the edges of the herd. The beastmen were facing away from them, all pushing north to get at the soldiers who had dared to attack them, and thus the slayers' first charge was more murder than melee. Gotrek's and Rodi's axes severed spines and hamstrung legs as Snorri's warhammer crushed skulls and rib cages. Felix and Kat stabbed and chopped to their left and right.

But as the beastmen in the last ranks died, those before them turned, enraged, and fell upon the dwarfs in a frenzy. The slayers laughed and pushed forwards to meet them, axes and hammer blurring as they blocked and countered a score of strikes. Felix and Kat stayed at their backs, guarding their flanks from the beasts that pressed in from the sides.

Gotrek looked over his shoulder as Karaghul deflected a spear tip meant for his neck. He glared at Felix.

'You shouldn't have followed, manling,' he said.

'I know, Gotrek,' said Felix.

Gotrek nodded and carried on fighting. No more needed to be said.

As the slayers pressed deeper into the herd, more beasts swept in behind them, cutting off their retreat. The slayers had done exactly what Plaschke-Miesner and von Volgen had done, but as Rodi had said, they were slayers. This is what they did.

Unfortunately, Felix and Kat were with them, and for a moment it seemed that they would be slaughtered as the beasts surrounded them. But then Rodi and Snorri turned and stepped in front of them, cackling as they slashed at the flankers. Felix and Kat edged back gratefully, and found themselves in the centre of a moving triangle formed by the three slayers. In this way the five companions fought slowly through the beasts – a three-headed snapping turtle crawling through a pack of wild dogs, with Felix and Kat stabbing out from within the slayers' protection wherever they were needed. Felix shivered at the turtle metaphor, for he knew that, without the hard shell that Gotrek, Snorri and Rodi provided, the soft middle that was Kat and himself would die instantly. His chainmail and Kat's light leather armour would be no protection against a full-on strike from one of the gors' massive weapons.

After that there was no time for thought. Felix fell into the clanging rhythm of the battle, letting his eyes and ears tell him where his sword needed to be and taking his mind out of the equation – a block, a parry, a stab, a slash, a hop to the right, a twist to the left, over and over. Kat and the slayers did the same. No one spoke a word. They worked together silently – a ten-armed threshing machine.

It was a precarious business. Despite the slayers' prowess, if the beastmen had mounted one concerted rush at them they would have been dead in seconds, knocked flat by the sheer mass of the gors' huge bodies, and then run through before they could recover. Fortunately, the beastmen didn't seem capable of such united effort. Instead, in their eagerness to kill, they fought each other almost as much as they fought the enemies in their midst – pushing, shoving and getting in each other's way – and the five companions were thus able to fight them in ones and twos, rather than as a single overwhelming unit.

Another thing that helped keep Felix, Kat and the slayers alive – though it terrified Felix almost more than the beasts themselves – was the sporadic firing of Plaschke-Miesner's mortars. His gunnery crews had found their range and were lobbing shots over the encircled army into the mass of beasts pressing towards them – in other words, they were aiming right where the five companions were fighting.

Every few moments a huge iron shell would whistle down out of the sky, then explode with a thunderous boom, splashing broken beastmen in every direction. One of these explosive rounds landed so close to the companions that the shock of the blast jarred Felix to his knees and threw Kat to the ground. Fortunately, the wall of beasts took the brunt of the impact and they had time to recover. Another time, a thrown beastman crashed into Felix and Kat's opponents and knocked them in all directions. Kat cut the throat of one before it stopped rolling, and Felix beheaded two more – then it was back to the endless dance as more rushed in to take their place.

That was the terrible, inescapable truth that gnawed at the back of Felix's mind. It didn't matter how many beasts they killed. There would always be more. Felix, Kat and the slayers would eventually be ground down by weariness and exhaustion and die not because the gors could out-fight them, but because they could out-last them. Already Felix's arms were tired. Already his legs ached. Already his breath was harsh in his throat, and they had not killed a thousandth of the beastmen who filled the field.

Strangely, he was content. There was no fear any more, and no regret. If he died here, he died among friends, in a fitting conclusion to his life. He could have wished that there were others at his side – Max, Ulrika, Malakai – but it was selfish to want them to die here too just so that his circle could be complete, so he did not begrudge them their absence. This was a good death. They had already done a great thing today, no matter what else they had accomplished, and to go down fighting by Gotrek's side felt fitting. He would be complete here. The notes from his journal – if it was ever found – all led up to this battle, and the rest could be filled in by some other chronicler, and the more exaggerated and legendary they made it, the better, Felix thought. A grand finish to a mad life.

He welcomed it.

A moment later they chopped their way through to von Volgen and Plaschke-Miesner's lines, and were nearly attacked by the terrified spearmen who faced them. Felix could see by the men's faces and their ragged line that their initial discipline was fading fast. If there had been anywhere to run, they would have broken. There wasn't, so they fought on, but hopelessly, mechanically, knowing – as Felix knew – that they were only prolonging the end.

Desperate fights raged to either side of them as the five companions slipped through the spear ranks to the inside of the square. To the left, Felix could see Lord von Volgen leading his knights, his eyes mad with battle lust as he wheeled his horse and slashed at Gargorath. To the right, Lord Plaschke-Miesner, his helmet gone and his pretty face hideously marred by a cut that showed his back teeth, fought a pack of blue-daubed beastmen with a half-dozen young knights at his back. Further on, one of the towering, tree-felling minotaurs was sweeping its man-high axe through the ranks of a sword company and killing handfuls with every swing.

Gotrek started towards Gargorath, growling low in his throat. 'Time to finish what I started,' he said.

'Snorri wants to fight the big one,' said Snorri, turning towards the massive minotaur.

'Not if I get there first,' said Rodi, hurrying after the old slayer and trying to get ahead of him.

Felix knew where he should be, and followed Gotrek. Kat came too. But as they moved down the back of the spear line to reach von Volgen, Felix saw a familiar figure fighting at the head of a sword company that was retreating hastily before a press of beastmen.

'Sir Teobalt!' Felix cried.

The gaunt knight was unable to fall back as fast as his terrified companions, and he was in danger of being surrounded. Felix and Kat pushed through the ranks of the fleeing swordsmen and ran to him.

The old templar was wheezing terribly as they fell in to either side of him, and seemed to be favouring his right leg. A heavy axe blow from a beast splintered his shield, sending him stumbling back, and he barely turned a spear thrust from another with his sword.

Felix stabbed at the axe-wielding gor while Kat swung at the head of the second. Felix's beastman turned on him, snarling, and the axe blade crashed against Karaghul's crossguard, nearly driving the sword back into his face.

It was reprieve enough. Teobalt thrust forwards with his long sword and drove it through the beastman's neck. Felix hacked through its ribs. It fell and he turned to the other beast.

Kat had left her axe in its back, and was dodging away from the questing point of its spear. Teobalt backhanded the thing with an off-balance slash and Felix sliced through its hamstrings. It fell shrieking, and Kat rolled aside and retrieved her axe.

The old templar fell against Felix, sucking air in great gasps. 'Thank… thank you, Herr Jaeger,' he said. 'I… have not the… breath I once had.'

'Keep your feet, sir,' said Felix, trying to walk him back to the sword line as he lashed out at encroaching beasts. 'We must get you to safety.'

Kat put Sir Teobalt's sword arm over her shoulder and they carried him back through the line, shoving the swordsmen aside.

Sir Teobalt groaned as they set him down behind. 'There is no safety. We will not... leave this place, thanks to those two... young fools.'

'Why did they attack like this?' asked Kat, opening her canteen and giving it to him. 'It was madness.'

'Madness?' said Teobalt after he had taken a drink. 'More like possession. I've never seen the like. One moment they stared at the flashes on the hill, biting their hands in fear like the poltroons they are. Then, when the bright light went out and the thunderclap came, they started raging like berserks, screaming for the attack to be sounded and howling for the blood of the beasts.' He shook his head. 'I urged them to wait for von Kotzebue, or at least hold to a defensible position, but they would have none of it, and led their knights in at a gallop, leaving all the rest to follow as they might.' He spat on the body of a dead beastman. 'Never have I seen lords show such flagrant disregard for the lives of their troops.'

To the west, Felix heard Gotrek's roar and looked up. The Slayer was charging Gargorath's retinue from the rear as the black-furred war-leader continued to trade blows with von Volgen. Gargorath looked back as his lieutenants screamed and fell, and von Volgen took advantage, hacking at the war-leader's neck with all his might. Had Gargorath stood still, it would have been a clean strike, but the beast lunged at the Slayer, enraged, and von Volgen's blade only glanced off his steel and gold armour, leaving the young lord half off his saddle and overbalanced.

With an annoyed bray, Gargorath lashed out behind him with the bird-headed axe. Von Volgen was fighting to stay on his horse and could not defend himself. The evil weapon ripped through his armour and bit deep into his chest. Felix shivered as he heard the axe scream like a vulture and saw its sapphire eyes glow bright blue. Von Volgen shrieked and clawed the air as the notched beak of the axe seemed to inhale the life out of him. The young lord's eyes collapsed into their sockets like dried peas and his face grew hollow and gaunt.

'Sigmar preserve us,' said Teobalt, making the sign of the hammer.

'It eats what it kills,' whispered Kat, her eyes wide with horror.

'And feeds its master,' gagged Felix, staring aghast.

As they watched, the blue glow from the axe's eyes spread across Gargorath's body and his myriad wounds knit together as if they had never been. Only the gash on his snout and the severed horn that Gotrek had given him did not heal, but all the rest were gone. He appeared at full strength again.

'Filthy magic,' Felix heard Gotrek shout as he swung at the huge war-leader. 'I'll give you a cut you won't recover from.'

Gargorath ripped the vulture-headed axe from von Volgen's chest and blocked Gotrek's attack with a deafening clang. The fight was on. Behind them, von Volgen toppled from his horse, nothing more than a parchment-covered skeleton in armour, as his knights wailed and cursed and called his name.

'I must go to Gotrek,' said Felix, standing.

But before he could take a step, a handful of beastmen broke through a line of spearmen to their left, roaring in triumph and attacking a company of unprepared archers who had been firing over the spear company's heads.

'Shore up! Shore up!' came a sergeant's cry, and Felix and Kat started forwards to help close the hole before any more gors could enter the square.

But Sir Teobalt stopped Felix and pointed at the beastman who led those who had smashed the line – a huge goat-headed gor that fought in a battered breastplate and a filthy loincloth made of some heavy material. Not so different than the rest, but what set the monster apart from ten thousand others was its weapon, a thick wooden club with a sword stuck sideways through it like a spike. Felix blinked. The sword was on fire, its flames blackening the wood of the club.

'The beast wears the armour of Baron Orenstihl, the grand master of the Order of the Fiery Heart,' said Teobalt. 'And that which it has driven through its club is the Sword of Righteous Flame. And the cloth belted around its waist is our banner.' The old templar fought to his feet and stood tall, readying his sword and shield. 'If the beast has stolen these things, I will have my revenge upon it. If the beast is Baron Orenstihl himself, I will put his poor tortured soul to rest.'

And with that, Teobalt charged at the gor and its followers as they pressed the archers back against the nervous mass of abandoned cavalry mounts that strained and squealed behind them.

'Wait, Sir Teobalt!' called Felix, racing after the limping knight with Kat at his side. 'We will help you.'

'No!' said Teobalt. 'This is my fight alone.'

Felix gave Kat a look and she nodded in agreement. They continued after Teobalt. The old templar was going to get their help whether he liked it or not.

'Grand Master Orenstihl!' cried Teobalt as they neared the melee.

The big gor turned from the retreating archers, its black eyes glaring, though Felix couldn't tell whether it recognised the name or was just responding to the noise.

'If it be you that wear yon sacred banner,' said the old templar, striding towards it, 'then lower your club and let me free you from your curse.'

The beastman cocked its head, as if confused, and dim recognition clouded its goatish face.

'It *is* you,' quavered Teobalt. 'Sigmar save us.'

'I prayed to Sigmrr,' snarled the beastman as Teobalt came on. 'He wss weak! He did not save me!' He raised the club with the burning sword stuck through it. 'The changrr is strongrr!'

'We shall see,' said Teobalt, and rushed to meet him, bellowing a prayer.

Orenstihl roared a response and a few of his gors turned from pursuing the archers to see what threatened their leader. Felix and Kat ran to block them as Teobalt and the bestial templar slammed together, swinging hard. The gor's sword-pierced club smashed against the old knight's blade with the force of an avalanche, and Felix thought the fight was over before it had begun. But Teobalt had been a knight for more years than Felix had been alive. He knew something of swordplay. He gave way before the blow, letting it take his sword around, then came up over the top of his shield and hacked down into Orenstihl's shoulder, chopping through his pauldron and finding flesh.

The other gors howled with fury and surged forwards to help the corrupted templar. Felix blocked a spear thrust aimed straight for Teobalt's head. Kat hamstrung a beast who was raising a mace.

Felix cast a swift look around as he and Kat fought to keep the knight from being flanked. Things looked grim. Beastmen were pushing back a spear company to their right, as their captain screamed, 'Hold the line! Hold the line!' as his soldiers tossed away their weapons and fled. Beyond that, a dozen gors tore Lord Plaschke-Miesner from his saddle as he slashed weakly at them. Near him, Rodi stood over the body of Snorri Nosebiter, defending it against a circle of beastmen. Was the old slayer dead? The massive corpse of a minotaur lay beside him, its skull a red crater, so if he was, he had gone as a slayer should. To the left, Gotrek cursed as Gargorath's axe fed on another soldier and restored its master's wounds once again.

The crunch of a heavy impact brought Felix's head around. Sir Teobalt was staggering back, his shield split in two, as Orenstihl advanced on him. With a curse, Felix disengaged from his opponent and lunged at the beast-templar, gashing his shoulder. He grunted and swiped the sword-pierced club at him without turning from Teobalt. Felix threw himself to the ground, the flaming blade flashing an inch above his head.

'Felix!' cried Kat.

Orenstihl's gors stabbed down at him. He flung himself aside inches ahead of their points. Kat hauled him to his feet and they danced back, blocking desperately as the beasts hacked at them.

'Hold on, Sir Teobalt!' Felix cried, trying to edge around the gors and get back to the templar.

Suddenly a handful of arrows thwacked into the beastmen and they screamed and twisted. The archers had rallied!

Kat cheered, and she and Felix cut down two of the pin-cushioned beasts before they could recover. Kat shattered the teeth of a third with her axe and it fell back spitting blood.

Together she and Felix leapt the dying gors and ran for Sir Teobalt. They were seconds too late. With a sickening thud, the beast-templar slammed his club into the old knight's breastplate and folded him up like a rag doll.

'Sir Teobalt!' cried Felix.

The knight's sword fell from his limp fingers as Orenstihl lifted the club, and Teobalt with it. Felix gaped, his stomach churning as he saw that a foot of flaming steel jutted from the back of Teobalt's cuirass. The beast had impaled him on the club's sword-spike, and was now raising it to shake him off.

'Sir Teobalt!' cried Kat. 'No!'

Felix charged forwards with her and slashed at Orenstihl's head as she hacked at his knees. The changed templar stumbled back, wrenching the club's burning blade from Teobalt's body, and nearly decapitating Kat with a backswing. She ducked and dodged behind his legs.

Felix shouted to the archers. 'Shoot it! Shoot the beast!'

But unfortunately the corrupted templar was too closely engaged with Kat for them to shoot. In fact, the damned girl had leapt on the beastman's back, and was clinging to his breastplate with one hand while trying to bury her remaining axe in his skull with the other!

Orenstihl roared and reached for her. She hacked at his fingers and sent one spinning. The beast howled, but still caught her wrist and flung her down on the ground in front of him. She landed hard on Sir Teobalt's body and bounced to the dirt, dazed, her axe flying from her hand as the beastman raised his terrible club to strike her.

'No, you cursed goat!' cried Felix, running forwards and slashing for the thing's unprotected waist.

Orenstihl turned his swing and the flaming sword-spike whipped towards him like the point of a scythe. Felix blocked the blade, but the end of the club glanced off his shoulder and slammed him to the dirt beside Kat.

'Are...?' he said, unable to draw a breath to finish the question.

'I'm...' She stopped and nodded, also unable to breathe.

They crabbed back from the beast-templar as he advanced, then scrambled to their feet as he swung at them.

'Now!' shouted Felix, glancing towards the archers. 'Shoot it!'

But the bowmen had turned to fire on another fight and didn't hear.

Kat made a desperate lunge for Orenstihl's ankles, but his club swung down and she dived aside, crying out.

'Kat!' called Felix. Was she hurt? 'Keep away from her!' He slashed at the beast-knight, trying to keep him from turning to finish her.

It worked too well. Orenstihl gave Felix all his attention, swinging the pierced club at him in an impenetrable X pattern that smashed away Felix's every attempt to stab through. Each blow felt like it was breaking his arms, and forced him back and back.

Then, just as Felix felt he couldn't raise his sword to meet another strike, the corrupted templar cried out and stumbled, throwing his left arm out to one side for balance. Felix took the opening, and stabbed him in the armpit through the gap between his vambrace and his breastplate. Orenstihl howled and raised his club for a last strike, but something flashed between his legs from behind and buried itself in his crotch with a sickening *chunk*.

Felix pulled his sword from the monster's ribs and jumped back as he whimpered, then toppled forwards onto his face. Kat was standing behind him, barehanded. Her axe was sticking up from beneath the beast-templar's loincloth like a wooden tail.

'Well struck,' said Felix, swallowing. It was the first time he had ever felt sympathy for a beastman.

She gave him a weary grin as she recovered the axe.

They hurried to Teobalt, and Felix was surprised to see that the old templar still clung to life.

He lifted his trembling head, looking blindly around. 'Is… is it slain?'

'Aye, Sir Teobalt,' said Felix. 'It is dead.'

'And the banner? The sword?'

Felix looked back, grimacing. The banner was soaked in gore and caked in filth. The sword was stuck up to the hilt through a heavy wooden club and bent halfway along the blade. A more degraded set of regalia Felix could not imagine. Nonetheless, he went back and cut the belt that held the banner to the beastman's body, while Kat grasped the heavy club that held the sword and dragged it back.

'I'm afraid they are... beyond repair,' said Felix, returning to kneel beside the dying templar. He held the banner out to him as Kat turned the club so that the hilt of the sword was at his side.

Teobalt shook his head as he clutched the banner and gripped the sword. 'That matters not. They are returned. The honour of the order is restored.'

He coughed wetly, spraying blood, then drew a painful breath and looked up at Felix with his pale blue eyes. 'The Order of the Fiery Heart is... grateful, Herr Jaeger. You have done well. You are... worthy of Karaghul.' He patted Felix's arm with a delicate hand. 'All is well,' he said. 'All is well.'

Then he laid his head back on the hard ground, folded his arms across the banner, and allowed himself to die.

Felix and Kat bowed their heads over him.

'Morr watch over you, sir,' said Kat.

'Sigmar welcome you,' said Felix.

A thunder of bestial hooves interrupted their prayers. A company of spearmen had broken, and a rush of beastmen was charging into the square. Felix and Kat jumped up, then tried to lift Sir Teobalt's body and drag it back. There was no time. The beasts were too swift. Felix and Kat turned and ran with the fleeing archers in amongst the herd of screaming, rearing cavalry horses behind them.

Felix looked around as he shoved between the surging beasts. The square was close to collapsing on all sides. The two young lords were dead. The companies were shattered, and the beasts were breaking through everywhere. The day was lost. It would be over in minutes now. He searched for Rodi again and could only see a heap of beastman corpses taller than Kat. He turned in Gotrek's direction and saw the Slayer still battling Gargorath while a scrum of beastmen and von Volgen's men-at-arms fought all around them. The black-furred war-leader was staggering from a dozen wounds. The Slayer looked little better.

'We must help him,' said Kat.

Felix shook his head. 'He will want no help. But I'd like to be at his side at the end.'

'Then let's go to him,' said Kat.

Felix looked at her smiling, bloodied face, then out at the roiling sea of slaughter that was between them and the Slayer. They would die in the attempt – but on the other hand, they would die standing here just as certainly.

He smiled back. 'Aye, let's.'

He pulled her to him and kissed her as they were knocked this way and that amid the surging horses. Though tinged with blood and dirt, it was as sweet as any kiss he had ever tasted.

They broke apart.

'See you in Sigmar's halls,' said Felix.

Kat grinned. 'I'll race you there.'

With twin battle cries they charged from between the horses and dived into the press of beasts and men, sword and axe whirling. Felix cut through a beastman's neck on his first stroke, and gutted another on his second. Kat severed the spine of a third. It was easy to fight when you had no fear, when you knew the outcome was inevitable, no matter what you did. A strange, savage joy welled up in Felix's chest as he fought on. Perhaps, he thought, this is what the slayers felt. Perhaps this was why they longed so fiercely for battle.

Ahead of him, through the mad jumble of murder that the battle had become, Felix saw Gargorath knock Gotrek back with a brutal blow, then sink his axe into the back of one of his own gors. The surprised beastman screamed, but not as loudly as the vulture-headed axe, which drew its life force from it and fed it to Gargorath.

As Felix and Kat stole horrified glances through their own fights, the war-leader's wounds once again closed up, and he was as whole as he had been at the start of the fight. Gotrek staggered up to face him again, as weary as Felix had ever seen him, and bleeding from a half-dozen deep wounds, but his single eye still blazing with fury. Gargorath was his exact opposite – for though his body was once again unmarked, and he still fought with unnatural energy, as he strode forwards, his glowing blue eyes registered fear and uncertainty. It was clear that he had expected the fight to be over long ago.

Then, with alarming suddenness, it *was* over. Felix caught a flash of inspiration in Gotrek's eye as he blocked another of Gargorath's brutal slashes. The Slayer backed away, feigning weakness, then, as the war-leader slashed again, Gotrek turned his axe so that the blade met the haft of the daemon weapon edge on. With an inhuman shriek and a blinding flash of blue light, the head of the vulture-headed axe was severed from its haft and spun away to bite the bloody ground with its glowing eyes fading to black.

Gargorath was left holding a sizzling stick.

With a triumphant roar, Gotrek charged in, bringing his axe up in an overhand swing that bit into the beastman's gold and steel breastplate so deeply that the rune-inscribed head disappeared entirely. Gargorath grunted and staggered back, tearing the axe from Gotrek's grip. He looked down at the weapon, blinking stupidly, then, with the slow majesty of a stone tower collapsing, toppled backwards to land flat on his back.

Gotrek chuckled, than stepped up onto the dead beast's massive chest, levered his axe free and spat in his face. 'Heal that, you overgrown sheep,' he rasped.

The other beasts had fallen back from Gotrek at the death of their invincible leader, but now they surged in again, howling for his blood. He roared in response and rushed to meet them.

Kat and Felix raced to him and fought at his side, still in the blissful trance of nothing-left-to-lose – though Felix was slightly sad for the Slayer. He almost wished that Gargorath had killed the Slayer, for it was certainly a grander doom to die fighting a great leader then to be laid low by the faceless numbers of the endless herd. He also grieved for Snorri, who would not now be supping in Grimnir's halls, but instead would wander as a forlorn ghost for the rest of eternity. But these were passing concerns, as all his being was taken up with the sheer physical joy of block and parry, strike and counterstrike. He took a terrible cut on the leg, but didn't feel it. A club numbed his off hand. He didn't feel that either. He was content to go down fighting in the middle of the great swirl of battle, knowing that he went with his friends at his side.

Then, at the edge of his consciousness, he heard a boom, and then another boom, and then a blare of horns and a roar of voices all raised in unison. He killed a beastman who looked away from him, craning its neck to find the source of the sounds.

For a moment, Felix could not conceive of what was happening. Since he had raced down into the battle from Tarnhalt's Crown, the scope of his world had been no more than the beasts around him and the short time he had to fight them, so this strange intrusion of distant sounds was as alien to him as air would be to a fish. But then, above the rising roar, he finally understood the words the far-off voices were shouting.

'Von Kotzebue! Von Kotzebue! The Empire! The Empire!'

TWENTY-TWO

It struck Felix as funny how quickly all his fear and pain and worry for the future came back with the knowledge that help had arrived. Hope was an evil thing. Without hope he had been at peace, knowing that his death was inevitable. With hope, suddenly he was desperate to stay alive and keep alive those that were nearest and dearest to him. Suddenly his heart was hammering with anxiety, and his limbs aching with fatigue. Could he stay alive long enough for von Kotzebue's army to reach them? Could he protect Kat? Could Snorri be saved? Was the old slayer still alive?

The wounds that hadn't troubled him when he knew that they were only momentary precursors to death now nearly crippled him with their agony. He felt faint and sick and weak, and wasn't sure he could continue to fight – something that hadn't mattered in the least only seconds before.

Over the horned heads of the beastmen that surrounded him and Kat and Gotrek, Felix saw columns of ranked cavalry pouring down over the hills to the east and west, with wide ranks of spearmen racing down after them, snare drums rattling and banners waving as cannons and mortars belched fire over their heads. A great cheer rose from the throats of the beleaguered men in the centre of the thronging beastmen at the sight, and Felix and Kat raised their voices as well.

Felix couldn't see the impact when the two prongs of von Kotzebue's army slammed into the flanks of the herd, but he could feel it and hear it – a heavy shuddering crash that shook the ground and caused a ripple effect in the beastmen, like a boulder being thrown into a swamp.

All around Felix and Kat, von Volgen's and Plaschke-Miesner's soldiers and sergeants were calling encouragement to each other and fighting with renewed vigour.

'Hold on, lads!' cried one. 'Help's on the way!'

'Saved, by Sigmar!' called another.

'Look sharp, now!' shouted a third. 'Don't want those damned Middenlanders seeing us look beat, do we?'

'All be over soon,' said a fourth.

Of course, there was a lot more fighting to be done before it was all truly over, but at least the tide had turned. Felix and Kat and Gotrek lined up with a company of swordsmen, and they presented a united front against the panicking beasts.

For a time, the gors fought savagely against the three fronts that were ranged against them, and hundreds of Von Kotzebue's men fell after the initial charge, as well as hundreds more in the deteriorating square of troops trapped in their centre, but after less than a quarter of an hour, as withering volleys of arrow fire ate away at their edges, and the spears of the infantry and the lances of the knights pressed in on them on both sides, the beasts finally could take no more and turned and fled south, clawing and killing one another in their desperation to be away.

After that it was butchers' work, with von Kotzebue's lances riding down fleeing packs of beasts, while his infantry closed the jaws of their pincer movement to catch the rest in the middle. It was not easy work, however. In fact, this was the hottest fighting of the battle for the survivors in the remains of the square, for the beastmen in their terror fought with the frenzy of trapped rats, and tried to tear a hole through the Empire lines in a desperate attempt to escape. There were a terrible few minutes where many men who had thought salvation was at hand were felled by flailing horns and clubs and axes. But finally von Kotzebue's men cut down the last few gors and the rescuers met the survivors in the centre of the blood-soaked and eerily silent field.

'Well met, cousins,' said a greatsword captain in blue and grey who stood beneath von Kotzebue's banner.

'Aye,' said a Talabecland sergeant. 'If a little late.'

The captain ignored his comment and looked around. 'Do Lord von Volgen and Lord Plaschke-Miesner still stand?'

'Yer a bit late for that too,' said a voice from the ranks.

'But too soon for me,' muttered Gotrek under his breath, as the conversation between the armies continued. 'Another few minutes and I would have found my doom.'

Felix rolled his eyes. 'I'm sorry you were disappointed.'

Then his pain caught up with him and he groaned and looked for a place to sit and bind his wounds. Kat did the same, as did the rest of the army. All around them the soldiers sank down in weariness and pain, calling for surgeons and drinking from canteens and flasks. The cries of the wounded and dying were pitiful to hear.

Then a deeper voice boomed over the rest. 'Gurnisson! Here!'

Gotrek, Felix and Kat looked up. Rodi was waving a torch at them from beside the pile of beastman corpses he and Snorri had made. He held Snorri's warhammer in his hands. Gotrek grunted, then stumped heavily towards him. Felix and Kat exchanged a look, then rose again and limped after him. Felix was certain they would find Snorri dead, and was saddened by it. What a terrible irony that only the one who could least afford to die had perished.

'Is he dead?' asked Gotrek, as they approached.

Rodi shook his head and Felix breathed a sigh of relief.

The young slayer was covered in gashes from head to foot, the worst being his left cheek, which was opened to the bone, but he seemed to be unbothered by any of them. 'He lives,' he said. 'But I broke my axe on a beastman's skull, and have need of yours.'

Without further explanation he turned and crawled up and over the ring of dead beastmen, using Snorri's hammer to balance himself. They followed, wobbling on the loose and uncertain ground.

In the centre of the ring lay Snorri, alive, but only barely. He was whiter than any dwarf Felix had ever seen, and bruised and cut all over.

He grinned weakly when he saw them. 'Snorri got the big bull,' he said.

'Aye, Father Rustskull,' said Rodi, pointing with the head of the warhammer. 'But the big bull got you too.'

Felix blanched as he looked where Rodi indicated. Snorri's right leg was a mangled mess from just below the knee – a tangle of shredded meat and shattered bone. His foot was missing entirely. A tourniquet had been tied above the knee to stop the flow of blood, but there was already too much on the ground.

'The minotaur hit him with its axe,' said Rodi. 'But it was dull from chopping trees. He needs a good, clean cut.'

Gotrek nodded. Felix winced, though he knew it had to be done.

Gotrek wiped his axe as clean as he could on the shirt of a dead soldier, then took Rodi's torch and held it under the cutting edge until both sides were black with carbon, then handed the torch to Kat.

'Sit on him,' he told Rodi. 'And hold the leg.' He looked at Felix. 'Manling, hold the good leg aside. Little one, bring the torch close.'

Felix nodded and squatted to grab Snorri's left boot as Rodi sat on the old slayer's stomach and pressed down on his upper leg, just above the knee, while Kat, looking slightly queasy, lowered the torch.

'Snorri is ready,' said Snorri, closing his eyes.

Gotrek stepped up and raised his axe, sighting down with his one eye to line up his swing.

Felix pulled Snorri's left leg away from his right, then turned his head so he wouldn't have to see. There was a swish and a thud, and Snorri grunted and jerked, then lay still.

Felix opened his eyes again and looked. The damage had been cut away, leaving a clean, straight cut through bone and muscle that looked disturbingly like an uncooked steak. Because of the tourniquet there wasn't much blood, which somehow made it even worse. At least he lives, Felix thought. At least Snorri still has a chance to recover his memory before he meets his doom.

Rodi stood and turned, looking pleased with Gotrek's work. 'All right, Father Rustskull?'

Snorri opened his eyes and nodded, though he looked even paler than before. 'Snorri is fine, but he would like a drink soon.'

'And Snorri shall have his drink,' said Rodi. 'Just as soon as we find a surgeon with some hot pitch.'

Gotrek wiped his axe clean again, then found two discarded spears and crossed them. He and Rodi lifted Snorri onto the spears, then picked them up like stretcher ends and carried the old slayer out of the ring of beastman corpses and across the field in search of a surgeon, with Felix and Kat following behind.

Felix shook his head as they walked, amazed that they had all survived. The battle he had been certain would be the slayers' doom had ended, and they were all still alive. Maybe they truly were fated for some great destiny. It seemed the only explanation for their continued existence.

A cold wind blew through the valley as they walked past the place where Gargorath and his headless axe lay on the ground. Felix shivered and pulled his old red cloak closer around him. The wind stank of death and moaned like a tormented soul. Then he paused, the hair rising on the back of his neck, and looked around.

Though the moaning and the chill and smell continued unabated, nothing moved in the wind. Felix's hair didn't flutter around his face. His cloak didn't flap around his legs. The banners of the armies didn't lift in the breeze.

He turned to the others. They had stopped too. All around the field, conversations stalled and the cries of the wounded died away.

Kat's eyes were as wide as saucers. 'Something... something is wrong,' she said.

Gotrek and Rodi set Snorri's litter down and readied their weapons warily.

'The light,' said Gotrek, frowning. 'It's the light.' He looked up.

Felix and the others followed his gaze, and a collective gasp escaped their throats.

The moons were colliding, directly over their heads. Morrslieb was eclipsing Mannslieb, sliding across it like a dirty coin covering a freshly minted one. As they watched, the Chaos moon occluded its fairer sister entirely, and Mannslieb's clean white light vanished, to be replaced by a sickly green luminescence that spread across the battlefield like a plague, making the wounded and the dying appear not only maimed, but diseased as well.

All over the valley, soldiers stared up into the sky, cursing and praying to their gods.

'It's the end!' cried a man. 'We have sinned and this is our punishment!'

'Sigmar save us!' wailed another.

A rustling from behind him made Felix turn. A wounded beastman was trying to rise, though it only had one hand. Gotrek kicked it in the head and it fell over. Felix blinked. The beastman had no intestines either. They had fallen out through the hole in its abdomen. Felix shivered. How was the thing alive?

Another beastman twitched and tried to stand. And another. Beside them, an archer with an axe through his chest and a missing arm opened unseeing eyes and sat up.

Felix stepped back and backed into Kat, who was looking at a drummer boy with no legs squirming on the ground and trying to turn over.

'What is happening?' she asked.

Felix only shook his head, unable to form an answer.

A heavy thudding and shifting to their left made them all turn. Kat gasped. Rodi cursed. Gotrek grunted. Felix stared, his heart pounding double time in his constricted chest. Gargorath was getting to his feet. Though Felix could see the monster's shattered ribs through the gaping hole Gotrek had smashed in his breastplate, the war-leader was somehow still alive.

'It's impossible,' Felix said.

All over the battlefield, broken figures were standing, both man and beastman, while soldiers cried out in dismay and fear.

Kat clutched Felix's arm. 'What is happening?' she asked again, an edge of panic creeping into her voice.

'It is midnight on Hexensnacht,' said a weird, shrill voice behind them.

They turned. A tall thin figure in plate armour was clanking stiffly towards them, its head cocked at an uncomfortable angle. 'The year has turned,' it said. 'The age of the Empire of man has passed.'

Felix stumbled back as he saw that the knight was Sir Teobalt, the blood still running sluggishly from the fatal wound the bestial templar Orenstihl had given him. His face, as he approached them, showed no animation. His eyes stared fixedly above them and to the left, and though his jaw moved, it was jerky and stiff, and not quite in time with his words. 'The age of the Empire of the dead has begun.'

'Grungni!' said Rodi. 'What's happened to him?'

'What has happened to him,' said the thing that had been Sir Teobalt, 'is what will happen to you all.'

Felix frowned. The voice wasn't Teobalt's, but he recognised it all the same. How did he know it? He couldn't think.

'My necromancy could not work with the herdstone present,' said the same voice from beside them. They turned and saw that Gargorath's jaws were moving too. 'But I knew your axe could destroy it,' the beast said. 'So I showed you the way to smash it.'

'And smash it you did,' said the same voice again from yet another direction.

Felix and the others spun around.

Lord von Volgen and Lord Plaschke-Miesner were lurching towards them, von Volgen no more than a paper-skinned mummy, and both dead from terrible wounds. 'Then I whispered in the ears of these young lords,' the corpses said together. 'Telling them to attack. Telling them of the glory to be found in death.'

As the dead youths continued speaking, the same high eerie voice began to echo from the mouth of every dead beastman and every risen soldier on the field. 'Now,' it chorused. 'Now I invite you to join them in that glory.'

The corpses of the men and beastmen laughed in shrill unison as they lumbered towards Gotrek, Felix,

Rodi and Kat, raising their weapons in their stiff hands, and though Felix had failed to recognise the voice that rattled from their dead throats, he suddenly recognised their laughter.

It was the mad giggle of Hans the hermit.

ABOUT THE AUTHOR

Nathan Long was a struggling screenwriter for fifteen years, during which time he had three movies made and a handful of live-action and animated TV episodes produced. Now he is a novelist, and is enjoying it much more. For Black Library he has written three Warhammer novels featuring the Blackhearts, and has taken over the Gotrek and Felix series, starting with the eighth installment, *Orcslayer*. He lives in Hollywood.

WARHAMMER

GOTREK & FELIX

THE FIRST OMNIBUS

TROLLSLAYER • SKAVENSLAYER • DAEMONSLAYER

WILLIAM KING